Day of the East Wind

Day of the
East Wind

Julia Shuken

CROSSWAY BOOKS • WHEATON, ILLINOIS
A DIVISION OF GOOD NEWS PUBLISHERS

Day of the East Wind.

Copyright © 1993 by Julia Shuken.

Published by Crossway Books
        a division of Good News Publishers
        1300 Crescent Street
        Wheaton, Illinois 60187.

Cover illustration: Chris Ellison

Art Direction/Design: Mark Schramm

First printing 1993

Printed in the United States of America

Excerpts from Molokan songs were taken from *The Molokan Heritage Collection: "Origins of Molokan Singing,"* volume 4, © 1989 by Linda Rothe-O'Brien. Used with permission from Highgate Road Social Science Research Station, Inc., Berkeley, CA.

Scripture references are taken from the *New King James Version* copyright © 1982, Thomas Nelson, Inc., Publishers and from the *New American Standard Bible* © 1960, 1962, 1963, 1968, 1971, 1972, 1973, 1975, 1977, by The Lockman Foundation. Used by permission.

With the exception of recognized historical figures, the characters are fictional, and any resemblance to actual persons, living or dead, is purely coincidental.

Library of Congress Cataloging-in-Publication Data
Shuken, Julia.
    The day of the east wind / Julia Shuken.
       p.   cm.
    1. Soviet Union—History—Revolution of 1905—Fiction.
2. Russian Americans—California—Fiction.   3. Molokans—Fiction.
I. Title.
PS3569.H764D38 1993   813'.54—dc20   93-12304
ISBN 0-89107-743-X

01		00		99		98		97		96		95		94		93
15	14	13	12	11	10	9	8	7	6	5	4	3	2	1

To the traveler come home,
The wayfarer now sheltered,
For David—husband of my heart.

With His fierce wind
He has expelled them
On the day of the east wind.

ISAIAH 27:8

Contents

I

The Power of the Earth

Transcaucasia—1905

Baku was in chaos. The rich oil city on the Caspian reeled under the impact of savage riots and sullen fires. Piotr Gavrilovich was glad to be leaving; that is—leaving *if*, and it was a big *if*, the trains would start running again. He touched his hand to his breast listening for the reassuring crinkle of paper beneath his uniform tunic and heavy military greatcoat. The passport had been signed in the early morning by his commissar, and with it was the disheveled letter from Semyon Efimovich that was bringing him home.

Piotr sighed and strolled across the tracks to the edge of the station yard. The February snow lay in a smooth blanket, but it was soiled with a metallic pall from the fires that had razed the Balakhani and Bibiebat oil works. The cracks and fissures in the snow gleamed livid, as though lit from beneath. Even the vigorous procession of oil derricks that marched down to the Caspian Sea and then stalked into it seemed to have lost symmetry. The crisscross of steel bracing looked jumbled and senseless, like metal filings drawn skyward by a powerful magnet. When the current failed, they'd tumbled into the shambles of the rest of the city!

In the upper town, detachments of mounted Cossacks patrolled the streets, enforcing a resentful quiet on warring factions of Azerbaijanis and Armenians and on the militant Social Democrats. But it was an uneasy peace — the peace of the tensed jaw and the silently clenched fist.

Piotr felt for Semyon's letter again and the precious passport. If the train for Tiflis (Tbilisi) did get underway, there would be a mad rush to get on it, and his military status would probably give him preferment.

But the Tiflis train was still standing as if frozen to the rails, as it had for days. The rumor was that the striking railway workers would be back on the job, but there were many rumors.

It was almost five o'clock, and a surly darkness began to gather. Piotr took a deep breath and returned to the station house. It was crowded with fleeing Armenians, a few Western businessmen, knots of wary-eyed Azerbaijanis, and a few Russian gendarmes—but no railway workers. Someone had heated the public samovars so that at least there was hot water. Piotr filled his tin cup and, throwing back his head, took a good look at the crowd. Most likely he would be spending the night with them. May as well make their acquaintance.

The Armenians huddled near the ticket windows, as though the intensity of their fear had created a powerful static that pulled them together. In the wake of recent massacres, they were desperate to leave Baku. Talented entrepreneurs in the oil-rich city, the Armenians wore their success discreetly—for Baku had had its way with them, prospering them just as it had impoverished the Azerbaijanis.

But now they seemed bewildered. The women's faces under diadem-like headdresses draped with dark veils were haggard with the long wait. The men were alert and watchful in spite of the fact that, like Piotr, they had been there all day. One young man with arched eyebrows under a black cone-shaped cap had taken it upon himself to make sure that the Russian gendarmes were still on guard. The little girl beside him, with the same arched eyebrows, would occasionally shoot a quick wincing glance at the group of Azerbaijanis near the door.

Piotr turned to look. Yes, there they were, a cluster of Tartars wearing baggy quilted jackets and *burkas* or skull caps. More than once he glimpsed the shaven head of the fanatic, proof of the mullahs' eloquence as they preached *jihad* against the infidel Armenians. No wonder the Armenians looked nervous. In the Tartar mind, "death to the Armenians" would not only win them entry into their Islamic paradise, but would also avenge their personal and social wrongs. Only Russia's show of force had stopped the killings—for now.

What a place, Piotr thought, *for a Molokan pacifist!* Everything was there—the patrolling Russians, frightened Armenians, bitter Tartars. They only needed a Social Democratic demonstration to complete the picture! Baku—"cradle of the winds" in the Persian tongue—was a seething cauldron of discontent. It was no place for a religious dissenter. He was glad to be leaving—glad! If only the strike would break and the trains would roll.

His cold fingers fumbled in his inside breast pocket, and he pulled out Semyon's letter. He didn't read it. He didn't need to; he knew every word by heart. But still he looked at it intently, as if he could draw some further meaning out of the old man's slanted scrawl. No doubt Semyon had been extremely agitated when he wrote it. The pen had dug into the paper so deeply that it looked embossed, and the splattering of blots seemed there, not by accident but for emphasis. But what did it mean? ". . . your mother, Galina Antonovna . . . seriously ill . . . make haste to come . . . we have called for the elders . . . be sure to come quickly . . ."

Come quickly, come quickly, Piotr's mind chanted. Yet here he was, stuck in a train station while his thoughts spun out and banked off of a host of woeful possibilities. Cholera? No, he hadn't read about any epidemics . . . typhus? A little early in the year for that . . . diphtheria? If so, already he might be too late. Piotr clenched his fists and sweated with a churning urge for action and the sucking pull of helplessness.

The crowded room began to swelter, and he made his way to the door. The cold, oil-tainted air struck his face like a splash of dirty water. He pulled his sheepskin cap down onto his head; the army kept his hair so short that his ears were always cold. The evening was dark, but a lamp hung out on one of the low, overhanging eaves. Its golden warmth melted the surrounding snow, magically turning the edges to fragile crystal. Melted drops fell precisely, one by one, making neat blue wells in the snow near the steps. It seemed miraculous, like something from nature—hopeful, yet beyond understanding. Piotr listened, expecting to hear a musical plink, plink. Instead, he started at a voice resonating from behind him.

"It's fine for cushioning a blow from a nagaika, but not much protection from a bayonet."

Two men, a little older than himself, stood in the shadows on the other side of the station door. The speaker wore a light-colored sheepskin that looked oversized and bulky even on his massive frame. His round face was garnished with a neat beard, trimmed at the bottom and shaven on the sides so that it made a circle within the larger circle of his face—like a dog's muzzle.

The small, dark-clad Georgian in front of him contrasted, not only with his companion, but with everyone. The anxiety and uncertainty that strained every other face did not touch this man; he seemed utterly sure of himself. No attitude of forlorn waiting here!

Piotr let a wry grin twist his mouth. *When you see the cranes flying, you know the ice will be breaking. It wouldn't surprise me if the trains rolled tonight after all!*

"Not that it's not a good idea, Koba." The big man was trying to lower his booming voice, without much effect. "You were clever to think of it. There have been plenty of times when those Cossack knouts have bounced off two layers of sheepskin instead of my own dear hide. But those devils keep getting more and more vicious. How much good would sheepskin have done for those poor wretches on Bloody Sunday?"

The man called Koba narrowed his eyes and aimed their glittering intensity at his companion.

"That's good," he said. "Excellent."

The big man shuffled around disconcertedly. But Piotr's attention was riveted on the Georgian. The light from the doorway spilled past him, but angled lamplight gilded the side of his face, diligently finding every pockmark, outlining every hair in his thick eyebrows and full mustache and throwing a triangular shadow alongside his nose.

Cynical indifference stiffened every feature but one—the eyes were lively with crafty intelligence and intense with the determination to assert his will, his only. Piotr prodded his memory. He had seen those eyes—that face—before.

A demonstration in January—that was it! Not long after Bloody Sunday in Moscow, the massacre of peaceful demonstrators had unleashed the fury of the Baku Social Democrats. Piotr's detachment was positioned along the massive medieval walls that separated the old citadel of the Khans from the modern Russian section. Ordered to stand with bayonets at the ready, Piotr had determined that he would not let an ungodly government mar his soul by forcing him to attack helpless people crying out for justice. He edged back from the milling, shouting crowd of demonstrators, his rifle dipped at a reluctant slant. He felt again a prickle crawling across his back as he had wondered if an officer would shoot him from behind.

Then this man's face had arrested his attention. Like Piotr, he seemed remote from the tidal tug and surge of the angry mob and surrounding soldiers. But he was cold, this Koba, inhuman in his indifference. When the Cossacks came charging straight for the center of the marching group, the blood had flowed! And Koba had come suddenly to life. The dying, the wounded—they were a feast for those glittering eyes. Piotr could see that it was not hatred that caused the transformation; it was more like lust—an unholy exhilaration. Intoxicated by the bloodshed, Koba flashed a comprehending look at Piotr, noting his unsoldierly stance. Piotr had turned away as though he had seen something shameful, indecent. He turned away now, but not before he heard Koba's voice slice into the present. "You want to make a revolution on the cheap."

Piotr winced at the words. *Without spilling blood, he means*.

"That's no use," Koba continued. "We must force the authorities to impose repressive measures. The worse they are, the better for us! They'll fuel the hatred of the people. Your tactics are not revolutionary. You are preventing the real revolutionaries from making a revolution."

Koba stood for a few more minutes, rock-still and expressionless, while his companion squirmed in his layers of sheepskin.

"The train will be starting," Koba said in his accented Russian. "We should get our tickets."

Piotr was not surprised when noises began to come from the station yard. He heard the clank of buffers and another sound, like crunching snow. Suddenly, the red lights on the train flooded out over the snow, painting it a tender pink.

Piotr followed the two mismatched revolutionaries into the station house at a discrete distance, grinning to himself. He could imagine Koba's expression if he realized that a uniformed Russian had overheard their conversation. But Koba had no way of knowing that the outward soldier was an inward Molokan, that Piotr would throw down his arms rather than kill. At least, he hoped that's what he would do.

Fenya Vassileyvna Kostrikin was the first to see him striding along in the unfamiliar military boots with his wide, bent-kneed sailor's gait. *What a walk for a Russian peasant*, Fenya thought, *as though the whole rough-crusted skin of the earth is likely to crumble, but he himself, Piotr Gavrilovich Voloshin, is determined to be the one steady and sure thing on it!* She screened her smile with her winter-tanned hand and moved closer to the trunk of the acacia tree so that she blended with the jumble of hedge, wattle fence, and snow-flecked wood piles at the edge of the village. The red sun behind her threw shadows in a mysterious script across the snow and blue-iced mud—a sign from heaven on the unheeding surface of the earth.

The sparrows roosting above caught her excitement and scattered impetuously, peppering the twilight air. But still he didn't see her. He never did. Fenya pulled her kerchief down to her eyebrows and quietly followed him down the sand-strewn lane, anonymous as only a plainly clad adolescent girl can be.

It wasn't hard to remain unseen, for the village was astir with swarming, noisy collective movement. Goodwives spilled from doorways, some carrying flaming rags, hurrying to light the evening fires. Speckled geese crossed the roadside, snaking their necks suspiciously. A Tartar lad in a tall lambskin cap prodded cows into a wattle enclosure. Soon the smoke-blue night gathering in the hills would creep down and quench the activity. But for now the villagers thronged into the streets, calling to each other and laughing, and night stayed at a wary distance.

Fenya could see that Piotr was glancing about eagerly. Well, he would find it all as he left it! Neatly placed huts of silvered wood, bright blue carvings garnishing post and shutter, lined the gentle slope up to the square. Brimful tubs of water, snatching at the last of the twilight, made circles of light that lay like silver coins tossed beside the community pump. Squares of wavering light began to glow from windows as the activity moved from street to hut.

Fenya kept Piotr in sight until he reached the tall thrusting trio of firs in the square. Their aloof grandeur called attention to the squat insignificance of the buildings. But the buildings had a warming homeliness to them all the same. Windows of the two stores glowed with stacks of gingerbread, honeycomb, colored jars of jam, and vivid bolts of the silk abundant in the region. Abajarian's was still open, exuding a warmth and a summons through its windows.

Fenya quickened her pace so that she outdistanced Piotr, keeping to the shadows. She looked back as he stopped beneath the shop window. Strong lamplight seemed to draw the bones right out of his face, sketching hard lines over the usually boyish contours. For some reason, the sight of that changed face filled her with dread.

Watching Piotr carefully, she paused with her back to a plastered wall. Its rough surface still held the sun's warmth, but the hard ground remembered winter, and she put one bare foot on top of the other for warmth. Then she turned suddenly and ran toward the stream-side path that would take her to the west where the Russian-style Molokan huts hugged the outskirts of the village. If she hurried, she could alert the Voloshins and still be home in time to light the fire.

Piotr mounted the wooden steps of the Voloshins' hut. His knapsack tugged at his shoulders—disjointed memories of his regimental life weighed like iron shrapnel, dragging him back from the slice of light shining out from the door. Impatiently, he hitched the pack forward, and the sudden lurch brought him into the light and warmth and vehement embrace of old Semyon Efimovich Fetisoff.

"Dzedha," Piotr murmured. Semyon clutched him and planted two haphazard kisses on his face. Piotr sniffed suspiciously; the hut exhaled the odors of a full-scale Russian feast. But wait! That didn't make sense if Galina was sick—seriously sick, if he could believe the note folded inside his tunic. All at once, the ring of his boots on the slatted floor boards seemed hollow and strange.

"*Stidna, stidna!* A sin!" Semyon was muttering. "A sin to see a Molokan in uniform—a crime against God!" The expressive movements of his mouth kept his stiff, white beard in motion, exaggerating the importance of everything the old man said.

Piotr stared down at the cap in his hand as though wondering where it came from. "I didn't choose my outfit, Dzedha," he said. "How is my mother?"

"You see for yourself." Semyon's gnarled hand began threading through his whiskers as though he were guiltily looking for something. "You're here now," he said, looking away. "That'll cheer her up!" The beard cut a side-to-side swath, and Piotr's face puckered in a smile at the familiar movement.

He called the old man "Dzedha," grandfather, but Semyon was actually his great-grandfather. At ninety-one, he was a figure of such power and authority among the Molokans that most had forgotten that Galina Antonovna was not his daughter but his son's child.

"Come on, come on," Semyon said, clawing at Piotr's elbow, "we'll see your mother."

Galina Antonovna was sitting on the narrow birchwood bed in the *gornitsa*, the best room. She was fully dressed, not even pretending to be sick. A flicker of gleeful satisfaction flashed across her features. But she quickly turned down her mouth and reached up to her son with one of her reddened, handsome hands.

"So you've come," she said. "How many times have I prayed for this day!"

"What else could I do?" Wariness and a hint of reproach edged Piotr's voice. Baffled, he searched her face for signs of the supposed illness. Galina was not a big woman, but her hands, feet, and face were proportionately large. She had a broad, childlike brow and beautiful eyes. But the lower part of her face was heavy with determination. She looked as though she were holding something in her mouth that she was unwilling either to swallow or to spit out.

"Dzedha's message sounded serious . . . I was . . . was worried . . ." Piotr found that he could not tell her about the hours of anxious waiting and the uncertainties of the railway journey, which should have taken twelve hours but instead took almost twenty.

Galina's eyes fell. "That was a bitter day—watching you go off to the Tsar's army and wondering when you would come back, wondering if you'd be sent to Manchuria to fight!"

"Only six months, Mother—it's not such a long time. After all, Russia is at war! Do we have a choice in these things?"

"Maybe more than you think, Petya. Let's go out to the kitchen."

From the looks of the kitchen, Galina had put in a day that would have exhausted the healthiest of women. The Voloshin table was set for a homecoming feast. Dishes of chicken and noodles, golden puffy *pirushkiya, blintzi* swimming in hot milk, and salted cucumbers competed for space on Galina's best tablecloth. Waves of savory air wafted from the stove.

The family assembled quickly—Semyon and Galina; Piotr's father Gavril Ivanovich; and the girls, five-year-old Dausha and fourteen-year-old Nadya. They prayed standing and then settled at their habitual places on the wooden benches. Only the old man had a chair.

Semyon couldn't wait to speak. "The time has come." He twisted his beard into two halves, revealing his red, scrawny neck and a protruding Adam's apple that jumped when he said, "*Pohod!*" Piotr stared at him. Could he mean it? *Pohod*—the journey, the pilgrimage.

"News, son, from Yerevan," Gavril interjected.

"Great news! God be praised," Semyon continued. "The boy prophet has told the Molokan elders in Yerevan that the waiting is over. The Molokans will be journeying again to a new land—this time of our own will."

"Now?" Piotr was shocked. All Molokans knew of Efim Gerasimovich Klubniken, the "boy prophet." As a child of eleven, Efim had received a vision in the form of a written message. The illiterate boy had laboriously copied the words, which described a coming time of turmoil when the Molokan believers would have to flee to a dry but fertile land on the other side of the world. Efim's carefully drawn map, also shown in the vision, had indicated the west coast of the United

States. Now, Piotr reckoned, the "boy prophet" was about sixty years old and still preaching the coming *Pohod*.

"What is your plan? Will you all go?" Piotr was suddenly agitated.

Semyon reached for a piece of heavy black bread. "Us? How about you?"

"I'm in the army. You know the price for desertion. I can't go anywhere. I have three weeks leave. Because," he bit off the words, "my mother is dangerously ill. At the end of that, it's back to Baku for me."

"Maybe not, maybe not."

Piotr's agitation increased. He glanced quickly at his father. Gavril looked away, controlling his face. Galina reached for Piotr's hand, a pleading expression in her eyes competing with that firm set of chin.

Piotr leaned back, palms outward. "It's not hard to see that you all have some kind of plan cooked up for me. If it's not too much trouble, why don't you tell me what it is?"

"A plan?" Semyon's tone was conciliatory. "Just some thoughts— that's all. Just thoughts."

"Just thoughts? I can see these 'just thoughts' hedging me in like a cow in a pen." Piotr glanced around the table. Gavril's broad shoulders slumped in a protective bend; Semyon chewed his lip above the splayed-out beard; Galina refused his look and flicked at crumbs with her fingers; the girls watched in baffled dismay.

Piotr drew forward with a disarming smile. "You tell me these thoughts, Dzedha! Your thoughts always hold an interest for me. Tell me!"

Semyon took a deep breath. His dark eyes probed the ceiling, hunting for words in the rough rafters, but the words scurried away, and the last of the winter cabbages had no wisdom to offer.

"Piotr, you know the history of our people—," he began.

"I know, I know. No need to tell me."

"Need to tell you—no. It's in your blood, in your mother's milk. Nothing will tear it out of you!" His eyes flamed, then grew moody.

"We are dissenters, always hounded by persecution. But God always opens a way of deliverance. Now He has brought us from the north to this place across the mountains. You have known no other home. But for fifty years, this prophecy has hung over us like a drawn sword. We wait, we forget, we think, 'No, it won't come to pass in my time.'" His look stabbed at Piotr. "Then it comes, unawares. And we are shaken. Shaken," repeated the old man. The quiver of his beard echoed the thought. He wiped a stray noodle from his mouth. "But we've been given a way out. And the time to take that way is now."

"We can see it come," put in Gavril, "turmoil and troubles—just as the prophet foretold. There are strikes in Tiflis almost every week now . . ."

"Baku, too," Piotr added. "You're right about the strikes. Something is bound to happen sooner or later. In Baku they say the strikes may force the industrialists to come to terms with the workers. It's a step in the right direction."

"A crust of bread," Semyon said gloomily. "No, the people are rebellious. No good will come of it. And we will be caught between hammer and anvil. We are dissenters as far as the government is concerned and reactionaries as far as the socialists are concerned."

"What is this way out you're talking about?" Piotr asked absently, his mind still on political solutions.

"What is it? What have we been talking about? The prophecy! *Pohod!*" The word exploded in a sputter of irritation. "What is it that every Molokan is talking about? The prophecy! Will we go? Will we stay? Every family is flying to pieces like a flock of chickens before a wolf. The Samarins and Melnikoffs have sold everything. They will go this April. From Marseilles. And you, Piotr, you will go too."

"Me!" The savory meat and cabbage filling of a *pirushka* turned to hay in his mouth. "Me! My life is settled so soon? You have one plan for me; the Tsar has another."

"Listen, the only plan for you is the plan of God."

"Go easy on the lad, Dzedha. This is a hard choice for him," interposed Gavril's heavy voice.

"Where is Piotr going?" piped up Dausha.

"God's plan," breathed Piotr. "It's not so easy to know what that plan is. Why are you so sure we should go?"

"We can't go. That's just the point," Gavril said. "Your Uncle Mikhail has too much to say about it. But you, Piotr, you can go. You can consider it. A new life—"

Semyon interrupted, "I know you will be the one to go, the one to carry on our heritage in a new land. I am too old. It's been almost seventy years since we crossed the mountains. I will die here. The others—who knows? Maybe they will follow later. Your chance is now. I'm sure of it."

"You can't be too sure," Gavril argued. "My brother is just as sure that this *Pohod* is a fool's errand. You can go down to the square and hear a dozen different opinions of Efim's vision. Some even think it's about

18

the end of the world! The fanatics sell everything—uproot whole families; the skeptics dig in their heels. I don't know. All we can do is wait. Wait until we get word from those who have already started."

"It may be too late if we wait." Galina spoke up. "I know as a family we have to wait. We have no choice. But Piotr—Piotr can go."

"Piotr should have something to say about it," Piotr insisted.

"Say on, say on—nobody's stopping you from talking!"

"Well, then, there's too much I don't know." Piotr tried to collect his thoughts. "How do you suggest I avoid getting shot as a deserter? That little point has some importance for me! How do you suppose that a poor Russian peasant is going to get from this village to the other side of the world? And without papers. And even if I got there, how would I live? Tell me that. Anyway, where is this place?"

"Ah." The harsh lines on Semyon's face melted to placid satisfaction. "That I can tell you. Efim had maps and charts to show us exactly where to go. I took them to Tiflis, to an educated man. He told me all we need to know. He even told me the name. It's called California."

Vigorous steps sounded on the porch. At the threshold, a blot of shadow separated into the figures of three massive men. The stove hissed and ticked as Galina flung more wood onto the grate. The flames leapt and cowered and played on the broad sweat-shining faces of Mikhail Ivanovich Voloshin and his sons, Trofim and Andrei.

"Well, nephew, tell me—have they got you all suited up to kill the Japanese for the glory of Russia's Tsar? Ha! You'll scare the daylights out of them. That's right, that's right," he said to Piotr's grin. "Bare your teeth at them, and you'll have them on the run." The big man guffawed his delight, then patted Piotr roughly, and gave him a straight look through his bantering tone. "Welcome back, son. So how long will you be here?" He stirred a spoonful of jam into a glass of tea with a work-blackened hand.

"Who knows? Ask Mother and Dzedha here. It sounds like they've been busy for weeks plotting out my life for me."

"Well," replied his uncle, "take your time. Don't be too quick to throw your life away."

"Throw away! It's the saving of the lad we have in mind," Semyon exploded.

"More prophecy talk! Let me tell you something, Piotr Gavrilovich.

God has given us hands for working and heads for thinking. We don't need to be led around by the nose because some peasant boy had some strange dreams. Probably from eating that rich Armenian food! A time of trouble and turmoil! Bah! You tell me when we haven't had trouble and turmoil. Better to face it on your own land with your own people.

"I say this," he continued, "if you see a good reason for leaving—fine, leave. But why now? Harvests are good; we have fertile land. Of course there are problems in the cities—but that doesn't affect us. Why go? People are running like scared hares—why? Because an old man in Yerevan says so. Just last week I bought two cows from Melnikoffs for the price of a sick goat. Prophet! Listen, your prophet is my profit!"

"You listen!" Galina was bent over the stove, pulling hot coals out of the grate and putting them in the top of the samovar. Odd apricot lights flicked at her features strangely. "I am just a woman, but I know when God is speaking. My heart tells me that He has spoken through Efim." Her voice hardened to bitter intensity. "Do you think I want to lose my only son? What I really want is to cling to him and keep him here. But my heart tells me he must go!"

"Your heart, your heart," muttered Mikhail, but he subsided at a warning glance from his brother.

Old Semyon ignored them both. A tattered copy of Efim's map appeared in his fingers, and he delicately smoothed it out on the table with his rough hand. Piotr watched him briefly as he drew all his wild, fervent energy into himself, excluding the others.

Later when their guests were gone, Piotr saw that the old man was still bent over the stained map, muttering to himself and making careful markings with a crude pen. His free hand wandered to the shiny bald patch that nested like a speckled egg in brambly tufts of hair. A mighty concentration split the skin on his forehead into arid fragments of flesh. Semyon blew on the pen nib, puffing out his cheeks, and then dropped his bony claw into his whiskers. The knobby wrist angled upward, and the pen dripped black stains into the silver-white beard so that his head looked like a rook's nest—black and white and covered with indecipherable signs. Piotr saw the shiny, mottled lips twist with the merest breath of a sound. But he heard it. *Pohod!*

II

The Gates of the Alani

Semyon threw down the pen to clutch at his beard with both hands as though wringing some stubborn hidden message out of it. *Pohod* was all he could think of. *Pohod* kept rattling through his mind like rusted cart wheels on a rutted road. He cast a sideways look at his great-grandson. Piotr's broad forehead and wide-set eyes were clear and untroubled, but a devil's store of obstinacy was set in that bold, hollow slope from cheekbone to jaw. Yes, the boy had his own dark eyes and, God help him, his own stubbornness.

Semyon shoved the map away. He went to the door and thrust his burning face into the icy air. A mournful bellowing reached him. *Nitwits! The giddy idiots have forgotten to milk the cows. Their udders will be hard as stone!*

"Nitwits!" he fumed loudly, and a shadowy form sprang up from nowhere. *Fenya! Ah, she'll take care of it. Why am I so agitated? I must have scared the wits out of little Fenya.* The girl had dashed across the yard to the byre, leaving oval footprints in the worn snow. Semyon glanced about sheepishly. A light powdering of snowflakes had begun to fall, but a fitful wind refused to let them settle. They swirled in the air in an annoying way, like clouds of gnats. The oval gray footprints remained.

Pohod! The wheels turned again, forcing his memory back to the time of the Exile. He saw her again—Yekaterina, his wife, his young wife—coming toward him across the steppe. She was walking slowly, steadily, with a measured weightiness as though her feet would leave scars even on that iron-hard steppe. And every place she set her foot was marred with an oval patch of blood—red, then quickly dark as the greedy steppe drank it in. She walked so steadily, so surely, and did not start trembling until he had his arms around her.

Well, they had known there would be trouble. They were religious dissenters in an era of orthodoxy, pacifists among a war-bent people, prophets in a time of impending doom! Of course there would be trouble! Molokans—"Milk Drinkers"—the Orthodox called them; Dukhovny Christiani—"Spiritual Christians"—they called themselves. Eventually both names stuck, and they became Dukhovny Molokans— or just Molokans. Their refusal to bear arms had earned for them this exile from the Volga plains to Transcaucasia. By the late 1830s the government of Tsar Nicholas I had grown weary of dealing with stiff-necked serfs who would rather die than kill.

Semyon shuddered, remembering the Exile and the wafting autumn scent of dying wormwood on the steppe. Ominous rumors of government atrocities and Cossack reprisals had hounded their steps as they set out for their new home. And, as if that weren't enough, the Muslim Imam Shamyl—swooping down from his mountain lair in Dagestan—had declared *jihad* against the *giaour*—the usurping Russian infidels. And this was the path they were forced to tread!

The plodding procession had done well at first, journeying alongside the Volga, stopping at river towns and Molokan settlements, then traveling south through the lands of the Don Cossacks.

Then in the no-man's land south of the Don, west of the Terek, they tasted war. Cossack horsemen shattered them—killing, kidnapping, raping with a ferocious lightheartedness. Scattered groups of panicking peasants were easy prey between sky and steppe.

Memory gripped Semyon's senses—cries, wails, thumps, and shuffling of frantic movement; a confusion of bodies; lathering horses flinging bits of feather grass and pungent wormwood from beneath their flying hooves; and another scent, clean and fresh, the smell of his four-year-old son's hair as Semyon held him through the fray.

When it was over, Yekaterina and a teenage girl were missing. They turned their carts and wagons off the road to follow the hoof marks, a phalanx of the strongest young men, Semyon among them, in front. At evening the searchers found them, the girl running ahead with an odd wobbly gait and Yekaterina behind, walking with that unearthly steadiness, her eyes locked onto his from afar.

The girl survived, but Yekaterina they buried in the steppe along with a premature infant. She was dressed in white—for white among the Molokans was the color of rejoicing, and Yekaterina had shrugged aside her broken body and had set off on the Beautiful Journey. But there was no joy in the gaunt faces who looked down at the young woman in the makeshift bier. They sang the songs that were their release from pain and prayed for her pilgrim soul.

Wormwood. The smell came back to him even now! The young men had torn up the wormwood that covered the unyielding ground to make a grave, and the bitter scent rose powerfully, encircling them with an invisible boundary.

Semyon walked next day with a heavy tread, his face showing no wonder as, at last, the mountains came into view. An elder, Ivan Fyodorovich, walked beside him for comfort, saying nothing. Semyon did not turn his head.

"We must fight," he said.

"You are heartsick, Semyon," Ivan answered. "But we cannot fight. If we resist evil with the ways of Satan, we become evil ourselves. We cannot fight! That's why we're here, because we cannot fight! Trust God, Semyon."

Semyon nodded. "We must fight," he said.

They fought. They faced off the next band of marauders with a thicket of scythes and pitchforks. The Cossacks checked their small, fiery horses and swerved aside, deciding to look for easier prey. A fierce exultation crowded Semyon's heart, and he began counting heads. From that moment, he became a leader—a phenomenon among the gray-bearded Molokan patriarchs! He determined that he would take those 247 peasants through the steppe and over the mountains with no further losses. He held onto his young son Anton and began to plan.

The next day he studied the mountains floating on the plain before him like some fantastic vision. He drank in their strangeness and beauty; then he turned to study the faces behind him, old and young, weighing their strength. The boy was trudging along beside him. Anton had changed in the past week; his face seemed to have thinned and blanched with night thoughts too hard for a four-year-old.

The boy looked back at him. "When is she coming?" he asked.

"She won't be coming to us, but we will go to her," said Semyon in the way of the old people.

But as he spoke, his eyes rested on the mountains and Anton followed his gaze. The pure, gleaming, ethereal mass had seemed to fix in the boy's mind with that other white image—his mother lying so peacefully on snowy linen. "We will go to her?" he questioned, and the thought became tangled in his vision of the mountains. After that,

Semyon noted, an eagerness came into his steps as they moved closer and closer to the Caucasus Mountains.

At the Ossetian town of Dzaudzhikau, they paused to rest before attempting the long trek across the main Caucasus range. Semyon screwed up his eyes and measured the rocky cliffs of Table Mountain outside the town. Monstrous, snow-slabbed ramparts bent white light onto faces strained with awe and fear. "This," they murmured, "this—between us and Russia!" The sight of that implacable mountain underscored their exile with bitter finality. But Semyon was determined that the mountains would not defeat them.

With the fear of early snow lapping at their heels, the Molokans met at the village of Redant with its guard tower, the first of many marking the way for them across the Georgian Military Highway. They began the mountain journey harried only by a dry east wind from the empty lands beyond Dagestan.

After a two-day march, they came to the mouth of the Drialskoye Usheliye—the Dariel Gorge. Semyon paused, thinking. He moved his broad shoulders this way and that to let the slow-moving pilgrims stream around him. They turned back to look at him, but he wrenched himself away from the compassion in their glances.

"It's not a road; it's a fairy tale," travelers in Dzaudzhikau had proclaimed. And they had told stories—folk tales and legends mainly—but already the towering gorge walls dimmed the sunlight to an otherworldly dusk where anything seemed possible. Before him rose the sheer rock cliffs where the "Gates of the Alani" had been hung, iron on wood, by those old ones who manned the mountain passes in the century after Christ. The Alani—some said that they were an ancient people, half-Ossetian, half-Persian; others said that they were the old Persian gods. Either way, their presence haunted this stretch of road!

Semyon trailed his people, a pace or two behind, because he could not control his face. The ponderous stone cliffs that rose thousands of feet on either side dwarfed the party. *A grave*, he thought, *a grave in its riven contours and a grave in its hunger to crush men's souls*. He had to crane his neck to see the sky at all, a narrow azure ribbon far overhead. An eagle screamed. Semyon jerked his head downward to see the silver River Terek leaping far, far below.

And there in the ravine on a jutting rock sprawled a decaying fortress—a fitting monument, Semyon reasoned. The castle, according to legend, was once inhabited by the beautiful but wicked Queen Tamara, who enticed handsome young travelers with promises of joyful love, but after a single night of pleasure, had the unfortunates beheaded and thrown into the Terek. *Tamara, the prophetess of life*. He chuckled grimly. *The lure of happiness, then the sudden sword stroke.*

A stocky farmer turned and glanced back at Semyon uncertainly. He seemed confused and lost in this mammoth landscape. A bent old woman turned too, her eyes pricking at him from under her calico *babushka*. *Don't look at me*, Semyon fumed inwardly, *what have I to offer you?* He slowed his pace, watching the group in front of him. Their movements had become ploddingly mechanical, and a dun-colored dust had settled on them so that they seemed part of the lifeless rock. *Move! You'll never get out of this ravine at this rate!*

Suddenly, Anton stood in front of him, letting the people flow around him like a small rock in a stream. His face was livid with expectation, and he was not afraid of the menacing cliffs or of the contorted expression on his father's face.

"I want to see the snowy mountain," he said.

Semyon picked up his son and shouldered his way to the front, again counting heads along the way. He urged the Molokans to a pace that won them the worst of the mountain pass before nightfall. And how quickly night fell—no benefit of twilight! The shadows seemed to bolt from that azure crack and fill the ravine like stricken night creatures that quickly drank up the silver stream.

The next day they saw Mount Kazbek, which the Ossetians call The Mountain of Christ, blazing with diamond brilliance. Anton's face filled with a peace and longing that spilled into Semyon's soul.

Finally, on a day of fine misty rain, they stood at Mleti Village where the road sloped gently down to a green southern country of orchards and vineyards.

"A land of promise," murmured Semyon. "Let us thank our God who carried us through." Two hundred and forty-seven Molokans fell to their knees in the mud of the Georgian Military Highway. The evils of the trek across the steppes did not revisit them; not a soul was lost in the mountain journey. They saw young Semyon as their God-appointed leader.

In the two years following, thousands of Molokans made the long migration. They settled in Kars, Erivan, Delizan, and Tiflis gubernias, building their own Russian-style villages—Malaya Tiukma, Nikitina, Golovinovka, Malhazovka, Voskresenovka. But most who had crossed the mountains with Semyon chose to settle with him in one of the vine- and wheat-growing villages near Tiflis.

And they had lived a good life, Semyon mused, as the snow twirled in ghostly writhings in the light from the doorway. Bountiful harvests and leisurely winters and an unruffled pace—the way the Molokans liked it. Until now. He shivered in the chill air, but he waited until Fenya, finished with her milking, went out through the wicket gate. *The days of complacency are gone*, he thought as he watched the girl disappear into mute stirrings of snow.

Fenya shut the wicket gate and walked with her crisp, light stride toward the west. She wasn't surprised that Nadya had forgotten to milk the cows. *I'd have forgotten too*, she thought. *It isn't every day that Piotr Gavrilovich comes home!* The snow danced in an airy spiral, then settled, as though it too were glad to be finished with its work for the night. The sky became wonderfully clear so that she could see the lights of home winking at her through the tree branches.

The Kostrikins' hut was a straggler. It hunkered into a slight hollow away from the other huts, wearing its thatched roof jauntily like a fur cap. Like Voloshins', it was built in the traditional style—a classic Russian *izba* with a long entrance hall that served as an air lock against the cold, the kitchen with its big stove, the best room lined with benches, and an attached shed for animals. The Kostrikin hut was smaller and poorer than Piotr's home, but it was also more decorative. Fenya's father wasn't much of a farmer, but he was a master carver, and his imaginative work decorated every post and lintel and beautified even the simplest piece of furniture. Her mother Anna was the clever, practical one. Without her ingenious management, they'd never get by.

Fenya slipped quietly into the warm kitchen; she had lit the stove earlier, and it was now blazing merrily. The golden glow enveloped her sister Natasha as she cut up turnips and plopped them into the pot of cabbage soup. In the other corner, where an Orthodox family would have kept its icons, was a small table and the family's most valuable possession, a sewing machine. It was one of only two in the village. Fenya's mother was able to bring in extra income by sewing for wealthier families. She was busy at it now, and the machine rattled away as she stitched on a gathered skirt in a rich brown merino woven from their own flock. The two older girls, Natasha and Fenya, would do the finish work and the embroidery later; no one but Anna was allowed to touch the precious machine.

Anna glanced up with one of her quick, harried looks as Fenya crossed the room. "God alone knows where your brothers are," she complained. "Did you see them in the village?"

"No, but they can't be too far off—the sheep are in, and I didn't bring them. I was at Voloshins'. The boys must have seen to it."

"Well, you'd better find them for me before you take your coat off. We need to eat. Then they may as well read while I'm finishing this. There's no point in wasting light."

Anna was adamant that her two sons, the youngest of her brood, learn to read. Among the Molokans, knowledge of the Holy Scriptures was considered the highest and most admirable trait in a man. The little boys were faithfully sent to the *zemstvo* (provincial council) school every day it was open.

For the girls, reading was considered unimportant; instead, they worked hard to free their brothers of chores so that the boys could pursue higher things. When the two tow-headed, ruddy-faced Kostrikin boys read to the family in the evenings, they'd all swell with pride. After all, it was a family achievement!

No sooner had Fenya stepped out onto the porch than she saw them, their silvery-blond heads gleaming like two little moons in the dark hollow. She laughed to herself as she wondered what unlikely portion of Scripture Misha and Vanya were likely to hit on tonight! They both had a knack for pulling Bible passages out of context in a devastatingly funny way. But her parents never laughed. They were awed and respectful of that ability to translate marks on paper into words. Never mind what the words meant!

Later when they had finished their simple meal of soup and rye bread, they sat around the table, and Misha brought out the Russian Bible. He opened it randomly and began to read in a childish monotone, syllable by syllable:

> "Until the day breaks
> And the shadows flee away,
> Turn, my beloved,
> And be like a gazelle
> Or a young stag
> Upon the mountains of Bether."

Misha continued to read, as though the words were not beautiful. But they went through Fenya like a shaft of light. *Until the shadows flee away*, she thought, *but now they are gathering*. She remembered Piotr's strained and anxious face as he came down the lane. *What will become of us?* she wondered.

Suddenly, she needed to be outside. "I'll check on the livestock," she told her parents and grabbed the ragged nankeen coat she shared with Natasha.

Fenya stood on the high ground, the hillside cradling her. Behind her, the mountains rose, dark and shapely. Below, the lights from the Molokan huts winked wistfully behind the winter-bare branches of the fruit trees. Around her the earth breathed out its essence through flecks of melting snow. She inhaled the cool scent and dug her toes into the prickly softness of last year's bracken. Its fragrance arose subtly, awakening that poignant loneliness within her that she fought or cherished but never forgot. And the earth opened its secret storehouse of memories and dreams and hope. The branch-drawn fragments of yellow light below her flickered in answer to the white pricks of light from the star-strewn sky. There would be plenty for her to do when she went home, but for now Fenya paused—surrendering her body to the power of the newly revealed earth and lifting her eyes, unashamed, to the sanctity of the stars.

III

In the Village

A fluff of gray-white cloud spewed out over the patchwork of field and hill like wool batting flung out of a torn quilt. An ancient scent of bare black earth rose with its haunting reminders of all the first spring rains since childhood. Piotr raised his head and saw that the cranes were already flying north in the frosty morning air.

He followed the lane behind the village to the stream flowing between the last row of huts and the vineyards and orchards to the south. The stream, like all streams in the Kura Valley, noisily fretted against its bed, the sharp edge of recently broken ice in its voice. Following its bank, Piotr spotted a small peasant in a peaked cap watching the water intently. He occasionally prodded at pebbles with a booted toe. Piotr called to him.

"Aleksei Davidovich!"

"God be praised, Piotr Gavrilovich. I guess they haven't sent you to Manchuria yet—but I suppose the fireworks there are just about over." Aleksei's darting black eyes took in Piotr's high-necked tunic and military boots. "A welcome to you . . . Rain, you think?"

"Seems likely."

"Well, God knows, God knows . . ." He seemed disturbed. "If this creek moves much more, it will be on my allotment. Then I'll have to pay quit rent on the fish in it. Who can tell how much they'll charge me for whatever fish may or may not happen to swim by!" Aleksei pulled at his luxurious wedge-shaped beard. "I'm wondering if I should try to dam it up on this side or let nature take its course. I have enough rent to pay."

"Can you do that?"

"Why not? I don't have so much land that I can afford to have half of it under water—you know what they say in Guria." He chuckled. "'If I tie up a cow on my bit of land, her tail will be in someone else's!' Not only that, but she'll be up to her knees in water if this stream changes course. You know, Feodor Slivkoff tells me he's careful not to let fir saplings from the forest take hold on his fallow field out to the west there. Otherwise, the government will come in, claim it's state property, and charge him quit rent on the timber!"

Aleksei held up a cautioning finger. "Ah, you have to be wily these days. Wise as a serpent, gentle as a dove. Smart as the devil!"

"I don't think that's in the Book, Aleksei," said Piotr, grinning at the man's rueful manner.

"Doesn't have to be! Wait until you try to make a life of your own. You'll see how you have to crack your skull trying to outwit the government. Pretty soon they'll claim my beard is state property, and I'll be paying quit rent on the lice in it."

"Don't tell me your troubles," Piotr joked. "I am government property and every minute of my time is quit rent."

The small intelligent eyes darted upward. "I know it's no joke." Aleksei made a wry mouth. "I'm careful not to let them see how many cow chips Old Betsy drops. Any increase in productivity means an increase in taxes. I suppose if I just nudge a few of these pebbles over here, I'll be hunted down as a revolutionary."

"Will you?" Piotr was suddenly serious. "Is there much talk of that in the village? I've gone six months now. Baku is boiling with it!"

"The whole Caucasus is boiling with it," Aleksei replied. "The war with Japan makes it worse. Especially since we seem to be losing. It gives the radicals a chance to condemn the government. You probably heard of the big strike in Tiflis in January. It was chaos—thousands of people screaming in the streets and bazaars. That Bloody Sunday Massacre in Moscow set it off. The trains were stopped. People were waving red flags, singing some French song—"

"'The Marseillaise.' Baku was the same—they call it 'the revolutionary hotbed on the Caspian.' And for good reason, I can tell you! I wondered if Tiflis was a little calmer."

Aleksei shook his head. "They've all been yelling 'down with autocracy' so they can set up some other anti-Christ government. Things have been quiet here, but even in Delizan there were strikes. The Cossacks came in and killed a few peasants, mostly Armenians. No Molokans. We don't get involved in such things."

"Why? Why don't we get involved? You're as unhappy with the system as anyone. Don't you want to see change?"

"Not that kind of change." Aleksei lowered his voice and nervously scanned the land and birch grove on the other side of the stream. "These Bolsheviks, believe me, they're Satan's illegitimate children! At least the Tsars are his legitimate children. A constitutional government—there's talk of that—well, that would be fine. But it's not going to happen.

"Too many have caught this revolutionary fever. Even some of the peasants and, of course, all of the factory workers, oil workers—everyone! Since those idiots in Moscow decided to persecute the Georgian church, they've even managed to turn the religious people away from them. Every time I go to Tiflis, the Social Revolutionary pamphlets are flying in the streets like dirty snow. I tell you, that madman from Gori is working overtime! They should have kept him in Siberia a little longer. What do they call him? Koba, that's it—name of a Georgian folk hero, but I've heard he's the son of a shoemaker named Djugashvili." Aleksei sighed gustily. "Meanwhile, we Molokans are sitting on the fence—until someone shoots us off!"

"Or until we leave. Have you thought of that?"

"The prophecy. Ha! I've thought of it—and thought and thought. That's another fence for me to sit on. Right now, I need a prophet to tell me if this crazy stream is going to jump its bed."

"Maybe it won't rain. Maybe the whole thing will dry up."

"Don't say that. Then they'll charge me for an increase in plowland!" He touched his cap as Piotr turned to leave. "Welcome back, Gavrilovich. May the Lord give you His guidance and wisdom. I think you will need it." Aleksei ducked his head and narrowed his eyes with a confidential air.

Could he possibly know? Piotr wondered. Aleksei, for all his barbed wit and joking manner, was a godly man; he would never betray him. But if his situation was common knowledge in the village, he was in danger. Even considering desertion could bring disastrous consequences.

Piotr absently followed the stream. Between the white boles of the birch trees, bare orchards and pruned vineyards sloped down the Kura Valley from the western foothills to the ranges of the lower Caucasus. Overhead, the cloud ceiling hovered close, its soft and maternal screen hushing sound and robbing the trees of shadow.

Whatever the talk was, Piotr mused, about his position or anything else, Sirakan Abajarian was bound to know. Sirakan knew everything.

He was the son of Aram Abajarian, an Armenian widower who had fled the Turkish pogroms into Georgia. Aram bought out the village store and promptly married a slender, fair-skinned Georgian woman, Maria Tcheidze, a widow with a five-year-old son, Noe. It wasn't long before she gave Aram his first and only daughter, Nina.

As his parents aged, Sirakan had begun to manage the shop, expanding its merchandise to include various dry goods and the exotic imports available in Tiflis. Even in these troubled times, Piotr noted, Sirakan's wily intelligence and gruff kindheartedness enabled him to keep the fragile balance of village relationships healthy—at least healthy enough for good business. *Yes*, Piotr thought, *Sirakan would know a thing or two*. He turned up a side lane lined with wattled fences and made his way to the square.

At midmorning, the village was quiet. A pale sun was just beginning to bleach the cloud layer. Dark-jacketed Georgian farmers, clustered in uneasy groups, had stopped glancing upward. The whitewash of houses and shops, the blanched stone street, and the dingy, porous patches of snow fused under a pallid sky. All the dark shades seemed to have been blotted up by the men's clothing and the fir trees.

In contrast, the rich color inside Abajarian's store seemed even richer as Piotr stood in the doorway, adjusting his eyes. Weak light came through the wavy bottle-glass window and fell with a greenish underwater quality on Nina Abajarian's pale face and dark turbulent hair and on the turned back of her half-brother, Sirakan. Behind her, a red and black rug from Azerbaijan proclaimed a fierce geometry.

Sirakan's deep voice doled out a heavily weighted collection of phrases. ". . . it'll be safer for you, Nina," he was saying without looking at her. "Don't turn from this betrothal. You know how things are with our people . . . These are dangerous times for someone like you." Piotr saw Nina stiffen against the Tartar rug, and he thought of the frightened Armenian faces he had seen in Baku.

"Safer," Sirakan repeated as the dark tilt of her eyes flashed, then wavered as she caught sight of Piotr. A scatter of petty coins fell onto the counter from her splayed-out fingers, and the noise brought Sirakan's head around. The Armenian leaned his swarthy arms on the counter while Nina turned and began arranging and rearranging items on the back shelf with elaborate attention.

"So, Gavrilovich, you've come home for your mother's funeral! Galina Antonovna always had great timing. Give her our hope for a miraculous recovery." Sirakan's red lips stretched in a smile beneath his glossy mustache.

"She is better . . . already," muttered Piotr.

"Good, good—and you, Piotr, I suspect you are doing some thinking."

Piotr nodded, trying to look noncommittal. Did everyone in the village know? His heart lurched in fear.

"Well, then," said the implacable Sirakan, "I'm going to help you do a little more thinking." He retreated to an alcove curtained off with striped cloth and returned with a creased paper, part of an editorial from the Socialist newspaper, *Sakartvelo*. Piotr could read enough Georgian to catch the heading: "Military Rule Foreseen for Guria."

"Can you understand that?"

"Yes, yes—martial law in Guria province."

Sirakan brought his face close to Piotr's and hit the printed broadside with the back of his hand. "Do you know what this means to you?"

Piotr was taken aback. His concentration fled, and the soldierly rows of black type were as incomprehensible to him as the whorls of black hair on Sirakan's arms.

"What do you mean, to me?" *God help me*, he thought, *does everything have to mean something to me these days?* He glanced at Nina's slender back, acute embarrassment flooding him. Her brother slammed the paper on the counter.

"Peasant! And the government gives people like you guns! Listen to me. Georgia is going up in flames. Right now Guria basically has its own government. This Socialist revolution has gone so far that the whole territory is in the hands of the Communist 'committee.' But it won't last. The procurator is calling for military rule. Listen to this! 'It is essential to send a strong force of troops into Guria without delay and place the area on a war footing for three or four months.'

"Who do you think is going to be holding a gun to the heads of these peasants? You!" Sirakan's finger jabbed at Piotr's chest. "You!" he repeated. "Tell me how you're going to like that. I know you. You aren't the man for it. I like you, Piotr Gavrilovich, so I'm going to give you some advice. Leave."

The door swung open and two kerchiefed women came in. Sirakan assumed a suave demeanor. "And what else can I help you with," he asked Piotr.

"C-cakes," Piotr stuttered, "a dozen iced cakes."

"Nina! Wrap it up for our young soldier." He turned his attention to the newcomers.

Startled, Nina twirled and tumbled some small cakes into a paper wrapping, dropping the pieces, then picking them up again. The more nervous she became, the calmer Piotr felt. He looked at her intently and at last she met his eyes over the clumsy brown package. He reached for it.

Sirakan stretched a muscular hand behind his sister, grabbing for an account book.

"Leave," he whispered hoarsely. "Leave."

Smoke was rising from the clay chimney of the dairy house as he came back to the hut. They were boiling milk for clotted cream. Nadya, with her rosy cheeks and pink smock, was a fresh blot of color in the drab, winter-worn yard. She swung up the porch steps ahead of him, carrying a brimful crock of sour cream against one rounded hip. He caught a glimpse of Fenya Kostrikin standing near the byre; she shot one of her vividly blue glances at him and then retreated with deerlike shyness, the point of her white kerchief flitting in a bright daub of sun. A *strange girl*, he thought, straining to make out her slender form against the weathered wood. In her patchwork dress, the colors of stone and wattle, she had a way of dissolving into her surroundings.

Nadya, however, was obvious enough. At fourteen, she was budding with womanly curves and full of village gossip as they sat down to dinner. Piotr listened happily, eager to forget about war or prophecy or revolution. He avoided Galina's probing eyes, laughed at the stream of cabbage juice running down Dausha's round little chin, and questioned his father about farm matters—livestock and new vines and the hardness of the ground after the first thaw.

"We need a rain . . . ," Gavril said, "but we'll be going out to the fields to establish our allotments this week."

Nadya waved the allotments aside. "Katya Shubin's getting married—did you know? To Fydor Samarin. Everybody's hoping for a summer wedding. I expect our cousins will marry soon, too. Uncle Mikhail is still the talk of the village. Everything he touches turns to gold. All the girls have their eyes on Trofim and Andrei—handsome and rich, too."

Her light tone changed suddenly. "But some people don't like it.

Kulaks, they call them." She dipped her wooden spoon into the common bowl of cabbage soup and gave Piotr a thoughtful look. "Uncle's not really a *kulak*. He doesn't get rich by using other people—he's just smarter than most. Anyway, he doesn't care what people think. He just laughs and says, 'If I'm rich enough to make them jealous, then so be it.'" She shrugged expressively, but Piotr glanced up in time to catch a worried pucker distorting Galina's smooth brow.

"Oh, and another wedding coming up," Nadya continued. "Nina Abajarian is engaged—finally! She's quite old, you know. At least twenty-two. But pretty—all the boys say so, even though she's *nynash*. She's going to marry a man from Tiflis. He owns part of a calico factory, so you can guess he's rich! But Sirakan wouldn't want anything else."

She chattered on, but Piotr's mind had stopped at Nina. *Nynash—not ours . . .* Of course, she would marry. That was no surprise. And he would marry someday too, but not *nynash*. Molokans rarely married "out." He would be counted as dead by his relatives, forced to live as an outcast.

A high price to pay, thought Piotr. *Too high. I'm not ready to make that kind of choice . . .*

Then he pictured Nina Abajarian with her vagrant eyes and trembling hands, and he was pierced with longing.

Later, at night, Galina came in and sat on the carved chest under the window. She held a wadded up quilt on her lap and kept plucking little bits of down out of it with her fingers.

"Piotr, I think you should leave." The left side of her face was lost in darkness; the other half was sculpted with a blue luster from the window.

"I'm considering it, Maminka," he said gently. "It's not so easy to leave everything behind."

"I know, I know—but I also know you can't stay. It's too uncertain. I'm afraid of what will happen to you if we don't listen to God's voice in this matter."

"Afraid? Listen, I've been in the army six months now. So far I haven't been sent to Manchuria, and I haven't been asked to shoot down any revolutionaries. Maybe it will turn out better than you think. There are rumors that the war is almost over. If I can manage to continue, things may change, and I can come back, and we'll all be back to our same old ways! Don't worry so much—young men return from the army all the time and take up a normal life. That's all I'm asking for."

"And that's all you can't have," Galina insisted. "Even if you came back, what memories and scars would you be carrying?"

Memories, scars. She left a pause, and it filled up with scenes from his past months of regimental life. In Baku, his religious background had made him an oddity—the shunned fanatic. Piotr looked away from her and fingered his scars. "Keep yourself separate," his family had warned during the emotional goodbyes. "Remember, we are a separate people. Be careful what you eat—make sure they aren't serving you pork."

The Molokans were strict about Old Testament dietary laws, careful to serve only kosher foods in their homes. But among the high-spirited Russians and Georgians in his battalion, Piotr's religious peculiarities became a subject for mess hall ribaldry—some of it funny, some of it cruel. *Scars, yes,* Piotr thought. *I managed to keep away from unclean meat and, as for the separateness, they never let me forget it!*

Galina was watching him. "Leave now," she said. "The life you know is failing. It will not be here for you to return to. You are young—you need to make a new way."

"What? And leave everything . . . you . . ."

"Yes. Leave." There was a heaving intensity in her voice, and the glow from outside touched on glints of moisture gathering in her eyes. Her proud face crumpled, and knotted furrows marred the beautiful forehead. Sobs struggled from the wide grimace pulling at her mouth.

Piotr watched her with an odd detachment. Galina was not ordinarily tearful. The swollen, animal noises coming from the woman by the window seemed alien to him, as though a stranger had crept in to beg some impossible boon. He twitched his shoulder with a cold repugnance. *Well,* he thought, *she won't cry a golden tear!* Then he was filled with horror at his own indifference.

Finally, exasperation won out over cooler emotions. He stood with abrupt anger and hobbled to the porch, one boot on, one off.

"What do you want of me?" he yelled back at her. "I didn't make my circumstances!"

As his leave time dwindled, Piotr's uncertainty increased. He found comfort in the small events of day to day. Bits of time, fragments of conversation, snatches of song—insignificant in themselves—together created the familiar, cherished pattern of village life. Everything not dictated by the demands of crop and weather was dictated by Molokan tradition. But each night, Galina came in to sit under the window and cried with woeful determination. Still Piotr could not make up his mind to go or to stay, but he lay paralyzed in a stifling web of obscure demands.

On Sunday the family dressed in their best and walked up to a steep-roofed wooden building for services. It was not yet Easter, but the western orchards flaunted the lace of early bloom. The first shoots of crocus sparkled against the dark earth in gallant blades, at war with the occasional patch of snow.

The Voloshins clattered up the slatted steps, scraping slush from their clumsy felt boots. As they entered the simple building, they bowed their heads, and a group of sixty or so Molokans stood respectfully to honor their prayer according to the custom. Galina and the girls sat in the women's section facing the preacher's table. Gavril and Piotr made their way to the "speakers" section.

Semyon strode to the front, looking at no one. His face registered watchful alertness as the group assembled. When the rectangular patch of sun shining through the east window touched the row of little girls in their starched kerchiefs, he turned to the "singers" section. "Gerrasim Alekseivich," he said quietly. Gerrasim, a portly peasant with a childlike pink mouth budding in his ink-black beard, began a traditional song.

Piotr studied the other "singers" assembled behind Gerrasim—each face was familiar. He knew their families, knew the burdens they carried in across the wooden threshold. He knew why Ivan Paveloff's shoulders slumped in weariness; he knew why Dmitri Bogdanoff, just sprouting the patchy beard of a newly married man, radiated joy; he knew why Fydor Samarin couldn't concentrate but kept glancing toward a certain lace-edged kerchief in the women's section. Piotr sniffed the smell of wet wool, listened to the restless shuffling of small boys behind him, and drank in the utter simplicity of Molokan life.

At the front stood Semyon, as he had stood every Sunday for as long as Piotr could remember. He swayed slightly to the slow-pulsed song, his erect form crisply outlined against the white hanging behind him. The Molokans sang with release, as though to break some strain that had gathered. As the tempo increased, they began clapping briskly, and a few women in the front rows raised their hands in an attitude of worship. When the song stopped, it ceased so suddenly that the silence itself rang.

Everyone's attention was riveted on Semyon as he took the Russian Bible into his hands, but he seemed completely unaware. His vibrant beard brushed the text as he read the fifth chapter of Luke. His paper-thin eyelids quivered, the blue-green veins that branched on his delicate temples throbbed, and his expressive mouth seemed to chew and feed on the words. The man's whole face was in motion, but his hands and body were absolutely still.

"'No one puts a piece from a new garment on an old one; otherwise, the new makes a tear, and also the piece that was taken out of the new does not match the old.

"'And no one puts new wine into old wineskins; or else the new wine will burst the wineskins and be spilled, and the wineskins will be ruined. But new wine must be put into new wineskins, and both are preserved.'

"God," Semyon told his people, "is preparing a new work among us— new. Every person here will be a part of that new work in some way. So each of us must search his heart with openness of spirit and see in what way His plan involves us. God is crying out to each of us, but to hear His voice, we must put aside old ways, old thoughts, old patterns of life.

"And Russia is old—old and sliding into a pit from which we cannot save her." There was a stir as the old man's eyes traveled the room, pausing, lifting, journeying on. They rested briefly on Piotr as if he were a stranger. "An old wineskin, patched and marred and leaking a sour, contaminated wine. But God will preserve His people."

In litany fashion, Semyon recounted the history of the Molokan people—always stressing the hand of God in the years of persecution, exile, and rebuilding. Change and upheaval, he assured them, became the vehicles of God's divine plan.

"Do not resist," he pleaded. "Do not fight the ways of God. Do not settle back into the smug contentment that kills the willingness of the soul. Do not be afraid to be cut off from Russia. You are Russia. Russia is in your soul. You will take her with you to the ends of the earth."

The singing started like something unleashed from nature. With crooked elbows, the men raised work-scarred hands, their bodies lurching with abrupt, jerky movements.

> "*Water our hearts with heavenly dew,*
> *As Thou gavest Thy people in the desert*
> *Water from a stone to drink.*
> *Lead Thou us into that good country*
> *Which Thou promised to give to Thine elect . . .*"

There was a heaviness to their chanting, like the heaviness and beauty of worked gold. But above, an unhindered soprano soared in lyrical counterpoint. Piotr fixed his eyes on the ceiling and sang as if to purge his soul of all the anguish of the past days.

Afterward, groups of men and women swirled in eddies, as fits and spurts of conversation, which would continue with more fervor at mealtime, began. Trestle tables appeared, along with dishes of eggs, pickled mushrooms, vegetables, and high round loaves. The eyes and mouths of the young children grew moist in anticipation. At a signal, the children went straight to the tables in the back. The boys played tug-of-war with the long strip of cotton toweling which was a sort of community dinner napkin, until a stern glance from an elder subdued them. The adults milled around a little longer in apparent confusion; then they settled down comfortably at the same tables they occupied every Sunday. The men put their wrists on the table in expectation, and the women moved their rumps from side to side like nesting birds.

Piotr, as a guest, sat at the head table with Semyon and the elders. Galina was serving at the foot of the table behind the samovar. Piotr's thoughts swerved in their own direction. His imagination filled with vivid pictures of drying streams, empty village streets, yawning black doorways in deserted huts. He saw a black crow aimlessly plucking at exquisitely colored bolts of silk scattered in the village square. Galina passed glasses of hot tea in steep-sided saucers. A platter appeared, and Piotr absently selected pieces of cabbage, cucumber, salted watermelon rind.

Semyon Efimovich was breaking up a piece of black bread with his strong hands. *Change and upheaval. Why? The hand of God shaping men's lives. Why? Why not shape us in peace?* Piotr mechanically took a crusty end of the loaf and chewed it.

Russia. An old wineskin. Beautiful, beloved Russia with her broad steppes, sky-locked peaks, vast taiga forests, great rivers. Russia—its thatched villages and fairy-tale domes and the mystery of the seasons moving across the land in powerful contrast. Russia—its poverty and corruption and the relentless tragedy that searches out every generation. An old wineskin, he thought, but filled with a new fermenting wine due to explode.

Savory steam struck his face. Soup. Tender homemade noodles swimming in a rich broth. *Lapsha*. He turned to take the bowl from Galina. Someone was saying, "No . . ."

"No, not immediately—it's too early in the year. The sea lanes aren't open . . ."

"The whole family?"

"All of them, yes."

"That must have cost a lot."

"They sold everything . . ."

Piotr glanced up as he lifted his soup spoon to his mouth. For some reason, everyone at the table was staring at him. They quickly looked away.

"An act of faith," said Semyon. No one contested him.

More bread, eggs, meat. The confetti drift of words fell around Piotr without effect. *Better to face it with your own people,* he thought. He glanced across the room and caught the eye of his Uncle Mikhail. Piotr was still not convinced he should leave Russia.

A looming disquiet shadowed Piotr throughout the next day. At dusk he wandered back by the stream, crossing at the small wooden bridge. Pilgrim geese and cranes were ruffled and restless on the choppy surface of the pond that straddled the eastern fields. The water was restless too, glinting with copper and lilac and sudden livid flashes. The air pulsed with wind sound and the fretful voice of the stream. Piotr shrugged deeper into his heavy coat, head down, so that at first he did not see Nina Abajarian lingering between the birches. He was surprised to see her at all—and surprised at his quick, unbidden notion that she came expecting him.

The wind took liberties with her. It turned her purple sleeves into flags and played about the surface of her dress to briefly mold thigh and breast, then billowed out as though in a huff to deny any suggestion of female form. It snatched her greeting but not her hesitant smile and the small jerking nod she gave him. *But wait,* he told himself, as his face betrayed a welcoming surge of feeling, *she's a promised woman.* Yet he was not only glad to see her, but also relieved—as though looking at her, talking to her could settle some vague and painfully unresolved matter.

"It's not a sin to talk to a Molokan, you know," he told her with a self-mocking grin, just to have something to say. "Just look at me as an ordinary soldier."

"A soldier?" she said with feigned disparagement. "That's not an ordinary business—for a Molokan. Do you plan on going back to it?"

"Who knows?" Piotr tossed caution to the wind. "It's difficult either way."

"It is difficult," she said with quick empathy. She seemed eager to turn her mind from whatever had been preoccupying her. "Sirakan is convinced that you should do anything to get out of the military just now. I think he's expecting some radical changes. I know that the Social Democrats are gaining power. I'm not sure what that means, but my brother seems to be waiting for something to happen very soon. Of course, he doesn't tell me this, but I can see. People come and go, and there's lots of talk . . ."

"Is he that involved?"

"Sirakan? No. Not directly. Noe is—our half-brother, you remember? It's his life! I think Sirakan gets his information from Noe. Noe is going to change the world!" Nina said, with a mixture of admiration and scorn in her beautiful eyes.

"He is, is he? What is this new world he dreams of? Has he told you?"

"No. People don't tell me their dreams. I have to make up my own. As for Noe and his friends, freedom and equality and the brotherhood of man—those seem to be their favorite words. And, of course, we bring about this brotherhood by tearing families apart!"

"So you don't agree with it."

"Oh, I don't know. Maybe we will be torn apart anyway. We may as well get something out of it."

"Well, at least he's choosing his war. Mine isn't of my own choosing."

She looked at him keenly. "You have some choices you can make."

"Not the ones I want! I'm being forced into a dark way—full of unknowns! How can I make a choice? I'm not a cause fighter like Noe. I'm not a fighter at all. I just want a normal life—a field to plow, some cattle to tend, a family. I just want to be left alone to be happy!" He gestured helplessly.

"Is that all?" Lights of humor played in her eyes. "How unusual! I'll tell you what, Piotr Gavrilovich—I want to be happy too. But I think that something has to happen to us first. Before we can be happy, I mean. Or even capable of happiness. For you, this is your ordeal. But there is something on the other side of it. Something you can win through to."

Piotr studied her earnest face with its delicate, downward-turning nose. *There's a surface gaiety about her,* he thought, *that plays across her nature the way the wind plays across her body; but inside, inside she's still and wary.* In Nina that inner pessimism called up a courage that somehow came across as charm. *But she's wrong,* he told himself. *I'm capable of happiness right now—if there's happiness to be found in the world. And ordeals?*

"Wait a minute," he joked. "Everybody's ready to shove me into some ordeal that I'm not ready for! To my way of thinking, ordeals are something to be avoided, and that's my number one plan—to avoid ordeals. Seriously, do you think we are in for big changes? Tell me what you think. What would you do if you were me?"

"If your plan is to avoid trouble, I think you will have it anyway—but won't gain anything by it. I do see changes coming. There's a restlessness, a hunger for action. I see it everywhere. When Sirakan and I walk past a group of farmers, they hush. Suddenly. Like a door being shut on a noisy room. Why all this secrecy? It's as though things that used to be set in the colors of ordinary life are suddenly black or white, and everyone has to choose. And with these choices come suspicions. You know what I mean, 'Where does he stand? Is he still safe?' People you have always known are different, and there's a secrecy about them. But you don't have any way of knowing what the difference means!"

"But some of us don't. Don't change, I mean. I'm the same, even if everything around me is shifting. The Molokans are that way. We've held to our customs for generations. Why can't we just continue?"

"Maybe you can. But I don't think so. It seems as though you will have enemies, whatever you decide. If you stay in the army and hope to come back to a peaceful life, you will be disappointed. I see the feelings in this village. If Georgia is put under any kind of military rule, as Sirakan says it will, and you are a part of that, you will be hated here. If you leave the army, you will be a hunted man, a criminal. The only thing left to you would be to flee, but that's an unknown too."

"Yes. America. The biggest unknown of all. And I don't want it. Everything in me tells me that I don't want that kind of exile. There must be another way."

"Talk to Sirakan. He may have some ideas. But talk quietly. Sirakan is very careful these days." She leaned against the bole of a birch tree; the notches in its trunk were set in gray wrinkled folds like weary, rueful eyes. Her own eyes were dark and shadowed now, and the lilac tints in the air stained the hollows beneath her cheekbones.

"I think Sirakan wants to see you go," she concluded.

"And you—what do you want?"

She shrugged and gave him a direct look. "Does it matter? Talk to my brother!"

IV

The Bartered Bride

Nina let the peevish stream lure her along its sandy bank. The wind tore at her, and she folded her arms against the chill, but she wasn't ready to go back yet. The water gurgled and hissed at the coming darkness, and obscure twilight shapes brooded under the trees. The first thaw had left the ground black and damp, but on the north side of each tree was a patch of snow like a starched bib. On the field, wan fingers of fading ice raked the dark ridges of last year's plowing.

Winter is breaking up, she thought, and a surge of wild misplaced joy scalded her. The water birds screeched and jabbered to make sure that her restlessness matched their own. A cacophony of discordant feeling went singing through her. *What a choice!* she mused, thinking of Piotr. *Flight to America—a strange land!* The idea was as alluring to her as it was repelling to Piotr. But Piotr, she realized, was tied to the Molokans with a soul-deep belonging that both baffled and attracted her. And now, now that it was in jeopardy, her feelings went out to him. Even Piotr seemed to sense an uneasy kinship with Nina Abajarian, the misfit!

Poised on the edge of two worlds, she could remember a time when it didn't matter that she was half-Armenian and half-Georgian. But those times were gone! "Safe—safer for you . . ." She remembered the concealed fear in Sirakan's tone as he insisted on her engagement to Mourad Mushegan. He had been elated when Mushegan had approached him after a church service in Tiflis and expressed a strong interest in Nina. Mushegan, Sirakan said with kindhearted insensitivity, was too rich to have to worry about social liabilities. He wanted a sweet and pretty wife, and Nina could be just that.

"And I can," she told herself as she made her way back to the shop. "I can!" She was willing to pay a certain price to have her own home, and family, and children.

She slipped behind the counter, positioning herself as usual beneath the bottle-glass window to see the clusters of Russian housewives, Georgian farmers, and village children crowding the square at sundown. She watched their dress and gestures as they tilted their heads together or called to each other in shared jokes—the jokes of those who belong to each other. Even their arguments seemed enviable! But the warp in the glass allowed her only bent and broken distortions. The clutter of merchandise, the scatter of coins, and the inexorable shapes woven on that Tartar rug behind her—those were her allotment!

Sirakan's level, soothing voice distracted her. He was explaining something from an account book to a Georgian peasant. The Georgian, she saw, was shaking with an agitation that quickly built to fury.

"What . . . what do I pay with? The scrap of land that you and those Russians have left me?" He gasped with the pain of it. "You leach away the best from us and then wonder that we can't pay for your filthy merchandise."

Nina looked at the man with wary sympathy. The Georgians, she knew, were chaffing at the Empire's bit and regarded the enterprising Armenians as greedy upstarts who had robbed them of the means they needed to break free. *I understand*, she wanted to say. *I'm one of you! Or half of me is.*

"You want me to pay? I tell you, I can't pay!" The man looked around wildly as people from the street pricked up their ears.

Fear sucked all warmth from her hands and feet and sent it flooding to her chest; the bursting tide of it tripped a hammering in her heart.

"No, no." Sirakan was calming, apologetic. "I'm not asking that . . . look. See this amount? That's credit to you. I'm saying I can't advance any more—"

"You'll starve us! Your greed will push us off of our own land . . ." The hoarse, hysterical cry set up a murmuring in the gathering crowd. Black-stemmed torch flames flowered here and there, tossing among shadow people with that pallid glow fire has at twilight.

With an angry sweep of his arm, the aggrieved customer shoved away Sirakan's account book along with several jars. All at once, glass shattered and noisy villagers burst into the shop. Nina stepped back, pressing against the wall as though to disappear into the black and red

44

shapes behind her. Sirakan stooped slowly, very slowly to retrieve his book. "Get out!" he rasped at her. "Get out now!"

Bottles crashed to the floor; someone grabbed a bolt of cloth and threw it to the crowd outside. The shining red-orange silk waved in upheld hands—a bright, undulating banner. It began to smoke with the unmistakable smell burning silk gives off. Then Nina saw the bonfire. Sirakan straightened, a raucous grin twisting his lips.

"Here," he said with flamboyant generosity. "Take it all; why not celebrate?" He grabbed a bolt of cheap calico and tossed it hard enough to stop the shout of the man who caught it. Nonplused, the man began unraveling the cloth. Laughing, Sirakan began smashing jars of pickles on the stone floor. Nina stared at him uncomprehendingly.

"We're neighbors," he shouted above the din. "We'll celebrate together." A heavy tang of vinegar soured the air. Nina, impaled against her rug, was getting very warm, but her eyes were glued to Sirakan in wonder.

"Wait, wait," his heavy voice boomed at the stunned faces around him. "Why have vinegar when you can have wine?" He began handing bottles of Tsitska wine around as he shouldered his way to the door. When he reached the roaring bonfire, he held the account book above his head.

"Look," he announced, "we'll celebrate together . . ."

He opened the book and read a name, "Patiashvilli." Without looking at it, he pulled a page from the book, balled it in his fist, and tossed it on the fire. "Vasadze . . ." A paper ball poofed and crumbled in flame. "Zhgenti . . ." Another one—ash. Nina watched in mute admiration as Sirakan read off name after name to the silenced crowd as their debts shrank and curled and disappeared. Broad grins began to replace bewildered scowls. If there were any two things the Georgians admired, these were courage and largess!

When it was all over, a lean-faced farmer stepped forward with all the poise and gracious ease of a people famous for their hospitality. He raised a cheap tumbler that Nina recognized.

"It is your glass and your wine, Abajarian, but we salute you. Neighbors!" he said, looking around to gather in the amused approval of the faces around him.

"We live together, we grieve together, we celebrate together!" The Georgian dipped his head to take the first sip.

It was as he said—they celebrated! Half the night. Nina had slipped upstairs to their living quarters, but she came down again after the last merrymaker left.

"It'll ruin me," Sirakan groaned as they began to put the shop back together. "The damage—well, it could have been worse." He smoothed his hand over the wooden counter as though comforting it.

"They could have burned us out. Do you know that? Burned us out . . . as it is, we've escaped lightly. Far more lightly than our brothers in Azerbaijan." Nina shuddered in the cold night air. The Tartars and Azerbaijanis had always been a shadowy menace on the edge of her world; recent killings of Armenians in Baku had brought the old nightmare back to life.

Sirakan stared at the blackening fire outside the door. When he turned his gaze back to her, it was thoughtful and worried.

"What I wonder is this—when troubles come in a village like this, who will they treat you as? The daughter of Aram Abajarian, the Armenian shopkeeper? Or the sister of Noe Tcheidze, their comrade in revolt?"

"I suppose after tomorrow, it won't matter," she said quietly.

"No, no, I guess not. After you marry, your fate will lie with Mushegan. The sooner, the better. It'll be safer for you . . ."

"And what about you, and father, and mother?"

"Who knows? Maybe we'll have to leave. This village is cracking at the seams. But there's nothing we can do about that."

Sirakan was quiet and grim as they set about restoring the plundered shop. *Safer*, she thought, as broken glass tinkled under her broom, *but at what cost?*

So tomorrow would be the day. The two families would meet and finalize a betrothal agreement. Tomorrow the Georgian half of her would retire behind some closed door in her soul, and she would become the Armenian betrothed of Mourad Mushegan.

The morning was crisp and still dark when Nina arose. A suggestion of gray dawnlight found its way into her room with its metal cot, white down quilt, and chaste little chair garnished with a faded blue and white striped pillow. She cautiously lit the lamp on the frail oval table in front of the window and went to open the chest placed on the rug at the foot of the bed. This rug was the only real color in the room. It was a deep Prussian blue, strewn with flowers in shades that varied from vibrant salmon to ethereal pinks and yellows.

Nina dressed slowly; today she would wear the Oriental dress of an

Armenian woman. She slipped a striped skirt of heavy silk over long bloomerlike trousers in indigo blue. Her white blouse was crisscrossed with a dark bodice, and both were belted in tightly by a vividly embroidered sash, wrapped twice around her slender waist. She went to the mirror, smiled anxiously, and stroked the thick glossy sweep of her brows. She had always thought of her skin as putty-colored, but it was finely textured and luminous so that its neutral hue reflected the colors around her. This morning those colors were shades of gray. Her face took on a stiff but earnest look, as if to say, "What will happen to you today?"

Nina's gaze wavered and dropped to the pretty sash, then to her hem and the blue trousers that hugged her heels above the Tartar slippers with their pointed toes. *These slippers won't do*, she thought. *It's just too cold. I'll have to wear my old boots.* The boots were soft russet leather, heel-less in the Georgian style. They were a good match for her russet cloak, but they were worn. She hoped that the rich Mushegans wouldn't notice scuffed leather beneath the jaunty, bravely colored trousers.

She could hear bumps and scufflings from downstairs as Aram and Sirakan went back and forth, loading the cart. Even the betrothal of an only daughter and sister was not enough to eclipse the possibility of doing some business in the city. Why waste a trip, they'd say!

Nina took a last look in the mirror, smoothed her stormy volume of hair, and crowned it with the Armenian headdress and long, silken veil that made every girl look like a princess. She cocked her head to listen and heard her mother's light step. This was serious, almost time to go! But something in her hesitated. She absently studied the face in the mirror as if searching for something. Then she went to the window. But there was nothing in the pale morning. She could see the loaded cart in the street below and the familiar row of huts beyond, backed by a twiggy exuberance of bare tree branches. And above that a moon, almost full, but worn and faded on the one edge like some ancient coinage too long exchanged.

"Nina!" It was her mother's voice. She left the window and went down.

"So you work in your brother's store!" Mourad Mushegan said this as if it were somehow amusing, as though she stood behind the counter as some young lady's idea of a lark. He smiled indulgently, creating for himself the image of a well-bred but whimsical girl who was not above entertaining herself with a shop girl's role. *Shall I disillusion him?* Nina asked herself. She tilted her head and listened to the dissonance within her and that crooked little desire to say something that would cause Mushegan to send her and her dowry packing. But she knew there was nothing that she could say that would influence him much. He spoke to her because he wanted to look at her face, not listen to her ideas. She gazed at him impassively and gathered her wits.

"Yes," Nina told him, "it's a wonderful opportunity to study human nature—and to survive. The two are so often connected!"

"Oh, and what have you learned?" His cheeks plumped in a smirk, and his temples moved up toward his hairline.

"Not as much as I'd like," she replied seriously. "I think I'm in the wrong laboratory! The problem with a shop is that people come in and honestly tell you what they want, and you give it to them. The rest of life is nothing like that." Nina let her eyes slide over her betrothed's face.

Mourad Mushegan was not a bad-looking young man. Just past thirty, he had lost the leanness of his youth, but had not yet acquired the heaviness of middle age. His skin was pale, with a sheen that was not the sheen of good health. His black hair was glossy, and even his clothes seemed to gleam. His hands were different though—pale, like his face, but dry and powdery looking. The change in texture seemed somehow disturbing.

"You are too pretty to be such a cynic," he commented with an arch look that dispatched the subject of human nature. "Dwell on the positive things! Just think, in a few weeks you will be my wife, mistress of my life, my home . . ." He looked around the room as if to acquaint her with splendors that should awe a simple village girl.

She followed his glance unobtrusively. Her future mother-in-law, Hamas, was sitting across from her in the formally decorated parlor, serving tea and cakes with a studied graciousness and exchanging dignified comments with Maria Abajarian. Nina's eyes took in the plush couch, the heavy draperies with their green silk tassels, and the gilt-framed family photographs. Could it be that she would really live here? She recited to herself all the reasons why it was appropriate, even necessary, for her to marry Mushegan. After all, what choice did she have?

He was smiling at her again with his humid eyes. He put his tea glass and saucer on the table with excruciating deliberation and placed his white hands on his knees. He had a way of doing this—his hand with the onyx ring would tighten on the striped cloth and hitch it up, revealing an inch or two of silk stocking.

Irritated and for some reason embarrassed, Nina turned her gaze to the window, but the early twilight robbed her of a view out. Instead the expensive glass mirrored the room and its occupants. She could just barely make out the plane tree outside, like a double-exposed photograph. It was an odd juxtaposition, she thought with her small, one-sided smile—the grand and shapely tree with stiff little people caught in its spreading branches, sipping tea. Sirakan looked particularly ridiculous and ill at ease.

She narrowed her eyes as a couple of barely visible students came into view, both of them wearing deep blue reefer jackets that were almost swallowed up by the dark street. Their pale faces and hands and the white papers they carried seemed detached from their bodies and wafted about in a ghostly, inhuman way. And the movement of those disembodied hands seemed portentous, an eerie mime holding a meaning both hopeful and sinister. Suddenly, the young men parted, and one of them began to distribute his bulletins across the street. The other was lost to view, but he couldn't have been far away because one of the printed broadsides came flying through the air and plastered itself against the tree trunk, moving up an inch or two as though trying to climb up into the branches above.

"The little fools don't know enough not to play with fire," said Mushegan, following her gaze. He looked stern, but then, breaking under the tension of the long look she gave him, raised his eyebrows and tried to sound droll. "Georgian independence! What a great, touching notion! But look where it got them up until Russia took over in 1801. How many times has Tiflis been invaded? Twenty-nine? Something like that. Not a desirable life even for the freewheeling Georgians."

"Every man wants his freedom." Sirakan shrugged in a conciliatory way. "You can't blame them for that, Mourad. Think of how you or I would feel about a free Armenia. People want to shape their own lives in their own way. For most that means some kind of national identity."

"Of course, of course. I don't deny them that. In fact, I almost admire some of them. Zoe Zordania and his Georgian nationalists are high-minded idealists. I can admire a high mind as well as the next person. What Zordania doesn't realize is that with these Social Democrats, he has a tiger by the tail that will turn around and rend him," Mushegan warmed to his metaphor, "and then the Russians will come in and cage the beast."

"Maybe," said Sirakan judiciously, "but Zordania is an astute politician as well as a high-minded idealist. I think he's a force to be reckoned with. I only hope the Russians are kind when they do the reckoning. Zordania is a real leader, and the people follow him because they feel he genuinely cares about the Georgian people. And he does! The only problem is that Georgia is no longer Georgian. Look at Tiflis. Mostly Georgian—but plenty of us Armenians, too. The rest are Russian, Turkish—a whole mixture of peoples. Meet the needs of the Georgians, and everyone else is in a stew. It's a complicated problem." He smiled in a self-deprecating way and glanced at Maria, apparently thinking of her Georgian blood. Nina noticed that she was pale and silent.

"Enough of politics," murmured Mushegan. "This can't be interesting to our lovely companions." He smiled encouragingly at Nina, and she felt a moment's panic. *Am I expected to say something?* She bit her lips nervously as though to incite them to action, but it was her father, Aram, who spoke up.

"Are you still importing cotton for your mills? I hear the price keeps going up and up."

Mushegan rolled his eyes and gave a grim chuckle. "I'm importing it from just about everywhere—the Indies, Africa, even America. They just can't seem to feed it to me fast enough. There have been times when I've had to close down for a few days just because there's no fiber to feed the mills. Believe me, it's a waste to have that expensive machinery sitting there idle. The only thing I save on is wages. Nobody works—nobody gets paid, including me. You would think that the peasants here and in the Ukraine would catch on and start growing more cotton. But who can understand the mind of a peasant! The fact that Russia is industrializing is nothing to them. They want everything as it always has been."

"We must have an unusually progressive village," Sirakan interposed drily. Nina noticed that he was stroking his mustache the way a man strokes a nervous horse to calm it. Not a good sign. "Some of our peasants are putting in cotton crops this year—although it's a risk for them. The Kura Valley may be a little cool for cotton, and if they lose a crop, they can lose everything. You know how the peasants are taxed."

"Of course, taxes are the price of peace."

"Well, they may be paying for it, but they're not getting it. No one could call Transcaucasia peaceful right now."

"Whose fault is that?"

"Good question. The answers, unfortunately, aren't so good. Who can explain what's happening in Guria?"

"The risings in Guria will be crushed." Mushegan's slick face had fallen into little pouches of discontent on either side of his short chin. "They're calling in the military," he added.

"I know, but look at what has already happened—landowners and *kulaks* killed. Factory owners will be next." Nina gasped. Sirakan had abandoned his usual diplomacy. "And it's not just another strike; these people have actually set up their own government by committee—a soviet they call it."

Mushegan lowered his head and looked up at Sirakan. Nina could see the red rims under his eyes and the pulse drumming in his temple. Although his face whitened with rage, his tone was light. "They are anarchists. How can they govern anyone? The role they have chosen is to be made an example of what happens to thieves and murderers who shake their fists at the established order. You'll see."

"I'm sure I will," murmured Sirakan. "Tell me, how do you deal with these anarchists in your own factory. I know they have been 'propagandizing the proletariat,' as they call it."

"I have no problem with that. I'm a genius at sniffing out Social Democrats and their tricks! Believe me, when I find them out, and I always do, I deal with them. But don't give me all the credit! The Black Hundreds have been very cooperative."

"Ah, well," said Aram, "business is complicated these days. Everything is changing. A man must look to his home for his peace and stability."

"Ah, yes." Mushegan moved his ashen hand on his knee, and Nina cringed as his sock peeped out. "Family life is the important thing— what a man works for."

Nina noticed that he said this in the same light tone he used to describe the thieves and murderers of Guria. *Odd*, she mused, *his voice makes even the most important things sound trivial, yet his painfully deliberate gestures make even the most idiotic movements seem strangely important.* She veiled her expressive eyes with her long lashes so that no one would see that she had decided that the rich Mourad Mushegan was a fool.

She glanced at her parents. As usual she could not read Maria's face. But Aram seemed totally unaware and was happily taking inventory of the elaborate Mushegan parlor. Sirakan's burly shoulders were hunched up against the carved and upholstered back of an English-style chair. Obviously he was ransacking his brain for a way to end the visit gracefully. Nina hoped he would think of something soon. Her limbs felt like lead, and she thought longingly of her clean, narrow bed and the little striped pillow on her chair.

Nina's mind the next day was full of Mourad Mushegan. Cartoonlike pictures of his unattractive traits flickered through her every waking moment. *The reptile!* she thought. *I'm already in bondage to him; he's crowding out my mind!* Her only comforting thought was that Sirakan's glee over the marriage had evaporated. Also, since Mushegan was a capitalist exploiter par excellence, she could probably count on Noe's help if she tried to elude the marriage trap Aram had set for her. Unfortunately, the radical Noe and his stepfather were always at loggerheads. What a joke! Aram was as likely to listen to her as to Noe! Besides, Aram would never willingly shame himself before the community by backing out of a formal betrothal. And the wedding was only three weeks away!

She lay across her cot face down and curled her fingers around a handful of quilt, as though she could anchor herself that way. How the day had dragged! She could hear Sirakan closing up shop below and then her mother's light footstep on the stair. She didn't turn when the door opened, but the rustle of Maria's skirts as she settled into the chair identified her visitor.

"I was thinking yesterday at Mushegans' of a girl I used to know," Maria began. Nina raised herself up on an elbow and gave her mother a listless look.

"She was from a good family, the daughter of a government examiner. But she went to work in a factory—to try to reach the people there. This was back in the '70s, and we wanted to raise the people out of their misery. And how else but to share it? So this young woman would work alongside the factory people and try to help them. She formed study cells for the Populists. But it was hard for her . . .

"Conditions were—horrible! She was so exhausted from the long hours and the terrible living conditions that she would slip away to one of the outbuildings and lie on the floor in the filth, just to catch a little quiet sleep. Finally her health broke, and she was forced to go back to her family.

"Then yesterday as we were drinking tea, her face came back to me.

She was a pretty girl, blonde and delicate. I wondered if there were girls like that in Mushegan's calico factory. It's been a long time since I've even thought about things like that!"

"Why did her parents let her do it?" Nina asked.

"They didn't. She left home and went out on her own. Some of us did that in those days; we would leave our families and get jobs or go to university so that we could reach the common people."

"We?"

"Oh, yes. I was one of the radical women of the '70s! I wore the blue glasses and the dark skirts and attended classes as though my soul's salvation depended upon it! And to do that I had to risk everything. Your grandparents are very bourgeois! It was years before they ever spoke to me again."

"How did you break away—how could you survive?"

"I married," Maria said simply. Nina looked hungrily at her mother's face, as though to pull out details that would hold some meaning for her. Maria was still a beautiful woman. Her austere face had darkened so that the shadows settled below her brows and nostrils and in the long lines on either side of her mouth. But this only accentuated the perfection of her features, like the black outlining on an icon. Oddly, she was holding a children's lesson book, too old to have been used by either of her own children. She kept caressing it with her fingertips. Nina looked at it curiously.

"There were plenty of us who did it back then. I won my freedom in a sham marriage. A terrible mistake, Nina. Marriage is a sacred thing, not something to be used toward any other end. But God was good to me."

"What happened?" Fascinated, Nina listened intently. Maria was trying hard to keep her tone clipped and factual, but her voice would catch and trip on furtive nuances of feeling.

"Well, there were dedicated young men who were willing to sacrifice themselves to free another 'worker for the people.' They didn't expect personal happiness anyway and so were willing to give up marriage in the future. Davit Tcheidze was one of them." Maria paused as though to savor the name—Davit, Davit—it was as though she were chanting it. And Nina realized it must have been years since she had spoken it.

"Davit was a friend of my brother's, and as far as my parents could see, he was suitable. Of course, they really didn't know him, just as they really didn't know me. When he presented himself as a suitor, they saw no problem. We married quickly, Davit and I, and took up our studies in Kazan. We didn't bother to keep up the pretense of living together."

"But Noe?"

"Yes, Noe! Don't worry, Nininka, I haven't forgotten how Noe came into the picture! I tried to keep my mind on business. I attended all the classes and the outside meetings faithfully. I didn't see Davit often, but when I did, I felt all fired up inside—as though I could love the whole world! Davit was my friend, my brother, my advisor—always with a calm unperturbed manner about him. And always maddeningly objective about me.

"So we continued like that through university; I lived on my dowry, and he lived on what he could earn and on gifts from his parents. When Davit graduated, he was sent to a remote village in the mountains to teach—a zemstvo job. He would write me occasionally, neat little letters that were both sensitive and cynical and, of course, maddeningly objective! I finished my course of study two years later. You see the picture there—that was taken about the time I graduated. See, there is Davit."

As she took a faded photograph out of her workbook, Maria shifted her body to tilt the picture toward the light. And all the shadows lifted off her face, and her voice was young. Nina studied the worn photograph. It was not hard to recognize Maria. She wore the severe garb and tinted glasses that were the uniform of the radical woman student. But on Maria the prim dark dress clung to her lovely form with a poetic carelessness, and the glasses did little to disguise the Byzantine beauty of her face.

Davit, disappointingly, was a blur. For some reason Nina felt that it was crucial for her to know his face, as if she would need to recognize it some day. She glanced at her mother and realized that Maria saw every feature with poignant clarity. The white crease that meandered across the shiny black and gray paper obliterated Davit's face, but did nothing to blur Maria's inner vision.

"I was surprised and pleased," Maria continued, "that Davit came back for my graduation. We both knew that the authorities would expect me to join him in his zemstvo post, but Davit let me know I could circumvent that if I wished to. I did not wish to. And I could see that Davit had changed during those two years in the mountains. The letters were a deceit, a screen to keep me at a distance! But when we saw each other again, we knew that God had given us a gift—a true marriage. See, look at him! You can see that hint of vulnerability in the way the shadows fall across his eyes. That was new. Davit looked more boyish at twenty-three than at twenty!"

Nina scrutinized the photo earnestly, but she saw nothing. Maria's manner cooled suddenly, and Nina wondered whether her thoughts pained her or whether she felt she should curb her enthusiasm about Davit Tcheidze to Aram Abajarian's daughter.

"Anyway," Maria concluded, "I joined him there in this primitive place. It was practically exile. I think the government was aware of Davit's political leanings and wanted to keep him at a safe distance. But we were so happy! We taught together, and we learned together. Especially, we learned that philosophy is not life. Our student pretensions and high-minded mistakes turned out to be frail things. Only when we tossed them aside did we really learn to serve. And, Nina, we found so much joy in doing that! Our life together seemed so simple and so complete. But I lost him. Cholera took him just as Noe was learning to walk."

Nina stared with unfocused eyes into the pause that Maria had left. "Why are you telling me this," she asked and moving her head slowly, slowly she met her mother's eyes. "Why?"

The older woman shrugged. "You are my daughter, Nina. I want things for you that you don't even know exist."

"I know they exist," said Nina bitterly, "but they don't exist for me. I am different somehow."

"Yes, you are. You are different," Maria responded quietly.

"What can I do?" Nina asked her. "Leave home to work in some factory? Then I would still be the chattel of some man like Mushegan. Talk to my father! Tell him to free me from this marriage!"

"I have talked to him. He will not move." Her eyelids flinched at some secret thought or feeling. Then she raised again the smooth defense that she had dropped so briefly when the name Davit Tcheidze came to her lips. Nina knew that Maria would never go against her husband, and a great loneliness came over her.

"Why did you tell me?" she asked again.

The road was hard and rutted. And the ruts were blue in the morning light, and the snakelike ridges between them pushed their way into her worn leather boots. But Nina walked and walked. She wanted to reach the eastern fields beyond the village and see a great and open expanse of land. She thrust back her head and looked at the telegraph wires that followed the road.

"I will go and be a telegraph operator!" She laughed and said, "No, I will go to Tiflis and work with Noe."

Behind her came the sound of singing. Strongly patterned Russian singing—the Molokans were coming out to work in the fields. She walked slowly, and the sound grew louder and louder until it enveloped her.

She listened. Every word and every note seemed exactly right—more than right—inevitable, as though no other word or note could possibly have fit. And the singing was like being in a leafy forest full of lights and darks—far more real than the ordinary-looking men who passed her in their caps and peasant smocks.

Then someone was beside her, walking and singing.

"Arise, new forces, for the time is long come.
 Set forth on the prepared path for peace and good.
The dawn is already rising in the heavens,
 for the sun is up; freedom is approaching;
spring, spring is coming.

Arise, all who are ready, having forgotten the hour
 of trouble; we are moving, new forces, moving,
  moving . . ."

It was Piotr Gavrilovich—singing in his strong, clear tenor. He glanced at her sideways and walked alongside her for as long as he could. She knew that he could not acknowledge her, but she felt acknowledged. She felt that everything within her was understood and expressed by the fields and the sky and the singing.

She turned as Piotr strode ahead, the last man in the group. The village lay before her, old and bare against the blue of the Surami Mountains. But the mountains themselves looked new under the sky. "I will go to the mountains and teach children or . . ." And she laughed out loud at the ridiculous idea. ". . . I will go to America with Piotr Gavrilovich!" She walked back slowly and not in a straight line, holding her arms a little way out from her body. The hard tubular ruts bit through her thin soles, but she curled her toes like a bird on a twig and reveled in the feel of the road. She knew only two things. She would leave the village, and she would not marry Mourad Mushegan.

V

The Reluctant Exile

The rain came and tabored on the window. It rattled the shutters and rapped on the clay-dipped thatch so that a musical percussion played on every side. Piotr pulled on his long *kosovorotka*, the side-opening peasant shirt with its upright collar. He jammed his heavily stockinged feet into *lapti*, woven bast shoes, and then wrapped his legs in linen puttees, his fingers quickened by the beat of the rain as he tied the leather thongs. It was not a day to be wasted! Spring rain meant spring plowing as soon as the fields dried.

In the kitchen Semyon was sitting at the table dipping twice-baked rusks into yogurt and glowering into the arched mouth of the oven. The damp-straw scent of fodder drying on the stove filled the room. Semyon skewered Piotr with a dark glance and grunted unpleasantly. *Devil take it!* fumed Piotr. *The old man knows everything! He'll pin me down with those sharp old eyes and spatter me with troubling words that'll stick to me all day like wet hen feathers!* Piotr eyed the door longingly as Semyon lifted his eyebrows in exaggerated surprise.

"So where are you going?" The smooth voice was deceptively mild.

"To Voloshins'—Uncle Mikhail's. They're just back from Vorontsovka, and he has some new machinery he wants to show me."

"Machinery." A triangle of goose-fleshed skin appeared between the unbuttoned collar of Semyon's shirt and the sweep of his beard as he turned his head. The bulging arteries in his neck jumped and squirmed as though pumping the unsaid words into his mouth, where they dammed up behind his tightly pressed lips.

"Machinery." Piotr nodded, with crisp resolve.

"Machinery!" The triangle of skin turned a pebbly magenta to match the moist rim of Semyon's eye. "Machinery—a plow, a harrow—a snare! A snare to you, Piotr. It will all rust! Rust!"

"It won't rust, Dzedha; it's in the barn."

"Don't play with me, youngster! You know well enough what I mean! Mikhail will fill your mind with his own schemes. And you're naive enough to be taken in by it. He'll roll out his riches like a Turk's magic carpet. A snare! A snare to him and to you! Mikhail will sell his soul to have the latest farm gimmick. He wants to be like all those *kulaks* over in Vorontsovka. Let him! But there are other things in store for you! Don't give me that mulish look!"

"You're afraid," stated Piotr cooly. "You're afraid that Uncle Mikhail may have some ideas of his own. Ideas that don't include *Pohod*." He flushed. His heart lurched with the audacity of his own words. But he would not take them back. No one would wrest this decision away from him! Not Semyon, not Galina, not Mikhail. The privilege of turning the course of his life with his own hand was worth some risks.

Semyon's bent-fingered hands scrabbled on the table as he levered his age-writhen body to a wrathful stand. Piotr shouldered past him with a smoulder in his eye to match the old man's. He sprang from the porch, scattering the fowl in the yard. His *lapti* slipped, then sucked at the sodden earth. Semyon was behind him, slower on his feet, but arms flailing energetically. Piotr turned and the drizzle sheeted his face as though its coolness would harden his obstinate expression.

Piotr stood his ground, letting Semyon's pent-up words flow over him. "The earth will be like soaked black bread—soft to the plow—and where will you be? Off to croon over Mikhail's tin and metal! Mikhail with the two sons to help in all his doings!" The old man waved his arms with a prophetic zeal that struck new panic into the hearts of the watching chickens. The rain beaded his beard and then spattered away with each jerk and nod of his powerful head. He stumbled forward, leaving a bast slipper stuck in the mud. Nonplused, he paused for so long that a stout-hearted hen approached, jerking her head back and forth in a suspicious way. She cocked her head to inspect the mired *lapti* as if to say, "What kind of fowl is that?" and pecked at it disdainfully. Chagrined, Semyon twisted his head to give the froward hen a hot stare. "Get out, you fool; leave it, you devil's spawn!" he shrilled.

Nadya poked her head out of the cow shed, her mouth rounded into a perfect 'O' while Piotr struggled with laughter. A welling up of love for the old man filled him. Piotr wanted to say something soothing, something that would still the ringing emotions and wipe the dismay from the old man's face as he stood with his tattered dignity and his soaked stocking oozing mire.

Semyon absently hitched at his trousers and looked around as though confused. Then he drew himself up. He screwed up his eyes so that the deep wrinkles radiated in sun-ray splendor as though daunted by a new bright awareness. The long look he gave Piotr was full of pity and comprehension. "You go now," he said gently. "Talk to Mikhail; talk to anybody. But in the end, listen to your own heart. And God go with you."

Semyon! Piotr's thought hovered around his great-grandfather with his quick-fire fury burning to fragrant ash! And from the ashes, some unexpected sweet-savored aspect of the old man's thought and spirit would ascend like smoke. How often Piotr had seen it happen! That rash inner flare would stoke a release—a great leap within to something entirely different, something very much like gentleness. And in Semyon, gentleness was a thing of great power.

Piotr's thought blurred and slipped away as he breathed in the rain-freshened air. The scent of stale ice was gone. The rain came down in undulating sheets, licking up the last of the snow. Piotr took the main village lane toward the west. Beyond the row of huts, a third of the grain fields showed a fierce combative green where the winter wheat had sprung up. Piotr had sowed some of it himself last autumn. With the thaw, another third would be sowed with the combination of barley, oats, and spring wheat that the peasants called *zhito*. The last third would be left fallow for the year. How yielding and inviting the fields seemed! His hands itched for the feel of the earth between his fingers!

The land began to bend and warp into little hollows and humps. Each rounded contour frothed with the pale springtime display of the orchards against the dark spruce higher up. Here and there, a thatched hut was tucked into a receptive fold in the land. To the south, the rain-swollen stream leaped with a spit and skitter, finding its way amid the rise and fall of the hills. But the lane carved a straight swath to Uncle Mikhail's, rose slightly to give the peasant carts and wagons access to the mill straddling the stream beyond, and then narrowed to a winding goat track that wandered back into the hills and was lost.

Piotr skirted the two-storied brick house with its tile roof and carved shutters painted a fresh blue. He glimpsed his Aunt Marfa shaking out a rag at the back door. Two of Uncle Mikhail's Tartar laborers huddled near the steps, smoking, and Aunt Marfa gave her cloth a fastidious snap in their direction. But the Tartars remained impassive, fixing Piotr with a stare both intense and indifferent. They raised their cigarettes to their mouths with languid grace in their fine-boned hands.

Mikhail and the boys, Piotr knew, would be in the barn preparing for the day when plow would be set to earth—for them, the first day of spring.

"Why do I even get involved?" Uncle Mikhail groaned as frustration moved in a wave from his blue-black widow's peak to the tip of his trimmed beard. But Piotr looked at him expectantly. Mikhail was not one to keep his opinions to himself.

They were standing just inside the large barn. Further in, shiny metal shapes mirrored gray rain-stippled patterns—glowing curves and bars of light hugging the contours of well-tended machinery. The rhythmic clank of metal on metal rang as Mikhail's eldest, Trofim, forced an attachment onto the new plow with his big smith's hands. The sound of the downpour outside competed with the harsh clamor. A bleating like the noise of weary, discontented children came from a far corner as Mikhail's flock added its forlorn note to the din. Piotr could barely make out the shape of Andrei, Trofim's younger brother, moving among the complaining sheep.

"*Pohod!* What hysteria!" Mikhail continued. "I've told my brother as much—you've heard me! Galina Antonovna has strewn little hints here and there that I should put up the money for them to go. They can afford your passage—no more. You knew that, didn't you? But why should I finance something I don't believe in? Sure, they'd pay me back—the money's not the thing. I'd be sending them on some fool's errand—something they'll regret. The future of the Molokans is here. In Russia."

"But then," interjected Piotr, "if I go, I'm cut off. I'll never see my family again."

"Maybe. Why risk it? What is there in America for someone like you? Remember, not all those who went to search out the land came back singing about milk and honey. Conditions are hard there. Most immigrants live in crowded, filthy cities. No Molokan can live like that! We need land. Some have said outright that California is no place for religious people."

"Is Russia?" Piotr argued. "We are forced into military service—or persecuted for resisting. Look what happened to the Dukhobors in Akhalkalaki Uezd. The Cossacks stormed into a crowd of two thousand—killing, raping, burning. The Dukhobors know how much kindness they can expect from the Tsar! They're leaving. They've had enough of Mother Russia."

"No one is accusing the Tsar of being tenderhearted, Piotr. But the Dukhobors bring wrath down on themselves. They demonstrate against the government and then wonder why the Cossacks are called in! Besides, that was years ago. The fact is, we Molokans are doing better than we ever have. Look at this," Mikhail waved his hand to indicate the equipment behind him.

Trofim stopped his hammering and looked up. "The best in five villages! And, let me tell you, it's not just for show! I've bought sixty more *desiatiny* of land from the count. That makes two hundred eighty! Not bad for a poor peasant. And land reforms are coming. Even the Tsar's minister, Stolypin, looks kindly on the Molokans because we've shown that the land can pay. American-style farmers, he calls us. You want to be an American? Fine! You can be one right here! Just wait a few years."

"I may not have a few years, Uncle. What if circumstances push me out? Prophecy or no prophecy, there are big problems with my staying in Russia right now, though God knows I don't want to leave."

"Sure, sure. But think ahead. The war with Japan is almost over. You're squeamish about the idea of shooting these revolutionaries, but I tell you it won't happen. They'll call in the Cossacks like they always do. Things will settle down, you'll serve your time, and then you'll come back here. What's five years to a young man? You have your whole life in front of you. Why not spend it where you want to?"

The earnest tension in Piotr's face broke into a grin. "I like your thinking," he said. "You're telling me just what I want to hear."

The big man grunted. "I'm not just tickling your ears. It's the truth." Piotr followed him into the dim barn. The odor of sheep, horses, and machine oil combined with the fresh scent of the rain. Andrei was spreading out fodder for the sheep and muttering to himself. His straight, dark hair fell forward as he bent his massive shoulders over the milling brown and white flock. His gray eyes were obscured by wire-rimmed glasses fogged by the damp of the day and the humid breath of the animals.

It was typical, Piotr thought, to find Andrei with the flock. He had none of Trofim's mechanical ability, but he was a clever farmer and husbandman. His father's attitude toward him wavered from pride to exasperation. For, unlike the docile Trofim, Andrei tended to think his own thoughts and go his own way. It was obvious to Piotr that he was thinking his own thoughts now—they were escaping from him like steam from a kettle.

"He's wro-o-ong," a singsong undertone moaned through the bleating and hammering. Piotr bent his own shoulders to the task of carrying arm loads of straw to the sheep enclosure. On his return trip, Andrei gave him a steam-mottled look and murmured, "We'll have to talk. Later."

"Good," said Piotr. "Tonight?"

"No. Not tonight. I'm seeing someone; we'll be walking together tonight—Natasha Kostrikin." He fought a smile and looked down as Piotr raised an eyebrow.

"We'll go outside—in a few minutes. You'd better go over there and sing the praises of that new plow."

Piotr strolled over to stand beside Trofim. *So,* he thought, *Andrei and Natasha Kostrikin! That'll put more of a wedge than ever between him and Uncle Mikhail.* In Mikhail's eyes, Natasha's stately beauty did not compensate for her lack of dowry. His practical uncle had never regretted his marriage to the big-boned, dour-faced Marfa. The union gave him the capital to become the richest man in the village. Mikhail had thought his brother, Gavril, a fool for marrying the winsome Galina who brought only her sweet smiles and lovesick eyes as a marriage portion. Marfa had brought him flocks and land and, best yet, a mill. What could be sweeter than that?

Mikhail's eyes now glittered with pride and anticipation as he watched his eldest prepare the new plow. Piotr was astounded at the complexity of the machine. Even the simple old steel plows were considered an innovation in a village where a third of the farmers still used wooden plows. The light, moving with the rain, picked out the word *Guenier.* There were three spoked wheels and a shining moldboard with a vicious edge to it. And, if you please, a seat—in case the plowman got tired. Piotr shook his head in bemusement. What would a man be thinking, perched on that steel seat, while the horses sweat with his weight and the earth broke and crumbled beneath him?

"What a beauty!" he remarked, running his hand along the seat attachment and stooping to inspect the evener where Mikhail's three powerful Dukhobor-bred work horses would be hitched. "It's not a plow—it's a work of art! It'll slice through earth like a knife through butter."

Trofim looked up and showed his white, overlapping teeth in a wide smile. "It will," he agreed. "We'll be through with plowing in plenty of time to rent it out to other farmers—double profit! Then we'll use that to sow *zhito*." He nodded toward a long box with a wheel on either end. Piotr looked over the new machine with something like suspicion. Apparently, it was pulled over the ground, and the boxlike device would spew out the seed. *But,* he thought, *it would have to be used on a well-worked, flat field.* Piotr stroked his chin as he imagined the clumsy box crawling over the fields, sending the seed from darkness into darkness.

"How about your new fields?" Piotr asked. "They were virgin forest just last spring. A contraption like that isn't going to waltz around tree stumps."

"You're right. We'll just scratch up the new field with the hand plow and sow oats. They'll grow anywhere."

"Good," Piotr assented. But he didn't like the sower. For him, the whole point of the back-breaking work of preparing the earth was to be able to sow—to walk upright and lift his unhindered hand to spread the seed. One of his earliest memories was following old Semyon up and down a well-plowed field, trying to imitate that expansive, generous sweep of the arm as the old man gave the seed to the custody of wind and earth and sun. There was such uncontained freedom and joy to that gesture! *Take it! Take it!* said the old man's outstretched arm. His long hair and beard would be pulled into spikes by the wind and by the force of his movement. He'd bend his knees to the vigor of his stride and flash his dark eyes around the tillage. *Take it!* And his arm would fling out in open-handed zeal.

Vibrant, pulsing colors sprang to Piotr's mind. The sun fervent on the bright ballooning skirts of the women as their arms rose and fell; the seed glittering gaily on the air and falling in a golden rain on the soft earth; the forest shadows lapping the edge of the field eagerly, and the trees themselves leaning forward receptively. No, thought Piotr, sowing was not for the niggardly! And Semyon was a great sower.

A couple of peasants came in. Mikhail's mouth took on a bold, forthright curve and his eyes a sly glint—his business expression. The men shuffled around casually, affecting an interest in the Dukhobor horses before they were drawn to the Guenier plow. Both were moderately well-off farmers and were probably looking over the new equipment with an eye to rental. One of them, a stocky peasant with an ash-blond beard, ran a reddened hand over the metal seat. An insolent black and white hen, happy to have escaped the rain, took a moment's perch on one of the two plow handles and fluffed out her feathers shamelessly, leaving a smear of manure behind her. The peasant absently wiped it off with a respectful sleeve and stooped to toy with the guide wheel. "Cunning people, these Germans," he muttered in amazement.

Piotr could see that Uncle Mikhail would have his hands full explaining the latest farm innovations. He nodded to the new arrivals and backed quietly into the wet yard.

Andrei was waiting for him by the threshing floor. With the rain lulled and the hammer stilled, silence settled, as fine-spun as the silvered strings of drops that garnished the edges of sills and eaves and rick tops. Moisture darkened the wooden planks and stone rollers of the threshing floor. Beyond, the yard stretched out toward the river. Along the water, a collection of disheveled shed-like *banya* leaned this way and that, like tossed dice.

"So," Piotr prodded his cousin, "it's to be Natasha Vassileyvna . . ."

Andrei drew his black brows together self-consciously and, ignoring Piotr's questioning glance, hurriedly said, "Natasha! That's another matter. You now, listen! My father's schemes aren't the only way of looking at things. He's so caught up in the farm, he can't see beyond a rick of hay and a pile of cow dung!"

"So you're with the rest of them! Wanting me to leave! You know what that means to me, cousin."

"No, but wait—father doesn't notice, but we're in real trouble here in the village. Not so much with the Molokans, but with the Georgians. *Kulaks*, they call us. And they're right, Piotr, they're right! Father stays within the bounds of what he thinks is right, but somehow he always comes out ahead. The envy festering beneath the surface breeds ugly things."

Piotr frowned in consternation. "What's happened? Have there been incidents here?"

"No. Not yet. But the peace is fragile as glass. A word out of turn, a careless slight—anything like that, and it'll be the worse for us. We'll be another Guria. Father has stretched out his hand to take for too long. It'll catch up with us, and I fear for us then. I fear for us!"

Piotr examined his cousin's face in the rain-washed light that streamed from livid edges of the breaking clouds. He saw unflinching honesty in the gray eyes; Andrei's face twisted as his eagerness to convince Piotr struggled with his determination to be objective, to let his cousin make his own decision.

"He seemed so optimistic—talking about land reforms, the future of Russia . . ." Piotr's voice trailed off dejectedly.

"Piotr, he's sure of nothing." Andrei's quiet voice shook with intensity. "The time will come when there's no safe place in Russia for people like you and me. If there's a place of refuge for you, take it. But think it through carefully; you need to be sure in your own heart. Your family isn't in the bad graces of every Socialist in the village like we are."

"What will you do, Andrei?"

"What can I do? Leaving is out of the question for me. Besides, if there is trouble, how can I desert my family? Then, too, there's Natasha." He leaned his head back so that his sharp young jawbone angled toward the changing sky. Blue rifts in the clouds threw jagged reflections across his glasses. Trofim's hammer again rang out with a heavy, regular beat.

"I don't know," Andrei murmured. "We may yet pay for our father's sins, Trofim and I!"

Piotr turned his face toward the swollen river, his mind tossed by Andrei's words. He took a few steps toward the water, close enough now to see the mill on a rocky rise of land and to hear the frenzy with which the stream accepted the melted snow and ice. Scraps of blue sparkled in the gray and white froth; the clouds had broken like torn paper, and evenly spaced azure cracks had appeared overhead.

Piotr was deeply troubled. In spite of the fury he had seen in Baku, the "troubles" had seemed to him remote—a grand sweep of history in the making, not an imminent tragedy that might threaten his own family.

Lost in thought, he started at a light footfall, a hand on his sleeve. It was Fenya Kostrikin. He drew back from her as though she were plague-ridden. Her face looked strangely unfamiliar. The kerchief had slipped back from her high, childishly rounded forehead, revealing the glisten of whitish down along her hairline and the thick sweep of the tow-colored hair. The smooth skin above each blonde eyebrow was knotted with stark fear. An electricity of urgency charged her voice and gestures.

"They're here!" Her whisper echoed the hiss and frenzy of the nearby stream. "Soldiers! Looking for you!"

"What? What are you saying? I'm not . . . there's no reason . . ." Piotr put a hand on each of her shoulders as if to shake the truth out of her.

"There are! They came to your cottage looking for you—said you were to go to Delizan, to the encampment there. Galina Antonovna told them you had already left, that you were on your way back to Baku. But they must have become suspicious. They started searching the hut—I think they'll come here next. Here to your uncle's."

Andrei was beside them. "So she's done it! Taken away your chance to choose. Your course is set now, Piotr!" His tone was bitter and passionate, and his eyes mirrored Fenya's fear.

"You'll have to hide—they'll question Father, maybe search our house. What has she brought down on us?"

"Wait, why not explain? Maybe they'll accept that there's been a mistake . . ."

"No! Don't risk it. Too many know what you've been thinking of. If they accept your explanation, fine. But if not, what will they do to you?"

Piotr shrugged. One risk seemed as good as another.

"Hide, Piotr," Fenya pleaded. She ran to the road, shielding her straining eyes with her palm, and was quickly back again, her hand outstretched as though she could not bear to let go of Piotr's sleeve.

"They're coming!" she reported with a shaking voice.

"The *banya*," said Andrei, pushing his cousin toward the river.

They were safely inside one of the bathhouses before the drumming of hooves added percussion to the stream's frantic music. Andrei closed the door and pulled the glasses off of his sweating face so that Piotr could clearly see his eyes widen with horror. The *banya* must have been recently used, for the coals on the grate glowed fiercely red, and the steam that filled the small dark space would be rising like a signal from the crude hole in the roof.

"God help us," Andrei groaned. "We'll be flagging them down—no better way of saying, 'Here we are! Take us!'"

Piotr jerked his head up to stare at the escaping steam, pulling the sleeve of his heavy coat across his drenched forehead. He and Andrei exchanged a dismayed glance; then Piotr began to strip off the wet sheepskin and fumbled with his tunic.

"Strip," he ordered.

"What?" Andrei was perplexed. "What are you saying? If we have to run . . ."

"Strip," Piotr repeated so sternly that the baffled Andrei obeyed. "If they find us, we'll tell them my mother was mistaken; tell them we're just taking an ordinary steam bath. If they find us dressed, it will be obvious that we're hiding—and you'll be in as much trouble as I am. This way, you're not to blame."

"You're crazy, Piotr. They're not going to lap up a childish explanation like that!"

"Maybe not. But it's our only chance—unless they're blind enough to overlook a *banya* with steam pouring out the top like a flag of surrender."

"It'll be no graceful surrender for you, cousin," Andrei whispered with a wry grin as he surveyed Piotr's tense, sweating body arched at an odd angle as he strained to hear through the cracks in the gray, warped wood. Piotr returned a thin smile, his ears alert to the rise and dip of voices in the yard. But he could see nothing through the ragged gap in the wood except Fenya Kostrikin's long, slender, mud-splattered feet. Andrei must have seen too, for he was quickly on his knees, mouth to the crack.

"Fenya," he hissed. The feet did not hesitate; in a second she was at the door. Piotr hurriedly pulled his *kosovorotka* around his loins. Andrei put out a hand and pulled her into the tiny space where she stood, confused but calm and steadfast, seeking Piotr's eyes in the darkness.

"Listen, Fenya, don't be afraid!" Andrei said softly, "If they come to the door—well, you know what that means for us. Better if you answer; if they think there's a bunch of girls in here, maybe we can throw them off the scent. Can you do that for us?"

She nodded, like a good, solemn child, still looking at Piotr.

"Fenya," Andrei explained gently, "you'll have to look like you're bathing—your smock, your skirt . . ." He hesitated. "You can pull your shift up, but—you'll have to hurry . . ."

"I know," she said firmly. "Don't look."

"No. See, my eyes are closed."

Piotr edged away from the wooden benches toward the door and the steaming coal bed in the corner. The moist heat scalded the one side of his body, while the other began to chill in the drafts that penetrated the poorly fitted door. Outside, he heard the jingle of harness.

"You two, check the ones on the slope," commanded a young, pleasant voice. "We'll look here."

Piotr's heart thudded in rhythm with the sudden pounding that shook the shoddy door. Then Fenya was there, and a vertical bar of light sprang from hinge to hinge as the door opened. He could see the young dapper soldier with his clear, curious eyes and thin curling mustache.

He saw the man's curiosity harden and condense into a fierce, avid interest as Fenya stood before him, holding her shift in front of her firm, young body.

"I'm looking for Piotr Voloshin," the corporal told her with an irrelevant caressing tone to his voice. "It seems that he . . . well, we don't know what to think. Have you seen him?"

Piotr looked quickly at Fenya as she shook her head. The steam roiled on a gust of fresh air, and the red-stained light flowed across the smooth skin of Fenya's bared shoulder like moving water. He could see little of her but the shoulder nearest him and the long, fair braid. The soft plane of her shoulder, so different from a man's shoulder, indented slightly as she leaned toward her questioner. Piotr could see the startlingly white nape of her neck. Her voice as it came to him in the darkness surprised him.

"The Voloshins you're looking for," she told the soldier calmly, "live further up the road, closer to the village center." Her voice was clear and fearless, with a husky suggestion of a flirt in it.

What is she doing? Piotr thought indignantly.

He dragged his eyes away from her and stared out at his adversary. The young man in the sleek uniform smiled and touched his mustache.

"We paid a little visit there already," he said. "The old woman rose from her deathbed to tell us that our young Molokan was so eager to get back to soldiering that he'd already left for Baku! She seemed remarkably healthy as she tried to keep us from being too zealous in searching for him. Just doing our duty! But somehow, my mind's not quite at ease about this Piotr Gavrilovich."

Fenya shrugged and the shift slipped a little. "It may be that he did leave early," she said helpfully. "The trains have been so unpredictable that getting to Baku is no easy matter. Maybe you could wire there tomorrow to see if he's back by then. You may find that he's not missing after all."

"That's true." He appeared to be satisfied with her answer, but he was obviously reluctant to let the conversation end. "It's not my business to go rounding up absent soldiers before they're officially missing. We're probably just wasting our time. Besides," he added suggestively, "maybe there are better things to look for."

"May the Lord help you find them," said Fenya demurely, but before she could close the door, two more soldiers appeared.

"Ho," said one, his eyes heavy upon her, "booty! Tell her to come out, and we'll decide how to divide her up."

The young corporal hooted with laughter as Fenya firmly closed the door. "I saw her first! To the victor goes the spoils."

"You're a lusty old dog. Why not share with your comrades? Besides, there may be more in there! Tell her to open up!"

Fenya pressed her cheek against the rough wood, listening for retreating footsteps. Piotr listened, too, but heard nothing except his own ragged breathing and Fenya's. She was so close that he could have touched her in the darkness. But he remained frozen, listening, listening, hearing the short fierce breaths tear from her body. Finally the corporal moved away.

"Well," he told someone, "that was a pretty sight to make the road shorter." He was answered by a murmur that was lost in the stream sound behind them. Then hooves sloshed and sucked at the ground, and a bawdy baritone caroled an old Cossack love song. The sound quickened and tangled as the horses broke into a canter, heading east through the village toward the Old Post Road that links Tiflis with Delizan.

Fenya let out a long breath; then she nimbly pulled her shift over her shoulders. In a moment she was transformed into the Fenya he knew, camouflaged again in her ill-fitting patchwork. Then she was gone without a backward glance. But as she passed beyond the door, Piotr saw that her face was wet with sweat, or tears, and her fresh young cheek, where she had pressed it against the door, was embossed with a wood-grain pattern.

For a moment, the cousins said nothing. Then Andrei sighed. "They are regular beauties, those girls! Queens!"

Piotr only looked at him in astonishment.

Long moments went by as the coals turned gray. A chill came in with the splinters of daylight, and they dressed hurriedly. Then they sat stiffly on the wooden bench in the way that Russians will sit before a long journey. Andrei was the first to break the silence.

"It may be," he said, weighing his words and looking sideways at Piotr, "that it has turned out for the best. I don't think that your mother meant to rob you of your choice. She probably blurted out the first thing that came into her head—with the idea of protecting you, giving you time. Think of this—if she hadn't told them that you were gone, you would be with them now, traveling south to Delizan. Is that what you wanted?"

"I don't know what I wanted." Piotr shrugged bitterly. "What does it matter now? What a fool I was! Carefully sizing up every side of this thing—tormenting myself with this first big decision. And here I am, like a penniless beggar self-importantly inspecting a prize mare while the seller laughs up his sleeve! What can I do now? I'll have to slink into hiding and then—America! I have no idea how I can even get there. Yet that's the big challenge of my life—how to get to a place I don't want to go to!

"Unless," he paused, considering, "unless I can make it true—what she told them. Get to Baku as quickly as I can, slip back into my military routine, and no one will be the wiser . . ."

"No! No, Piotr. You heard them out there! They're suspicious of you now. You think you were harassed before—just wait! They'll waste no time in shoving you into situations intolerable for a Molokan. Or worse. I heard you telling Father about that incident with the Dukhobors when we were boys. Remember, at that same time the Dukhobors of Akhalkalaki Uezd had a dozen men in the army—and nine of them were tortured to death! You'd be a fool to put yourself at their mercy after what's happened."

Piotr looked across at the coal bed, gray-white and dead now except for a minute cave of orange fire that glowed piercingly bright, yet remote.

"You're probably right," he admitted. "But if there's any way I can stay in Russia, I will find it!"

"Well, you'd better find it soon then. When you don't show up in Baku, they'll come looking for you. You'll have to go underground, as the radicals say."

"That's right. That is what they say, isn't it?" The anger drained from Piotr's face like water gone into earth. "Maybe that's the solution for me."

"What! You would cast your lot in with them? They're a godless people, bent on destruction."

"Listen, Andrei, I'm not accepting their deeds or their beliefs—but in time of need even King David took refuge with the Philistines."

"He was insane when he did it."

"No—pretending to be insane. It's not the same thing."

"In your case, Piotr, I think it is!"

But Piotr wasn't listening. "Just think, cousin. As of now, I'm a fugitive—I have no choice. But if there is a revolution, a new regime, then my position will be entirely different. It's a chance!"

"A chance, yes. But in the end, it will betray you."

Piotr gave him a cold glance. "What is betrayal to me? My own family has betrayed me."

"Don't worry, they're gone." Sirakan's tone was reassuring, but he almost knocked Piotr over in his hurry to pull the shade and bolt the door. "I saw your gallant friends gallop by a couple of hours ago." The Armenian pulled Piotr behind the blue and cinnamon striped curtain between shop and storeroom. He absently picked up a crock of pickles and dusted it thoughtfully. The look he gave Piotr was both bracing and sympathetic.

"Why beat around the bush?" he said as his hairy fingers fidgeted among the crocks and jars. "You've lost; Galina has won. At least you have the chance to start over and make a new life—maybe that would have been the best thing after all. Where's your spirit of adventure?"

"I know, I know. So I have to leave the army. I'm already a deserter! But do I need to leave the country —that's what I want to know. I keep thinking, there may be a way—leave the army, but not Russia." Piotr was finding it hard to talk, as though the knot in his jaw were distorting every vowel.

"Sure, sure, if you don't mind being shot at regularly. What? Do you think you can disappear?"

"For a time, why not? I'm sure others have done it."

"You're a fool, Piotr. Are you kicking against the goad just because you don't want to feel that your mother has pushed you onto a path in life? Be reasonable. Get out of here—lose yourself in Batumi until the sea lanes open. Then take the first boat you can get."

"What about Noe? Noe disappears from time to time. How does he do it?"

"Noe! Noe's a weasel!" Sirakan gritted his short square teeth in chagrin and admiration. "It's true; he's remarkable. So is the devil. Only by God's grace has he lived so long—twenty-five years! You want to live like Noe? You're crazy! You don't know what you're talking about."

"Only for a time, Sirakan. It . . . it will delay things, give me time . . ."

"Delay is the last thing you need. You need to act decisively. Now!"

"No, listen. I need time." Piotr sweated into his already damp clothes. "I want to slow things down so I can think—"

"What are you waiting for? Nothing's going to change."

"It may. Give me the chance. You know us peasants, tied to the land—"

"You'll find yourself tied to a gibbet," Sirakan grumbled, but Piotr could tell that he was softening. "The only thing that could possibly help you is if there's a revolution, a new regime. But that's a far-flung star to reach for! I wouldn't advise it."

"Maybe that's the only star left to me," Piotr said grimly.

Sirakan's hands were suddenly still. "So you think you'll find that history is your friend. You are a fool, Gavrilovich! Any Armenian can tell you man has only one friend, and it isn't history!" His eyes narrowed and locked onto Piotr's in a combative, evaluative stare. "What are you really waiting for?" he asked softly, and Piotr felt the knotted muscles in his face slacken and tremble.

The big Armenian pushed aside the striped curtain, his bearlike frame filling the doorway. "All right," he said. "On Monday we'll go to Tiflis for supplies. You can go with us, and I'll tell you where to find Noe. If Noe has some brilliant idea for you—fine. If not, you can take the train to Batumi and stay quiet for a month or so—until you can get out. Either way, Noe can get you the papers you'll need."

Piotr closed his eyes and breathed out relief. "Thank you. God bless you for your help!"

"Don't say that to Noe! He'll choke you with arguments that will clog your brain for a week!"

"Why should he do this for me?"

"For you? He wouldn't do it for you. He'd do it against the government. That's what motivates Noe," Sirakan replied as he moved with heavy grace to the front room. "By the way, when does your leave expire?"

"Wednesday."

"Thank God. You'll make a smuggler and abettor out of me yet, Piotr Gavrilovich. But not this week at least."

Piotr trudged back to the Voloshin hut with reluctant steps. He clenched his fists and trained his unfocused gaze on the mire of the road. He sweltered in the humid trap of his clothing despite the fresh breeze that licked about his damp hands and face like a friendly dog.

He heard the voices from halfway across the yard. Gavril's stern, accusatory tone, so unusual for him, rolled in resonant outrage past the porch posts. And that harsh, rasping grief that sawed at the darkening air! That was Galina—keening out the pain of her betrayal. Piotr hardened his heart, but could not shield himself from the stinging pain. The words were nothing; it was the rage and bitterness and heart-searing remorse that inhabited them as they spilled from door and window.

Piotr stood at the porch steps, but they seemed too steep to climb. He turned aside and leaned into the wall of the hut, with his two palms spread against the siding and his forehead pressed hard into the wood. He closed his eyes, his fingers moving slightly on the spongy surface of the wet wood as he groped for comfort.

He turned his head roughly and saw that Fenya was standing within arm's reach. Her shoulders were braced against the wall, and she stood with one foot on top of the other. Her vividly azure eyes were trained intently, but he knew that there was no object in the midspace of the yard that she could possibly be focused on. The blue beneath the thick golden lashes deepened as though it were gathering the darkening shades of the coming twilight. And he saw his loss in her unmoving eyes.

Finally, she stirred and, reaching up one of her rough-skinned, delicately shaped hands, she touched his forehead. "The wood has marked you," she said. "It makes you look like an old man. Like Semyon." He could not answer her, but turned back to the wall and in a moment he sensed that she was gone.

The rain began to fall again, gently. But he did not move. He knew that he would soon go in, eat cabbage soup and black bread, and sleep a last night under the familiar quilt. But it would be a stranger's sup and a stranger's bed. He was already an exile.

VI

The Mark of the Wood

I'm all hollow inside, Fenya thought, returning to the Kostrikin hut at twilight. *Scooped out at the core of myself—that's it. And will this empty feeling go away, or will I carry it with me until, until . . .* Her untutored mind stopped tiredly, and she looked down in surprise at the hut. Why, every light in the place was lit! She quickened her steps and sprang up the steps to the porch.

Vanya and Misha were collecting the containers of seedlings she had so carefully planted and set out anywhere there was a suggestion of light. Anna was ransacking the wooden chest in the best room, finery from her dowry of twenty years ago spread out around her. Her father, Vassily, stood by the stove, his face working with the strain of forcing deep chagrin to pose as humble decorum. Fenya knew that expression—knew that it meant that some special occasion was coming up, something that would force them all to wring what they could out of every pittance of a resource they had. They'd straighten their backs and sprinkle dust in the eyes of their beholders—the dust being the display of Anna's ancient silks and the exquisite array of pastries that would cover the dilapidated table—disguised, of course, with satin damask. *We're not so badly off after all*, eight pairs of blue eyes would declare! *Just don't lift the table cloth!*

Then, Fenya knew, life would contract into a dreary, anxious scrambling to put food on the table. Cabbage soup and turnips for two weeks—no bread. Unless someone from the church remembered them, as they often did. After all, no one was fooled. They knew what she looked like every day—and Natasha and Tanya and Luba and those two little tatterdemalions, Misha and Vanya. Ah yes, Anna would filch

74

what little refinement she could, and it would cost them all. But it was little enough for a woman as stately as a queen. Fenya sighed and turned her attention back to the seedlings.

"What are you doing?" she demanded of the two boys.

"Cleaning, that's what. Mother doesn't want these dirty old plants cluttering up every window and door. There's company coming, so you'd better pitch in, too. We were wondering where you were," answered Misha.

"Give them to me," Fenya said. She had been cherishing the cotton seedlings since late winter, hoping to give the plants a good start to make up for the short growing season. A successful cotton crop could give them money—maybe enough for *Pohod*. "Grow, little seedlings," she had whispered in winter's cold dark days. "You have a chance here. Grow."

"Fenya," Anna broke in, "where have you been?" She didn't wait for a reply, but kept talking, her voice jumping with nerves and exhilaration. "Come here. We have so much to do. I don't know how we're going to be ready by tomorrow."

"Tomorrow? For church?" Fenya asked stupidly, her mind still on her precious cotton. Anna laid out the two silk dresses—a prescribed part of her Molokan trousseau, and the small room filled with the scent of dried, dusty thyme and cedar. The fragrance sent memories ghosting up from Fenya's childhood when she and Natasha would open the old chest with quiet reverence and peek into the dark interior. Rose silk and blue silk glowing like flowers! Ivoried webs of old lace. White linen handkerchiefs embroidered in red and blue. Afraid to touch even a thread, they'd poke their little noses in and breathe in that lovely, musty scent that seemed to come from another world.

"No, no, not church!" Anna exclaimed. "After church—after, Fenya. Ivan and Aksinia Bogdanoff are coming from Delizan," she continued with a rush. Then she paused and, looking into Fenya's eyes, said in a measured way, "And do you know why they are coming?"

Fenya's eyes widened. Bogdanoff? She had never heard of them. But there was no doubt that it was important. Very important. "No," she whispered, "why?"

Anna held up a faded felt skirt and folded it with a snap. "As matchmakers. Matchmakers for Voloshins. Andrei is asking for our Natasha! . . . Yes, it's true!" she exulted. "Mikhail has given his blessing—it will all be arranged for this summer, just before harvest—that is, if we can scrape together enough for a dowry. Bogdanoff is Marfa's brother, so he will speak for the young man." She pushed an assortment of aging garments aside. "We have plenty to do! I expect we'll be up all night!"

"Where's Natasha?" Fenya wondered, looking around as though she had lost something.

"At the *banya* with Luba. She's getting herself all spruced up for her betrothal day."

Anna was right. They were up all night—cleaning, baking, preparing. Natasha came back and joined in. The boys were sent in to sleep on the bed in the best room rather than on the sleeping benches in the kitchen. Anna threw herself into a frenzy of activity, but every now and then she'd stop and look around as though suddenly bewildered. "A hovel," she'd mutter grimly, "a hovel."

Fenya glanced guiltily at her father standing at the window with his back to them. There was no change in the bend of his shoulders or in the pose of his head with its thinning flaxen hair. But she could see his ears moving on either side of the red, cracked skin on his thick neck, and she knew that he was chewing the end of his whitish mustache. And she knew the frustrated expression on his face as surely as she knew the cracks in the wall that she'd stared at since birth.

Natasha caught her eye and shrugged. "Too much work, too little joy," she murmured. "They are neither one to blame. It's our poverty . . ."

"Well, sister, you are getting away from it," Fenya said softly.

"Oh, no. You never get away," she replied, and Fenya could not understand the sudden cloud of sadness that passed across her eyes.

Tanya came in, her square, buxom body bursting with excitement and energy as she tugged off her clumsy padded coat. This betrothal had filled them all with hope! *Except for me,* Fenya thought. She took the coat from Tanya and slipped out, taking her rescued trays of seedlings. She had stashed them carefully on the porch, but they'd need a safer place to hide from their exalted guests. She took them to the shed and set them up in the sagging loft where the geese and goats wouldn't knock them over.

"A few days of darkness," she told them, "and then I'll put you in the field where you can grow." She imagined where she'd plant them. Most of the ground would have to be seeded, of course. But she'd set out her special plants along the eastern edge where they wouldn't block the afternoon sun for the later seedlings. Then in September they'd burst into white puffs of healthy cotton. By then Natasha would be a wife.

The door cracked open, and the geese began to hiss. Vassily came in, rubbing his hands from the cold. He smiled when he saw her, his teeth a darker ivory than the tow-colored mustache and beard.

"So, little daughter, you've come to get out of the way, too," he said ruefully.

"I'm just hoarding up my seedlings; see, they're all snug for the night in the boxes you made!"

Vassily gave them a serious look. "Yes, they've gotten something of a start in this hard world. We'll see how they do in the field."

"We'll see," echoed Fenya. "Maybe the crop will be better than we think."

"Well, it's a start. The growing season may be a little short for cotton, even with a head start. But we'll see, girl. We'll give it a try." The words plucked at an unpleasant awareness in Fenya. She looked into his face, worn out with "giving it a try," and doubt began to sip away at her glad plans. Vassily gave her a steady unflinching look, as though he had read her thought and he, too, could understand her doubt. She felt suddenly ashamed.

"Don't look too high, Fenya," her father cautioned. "Even with the best of crops, *Pohod* would be too expensive for us as a family. It would take years of good yields to get that much money. Remember, there are eight of us. Although, after this summer, I suppose there will be only seven. And with you and Tanya growing up before our eyes, I may lose a daughter every year.

"It's like the old tale of the farmer who told the Tsar that he spends a fourth of his income on taxes, a fourth on a debt, invests a fourth in the future, and throws a fourth out the window. The puzzled Tsar asked the peasant what he meant, and he said that he supported his old father, which was paying a debt; he kept his son, which was an investment in his own future; and he also kept his daughter, which was throwing money out the window because, as you know, a daughter marries and is gone. She becomes a part of another family."

"So, poor Father, you are throwing a lot of money out the window!

No wonder we're so poor! But perhaps I'll never marry. I'm no beauty like Natasha."

Her father bared his dark teeth and chuckled. "You say that now. Just wait a year or two! See, you're like this seedling. It's pale and spindly now. It just hasn't gotten enough light. But wait until it's set in the field."

Fenya gave him a suspicious sideways glance. Was he laughing at her? "What do you mean light. I understand light for a plant, but what's light for me?"

"A man's eyes, that's what. Not only his eyes for that lovely little face you keep hiding, but his eyes for your inner self, your soul. And your soul, little Fenya, is as straight and healthy as a young tree." Fenya pulled her kerchief over her eyes and ducked away in embarrassment as he chucked her under the chin with a rough, red hand. But she remembered his words. Even when she was an old woman, she remembered them.

Who would recognize us? Fenya asked herself. *We're like butterflies in sudden glory!* The Sunday morning dawned silver-gray in the aftermath of Saturday's storm. But the Kostrikin hut glowed like a garden with unaccustomed color.

Like many poor families, the Kostrikins bought their fabric for clothing by the pound rather than by the yard. It was especially practical for Anna's children since she had a sewing machine with which to piece together the patchwork garments they wore day to day. The finely woven merino skirts and caftans were made to sell, not to wear—so they were like some of the poorer dairy farmers who couldn't afford to eat butter.

But this morning, Fenya observed, Natasha and Tanya looked like boyar's daughters—except, of course, for their shoes. Natasha especially looked lovely. She was tall and stately like Anna, with skin like a lily, pale yellow hair, and serene gray eyes. Age had given Anna's old blue dress an iced sheen that blended with the girl's ethereal coloring. *She looks like Snegurochka, the Snow Maiden,* Fenya thought, *with her delicate features and that crystal light of happiness in her eyes. What will Andrei think when he sees the beauty he's won?*

And Tanya—Tanya was like a ruddy rose. The faded red silk had taken on a flower's tint that enhanced her buxom prettiness. Her dark gold hair was set off with a kerchief of starched lace, and she held a stiff linen handkerchief in her plump, pink fingers.

Anna was wearing the green wool skirt she wore every Sunday. The silks, she insisted, were for her daughters to wear. After all, there would be matchmakers in the house from far-off Delizan. She wanted her girls to be shown off to advantage. Who knows? There were plenty of good Molokan boys in Delizan . . .

Fenya, still in her shift, helped ten-year-old Luba into her everyday patchwork and then began to pull on her own work-worn skirt.

"Wait," said Anna, "not that. I have something else for you."

Fenya looked at her questioningly. Any other garment in the house would have been made to order for some well-off farmer's wife or daughter. But Anna was unwrapping a woolen dress with a determined look.

"It's not ours, of course," she was saying, "but who will know if you wear it for a few hours? Darya Efimnovna lives in Vorontsovka, so what's it to her if you make use of her dress? She's about your size . . . here, try it."

Fenya reached for the bundle of soft wool and slipped the dress on over her full-sleeved peasant blouse. Anna stood back and looked at her. "It will do," she said cryptically, but she nodded with a glint of pride in her eye. Natasha turned and gasped, "Why, Fenya, you're a little beauty!"

A hot, bursting blush made Fenya feel as though her skin were too small for her, and she looked down at the new dress—the first new garment she had ever worn.

Anna's look of pride was understandable. It was, indeed, a special dress. Patterned in the old way, it was a traditional Russian *sarafan* woven of soft, brown merino wool. The high neck and the front of the jumper top were embroidered with a leafy scrolling in vivid green and a pale wheaten yellow—the color of Fenya's hair. The skirt was bordered with a profusion of golden sunflowers, springing up joyously with green leaves and pale tow-colored tendrils.

"Well," said Anna, still with her eyes on her daughter, "Darya will pay dearly for all the work that went into that—but it looks better on you than on her!"

"It does," Natasha agreed. "It suits you somehow—like something sprung from the earth—but so lovely on you, Fenya! And really it doesn't even look too bad with bast shoes. It seems fitting with all those sunflowers. If only Piotr Gavrilovich could see you today!"

Fenya backed away, stung with shame. It shocked her to hear his name linked with hers. She hung her head and began to unbraid and comb her hair, letting it slip over the rich brown fabric. It was long enough to fall among the sunflowers that opened with an artless silken shimmer above her clumsy lapti.

But Tanya had already turned to look. "She's right! You're like a wood sprite! And Natasha's an angel from heaven. So what am I?"

"What is she?" young Vanya interrupted, fixing Anna with a hopeful look, as though he expected to hear that practical Tanya had changed into some exotic creature.

"Enough foolishness," Anna said impatiently. "Put on your kerchief Fenya, we're going . . ."

Ivan Bogdanoff and his wife, Aksinia, both had the open-handed, easygoing nature of people who believe that there is plenty of everything. A young couple, like most Molokan matchmakers, they came in with the Voloshins, bobbing their heads at greetings and exclaiming over Vassily's woodwork and Anna's beautiful food. The fact that they carried in two babies instead of one seemed fitting to Fenya. Something inside of her relaxed as she saw Anna's pleased smile and Vassily's shy look of relief. Maybe this wouldn't be such an ordeal after all!

Fenya watched Aksinia with curiosity, attracted to her simple, childlike smile as well as to her expansive and, to Fenya, utterly strange point of view. Aksinia was both very fat and very pretty. Her silken peasant skirt was striped with red and white and covered by a white linen apron edged with lace. Her full-sleeved printed blouse was bursting with floral color and with her huge bosom. Her twin infants were entirely at home sharing these ample contours. Aksinia would let the one curl up on her lap and hold the other up over her breast where it would cling like a kitten to a haystack. Occasionally, she'd rotate them. Her red-cheeked face and smooth brown hair shone as though smeared with butter. *Why, she's just like a giant Matrushka doll,* Fenya thought in amazement, *one with lots of varnish on it.*

Ivan, too, had a substantial and expansive way about him— although it was true he seemed a bit dry and pale next to his colorful wife. Fenya liked the simple generosity with which he approached the business of matchmaking. Ivan Bogdanoff, his wife Aksinia, Mikhail and Marfa Voloshin, and Andrei and Trofim gathered around the Kostrikin table with Vassily and Anna. The children had been sent out to play; Tanya and Fenya stood by the stove ready to serve their guests, while Natasha sat quietly in the best room, waiting to be summoned.

In keeping with Molokan custom, Ivan wasted no words in the negotiations. "Andrei has offered for your Natasha. Do you agree?" he asked.

Ordinarily at this point there would be some demurring by the bride's family. "Oh, the loss of a daughter, such a worker, too . . ." or "What are you saying? She's scarcely out of the cradle . . ." But Vassily knew such ruses would fool no one. He had a girl ripe for marriage, and one of the richest young men in the village wanted her. The only question was the dowry. Vassily ducked his head with a humble, worried expression. Fenya knew that Natasha's trousseau had been preying on his mind for weeks. Would his meager provision rob his daughter of her chance of happiness?

Ivan gestured to Andrei, and the young man stepped forward, resplendent in a new embroidered *kosovorotka*.

"Such a groom!" Aksinia spread her hands, palms outward, and one of the babies took a tumble onto the earth floor. "You might search far in broad daylight with a lantern and not find another like him! A husband worthy of any . . ." She retrieved the infant who, undisturbed by his fall, was picking bits of lint off the floor. Aksinia, enjoying her role, continued to pour out a flood of soothing words, praising Andrei, the Voloshins, the match, and the holy estate of matrimony. She threw the one baby over her shoulder so that he was staring at the floor behind her and bounced the other one on her lap, so vigorously that the solemn little thing seemed to be wisely agreeing with her pronouncements.

"Do we want evil for our children? Ask anyone in the village—Voloshins know how to live. And Andrei—why the work burns in his hands! Anyone can see what they've done with their farm—a blessing for any girl. We've raised the matter; now let's settle it for the happiness of our children."

Fenya restrained a smile as the baby bobbed its head sagely. She stepped behind Aksinia and took the other child from her, darting a swift, curious look at Andrei as she did so. How tense his face was with that lock of straight black hair falling over his brow! He kept adjusting his glasses to hide the fact that his eyes were straying toward the door of the best room. His hand shook slightly as he handed a purse, bulging with rubles, to Anna. The money, Fenya knew, was *kladka*—the price of "buying the bride," which is supposed to vary depending on the girl's beauty. Anna made a little ritual of counting it out. *No wonder the purse is so fat*, Fenya surmised, as Natasha appeared in the doorway.

Natasha had never looked so beautiful—or so stiff. It seemed that the glacial hue of her faded dress had frozen her heart and forced her slender body into that erect, rigid pose. Her hands were clenched, and Fenya could see that she was near tears. Aksinia clucked solicitously. "Ah, she's shy," she said in a loud aside. "Don't be afraid, dearie—it's woman's lot; we all must bear it." *She is afraid*, Fenya acknowledged, *but not of marriage. She can't believe her happiness, and she's afraid that it will somehow slip away from her.*

But the weight of Andrei's *kladka* was too substantial to slip easily away. Anna's hands with their beautiful bones and ugly skin passed the money into Natasha's younger version of those same hands. The weight of it seemed to anchor her somehow. She looked up; her eyes met Andrei's, and she was suffused with warmth.

Without taking her eyes off his, Natasha transferred the purse back to her mother and pressed a silk scarf into Andrei's hand. He looped it around his neck as a sign to the village that he had a bride.

"That's better!" Aksinia rejoiced. "They've played *lapka*, *krugi* and *gorelki*, and young Andrei has chosen a beauty for himself. And now she's smiled on his petition. What more is needed? God be with you."

She eyed the laden table. Vassily, intercepting her look, stepped forward with a stiff bow.

"Eat," he enjoined them, "and Christ be with you."

Fenya and Tanya began handing around tea towels and platters of food. Fenya glanced nervously at her father as he began picking at his food. Custom dictated that the feasting of the matchmakers was the time for discussing *pridanoe*—the bride's trousseau. She could see that Marfa Voloshin was giving her husband a questioning sideways glance. *Talk*, her eyes said, but Mikhail was complaisantly swallowing mouthfuls of *lapsha* from the common bowl.

He reached for a piece of roast lamb with a clever gleam in his eyes. He knew well enough that Vassily would be hard put to it to scrape together a trousseau for his eldest. But what would he be willing to accept?

"*Pridanoe* now," he began, and Vassily began to chew the ends of his mustache. "Coats, dresses, linens—we all know what's customary. The important thing is the chest that you provide for storing it. We would like a birchwood chest with a carved lid—"

Marfa couldn't stop herself. "A velveteen and a leather coat for

Andrei, a down mattress and quilt, silk and everyday dresses . . ." She held out her fingers for the traditional count of clothing and household goods. *And she has plenty of fingers left,* Fenya thought in alarm. Mikhail lowered his head like a bull, and Marfa's inventory faltered. Vassily absently stroked the damask tablecloth like a blind man trying to identify something he'd never come across before.

"The chest is the thing," Mikhail pronounced. "I don't need a woman to tell me what my son needs! When has Andrei ever been threadbare?" His keen eyes sought Vassily's. "Agreed?"

"Agreed," affirmed Vassily, trying to keep the relief out of his voice. "I have the chest ready. By August we will gather what we can to fill it."

"Praise be!" Aksinia put in. "There's no use holding back a young man's love for a coat he doesn't need! God will provide. The body is more important than clothes."

Fenya pressed her nose into the soft down on the baby's head and gave Aksinia a grateful, smiling look. The older woman answered with a friendly smile. "Ah, the beauties you have in this family," she said to Anna. "God grant that my little Valentina will turn out so pretty!"

The little girl on her lap puckered her brows in a doubtful look and began pulling at the tablecloth. Fenya, too, looked at her in doubt. Then she remembered that she was wearing the beautiful dress and hurriedly put a rag under the baby boy's chin. "I'll put them to sleep in the best room," she offered.

"Bless you, dearie! They should sleep this afternoon. They've had a big day of it."

Fenya settled the twins on the birchwood bed. The little boy curled up drowsily, but Valentina looked around wildly and began working up to a good, loud cry. "Shush . . . sh . . ." Fenya patted her soothingly. "Quiet, little girl," she whispered, "they're talking and I've got to hear." She held her breath and listened. She caught the harsh consonants of one word—a word that strummed on her heartstrings every time she heard it. *Pohod!* She pricked her ears as Valentina began to gurgle a lulling little gurgle to herself.

"Delizan has been stirred up like a beehive." The taciturn Ivan had found his tongue. "Many, many families are going—Tarnoffs, Samarins, Fetisoffs—some next month, others after harvest. That's when we'll be going. Just after the wedding."

"God help us," sighed Aksinia, reaching for a pastry. "Such an outlandish journey! Just like the old tales our Granny tells about Ivan the Fool traveling beyond the thrice-nine lands to the thrice-tenth kingdom." Ivan shot her a quick, suspicious glance. "Not you, dearie," she said quickly.

"What about your old granny," Mikhail asked, hiding a smirk. "She lives with you, doesn't she? What will become of her when you've all forsaken Russia?"

"Oh, she'll come, she'll come," Aksinia replied, waving a spoonful of jam. "As soon as she heard, she jumped off the stove and started making pies. 'Granny,' I said, 'You need to rest.' But nothing doing. 'I've worn out my sides with sleeping on the stove,' she says. 'What do you think I've been resting for all these years? So I'd be ready for *Pohod!*' Well, truly we thought she was getting ready to die—God knows, she's all scrunched up with age. But no, she says, 'I'm not going to die, dearie. My soul won't part from my body until I've seen this California.' So she'll be coming. And for my part, I'm glad. My heart was heavy at having to leave her. . . . But she's no good with the babies. She's vague now. She'd likely drop them over the boat rail thinking it was a crib." Aksinia sighed, a sound that had no breath of discontentment in it.

"God has seen fit to tear us from our homeland and send us who knows where. He only knows how I'm going to manage with two babies. It would be next to impossible with one—but two . . ."

"She drones on like a weir about it!" expostulated Ivan. "I'm not asking them to swim!"

"What do you know? I'll be worn to a frazzle trying to manage the two of them on the ship. We'll need some help, a young maid servant whose heart is burning for *Pohod.*"

"You're dreaming, woman. What girl would sail across the world to burp our overfed infants?"

A wide-eyed alertness pulled Fenya to the door. Aksinia's eyes met hers in understanding.

"Some may be willing. God has His purposes." Aksinia's bright eyes under their arched brows never left Fenya. But Anna stiffened and shook herself as though someone had put a handful of prickly straw down her back.

"Few parents would let a daughter go so far alone," she said pointedly. "You know how it is with us farm folk; we need our daughters for the work."

"Of course, we all end up losing our daughters anyway when they marry." Aksinia sighed sympathetically. "But who's to say? Maybe they'll marry better in America. My little Valentina, she'll marry there."

Fenya's alertness whipped up to a heart-pounding intensity. But

Anna shook her head. "It would be a cruel thing to take a young girl so far from her family."

"It's as God wills it," Aksinia demurred, but there was a benevolent, purposeful lift to her head as she turned her eyes away from Fenya.

"It's God's will for all to go!" declared Ivan.

Mikhail ground his teeth in a grim smile and opened his mouth to say something, but Vassily intervened. "It's God's will for all to follow Christ," he affirmed, quickly dousing the flare of controversy. "Some will serve Him here in Russia, others will follow Him to America. The thing is to remember who we're following—Christ, not a prophet. Too many are harkening after Klubniken and forgetting Christ.

"But now I want to show you the chest for Natasha's trousseau. You tell me if it's fit for the young couple . . . Fenya, help me bring it from the shed."

Fenya raised her eyebrows. A chest? In the shed? She certainly hadn't seen it. Her father must have worked on it in secret. When they returned to the kitchen with it, all their guests gasped in wonder.

"A work of art!" Aksinia exclaimed. "Look at it! Why there's months of work there. Who would have thought to carve leaves and branches so?" She chattered on while the others clustered around the wooden box. Natasha stooped to stroke the richly carved lid and to hide her face, for Fenya could see the tears sparkling in her eyes.

Vassily bent to smooth away a stray filing. Keeping his eyes averted, he diffidently explained his work. "A vine, you see," he said caressing the shapely, twisted trunk of a mature vine that branched into overlapping leaves. "I can't read the Scriptures, much less carve them on wood, but the idea I wanted to send off with my daughter is that of Christ as the true vine."

He raised his head now and spoke clearly. "'I am the vine, you are the branches'—Christ's words to us. This is the thought I want you to hold to tightly, Natasha and Andrei, in your marriage. Abide in Him, in His love, and you will bear much fruit, and your joy will be full as He promises. The chest—it's to be a reminder of that," he said, shy again. "I'll line it with cedar and have it ready by August."

Later, when their guests had gone and the children had eaten their fill of left-over delicacies, Vassily brought the Bible to young Vanya. "Read," he said. "Read the Evangelist's words about the vine." Then he went to stand by the window, holding his arms across his chest as though cradling some pain. Anna came to stand beside him. Fenya saw that she was subdued, almost tearful, in the emotional silt left behind by the day's events.

"The chest, Vassily—it's so beautiful," she offered. The tilt of her face, the slump of her shoulders, the whole posture of her tired body was an apology—and Vassily did not fail to see it.

"It's little enough we have to offer," Vassily murmured shaking his head. But his hand came round and began caressing the soft skin above his wife's elbow.

Vanya had found his place and began reading. "Without Me you can do nothing . . . ask what you desire, and it shall be done for you . . . abide in My love . . ." Natasha, weary and peaceful, was dreaming by the stove. Tanya was fidgeting behind her, picking at the last of the pastries. "These things I have spoken to you, that My joy may remain in you, and that your joy may be full . . ."

The boy's voice wavered childishly, but the words cut into Fenya. *A place in the heart of Christ . . . fullness of joy . . .* The little boy's thin voice carved into her heart! Like Vassily, Fenya folded her arms over an aching fullness of joy or pain. Then she edged toward the porch.

"Take the coat, ninny!" Tanya's voice followed her.

The village slept. New grass and clover on the hillside squeaked juicily under Fenya's bare feet, sending up a green, fresh scent to meet the bracing fragrance of pine coming down from the hills. The earth, black and receptive, rested its mysterious power in that brief space between last thaw and first growth. She watched as the lights in the Kostrikin hut winked out. Now there was only one light shining in the village—the light coming from Piotr Voloshin's hut. Fenya fixed her eyes on the window's feeble yellow glow. Piotr Gavrilovich's last hours in his native village were slipping away as the moon waned and the mists closed in and a muslin slip of cloud sponged up the stars.

"I'm all hollow inside," Fenya whispered. "Knock on me, Lord, and you'll hear an echo . . ."

VII

The Land of the Philistine

Galina's face had changed. She had spent the night stitching ruble notes into the felt lining of Gavril's big leather boots, and it had done something to her. Her magnificent jaw had lost its combative pose, and her skin draped slack and deflated from the prominent cheekbones. Piotr eyed her with annoyance. *You've got what you wanted*, he inwardly scolded her. *Look happy . . .* His knapsack leaned against the door post, stuffed to bursting.

"One more thing . . . ," Galina kept saying.

Piotr, feeling badgered and perverse, kept rebuffing her. "I'm a refugee—not a traveling sultan. No, no more."

Crumpled on the stove bench were his military tunic and trousers. Tomorrow they would be smeared with goat's blood and presented to the commissar as evidence that Piotr had been killed by wild animals on his way through the forest. A common story for absent soldiers— sometimes it was true. Dausha was curled up next to the pile of clothing, a rumpled little pile herself, watching everything with half-closed eyes. Nadya busied herself around the stove, deftly turning pancakes and casting an occasional forlorn glance at her brother.

Piotr crammed his feet into the clumsy, ruble-lined boots. When he looked up, Galina was standing over him holding out a beautifully embroidered peasant shirt. "For you," she said, eyes pleading.

Piotr wrenched his head back, looking into the exquisite stitching along collar and cuff. He thought about the long hours that went into such intricate work, but it only reminded him that his exile was planned and that it was Galina who had done the planning as she stitched away the winter evenings. "I can't take it," he said curtly. "I have too much as it is . . ."

He turned from her and went to the table where Semyon and Gavril bent over the dog-eared map that told the way to California. Semyon's strong knotty fingers moved purposefully as though he were kneading Piotr's future into the much-creased paper. His written instructions and reminders bordered the page, the Russian characters penned at a mad tilt, like fleeing animals.

"Remember to keep your face out of sight," Gavril warned him. "After tomorrow, you're supposed to be dead."

"Don't worry," Piotr replied, "that's one part I'm up to playing."

Semyon shot him a sharp look and then returned to the map, shaking his head so that his long whiskers brushed the paper.

"Keep those boots on, Petya. They're your fortune," Gavril was saying. "Don't part with them for anything."

"No," said Piotr beginning to strap on his rucksack. Semyon wouldn't look at him but kept on shaking his head.

"All right, I'm ready," Piotr said quietly. Gavril kissed him, roughly rubbing his big hand on the back of Piotr's head. Piotr stood woodenly as Galina held him. She raised her eyes to his, but he looked away. A wiry strand of hair escaped her kerchief, tickling his chin. She looked old. He didn't want to remember her like that. He didn't want to remember the desolate look in her eyes or the defeated set of chin.

Don't look like that, he wanted to shout, *for all you know, I may be back! I'll surprise you all!* . . . *But then, again, I may not.* The thought slipped in for long enough to awaken a moment's pity for her, and he patted her clumsily and returned her kisses.

The predawn air clamped down on him like cold metal as Piotr turned his back on the hut and followed the silent back lane to the square. He knew that Gavril, Galina, and the girls crowded the porch in a single lump of shadow against the doorway's feeble light. He did not look back.

Stealthy lights from Abajarian's splotched the street. Sirakan hoisted an empty barrel into a wooden cart while three mismatched horses stolidly puffed plumes of frosty breath into the air. Piotr slid his sack under a crushed tarp and slumped between the barrel and the driver's seat.

"Where did you get these beauties?" Piotr joked, nodding toward the sway-backed shaft horse that, from his angle, looked like an old battered couch.

"Looks aren't everything, Gavrilovich. You'll find that out if you ever get to be that old," Sirakan replied with patient condescension, "but if my travel arrangements aren't to your liking—"

"Oh, no, I'm more than thankful for them. I'm sure they're much more comfortable than what the Tsar has in mind for me."

"Make yourself at home then," Sirakan said with exaggerated hospitality. "All the comforts of my humble cart are at Your Excellency's disposal." He tossed a stinking load of half-cured hides beside Piotr.

"For the shoe factory," he explained. Nina, who had just stepped out of the shop, smiled vividly as though he had said something very witty. She climbed into the cart facing Piotr and drew up her knees. Nina was quiet, but there was something breathless and aware in her silence. The growing light brought out burgundy lights in her dark hair and revealed the deep pansy softness of her tilted eyes. Her pure profile was as pale as ever, her neutral skin tones a lovely contrast with the rich nuances of color in hair and eyes.

A sweet, languid weight settled on Piotr. He sighed and looked away. From his nook behind the barrel, he surveyed the empty street. There was little to see at this hour—just the huts with the budding trees behind them holding out small dollops of life at each twig tip. And in the shadows, an old man, his sumptuous beard giving the moon's light something to work on. It glittered so fervently that Semyon's eye sockets deepened to dark caverns. But Piotr, looking hard, caught the glimmer of his expression beneath the heavy brows. The cart lurched forward, and their eyes locked in an unwavering steady gaze that caught and held until the road dipped and the square was gone.

They came into Tiflis, turning onto Vorontsov Street. The purplish browns and peaches of the old houses swam in the sultry haze that drifted up from the river. Intricately carved balconies on old brick houses conspired overhead. They plodded past the university and then out toward the Kura where the houses clung crazily to a steep-sided cliff above the boiling waters. The Kura frothed discontently at its restrictive banks, while the drab-colored houses looked down from their perches in consternation.

They followed Golovinski Prospekt along the river. This was the "New Town" with its government offices and stylish shops and cafes. The avenues were lined with stately pine trees and equally stately buildings which combined Russian classicism with the old Georgian style. The streets teemed with handsome Georgians in dark *papachkas* and flowing Circassian coats crossed with grouped cartridge holders, Russians in high-necked shirts or dark European-style suits, and Armenians wearing tradesmen's caps and jackets. Pretty women in long dresses rode in carriages or strolled with Parisian gaiety on the arms of fashionable young men. But at the edges of the nineteenth-century town center huddled the other Tiflis, the Tiflis of ancient warring cultures: Circassians and Ossetians, Jews and Armenians, Gypsies and Tartars.

Resilience and dash, thought Piotr, craning his neck around the shielding barrel. Tiflis showed its strength like a generous courtly gesture from a well-muscled arm. It had the uncanny ability to grasp widely flung themes and integrate them into a fascinating pageant of city life. During its turbulent history, the city had been pillaged forty times and completely devastated twenty-nine times, but each time it had risen again—as effervescent and indestructible as its mixed populace. Tiflis managed to take the scars left by Khazars, Huns, Persians, Byzantines, Arabs, and Mongols and wear them as ornaments. And for the past century, mused Piotr, Russia had provided the backdrop for this flamboyant cast—but for how long? Tiflis was convulsed in revolution. Even without the signs of strikes, violence, street meetings, Piotr could sense rebellion like a tang in the air.

The cart wheels rocked and protested as they left the wide, well-paved avenues for the narrow streets of the "Old Town." They soon stopped at a tall brick house with wrought-iron trim, and the ugly shaft horse turned to give them a martyred look. "Carts are impossible in this rabbit warren," Sirakan complained. He and Nina would spend the day going from street to street for merchandise. In Tiflis there was a separate street for each trade. Shoemakers, weavers, silversmiths, perfumers, dyers competed in medieval conviviality so that buying was an all-day affair.

"We'll have to meet here later," Sirakan grumbled. "Who knows what scheme Noe will cook up! Pull your cap down, Gavrilovich. You look like a Russian. Do you know where you are? If you don't come back here to report, old Semyon will string me up and flay me alive with those sharp eyes of his. Noe lives in Nadzaladevi. You can probably find him at the Armenian cafe near there. Understand?"

"Right." Piotr tried to hide his feeling of disorientation. "Here, then, at sunset . . ." The warming sun stirred up the odors of the alleyway—garbage and melted butter and cloves and the rank odor of the half-cured hides beside him. He clambered out of the cart, feeling dwarfed by the unwelcoming brick walls looming around him. He took off his cap and crushed it between his fingers.

"Sirakan, you've been a good friend . . ."

The burly Armenian grinned ruefully. "Just scamper now, Piotr—that will be thanks enough. You're subversive and illegal enough by now that Noe will welcome you with open arms. Give him our greetings."

Nina, kneeling in the cart with one hand on the railing, gave him a merry, secretive smile. He held up the cap in a half-hearted goodbye and made his way through the narrow, twisted streets to his meeting place with Noe.

Dedujian's cafe was not hard to find. It straddled a sloping street corner—bulky and thick-walled with much replastering. A glass case filmed with grease and dotted with flies displayed honeyed sweets and baklava. A savory aroma of roasting lamb wafted from the open door. Several tables with printed cloths crowded the room. Most of the wooden chairs, covered with peeling paint that was once Uzbek blue, were occupied. Thick smoke and the buzz of conversation closed around Piotr as he stepped inside.

In the back he could see a balding man with an enormous mustache ladling thick, sweet Turkish coffee into cups. A girl in a claret-colored skirt and leather belt waited with a tray.

As Piotr moved into the room, gazing intently about him, the noise faltered. He noticed that several pairs of suspicious eyes had switched to him with machinelike precision. He flushed, realizing how out of place he looked with his sheepskin cap and Russian clothes. Except for a few Georgian workers, most of Dedujian's clientele were Armenian.

Piotr hurriedly scanned the room until he spotted Noe's dark head near the back. The young Georgian's wiry frame relaxed in one of the primitive chairs across from two of his countrymen. The angle of his elbow, his leveled line of vision, and the ash-tipped end of his cigarette all pointed to the waitress in the claret skirt. She stood impassively with her tray, her haughty gypsy face framed by short black hair and gold earrings.

Noe's own face suggested something of the gypsy with its dramatic play of horizontal and vertical lines. An early crease scored his forehead; the long, beautifully shaped aquiline nose drew the line downward to the gap between his front teeth and the cleft in his chin. This center line was barred by straight, intensely dark brows and an equally dark mustache.

As Piotr approached, all of Noe's concealed energy was riveted on the girl; he was laughing at her and then, with a sinuous movement, he turned to douse his cigarette and caught sight of Piotr. His eyes widened; he nodded with a serious look and reached for a fourth chair. The girl stared at Piotr curiously and wove through the tables with narrow swinging hips.

Piotr wedged his long legs uncomfortably under the rickety table. He put his cap on the table in front of him until one of the Georgians stared at it with a fierce offended look. Piotr quickly snatched it out of sight while Noe sized him up, smiling, speculative.

"This is Piotr Gavrilovich," he said in Russian to his companions, "from our village." They gave a perfunctory greeting, then exchanged a few words in Georgian. They seemed put out at the newcomer and left as soon as they finished their coffees.

"Nationalists," said Noe.

"Oh . . ."

"Good people, but a little dogmatic. I hope they get what they want. Or some of what they want."

"Yes."

Noe laughed suddenly and then leaned back against the stained wall with narrowed eyes.

"So, why has Sirakan sent you to me?"

"He thought, that is, I thought you might help me . . . I'm in a difficult position."

"What? Say, weren't you in the army?" Noe's eyes raked Piotr's peasant dress. "Wait. I see." He softly whistled between his teeth and looked hard at Piotr. "And you want to leave the country?"

"No! That is, I don't know . . . I hope to stay."

"You have big hopes, Piotr."

"I know."

Noe tilted his chair back against the wall. His eyes had a demure look as he scanned the busy room, but there was nothing demure about the coiled stillness of his body. Piotr could read the intrigue gathering in his hazel eyes and in the corners of his wide mouth. Sensing his pre-occupation, Piotr let his eyes wander about the crowded cafe.

In the center of the room, six or seven Armenians clustered in low-voiced conversation. One of them, a heavy-set man with a prow of a nose and a weak chin was earnestly explaining something—his fingers splayed out on the flowered cloth and his eyes begging for understanding. Near the kitchen a man stared fixedly in their direction. His aristocratic features contrasted sharply with his shabby dress. Across his forehead a blue-green vein branched up to his recessed hairline. It was hard to look away from the fascinating throbbing of that vein, as though it were pumping poison into the man's brain to cause the wryness of his mouth.

"An idealist," Noe said.

Piotr gave him a questioning look. "There's a bitterness to that one."

"Well, there are only two kinds. Either they're naive or bitter. The bitter ones are more effective."

Piotr was taken aback. "Aren't you an idealist?" he asked with a short, baffled laugh.

Noe looked at him strangely. "Let's go; we can't talk here."

He strode into the brightening afternoon with Piotr following, awkwardly clutching cap and satchel and sweating under his heavy coat. They walked quickly toward the working-class quarters of Nadzaladevi. Noe led the way up a chute of a stairway to a small, disheveled room on the third floor. The Spartan bed with its mottled green coverlet was strewn with copies of *Sakartvelo*, the Georgian revolutionary paper. In a corner were boxes of printed material.

"Your first problem is that you look like a Russian," said Noe, closing the door. "That's what they'll be looking for. Try this." He tossed him a short workman's jacket and cap.

Piotr shrugged into the stiff unfamiliar material. The blue fabric stretched across his powerful shoulders. He hunched to accommodate it as Noe cocked a brow at him.

"You still look like a Russian," he said disgustedly. "But there's nothing we can do about your face. Pull your cap down, and try not to look at anybody."

Piotr gave the cap's beak a determined wrench. "How's this? My ears are displaced by at least an inch, and I feel like I have an iron band around my chest!"

"Just what you need—a little rearrangement of the anatomy.

Believe me, if they catch you deserting, they'll rearrange your anatomy for you! I've seen some of their best work."

"Don't describe it," Piotr groaned. "There's no room for any more worries under this cap."

"Now," said Noe, straddling the only chair, "tell me."

Piotr eased himself onto the sagging cot and told his story. The young Georgian listened with an abstract, restless attention. He would remove the cigarette from his mouth, stare studiously at the butt, and then forget it until it burnt down to his fingertips. Then he'd light another with a graceful automatic movement. Despite the fidgeting hands, Piotr had no doubt that Noe was absorbing every detail.

"If this were happening a year from now, there's a chance that there would be a completely new government—and no war with Japan," was Noe's first comment.

"But too late for me, you're saying . . ."

"Not necessarily. Things have been happening fast this winter—faster than we ever expected. But there's no way of knowing. You'll just have to act—and take the consequences."

"Fine. But how do I know what the best course of action is? I've been battered this way and that for weeks over this. Act, you say! But what I want to know—"

"That's just it! You want to know! That's the fallacy you people live with! And it's bound you hand and foot." Noe indicted him with a long tip of dead ash. "You think you can control things by knowing; that's naive. You can't know. You can only act. And in acting there's power. That's how you can exert control. There's no power without energy and no energy without action! You aren't real until you act." The ashes scattered with another quick gesture.

Piotr was taken aback. "Forgive me," he said. "I'm not educated. For us, if there are two choices—one good, one bad—we choose the good. In this case, it's hard to see what is good. It's in God's hands—"

Noe's grin was edged with derision. "Good, bad—how do you know? And remember this, Gavrilovich, you aren't in the hands of God. You are in the hands of history! There's a momentum building that will sweep you along its path like a bit of dust in front of an old hag's broom."

Piotr shrugged. "Well, while I'm waiting for the beat of the old hag's broom on my backside, what do I do?"

Noe smiled broadly, affectionately. "That, friend, is simple. You disappear."

"Disappear. Now that's an idea even a simple peasant can understand. I like that," he continued with mock awe. "I can only become real by acting, and I can act by disappearing; therefore, I become real by disappearing. So, teacher, how do I disappear?"

Noe laughed delightedly. "You and I are going to get along, Piotr. As I'm sure Sirakan has told you, I'm a master of disappearances. I'll tell you my plan. Later. But first I have some business this afternoon. A little demonstration. I'll show you Tiflis, and you can be a Social Democrat for a day—no better disguise for a Molokan peasant! Here, take this."

And Piotr took it—a cardboard box sagging under its weight of printed propaganda. "UNITE!" screamed the headlines as Noe began stuffing flyers into canvas sacks. *Unite*, echoed Piotr and wondered what he had gotten into.

The crooked stairway spewed them out again into the ramshackle alleyway. A warm spring day greeted them; the fresh scent of blossoming apricot trees conjured away the fetid smell of too many humans living in too small a space.

They made their way to the old south section of the town—new to Piotr. Cobbled streets and lanes crossed and knotted in a complicated labyrinth lined with cavelike shops and bazaars. Noe led him down a dyers' lane where red and black and indigo banners of drying wool hung in heraldic display. A complex, unnameable longing awoke in Piotr as he breathed in the mingled smells of wool and dyes, perfume and spices, baking bread and savory meats.

Exhilarated by the newness, Piotr kept turning his head to see another side alley, darkness pricked by the sudden gleam of copper or silver or rich silk and redolent with exotic odors.

Noe strode alongside him with his springy walk and gleaming smile. "I'm hungry," he announced suddenly. He dived into the mouth of a little shop which soon ejected him on a belch of hot, yeasty air. They ate *lavash*, Georgian flat bread, as they walked, cramming the warm, crusty stuff into their mouths. Piotr followed his friend closely as he dodged gesticulating vendors, calico-clad housewives, mullahs in silk turbans, and gorgeously arrayed Georgian bravos. Here and there Muslim maidens, swathed head to foot in black purdah, blocked the color like moving shadows.

Feeling bold and carefree, Piotr pressed into the crowd, occasionally stalling to give a second look to some slender Georgian girl. The Old Town airs wafted and changed subtly, and Piotr could tell that they were closer to the river. The pale blue walls of a mosque rose before them, and they turned back toward Sioni Cathedral, passing an old *caravanserai* building at the end of Sionskaya Street.

"This is where we will meet this evening—here on the steps of the cathedral." Noe lounged against an evergreen tree and scanned the agitated Kura. "There, you see, across the river? No, a little further that way—on the hill. That's the Metekhi fortress. It's very old, but they still use it. For political prisoners. Sirakan is convinced it will be my future home. He doesn't know how slippery I am."

Piotr probed the brown-gray walls with cautious eyes. The building looked formidable, probably riddled with filthy cells filled with rotting "guests of the government." But to the front and to one side was the lovely dome of the Metekhi chapel, its silhouette distinct against the hillside. "Pretty," said Noe, following his glance, "but it's used as a prison too."

"Why do you do this?" Piotr asked wonderingly, his eyes still on the chapel. "Why would you risk imprisonment—or worse—for something you can't even name?" Then he was struck by the thought that as far as the government was concerned Metekhi prison was as proper an abode for deserter Piotr Gavrilovich Voloshin as it was for political agitator Noe Tcheidze. "Why?" he muttered again, more to himself than to his companion.

Noe took out a cigarette and studied it. "I live for change, Piotr. Who can know what is right? I only know what is wrong. And it's the wrong that creates discontentment; and discontentment fuels revolution."

"Revolution! What good will it do? To you, personally. Do you trust the people who will rule if you succeed? As the old people say, the only strong birds are the raptors—Tsar and Communist alike."

"The government will be one of the people," Noe broke in. "But that's not my business. My business is change. Now. History has tossed me into this time of ferment. And so I throw myself into change. I do everything and anything I can—big or small—to overthrow the system. That's what I live for! After all," he added in a reasonable tone, "why do you think I'm helping you?"

"I wasn't sure," said Piotr. "I didn't realize your motives were so lofty. But you, yours seems a strange and haphazard way to live! Don't you ever think of the future?"

"Never. Any thought for the future will deplete me, erode my power . . ."

"Your power! I see—to work change. But how about God? Are you an atheist?"

"No, no . . . I don't exactly disbelieve . . . in some kind of power," Noe threw back his head and tapped his chest in a parody of conceit, "that's greater than my power! Only the true idealists are really atheists—the bitter ones! And I'm not bitter. I'm young and life has a sweet taste!" His hazel eyes took on a distant, brooding look, and for some reason Piotr thought of the Gypsy waitress at Dedujian's with her proud bearing and striking face. Piotr snorted a confused laugh. The conceit, he thought, was real; so was the sudden flare of passion. But one thing was true—there was no bitterness in Noe Tcheidze.

Noe detached himself from Sioni's shadow and led Piotr west to where the sheer wall of Mount David rose ahead of them. Joking and arguing both with each other and the street vendors, they bought tomatoes, goat cheese, and more bread. They slung their jackets over their shoulders and strode up the slope toward the mountain. Both Noe and Piotr were warm with the walk and quieter by the time they reached the spiral stairway that coiled up to St. David's from Golovinski Prospekt. Litter from the construction of the new funicular railway cluttered the area, so they skirted the mess and climbed to the church—St. David's on Mtatsminda Mountain. The mauve-colored haze lingered on the outskirts of the town and simmered in the pastel undulations of the surrounding hills—a gauzy, alluring enhancement to the strange, mythical quality of the city spread out below them.

But on Mount David, the air was clear and invigorating. The cheese and bread tasted especially good. Noe sighed with satisfaction and stretched out on the lawn with his dark head propped against a sack of propaganda. Piotr studied his strong, beautiful profile. Then he wandered toward the church. Long blades of charcoal tree-shadow scissored the late afternoon light into glowing triangles. As Piotr walked on them, a hush settled into his soul. An onyx gleam caught his eye, and he strolled toward it. There in the church yard was a black marble tomb decorated with a bronze crucifix. "Griboyedov" said the carved letters—Griboyedov, the Russian writer beheaded in 1829 while serving as ambassador to Persia. His young, beautiful wife survived him. Piotr's attention lunged toward the mourning female figure laved in satin light on top of the tomb.

The curve of her back, the posture of her bowed head seemed poignantly familiar. The whole figure was bent by loss in a way that forced his memory to Galina and her changed face as she had said goodbye. Her image slipped between him and the black marble—pleading eyes, fingers caressing a peasant shirt, ornamented with the labor of hours. Piotr shook his head like a wet dog. "Why didn't I take the shirt?" he asked himself.

Unwillingly, Piotr remembered Dausha's little form curled up on the stove, Nadya's shadow in the doorway, Gavril's shuttered expression, and Semyon's dark eyes in the moonlight. "That was only this morning! Is it possible?" he wondered. He moved a hand across the cold marble, and it sent a shiver of foreboding through him. "Could it be that I'll never see them again?"

Piotr shook his head again as if to throw off the pestering ideas, but they stuck to him like burrs. *I should have taken the shirt.*

As the air cooled, subtle changes of light found their way onto the chiseled surfaces of the grieving statue. Piotr stood rooted for so long that the chill of the earth seeped into his boot soles. Finally, he sighed and turned. Noe, his head still pillowed on a stack of broadsides, was watching him closely—an inscrutable look on his handsome, dark face.

VIII

Man of Steel

I don't belong here, Piotr thought as the teeming mob at Sioni
Cathedral began to close in on him. He and Noe had wedged their
way right up to the front—so close that he could see the flat, gray
eyes of the first speaker flicking around the growing mob like pewter
disks.

Piotr let the heavy sack of flyers fall to his feet, and his eyes sought
Noe's. "This is not for me, friend," he declared. A growing dread began
to knot his stomach.

"Don't worry," said Noe good-naturedly, "it's a little early in your
education to expect you to get inflamed about the rule of the proletariat—or Georgian independence for that matter."

Piotr was relieved that he was not offended. Noe's inner fire seemed
to be stoked by the excitement building around him. Something elemental in Noe sprang to the surface and flickered out in his swift assess-
ment of the crowd, his quick greetings to comrades. But Piotr felt
trapped by the pressing mob and confused by the booming, chaotic
noise of hundreds of conversations.

"I'm not a philosopher, I'm a workhorse," Piotr apologized. "When
you have a free Georgia, I'll gladly plow your land and feed your children. Meanwhile—"

"Meanwhile," Noe finished for him, "you can find some neutral
ground on the fringes. Better for you not to be seen right now anyway.
But find yourself a dark alleyway to listen from. You may learn
something."

"Who's speaking?"

"The usual assortment of Zordania's Socialists. I'm not sure what

99

they want more—radical overthrow of the system or a safe little berth in a free Georgia."

"Can't you have both? Besides, I thought you liked Zordania."

"I do. For the most part. But I'm at a turning point, too. Zordania and his Mensheviks are sliding toward the liberals—putting their hopes in nationalism. Before you know it, they'll be mewling about constitutional pablum! But the Bolsheviks are the true revolutionaries. Their vision includes the world—not just this little tidbit pronged on the tip of the Caucasus! There's a man I want to listen to—he's called Koba, but his ideas—"

"Koba!" Piotr interrupted roughly. *Again! The man turns up like Satan himself!* "Do you know him?"

"A little. Enough to know what he stands for."

"Bloodshed," snorted Piotr. "That's what he stands for."

"Yes, blood," replied Noe hotly. "The autocracy has bled the people for centuries. Now is the time for reprisals—not the time to flinch. This Koba—he doesn't flinch. He's like steel. Stalin, they should call him—man of steel."

"He's not a man, he's a wolf. He likes the scent of blood . . ." Piotr was suddenly aware that he had raised his voice to combat the din of the mob.

"You think you're too pure for all this, Piotr, but someday you'll find you can be infected, too!"

"It's not our way . . . ," insisted Piotr. But Noe was no longer listening. The beautiful waitress from Dedujian's had appeared.

"Irina!" shouted Noe.

Piotr backed toward the edge of the crowd. He could still see Noe shoving sheafs of flyers into the hands of anyone who would take them. The white leaflets passing from hand to hand from Noe's central position looked like a pale, ragged flower opening on the dark storm of humanity.

Curious, Piotr hung on the fringes of the milling crowd. Most of the demonstrators were obviously from outside the primarily Turkish sector around Sioni Cathedral. Only a few turbaned heads passed by, going about their own business or pausing to look on with brief, contemptuous curiosity.

Piotr strained to hear the speaker who had just mounted the steps—the one with the gray, darting eyes. He spoke in Georgian, but Piotr could catch random words: ". . . brothers . . . unity . . . a long and difficult struggle . . ." Then more clearly: "The call of the times is for freedom, and freedom is not possible in Georgia without sovereignty and independence!"

True, thought Piotr, *a good and wholesome desire—if they choose the right means to get it.* If the "legal" Social Democrat leader, Zoe Zordania, moved toward a more moderate position, the dream might come within grasp, Piotr speculated. *If these violent Bolsheviks like Koba don't wrench it away from them!*

There he was, Koba, mounting the steps—small but powerful. Piotr remembered the tobacco-hued pallor of his face. Koba held his shoulders oddly as he turned to confront his audience, and Piotr could see that one arm was shorter than the other. Koba's voice carried easily; besides, he was easier to understand than the previous speaker because he spoke Russian.

Nothing he said was new, any more than the rugged side of a mountain is new, but a certain kind of raw light can make the familiar look monstrous and menacing. *Koba has a way with that kind of light*, thought Piotr, *he has a way with it!* Koba scoured the autocracy with a grating sarcasm that rough-hewed the crowd's formless discontent down to its elemental core—hatred. And he made it sound so reasonable, in fact, morally right, to hate.

Koba summed up with generalities the rock-hard undergirding of all revolutionary thought, whether Socialist or nationalist. His clenched fist punctuated the now-familiar phrases: "We must struggle constantly against the government, overthrow autocracy, loudly and insistently call for an end to the senseless, unnecessary, and cruel war in Japan . . ."

Piotr had heard enough. He detached himself from the crowd and backed into a recessed doorway under a balcony. But Koba's voice followed him: "The proletariat cannot live or breathe without political liberty. Like air or food, we need freedom of the press, of speech, of association, assembly, and strike action. And to achieve this we can only count on ourselves. Of course, the liberals want political liberty—but they want it for themselves alone. We, the workers, desire it for the entire nation. Only when the fetters of slavery fastened by autocracy on every living creature are broken can the working class develop its full strength and win for itself a better life, a socialist system of society!"

Suddenly, the dogmatic rasp was cut off by singing. Soft, lyrical, haunting, the melody framed the words of one of Georgia's great poets. One by one, the demonstrators took up the song until it swelled and grew like a living thing inhabiting the air above the people. Piotr, listening, was filled with a great pity for them. His mind awakened to the beauty of Georgia, and he wanted them to be able to hold it as their own, to live in peace, glorying in their unique gift from God.

The music muted all other sound so that Piotr saw the first line of a Cossack detachment before he heard them. The pitch of the singing tightened into a scream as the horsemen collided with the waiting crowd.

Piotr pressed himself against the wall, taking in the limited scene allowed him by the shadowed doorway and failing light. The screaming stopped as suddenly as it had started. The chink of hooves, the creak of saddles and gear, sounds of scuffling, odd thumps and groans came to him in his seclusion. A shadowy Cossack rode past him, sabered a fleeing youth, and then wheeled his mount back toward the church. A moment later, a stout, rosy-cheeked woman leaned over the fallen student. She tore strips off her petticoats, her mouth set in a concerned line. She kept straightening her white kerchief, which kept slipping over her eyes, with an almost coy gesture—absurd in the circumstances. A second rider on a dappled horse came at a trot and brained her. The kerchief slid over her face and turned red as she slowly slumped to one side.

Horrified, Piotr froze into his corner, drawing back his head. The veins stood out like whipcord on his broad neck. He strained to hear, oblivious of the muscular tension created by his awkward position. A metallic scrape on the stone street jerked his head to the left. He found himself staring into the impassive face of a young Cossack mounted on a Kuban mare, a bayonet held carelessly in his hand. A maelstrom of emotion smoked in the look that passed between them.

The Cossack was enough like Piotr to pass for close kindred—the same broad cheekbones, the trapezoidal slant of bone to the firm jaw and straight mouth. The eyes were different though—slanting Kirghiz eyes with avid curiosity spurting from between the narrow lids. Piotr felt himself responding with an odd recognition. The soldier continued to hold his look as he casually moved the tip of his bayonet. The blade pricked the fabric of Piotr's blue jacket, deftly drew it aside, and traced the line of his collarbone. Piotr shuddered and closed his eyes, breaking the strange bond.

The Cossack moved his hand in a leisurely, mechanical way and thrust it so that the blade deflected off the collarbone into the soft flesh between neck and shoulder. Gasping with pain, Piotr opened his eyes; he was pinned so that any movement was agony. The Cossack looked at him for a long, satisfied moment, then drew back his weapon with all the savagery lacking in his earlier gesture. He showed his teeth in a gleaming smile, and the smile ignited a fierce hatred in Piotr.

Putting all the strength of his plowman's back into the movement, he grabbed the muzzle of the man's rifle and wrenched it away. He swung the butt of the weapon in a bone-cracking blow to the man's ear where his head was not protected by the sheepskin cap. Blood spurted from his ear, and his face flamed with astonishment. The Cossack fell with a squirming movement, his fingers clawing toward the revolver at his belt. Piotr put his booted foot on the man's wrist and pushed hard with his heel, feeling the skin slip over the bone. The Cossack groaned and was still.

Panting, Piotr curled his fingers; his diaphragm rose in revolt. "*Stidna, stidna . . . a sin . . . ,*" chanted a voice inside him. He slumped to his knees, his own blood mingling with the blood pooling beneath his enemy's head. "God help me," he prayed. "I've killed him . . . *stidna* . . ." He retched and his fingers slipped in the blood and filth. He fought for consciousness, welded to reality by a triad of sensations—the chill of the pavement, the pounding of his heart, and the agony in his shoulder. From a window above him floated the sound of a Caucasian clarinet. Its bleating resonance dipped and soared with a Middle Eastern skirl and then faded into the night air.

Piotr forced a stiffness into his knees where they were inclined to buckle and inched himself up against the wall. Cautiously, without looking at the fallen Cossack, he stumbled toward the open street. The bodies of the young Georgian and the woman with the kerchief were gone. A few men clustered in the doorway of the church; a heavy-set man lay in the square like a discarded bundle; another, a tall Georgian, was lying face down in the gutter, the skirts of his flowing coat pulled over his head. A third body sprawled in a pool of blood on the steps. Piotr's heart lurched with fear as he recognized Noe. Forgetting himself, he wobbled toward his friend. A shadowy form was there before him—Irina. As Piotr approached, she cocked her head and rudely nudged the prone form with a bright blue boot. Noe sprang to life.

A ghost of a smile flickered across Irina's face as she saw Piotr's face contort with sick shock. "It's one of his tricks," she explained. "He's done it before—playing dead when the Cossacks come in."

With a quick movement, Noe was beside Piotr as he began to sway. "Can you walk, Piotr," he asked with such gentleness that Piotr barely recognized his voice.

"I—can—walk."

It was very late at night when Piotr awoke to the rattling and creaking of people moving up and down the stairs at the back of the house. What house? He struggled against the lethargy tugging at him, pulling him into unconsciousness. He was lying in a clean bed; he had been washed, bandaged, and was wearing a clean shirt. He had no other clothes on except, to his surprise, his boots—lying clumsily on the fine, white sheets.

"You wouldn't part with them," said an amused feminine voice. Piotr started at the sound. Nina! He drew a shame-faced grin.

"You fought as hard for those boots as Noe fights for the future of all Georgia!" Nina chided him.

"They have a sentimental value," he told her looking into her face. Her eyes, smudged with sleepless concern, belied her jaunty words.

"Your sentiments run strong then. Noe and Sirakan gave up on you!"

"Well, you can tell Noe that the Tsar's army—even with a war on— is a good bit safer than his escapades."

"Tell him yourself," she threw back at him.

"Tell him what." Sirakan's heavy tread sounded on the floor boards.

"Not you—Noe," said Nina.

"Noe," the big Armenian rumbled. The word had obviously been mulled in hours of anger. "He went for your things—he'll be back. What he'll have to say for himself, I don't know."

Sirakan stopped beside the bed, drew back the coverlet, and examined the bandaged wound. "Stopped bleeding," he commented.

"I can't see it. Hurts to crane my neck like that. How big is it?"

"A little more than an inch long. Much deeper than that, of course."

"An inch!" Piotr was amazed. An inch, yet his whole body was shaken!

"So-o-o," Sirakan drew out the word on rounded lips, "you took my advice, and this is where it got you. What will I tell your folks, old Semyon?"

"Nothing," Piotr begged. "They don't need to know. Tell them I'm safe—"

"I owe them more than that—so do you. How do you feel?"

"Better. A little shaky, but ready, able." He sat up with a wince.

"I see. I think you will need to be able, ready for anything tonight, Piotr Gavrilovich."

As he spoke, a shadow parted from the darkness of the doorway. A stately, heavily veiled Moslem woman stood silently, waiting for them to acknowledge her. Surprised, Piotr noticed that she was carrying his knapsack and sheepskin coat, and she had another jacket slung over her arm. She abruptly dropped the knapsack, groped in the jacket pocket for a cigarette, and strode toward the bed, drawing aside her black veil.

"Noe!" Piotr cried.

The Georgian locked his teeth, cigarette and all, in a cagey grin.

"Well, who else? How many harem beauties can boast a mustache like this one?"

Piotr shook his head painfully and shrugged, also painfully. As Noe backed away, surveying his young charge with a critical eye, another black-swathed shadow slipped into the room. Piotr had no trouble recognizing Irina's abrupt, sensual movements. Noe glanced briefly at her with that inadvertent flare to eye and nostril that Piotr had come to know.

"We often dress like this," Noe explained, "for our own nocturnal jaunts. I'm not sure who thought of it first, but it was such a good idea that a lot of us put on the veil when we don't want to be noticed. The police are probably amazed at the sudden increase of Moslem women in town. We'll be in purdah tomorrow, too," he added. "For our trip."

"Trip?" asked Piotr.

"Yes. You remember I promised you an adventure. It starts tomorrow."

"I was under the impression it had already started," Piotr said dryly.

"It's started, all right. You'll be wanted for manslaughter as well as for desertion. If we don't contrive your disappearance, the government will."

"Enough of your nonsense, Noe," interposed Sirakan. "We need to make our plans—then get what little sleep we can. Nina, go to bed."

Looking thoughtful and remote, Nina obediently left the room, turning at the doorway to give a last long look at the bed. But Piotr could not meet her eyes. *Manslaughter*, he thought, *so it wasn't a nightmare after all.*

They made ready while the white stars faded over Mtatsminda. By the time dawn gilded the tarnished gold and silver of domes and spires, they were gone from the city. Sirakan's cart lumbered north on the

Georgian Military Highway which cut straight into the heart of the mountains. Piotr, fully awake and throbbing with pain, set his body to absorb each shock that the road sent through the wood of the cart.

The morning was crisp, and he pulled his skirted coat closer; his cap, wadded against the cart railing, buffered his injured shoulder. It seemed impossible that he had left his home village only twenty-four hours before. He felt like an old, old man jolting along in his own funeral procession. The purdah-clad forms of Nina, Noe, and Irina contributed to the impression—except that Noe was smoking furiously, sifting pale, gray ash onto the front of his black robe.

The flat farmland fell behind the cart. To the north, the land began to rise, toying with the geometry of orchard and plowland. The cart wracked to one side, and Piotr shifted to absorb it. *Absorb, absorb*, he thought. Pain pummeled him into a tender receptiveness of the savage beauty of the Caucasus. *Absorb it,* he thought, looking out at the fields flanking the road. *Take it in; you aren't the first to feel pain!* His yearning eyes roved around the landscape, searching for images to replace those that haunted him—his broken family, the blood-stained body of the Cossack. *Stidna,* echoed the hills. Piotr stiffened to absorb the pain.

The mountains shouldered forward. The land broke from the smooth curve of the earth and crusted into a piled-up rubble of stone against the brilliantly blue sky. It was a young, aggressive geology—one that still remembered the ancient thrusting forces that had birthed it. Far away, silver filaments of snow and ice threaded the flanks of distant peaks, crossing and meshing into pure white ice caps. The cart lurched and swayed; Piotr braced to absorb it.

As the morning drew on, the road from Tiflis to Mtskheta was peopled with peasants going to market. Shepherds in tall knitted caps coaxed their flocks along. An outlandish cart pulled by twelve white oxen rumbled past them. Piotr crouched and Noe doused his cigarette as a troop of Cavalier Guards approached. The road smoked in the dust of their going, and the white crossed straps of their gray uniforms twinkled on their breasts.

The flanks of Mount Kartli came into view at the joining of the Aragvi and Kura Rivers. Mtskheta nestled in the hills, the legendary capital of Georgia until the fifth century. But they kept on toward the higher mountains. Deeply cloven canyons opened, first on one side, then on the other. Their echoing walls rudely exaggerated the secrets of the spring-swollen streams.

Past the village of Passanauri, they turned off the road and stopped in a copse where the dogwood blossoms opened like stars against the dark firs. They picnicked on cold chicken, *lavash*, and olives. Piotr watched the others moodily. The quivering in his diaphragm robbed him of any delight in food. Nina and Sirakan were preoccupied with a low-voice debate. Irina perched on a rock next to Noe, her face uncovered but its stern beauty still framed by the black veil.

Piotr was piqued by their relationship. Irina seemed careless and flippant in her treatment of Noe, yet she was always there with her beautiful curved nose and huntress eyes. She'd tilt up her chin and glare defiance at him through lowered lids—a look that would be an insult from a man. But Noe would flame at it. It was obvious that they were intimate, but it was an intimacy full of challenge and unknowns.

They're alike, those two, thought Piotr. *Intense, the both of them.* But Noe's intensity was scattered and diffuse—it could build to a storm front and then dissipate in a hundred directions. Irina's was focused. She was the kind of woman who needed one object. And it looked like that object was Noe.

Piotr flexed his hands; even the uninjured arm was beginning to numb. He crossed the road and looked out on the deep valley, loud with water sound, that opened almost at his feet. Nina came up quietly beside him, shading her eyes from the late afternoon sun.

"The two stay separate," she said, nodding toward the rivers that struggled over an untidy rubble of rock. "See, the White Aragvi and the Black meet here—but they don't mix. The dark stream on the left stays black and the light-colored White Aragvi stays on the right. They go on that way for a while. Until the village of Bibliani, I think. It's mysterious, isn't it?" she asked, looking deep into his eyes.

Piotr stared at the river below him. She was right. The waters foamed and scrubbed at the rock, but they could not erase the clear division between the two Aragvis. It did seem strange. Strange and troubling.

"Where are we going, Nina? Do you know?"

"Further into the mountains. Noe has a contact in one of the mountain villages. They've been succoring revolutionaries and other undesirables for years. I don't know much more than that except that a rope over a cliff is the only way in, and there's no way out until the snows in the high passes melt. Which makes a snug little refuge for troublemakers like Noe. The police can't get to it."

She paused, as though carefully considering what she was going to say. "I'll be going with you," she stated. "Sirakan has agreed, and he's arguing it out with Noe right now."

"Your betrothal . . ." Piotr began.

"Over," she said with such finality that he swallowed his questions. "Noe wants to be over the cliff and into the valley before nightfall, so I think we'll be on our way," she added.

As the air cooled, the numbness in Piotr's arm increased, and dizzy spells plagued him. Shadows gathering at the roots of the great mountains began to blot away the contours of trees and rocks. But the sky burned with a rosy fire. Oval patches of light punctured the dark silhouettes of pines, hanging like fire opals in the webbed branches.

They came to an ancient stone wall flanked by a stand of pines that leaned in misshapen obeisance to the east wind. *Now for it,* thought Piotr. *Here it is—the cliff, the rope, the valley. The rope and the cliff,* he worried, *are going to be a problem.*

Sirakan and Noe carefully looped the rope and lowered Irina and Nina into the darkly forested valley. Piotr followed, trying to steady his grip with his sound left arm. But it was a long way down, and he could feel the warm spreading sensation of an opening wound before his feet touched bottom.

"Are you down?" came Noe's question from high above.

"Yes."

Noe's wiry body, twisting as he moved hand over hand, appeared on the cliff side.

"Are you down?" yelled Sirakan as he dropped knapsacks and bundles to the waiting group. The rope slithered up. They were in the valley.

Noe led them through the forest, moving confidently along a sandy path silvered by the moon. No longer in purdah, he was the only one in the group that Piotr could clearly see. The girls' shadowy figures were often swallowed up by tree shadow. Piotr trained his eyes on Noe's blue jacket, willing his limbs forward.

The trees ended. The valley opened before them, bounded on one side by a small river. A riprap of broken rock had tamed its turbulence and spread its waters smoothly over the valley floor. Its banks were dotted with piles of bear dung and guarded by several tall poplars on the far side. Beyond them, past an opening, a jumble of square stone huts clung to the mountainside. Crumbling towers with notched parapets presided over them.

Noe stood at the river bank, waiting for the girls and keeping a careful eye on Piotr. "I'm behind you," he said as Piotr waded into the stream. The water was icy cold. Piotr tried to breathe normally as he toiled across. A few yards from the opposite bank, he stopped. The water slipped over the sand, smooth as silk. Sinuous strands of light coiled over the black current like eels. The movement made him sick. Daunted, Piotr looked up.

A blur of cloud distended the moon. There was a heaving in the air like the heaving of the sea. But it touched only the tops of the trees, flipping up the milky blue undersides of the poplar leaves. The tossing trees and unquiet sky seemed akin to him. For some reason, he felt he should kneel in the stream. He swayed slightly, and Nina came up behind him, wading clumsily and breaking the water's smooth surface like shattered glass. Piotr pulled his eyes from the glitter and met glitter again on the bank—something sparkling under the moon like fishes' skin.

A man stood there, clad head to foot in steel mail. He carried a drawn sword like the angel guarding the Garden. Latin letters beneath a silver cross emblazoned his yellow surcoat. Piotr looked back at Nina. Her face was blanched and tense; her lips were parted but not with fear.

"Noe," she asked without taking her eyes from the man, "what do the Latin letters say?"

"*Sollingen*," said Noe.

"*Sollingen*," she repeated, as though that explained everything.

IX

The Cleft of the Rock

The mail-clad stranger sheathed his sword and swept his hand out in a grand, archaic gesture. Was it grace—or menace? The man's mouth moved, but Piotr could hear nothing but that great tidal movement in the trees above. He could see little of the features on the bulletlike head enclosed in metal mesh. Triangular moon-shadow beneath brow and mustache gave the man's face an inhuman appearance.

As they climbed the river bank, the striated light beneath the poplars played tricks with the metal scales, so that at times Piotr saw only a moving collection of silver dots. But as they crossed the empty fields, the armor rippled over their host's powerful muscles with a dazzling sheen.

No one spoke. Piotr listened for the sound of their footfalls on the hard plowland, but he was still hearing the heave of wind-sound above moving water—or was it the rasping effort of his lungs?

The ground rose and a white, stony village gleamed in a jagged cleft of the mountains. Above it, a splay-fingered patch of snow clawed at the mountainside; below, constellations of dull orange fires burned sullenly. Piotr struggled to find some order in the confusion of ash-white shapes. A senseless jumble of rock turned into a teetering wall at the edge of the fields. More rubble spawned clumps of stone huts, then piled up to slab the rugged sides of a guard tower. Piotr looked up; the pointed teeth of its serrated parapet snapped at the feeble stars.

Piotr strained his eyes and stopped. He was listening to the stirring of unquiet air in invisible treetops. He saw Noe's lips move. He was sure that he had said something, but the words were lost to him. A cry from

Nina pierced the hypnotic ebb and flow of sound. He felt Noe's hand come softly on his shoulder; the light touch bore him down to the ground. Somehow he was lifted and carried like a child, with the cold touch of steel against his face. Then a slow-coming darkness dissolved stone and metal.

The darkness smelled of clay, smoke, and animals. It teemed with unnameable things. Piotr's nerves stretched taut with an urgent craving to identify his surroundings. But the darkness defeated him. Scents, harsh or cloying, gusted on currents, now humidly warm, then suddenly chill. Sound ferreted softly and stealthily—or came clamoring at him. The light from a high lancet window was the only clear thing in the room. Piotr's eyes clung to the bright rectangle as it roved around the room in answer to the sun's position.

The light captured things—an old man's face grooved with wrinkles and ridged with old scars, his eyes gleaming like two bright commas. His right ear lobe was missing entirely, but that didn't stop him from smiling inanely, showing huge gaps in his teeth. He fingered the gray hairs that covered his dark, naked chest like a smear of ash and then passed into the darkness.

Piotr closed his eyes. But the insistent, secretive noises stirred him up again. The light had pounced on something else—a princess this time with a soft, round face under a rolled velvet headdress. There were bits of shiny glass and mirror stitched onto her bodice, and the light exploded them into dazzling sparks that hurt the eyes. Piotr turned away into the dank rustle of the straw beneath him.

A soft voice drew him back. Soothing words. He tried to understand, but meaning eluded him. It was enough that friendly hands were on him. They gently bared the skin on his shoulder and secured a fresh bandage. Piotr opened his eyes. Nina Abajarian's white hand moved across his collarbone as though it could lull the pain. She put her cool palm on his forehead in a way that made him turn his face to her with such yearning that she stepped back a pace. A low-hanging chandelier of pierced iron meted out small silver star-bursts of light that quivered around Nina on motes of dust and smoke. The man behind her stood shock-still in his watchful pose, but somehow the shimmer in the air and on his mail coat became fluid—a liquid membrane of living light that flowed around and between the man and the woman. Piotr's mind turned to the ford under the poplars and the sparkle of breaking water and the expression on Nina's face as she stood with the dark waters tugging at her. Dark swirling waters—they were tugging at him, too. He'd sleep now. Sleep for a long, long time.

The click of a rifle shocked him to attention. A blue bar of light defined the long muzzle with its unusual triangular mechanism. *Stidna!* The frantic reflex of raw memory forced Piotr's blood to his heart. But the blunt-fingered, clever hands on the rifle were deftly taking it apart. *No threat here*, Piotr comforted himself. Behind the rifle and the hands, he could barely make out the face of a warrior. Young, with fearless tawny eyes, a blunt nose, and a pale scar on his tanned cheek. His faded brownish-red shirt was belted with black leather studded with curiously shaped silver medallions. No armor, but Piotr recognized him immediately. *Sollingen*. The strange word had taken lodging in Piotr's mind in a friendly, comforting way. The young knight's head was bent to his task. Coarse sun-bleached hair framed the oblong planes of his face, and a luxurious, rusty-tipped mustache draped over his mouth like a garland over a door.

Sollingen. Piotr rolled the word over in his mind. There was something he wanted to say to the young man. He was forgetting—what was it? He shook his head with the effort to concentrate, but his thoughts scattered like scared birds. *Sollingen*. He knew it was important. Too much effort. He'd remember later. Piotr surrendered to the heavy inertia that pushed him down into sleep.

The harsh beat of metal on stone assaulted his ears. The door was open now, and he could see more of the interior of the hut. He was lying on a pile of straw and wolf skins. Strange, richly colored hangings adorned the stone wall opposite him. No, not hangings. They were tunics, medieval surcoats decorated with heraldic devices—a crown, an eagle, a cross. They were marked with strange words: *Genoa, Vivat Husar, Souvenir*.

Where on earth was he? Broadswords, round metal shields, and ancient armor surrounded the tunics. Piotr turned away. His head was bursting. That metallic racket was drumming agony into the very marrow of his bones! How could he think? And he needed to think!

The noisy timpani was coming not far from his feet where a naked infant was banging a brass ewer against the stone floor, his little face bunched with determination.

A plump young woman gently pried the pitcher from the baby, murmuring and clicking her tongue. He flailed out energetically with both arms and legs. The mother, entranced by this behavior, spoke a few words into a murky corner and was answered by a deep chuckle. Then she turned to give a compassionate glance at Piotr and stepped outside with her ewer.

She was back in moments. She closed the door, narrowing Piotr's world again, and came to bend over him, the sparkling coins on either side of her headdress swinging. She fingered his hair and then poured the contents of the pitcher over his hair and head. The liquid was warm and sourly acidic. *Urine*, he thought. He wrenched his body forward, shouting and gagging, but violent pain slammed him back against the stinking straw. With a kindly bewildered glance, the woman took her empty pitcher back to where her baby kicked in the dust. The little boy grabbed the brass handle gleefully and began hammering at the floor.

"God, Father, let me pass out," prayed Piotr. But he stayed relentlessly awake. Frustration choked him from within as he strove to make sense of the chaotic tumble of life inside the stone hut.

Even after nightfall snuffed the lancet window, Piotr's fear forced an alert on his exhausted body. He probed invisible corners with starting eyes and strained after every small noise. But the only message his fatigued senses could find was the ammonia stench of cold urine that came from his head.

He awoke to the smell of cigarette smoke. The odor seemed clean, familiar and welcome. Noe was sitting beside him, watching him cooly from behind a waft of blue smoke. Noe looked more serious than Piotr had ever seen him. Boredom, Piotr suspected. But Piotr warmed to him instantly. Noe, his good old friend of three days!

The young Georgian's expression changed as soon as their eyes met. He looked almost guilty.

"Welcome to our mountain refuge," he began. "You're probably wondering where we are."

Piotr answered with a receptive quirk of an eyebrow.

"We're honored guests! Guests in a Khevsur village in the mountains above Passanauri—beyond the valley of the Black Aragvi."

"Khevsurs! Haven't I heard . . . something, I don't remember . . ."

"They're one of those mysterious mountain tribes. No one knows where they come from. Some people think that they're descendents of lost crusaders—seems plausible; they dress the part, don't they? But then they speak a Georgian language. So, who knows? The fact is, they've been a boon to us. They hate the Russians and will go to any amount of trouble to help anyone unpopular with the government. At any rate, they're an odd bunch. Strangest mixture of squalor and nobility you'd ever care to find. But you're quite safe—in spite of your unfortunate nationality. They'd never insult a guest. Hospitality is part of their religion."

"Are they a Christian folk then?" asked Piotr, much relieved.

Noe paused and cradled the glow of his cigarette with his left hand. "No. At least not what I think you would call Christian. They seem to believe mainly in Saint George. 'Tetri Giorgi,' they call him—White George. Somehow they've associated him with the moon. I don't really understand it.

"But I sort of admire them. If you're going to be mindlessly superstitious, you may as well go all out. And I tell you, these Khevsurs go all out! They have four feast days a week—no less. They keep Friday holy out of respect for their Muslim neighbors and Saturday for the Jews; Sunday they celebrate because they consider themselves Christian, and Monday just to show that they're free Georgians of the mountains! I like that!"

"I'm not sure I do," Piotr considered. "I see the crosses—don't they know about Christ?"

"I don't think so. I think they worship the crosses as symbols. They don't really know what they represent. They worship the fertility gods of the woods just as fervently. Trees, the moon—they worship it all! They pray to a deity they call "the old man of the forest" before a hunt. And you should see their temples. They hang them with hundreds of little brass bells. The more bells, the holier the temple. On important feast days, they make beer out of barley flour and consecrate that. It's wonderful stuff—they strain it through an old bag made of horse's mane. And on the most important feast days, they sacrifice sheep—to invoke the glory of God and to satisfy the moon and stars, they say. They behead the animals and make a cross with the blood—"

"A cross! Yet they don't know what it means!" Piotr exclaimed. "Strange! They pick up little pieces—slivers of truth here and there—along with these pagan ways. Where did they get them?" An image rose in his mind—men with stalwart earth-hewn bodies and noble faces with their hearts caught by the glory of the moon and stars and their hands soiled in the gore of blood sacrifice.

"Who knows? If you want to know, ask Grigol."

"Grigol?"

"The Khevsur who met us on the path."

"Oh." *Sollingen*, thought Piotr. "Does he speak Russian?"

"Very well. He's a metal-worker and apprenticed in Vladikavkaz. He's probably the most knowledgeable man in the village—about the outside, that is. And respected, too. In a culture where weapons are more important to a man than his house, his wife, or his fields, a smith is a very important man!"

Piotr snorted. "Murderous weapons and kindly hospitality—what a combination! How does your fierce friend feel about harboring a Russian?"

"Don't worry; you're relatively safe—at least for the time being. But the Khevsurs can be unpredictable. A few years ago, a Russian ethnologist came into one of the villages to study their ways. They treated him like a long-lost relative while he was there. When he left, his host thought about it for a while, then followed him on the trail, and swapped his head off before the poor scholar could say 'cultural anthropology.'" Noe seemed to be relishing his story. "I suppose all the questions made the man feel threatened."

"You're a different case though," he added in a comforting tone. "I told him that you killed a Cossack, so you're a hero in his eyes. You'll fit right in."

Stidna! Would he ever be allowed to forget? The Cossack's astonished face, the blood, the slipping of bone beneath his boot. Again the familiar twisting of dread torqued Piotr's spirit. He shuddered against the rank, squeaking straw. Noe touched his arm in quick sympathy. "You're safe," he assured him, and Piotr did not bother to explain that it wasn't fear for himself that tormented him.

"When do we leave here?" he asked instead.

"Not until the snow melts in the mountain passes. A matter of weeks, I expect."

"Weeks!" His dismay resonated in the small space.

"Weeks." Noe eyed him ruefully. "I see, or smell rather, that they've anointed you with their favorite potion for lice control. These women have a way of making a cosmetic out of just about anything. They wash their hair in cow urine regularly. It's considered a luxury. So you've been honored."

"I don't feel honored. I feel filthy. I hope they don't honor me again—before I can get out of this place."

Noe began laughing irrepressibly. Piotr pulled a reluctant grin.

"They'll do it again," Noe predicted gleefully. "Believe me, Piotr Gavrilovich, by the time we leave Khevsuretia, you will understand futility, alienation, and all the forces pushing us to revolt. You'll be standing shoulder to shoulder with us before it's all over!"

Piotr eyed him with disgust and recoiled into his odorous straw, pretending to want sleep.

As his strength returned, Piotr began to get acquainted with his surroundings. His host, he learned, was a taciturn Khevsur of about forty with cropped hair that hung over his forehead in locks like wide black noodles. The young mother was his new wife, Fardoua. His previous wife had been sent back to her family with a gift of five cows because she had failed to produce a child, so Fardoua was particularly proud of her robust son. On the surface, the couple were cold and distant toward one another. They never touched, and Fardoua would haughtily refer to her husband as "Fepkhvia" or "Panther" in public, although his real name was Shota. In private they were plenty affectionate.

The hut, Piotr discovered, was really a small tower with three stories. The top space was used for storage. The second floor was reserved for the men and their armaments. The first floor was for the women, children, and animals. But in the late evening, Fardoua would quietly slip upstairs, and her laughter would waft through the opening in the ceiling that was supposed to carry away smoke, and the iron chandelier would begin to sway.

The battered old man was Shota's father, a tribal patriarch much respected for his numerous scars and wounds. The teenage girl in the princess-like headdress was Fardoua's sister, Mzia. She would often appear in the afternoons with Nina, and they'd drink tea and chatter in Georgian. It was considered inappropriate for an unmarried girl to tend an unknown man, so Fardoua was usually the one who brought

Piotr the Turkish beans, millet, and dried meat that made up their early spring fare.

Sometimes Grigol would appear at odd times of day, accompanied by a boy of about six and a yellow dog with a mangled tail and shiny black lips that curled in a perpetual smile. The mongrel had a way of looking at his rear every now and then with an abashed grin that gave the impression he was ashamed of the disreputable state of his tail. The boy was a young version of Grigol. He had the same dark hair with its scorched-looking rusty fringe, a small likeness of Grigol's blunt nose with the shallow dent in it, and the same big square grin that showed both his upper and lower teeth. His yellow shirt and indigo blue leggings were ragged, but his silver-studded leather belt was a work of art. Grigol would call him "Loma"—"Lion"—in a stern voice and then touch him on the back of the neck or ruffle his hair, pulling his mouth down to hide the affection that shone from his tawny eyes.

When the fever left him, Piotr took to sitting outside in the afternoons, absorbing the sunlight that bounced off the westward-facing wall. First the dog would join him, sidling up to him with a snakelike wriggle and panting joyfully as Piotr's hand came down on his head. Then the boy would show up carrying a small wooden sword or sometimes a bow and arrows. He'd shoot at a charcoal smear on a rock or dash around making elaborate feints with the sword, glancing occasionally at Piotr to make sure he was watching. Piotr's encouraging smile would draw him, and he'd kneel next to the yellow dog, massaging its ears and asking questions in his halting Russian. His russet-colored eyebrows would slip back toward his ears in amazement at Piotr's replies. Finally, Grigol would appear, and the boy's face would take on a confident expression, as if to say, "Good. He's here now. He'll set you straight!"

But Grigol showed no inclination to set anyone straight. His cache of questions was as brimful as his son's. Piotr found that, as Noe had told him, Grigol was a man of some experience. His Russian, though heavily accented, was good. He had apprenticed in Vladikavkaz—a Russian military and mining city that had once been the Ossetian town of Dzaudzhikau. Apparently he had learned more than smithing. Grigol had worked for several years as a journeyman and then came back to his village to marry a fair-haired girl of the Svann tribe, Tetroua. He was past twenty, and it was time to start a family.

"But hard times came upon us," Grigol told Piotr. "Even in good years it's hard to scratch out a living in these mountain valleys. People in the village were starving, so I went to Tiflis to find work. When I came back, Tetroua was dead, but she had left me a gift—my little lion cub here." Grigol's hand came down on Loma's neck, and the boy, with the fervent joy of early childhood, sprang up as if the touch had given him an electric jolt. He capered around in an imitation of the Caucasian "dagger dance" and then came back to sit near his father, a little closer this time.

"So," Grigol was saying, "I sacrificed a goat and gave eight silver rubles and reckoned that my wandering days were ended. But everywhere I go, I talk to people. Maybe you think I'm too quick with the questions, but that's my way. I'm like that with everyone. Folk everywhere have different ways of looking at things, and there's only one way to find out."

Piotr found that Grigol was true to his word. He wanted to know everything about the Molokans—how they farmed, what yields they got, whether they had their own smith, what kind of equipment they used. He had a way of snatching at a new piece of information and connecting it to the other things he knew with a swift creativity that won Piotr's admiration.

Grigol kept coming back to two things—war and marriage. He'd probe Piotr's thoughts and rifle through his beliefs like a bargain-hunting old woman on market day! Pacifism—what a thought! "May as well give up and live as a—a plant! At the mercy of every shift of weather the mountains can fling at you!"

Grigol had no trouble understanding Piotr's reluctance to serve the Tsar. But he was astounded at the pain that flickered across his face when he brought up the dead Cossack. "It hurts you, doesn't it?" he challenged him, looking keenly into his eyes. "You're grieving because you killed a man! Save your tears, Piotr. He wasn't your brother; he was a snake. Crush the vermin before they can strike. That's our way. If the Tsar and his cohorts had their way, the Khevsurs and Svanns and all the mountain peoples would be transported to the south—as slaves to work their plantations. For a free Georgian, death is better."

"For me," Piotr muttered, "death would be better than the thought of that killing tearing at my soul."

"You're a fool!" Grigol was so upset he stood up and then sat down again. "It's a good thing to kill an enemy. Those timid old grandfathers have scrambled your brains. You're all mixed up."

"Maybe. But I'm still sorry I bloodied my hands."

Piotr studied his hands—they weren't quite steady these days—and retreated into his own dark thoughts. But Grigol wasn't finished with him. He pried him out of his shell and started rummaging through his beliefs on marriage.

To Grigol, the Molokans' insistence on marriage within the culture seemed bizarre. Love was an exciting, exotic adventure; to restrict the choice to demure Molokan maidens was going against nature! With the Khevsurs, it was taboo to marry within their own village. A young man would set his eye on a girl in another village; there would be brief negotiations between the families; then the Khevsur brave and his comrades would ride through the village on a surprise raid and kidnap the bride. It was as simple and as grand as that!

"But wait," Piotr argued, "what if the girl doesn't agree . . . you're— why you're just ravishing her."

"Agree? Of course she agrees! What girl doesn't want to get married?"

"Love, Grigol. I'm talking about love."

"Of course there's love. What man would take a girl unless he loved her? Besides, don't you Russians give your daughters away? The parents don't bow down and ask their child's permission, do they?"

"No, but good parents want happiness for their child." Piotr faltered, thinking of Nina Abajarian. Wasn't this the very thing that had forced her into this mountain exile? *We've both been uprooted*, he thought, *me by war, she by marriage*.

"What's in your mind?" Grigol commandeered his thoughts.

"Nina. Noe's sister. She's no political refugee. She's a refugee from marriage!"

Grigol pierced him with a quick, fierce look. Then his lowered brows forced inscrutability on the rest of his face. "A refugee, you say— has she been given away?"

"No. She's freed herself from an arranged marriage. But what will happen to her now? Her parents are shamed in front of the whole village; she can never go back. I suppose she'll have to depend on Noe or Sirakan—"

"Noe is not a good protector for a girl like that. He can't even protect his own woman," Grigol said grimly, and the scar on his cheek whitened.

"Irina? What do you mean?"

"Just this—she's an unmarried woman, and the whole village knows she's sleeping with him. Do you know what can happen to a woman like that in this village? I'll tell you a story. A man had a wife.

She was beautiful and—and free in her manner. When she became pregnant, he started torturing himself with the idea that she was false to him, that the child wasn't his. The custom here is to cut off the nose of a faithless wife. But he did love her! He couldn't bear to destroy that smooth, fair face. So he took her to the elders, and they cut off her ears instead. That's acceptable, you know; it doesn't have to be the nose. Later, he found that he was wrong. The child was cut out of the same piece of cloth as his father! But by then, she was dead . . ."

"Tetroua?" Piotr ventured softly.

"Tetroua!" grated the answer. "But tell me this—did I choose to defile a human being, or did the ways of my people push me to it?"

Piotr's eyes widened. "Why, you're like me! You've stretched out your hand to crush a life, and you can't live with it!"

"I live with it. I live with it every day. You see my son—stamped out in my own image, except for his eyes. His eyes are Tetroua's; and even when they're filled with love, they accuse me—they accuse me!"

Sometimes Noe would break into their conversations, usually bending the flow of words to the "people's struggle." It was obvious that Noe had decided to "work on" Piotr; Grigol would yield the conversation with a yellow glint of amusement beneath his straight reddish lashes. He usually had some bit of metal and tools about him, so that his time was never wasted. He kept his eyes on his work, but Piotr knew that nothing escaped him.

"We're brothers, Piotr," was Noe's first tack. "Even Lenin says that persecution of sectarians in Russia has gone so far that even the stones cry out! Those are his very words. So you can see we have common cause."

"Isn't Lenin an atheist?"

"Sure, but that doesn't stop him from seeing injustice and reacting to it. Look." Noe rifled through his pockets and pulled out a pamphlet. "This was published just last year especially for the Molokans and Dukhobors and other sectarians. Have you seen it?"

Piotr glanced at the title page: "Rassvet"—"The Dawn."

"Yes, I've seen it. It's been all over the Caucasus. But I haven't read it." He didn't mention that he had seen it in his own home, but that Semyon had used it to light the stove before he could get his hands on it.

"The devil's work!" the old man had said. "It belongs in the flames!"

"You should read it. You sectarians have suffered to gain freedom of conscience—that's what this revolution is all about. Molokanism is a form of social protest against the feudal oppression of the Orthodox Church. Political protest in religious guise! Look here—Lenin himself says that the sectarian movement in Russia is 'one of the democratic trends directed against the existing order.'" Noe began patting his pockets in search of tobacco.

"So you're saying we dreamt up a new religion because we had this need for equality or freedom?"

"That's too simplistic. You have to admit that there are inequalities everywhere, and these create a profound unrest, not only in society but in the heart of man."

"That's true," Grigol broke in. "There is unrest in man's heart— some kind of restless craving. But if we were all equal, it would still be there. It's not just equality or freedom that man needs; a strong man can take both of those with his two hands!"

"He's right," Piotr agreed. "You're saying that we've created our religions because of social needs; I say man creates religions because he needs God. And how about the religion that God Himself creates? True, there's this vacuum . . . and we can't live with it, but if God Himself steps in to fill the void . . ."

"All the religions say that. Each one claims that they're the one ordained by God."

"They may claim that, but it's not so." Grigol was following his own train of thought, his hands busy with a file and some intricate bits of silver. "I was in Baku a few years ago. You've seen the minarets there. They spire up as though they'd puncture Heaven itself. A mullah stands atop this high tower several times a day, and he cries out to the one God to come out of Heaven." Grigol paused, the file quiet in his hand. "Who knows what words he's saying; I don't know the Arabic—but it's a tongue for yearning. His voice is the voice of some keening creature. And the Moslems in the street—why they fall down with their faces to the street! As if they expect God to appear and are afraid to face Him! But the mullah—he keeps bleating away—calling out to God from his high tower. He does this every day. He knows God won't appear, but he's grieved about it all the same. When you're alone in a city far from your native village, that cry is the loneliest sound on earth."

Grigol moved his hand, and a beautifully hammered triangle of silver glinted in the sun. He didn't bother to raise his head or search their eyes. They had forgotten Lenin and were thinking of a man's loneliness and of God and of a trapped people living in the shadow of the snow-barricaded ridges.

Noe had found his tobacco pouch and absently rolled a cigarette with a page of "Rassvet." The orange glow quickly ate into the black letters.

Grigol had been gone for two days. Piotr and the boy spent the afternoons lounging around the village in a desultory way. "He's hunting," explained Loma. "When he's back, there will be a feast. He'll bring us bear or a roe or at least a brace of hares."

Piotr was not encouraged. Bear and rabbit were definitely not in the Molokan diet. *But what does it matter,* an inner whisper niggled him, *after all, I've killed a man. What's hare or even pork to that?* Sometimes at night when the fever came stealing back into his bones, he'd wonder whether he could still consider himself a Molokan at all. *May as well eat bear meat and love Nina Abajarian.*

For Piotr, one benefit of Grigol's absence was that he saw more of Nina. For some reason, she kept her distance when Grigol was there. Whether out of deference to some village custom or for reasons of her own, Piotr didn't know.

Nina seemed to slip into the pattern of Khevsur life with ease. And there was something freer, more childlike about her these days. He could see that Loma liked her company; she always had a comment or a story that would capture his swift-moving attention.

This afternoon as she came walking up the bent stone street with Mzia, she looked like a new person. She was dressed Khevsur-style in a dull red skirt with an embroidered border and an elaborate bodice. Her head was covered with headdress and veil, but her dark curly hair escaped and fell over her shoulders like bunches of fruit. She exuded well-being, but a nagging anxiety ruffled Piotr's spirit as he watched her. Against the razor-cut edges of the charcoal peaks, her beauty seemed a fragile thing—easily crushed.

But Nina, decked out in her Khevsur red, seemed completely unconcerned. The two girls perched on the low stone wall that girdled the village, and Nina turned to scan the dark jagged band of forest beyond the fields. Mzia's warm smile curled into her plump cheeks as she watched her friend.

"They've started plowing," Nina observed.

"You're not looking at the fields; you're looking at the forest!" laughed Mzia, with a you-can't-fool-me taunt in her voice.

"Silly! What's in the forest?"

"A bear, a lion, a hunter . . ." chanted the younger girl.

"Shush!"

What are they talking about? Piotr wondered. He leaned against the wall, facing outward—toward the fields, the forest, and the ramparts of the northern mountains. He took a good look. So this was it! This unrelenting geography was the trap that had snapped down on Piotr Gavrilovich Voloshin. The valley of the Khevsurs had been scooped out of tiers of peaks on every side—and it had been an untidy job. Piles of rocky rubble littered the valley, as though it had been hastily constructed by some careless work crew with better things to do.

Every angle of those adamant peaks drew the eye up and out. Even the dark shapes of the trees arrowed upward—pointing—that's the way! Take it! If you can fly.

The village itself straddled an eastern spur of rock. The main street zigzagged up the slope, and the huts lining it looked as though they had been shoved out of the earth in some dire upheaval. *Only a day's journey from my native village*, thought Piotr, *yet it's like another world, like living on the surface of the moon!*

"It's a barren, forbidding place," he commented to Nina.

"No, not barren; look, they're plowing."

"The soil is poor; they won't get much for their pains."

"They have to live—like anyone else."

"It's a poor life," he insisted, testing her with his eyes.

"It's a life," she contradicted. Mzia edged closer, wanting to listen. The glisten of her rosy cheeks was a contradiction, too. Loma appeared and his wooden sword crashed on stone between them.

"Tell me a story. Tell me about Shamil and his warriors again!"

"That's an old story. I'll tell you a new one—about the evil Gud and the shepherd boy Sasiko."

"A shepherd? No! Tell me about Hadji Murat and how the Russians cut off his head."

"Head slashings, murders, and wars—you're on the warpath today! How's this? I'll tell you about Shamil and how he kidnapped Shouanette for his bride, and her rich Armenian relatives couldn't ransom her because she decided to stay kidnapped—"

"Girl stuff," roared Loma, and the sword came crashing down. Then he shrieked again—this time with joy. Grigol was striding up the slope with Shota and a third Khevsur. The "man of the forest" had been kind to them. Grigol's companions carried a skinned elk; Grigol had four plump woodcock stuck into his belt by their necks. His shirt was open and covered with dark bloodstains. More blood from the dead birds striped the lower part of his shirt. The yellow dog, trotting alongside, would worry the tail feathers of a cock, then turn his shiny black smile toward his master.

Loma, heedless of the mess, was soon in his father's arms. Then he sprang back toward Nina, tensed with excitement.

"A feast!" he exclaimed, hugging her. "Tonight there'll be huge bonfires and a great feast!"

"Yes, a feast!" she repeated. Her hand fingered the dark red stain that had transferred from his shoulder to hers and then settled on the boy's head. But her eyes turned to the men on the lower slope and came to rest on Grigol's dark exhausted face.

X

The Valley of the Khevsurs

Morning and evening—to Nina the days sprang forth with shining newness over the jagged rim of the Khevsur valley. Dawn would bring the morning mist spilling out of the slot in the southern ridge like milk out of a spout. The twilight trembled, pink or apricot, with timid uncertainty. Then the black shadow of the western peaks would slam across the valley floor so violently that she was always surprised. After that, the fires would start, winking to life in the shelter of a rocky overhang or near the twisted wall or alongside a stone hut. Tonight they'd flare all over the valley announcing the feast.

Nina spread out the stiff folds of her red skirt. The embroidered border with its interlocking forms of indigo, yellow, and bright red lapped about her feet—*an enchanted circle*, she thought. The velvet headdress pressed down with a weight that seemed both pleasant and fitting.

Her thoughts drifted back to the first days of their arrival—tormented days for Piotr. How his hot, parched mind had wandered in the paths of Molokan wisdom! His lips were cracked and his voice too, but the words themselves were sure and apt. "Why is my soul so troubled . . . He will send you trials that you shall know all griefs; He will send you consolation so that you will no longer suffer . . ."

Piotr had shuddered; the straw rustled and a stench arose, but she bent listening. She turned. Yes, he was still there—Grigol—standing, listening, too. His bright mail collected bits of light from the ancient iron chandelier, and they sparkled on his body as he listened to Piotr Gavrilovich pour out the songs inscribed on his heart from birth.

Piotr was muttering now. "I don't want it! Why? Why didn't I take the shirt?" Then, "Fenya . . . close the door. Don't let it happen . . . Fenya . . ."

The Molokan songs began again. "He raises up and casts down all; He slays all and makes all live . . . You are my strong refuge . . . You only . . ."

Nina twisted to let the ache in her torso shift to some less punished area of her body. "You only . . . my salvation . . ." She let the words pelt her—a sustenance in that dark place. She remembered old Semyon telling her, "The Molokans are a people that sing the Psalms." At the time she thought it a lovely custom; now she saw that it was more than that. For Piotr, the words staunched some inner agony and held at bay some terrible, troublesome darkness.

Nina had waited until Piotr was resting easily before she left Shota's hut. By that time dawn had come. Grigol followed her and touched her arm with his warm hand.

"Who was he talking to?" he asked.

"God, I think."

"Who is Fenya?"

"A girl—a girl in the village . . ."

"His sister?"

"No. Another girl."

"Ah." He walked off, well satisfied.

After that Grigol came to sit by Piotr every day. He always had some work or other in hand, and he seldom spoke. But he'd watch the sick man and, when Nina's eyes were turned away, he'd watch her.

A glowing white starflower at the core of the fire bloomed and contracted as the blue-gray smoke of roasting meat rose to the night sky. The men, all in their crusaders' finery, had assembled around the bonfire at Grigol's forge. The women sat in clusters on the outside. Next to Nina, Mzia and Fardoua were whispering while Shota, in the inner circle, stood to describe the hunt. He spoke in a practiced way using formulated phrases that were part of a Khevsur's early training. He joked about "the old man of the forest;" apparently the hunters' deity was not taken very seriously. Then, more solemnly, he beckoned toward the crescent moon—Tetri Giorgi.

Nina lifted her face; a sliver of moon hung low in the sky like a child's cradle surrounded by the fragile stars of early spring. She turned her attention back to the leaping, quivering center of the fire. It was a fallen star, she thought, with one prong anchored in the ashes, another spurting upward, longing to shoot homeward. The light laved the ground, shaping the shadows of Noe and Grigol just in front of her. They were deep in conversation. She leaned forward. Noe's face was shadowed, but she could see the firelight stroking the side of Grigol's face like a luminous hand.

Grigol's voice was questioning. Noe's hands moved as though sculpting explanation out of smoke. Nina realized that they were talking about a woman. *Me?* she wondered as the words *free* and *choose* sifted down. *No*, she decided, *they're talking about Irina*.

"We've grown beyond the old ways," Noe was saying. "A woman can make her own choice. Why should the old people have anything to say about it? Every human being, man or woman, has a right to make his own life."

"But wait—if you choose so freely, how can you live in peace with the elders? Like it or not, they're a part of things. With us, the blood would flow if we were so quick to act without consent. There would be a blood feud. It's true, we usually abduct the bride, but there are customs to be followed first."

"Sure, in a remote village like this or with some backward groups. But things are changing. Women are fed up with being possessions. They want to reach out for some joy for themselves."

"But is that what you would want for your daughter—or your sister? Tell me as a father—as a protector."

"Of course. That's what I've been saying all along! I would want what would bring the girl the greatest happiness."

Grigol's profile stiffened. "Happiness. Maybe you need to think about how much joy you are bringing to your own woman. Your love has put her in a dangerous position. And I can tell you, happiness and danger don't mix."

"Oh, no. You're off there," Noe replied. "Danger sharpens the edge of joy. You tell me if you think I'm wrong!"

Nina drew back. The hand she put out to steady herself just missed a blue heelless boot. *Irina. She must have overheard, too.* Nina glanced up just in time to see a faint tendril of a smile twist those chiseled lips and then disappear. The challenging, scornful look was back. But something about that vulnerable wisp of expression made Nina's heart ache.

More women were coming now, bringing dishes of millet and beans. But Nina followed Irina as she strode away from the crowd, catching up to her as she turned onto the pathway alongside the low wall at the field's edge.

"They'll be serving soon," Nina said. "Shall we go back?"

"Back to what?" Irina shrugged. "I've seen men get drunk on beer before."

"No. I just thought you'd be hungry . . ."

"Don't look at me like that! I don't need your pity. Keep it for your lost little Molokan boy—or keep it for yourself. You may need a little pity. I'm free, but you've gone from one trap to another."

Too baffled to say anything, Nina stiffened. *So,* she thought, *Noe's easy banter was squeezing the shame out of Irina, and she is chaffing under it. She knows I heard, and it hurts her.*

"You think he's using me," Irina continued in a hot, raw voice. "But I'm using him."

"He's my brother, Irina. I think he loves you. There is some using in his love, but it's love all the same."

"Oh, I know that. You wait. He'll miss me. Then we'll go off to the forest. You know what that means. In the villages they say a good girl courts by 'walking out in the village.' But the bad girls 'walk in the forest' with their lovers! I know your village ways. So I'm a wild girl of the forest," Irina said bitterly.

"It's better not to go to the forest with Noe," Nina warned. "Things can happen. These are a strange people with unaccountable ways."

"I'll choose it if I please," Irina answered. "I'll decide whether to risk it or not. I don't have to be dragged down into primitive ways that mean nothing to me." Her proud face softened as she turned away. "I know you're concerned for me, Nina. You be careful, too. You're more likely to be captured by these people than I am."

Nina shook her head, exasperation and fear tugging at her. Irina was so quick and adamant in her assertion of her own way, but there were mysteries around her that she wasn't taking into account as she marked her path! *I'll have to warn her more clearly. Tomorrow before she goes to the forest to meet Noe, I'll stop her. But tonight I'll go back.* She thought of the red magnetism of the fire by the forge. She wanted to sit with Mzia and the other women and share roast meat and bread. She wanted to hear Shota tell his outlandish battle tales and see Loma's eyebrows slip back with astonishment. And she wanted to watch Grigol's face, impassive under the caress of moving firelight.

"I thought that you didn't want to partake with us."

She started and turned. It was Grigol, standing there with portions of meat and bread on an upturned round shield. "You see, I came to look for you."

"I was just going back. But you've brought a portion for me."

"We'll have our own feast. There's plenty for us both. To let a guest go hungry is a great shame with us."

"But you'll miss your fire. And the stories."

"Loma tells me you have the best stories. I'll miss nothing. Look. We'll have a fire of our own."

He gave her the metal shield, and her fingers curled around the rim. She held it tightly; the crude pitted silver encircled rough rounds of bread and cubes of meat. *A portion and a measure*, she considered. *Someone has taken thought for me*. She stared at the food, pierced by sweet comfort and promise.

Grigol soon found kindling, and the flames began to take shape under his hand. It was more windy here outside the wall. The long flames bent under the force of air and then sprang straight up as though suddenly released. Nina and Grigol sat side by side with the silver circle between them and talked of this and that. He began telling her about the strange people he had met on his travels.

"All kinds of folk—beggars and intellectuals, peasants and artisans. Everyone's pouring his soul out these days. Someone's pulled a cork out of the bottle—whatever's been fermenting in the darkness comes gurgling out. Even the tramps have their ideas. Yes, even the ones with black, ringed eyes that look as though every thought has been burned out of their heads.

"The tramps in Russia build fires like this at a crossroads," Grigol told her. "A few winters ago, I was warming myself at one of them outside of Vladikavkaz. There was a man there, a Russian with a broad face and the lines of some kind of torment on his brow. Well, this Russian was fascinated with fire. A burning house was better than a feast to him, and a roadside bonfire was his delight. He told me so himself. 'See how sly it is,' he'd say. 'It gnaws at wood like a mouse at cheese.' Then he'd go into all kinds of fanciful descriptions of fire, comparing it to the creatures of field and forest.

"Looking at his brooding eyes, I thought, *Good—let him take pleasure in fire; there's little enough joy he's had of life*. One of the vagabonds standing there was a holy tramp, the kind you see all over Russia. Bast shoes and a long beard so tattered at the ends you could see the rags of his shirt through it. His eyes were red and blue. Eyes that look like they're trained on a distant place even when they're looking right at you.

"'Our God is a burning flame,' he said. Well, the fire-lover pricked up his ears. 'Why do you believe in God, old man?' he asked, respectfully enough.

"'I believe—that's enough,' said the tramp. Then he bent his old body back to look into the sky. 'The heavens declare His glory, the stars utter knowledge!' I knew well enough that there wasn't a star in the sky. It wasn't yet twilight. Besides there had been a gray pall on the day. But those strange old eyes had a way of forcing the holy man's vision into your own eyes! I looked up, and the constellations were wheeling overhead with a smooth intelligence. But the fire-lover was still watching the flames, shaking his head. 'Man is the axle of the world,' he murmured. But he was a listening sort of a man and didn't say much more.

"Darkness was coming and, with it, the cold. A few more vagrants turned up, crouching and crowding to get closer to the fire. But the holy tramp stood a bit away, ramrod straight. I noticed that he was moving his lips as though talking to someone.

"A dark little man squatted near my elbow. His skin was dry and shiny, as though he had been hung up to smoke in a chimney. 'Who is that?' I asked him. 'That's Gorki,' he said. 'The writer.' He was talking about the fire-lover. But Gorki was nothing to me. I meant the tramp. So I just walked away. As I was leaving, I heard the writer's voice again. 'See how sly it is,' he was saying. 'It'll slither into hiding in the black ashes, then spring out again . . . No, it hasn't finished it's work yet!'

"I think of that night by the fire every now and again. Something about your friend Piotr reminds me of that old tramp. He talks to God, and you sense a Presence bending down from Heaven." Grigol paused for a moment, looking at her. "Besides, even in daylight smothered with cloud, the stars are still there."

Nina was so absorbed in watching his face that she let the pause draw out. Heavy molten light bronzed the edges of his rough hair, poured gold into his eyes, and brought out the white scar. That scar, she learned, was a better indicator of Grigol's mood than either his sternly composed mouth or his straight gaze. Now when he was speaking seriously, it stood at a vertical alert. If something struck him as funny though, his white teeth would gleam under the lavish mustache, and the scar would tilt out to a merry angle. But in moments of deep emotion, the scar seemed to whiten and detach so that it stood out from his face like an exclamation point.

Nina forced her gaze back to the fire. "You seem to be curious about Piotr. About his faith."

"I know this," Grigol answered, "there are certain times when a man is not in control of what pours out of him. That's when you see what he really consists of. I see the goodness in Piotr, and I see that he draws it from somewhere outside of himself." The white scar stood out like a warning post. She knew not to ask questions.

"I'd heard of the Molokani in my travels," Grigol continued, "but Piotr is the first I've met up with. There were Molokani villages in the steppe north of here. They were known to be a hard-working, religious people that kept to themselves. But we're isolated here and don't have much contact with the outside."

"Why do you stay?"

"I won't, always. And, in fact, except for my early childhood, most of my life was spent outside of the village. But my son was born here, and here there was care for him when his mother died. Tetroua's mother took him in hand, but she has been dead for over a year now. When Loma is a little older, we'll go back to the city and make our way there. But the boy needs a little more growth on him; and I, myself, feel I need to strengthen myself somehow before I take up a new life. But," he said, "I'm making plans." And he gave her a straight, stern look that could mean anything.

They watched the fire spurting blue and orange until it shrank into ash. Then Grigol stood and tossed a last brand into the coals, and the hot embers flew up like glowing red moths. "Look," he smiled, "when I see something like that, I think of the writer, Gorki, and I wonder, well, is man the axle of the world?" He paused and looked up. The cool weight of the night sky pressed on Nina's face as she followed his gaze. The whole vault of the sky, arched between the dark mountain ranges, thrummed with fluid motion. The gauzy wheel of the Milky Way traced its slow spin from peak to peak. The nearer stars flared and faded as though tapping out messages to each other.

Grigol's eyes brightened and he chuckled. "That old tramp was right though. There is knowledge with the heavens."

He stooped to pick up the silver shield at Nina's feet and straightened suddenly, bringing his right hand up to gently cup her chin. She did not turn away as he looked intently at her for a long moment. The scar burned with white heat. Then he dropped his hand, and they made their way back to the village.

Morning and evening—the days came bright and mysterious. Nina sensed the unexpected crouching behind stones, lurking in the shadows of the mountains, hiding under the dark drape of the forest. *Anything could happen here!* she exulted. Possibilities took alluring shape in the unacknowledged spaces of her imagination.

Today she saw that a wispy, fragile spring was beginning to infiltrate rock and rubble in surprising places. Delicate yellow and purple wild-flowers took tentative root along the rough plowed edges of the fields. Tiny clinging rock flowers in translucent pink nestled in impossible crevices on forbidding stone walls. Absurdly feminine garlands garnished hulking rocks. *They'll throw them off in a fit of male pique,* she joked to herself.

Nina stood in the doorway of Mzia's hut and surveyed the village as it began to come to life in the cool morning. Behind her, Irina was still sleeping, but Mzia's mother had begun to make herself busy around the odd, conical oven. Mzia herself was perched on a three-legged chair with a leather seat and a high back shaped like a board, but carved, every inch of it. The Khevsurs incised their fitted geometric patterns on any available surface.

Nina could see that the old woman was rummaging around for fuel.

"I'll get it," she offered and set off to fetch *kizyak*—dried dung bricks—from a collapsing wall at the village edge. Her russet boots obeyed the downward pull of the steeply curved road, but her eyes strayed to the ring of mountains. She skirted a collection of huts poised on the cliff side. *How adeptly they balance,* she thought, *angled so tenaciously on that slanted slope!* Squares, cubes, blocks sprang at her—doors opening on stairways, windows opening on rooms, passageways tunneling down to fields. Stone, everywhere—but here and there the astonishment of fervent color met her eyes in a wrought geometric rug, an emblazoned coat, a child's bright frock.

One black doorway framed an old woman with a crabbed face and shiny black eyes who smiled at her. Nina rejoiced in her approval.

She was almost at the bottom when a shout spun her around. Loma had catapulted out of a hidden doorway and came bounding down the hill at such a mad tilt he seemed to bank off the stone walls. Nina laughed and watched his excited face and agile little body come closer. He couldn't have been up for long, she observed. One side of his face was rosier than the other, and his wild tufts of hair were pulled in every direction and sprinkled with lint and straw.

"I'm hunting today," he announced. "Look, I'll have my own weapons and we'll shoot—Father and I." He waved his arms and kept looking behind him as if the adventure would slip away if he didn't keep his eye on it.

Nina stooped to look into his face. "What a brave boy! What will you shoot?"

Loma hesitated as cool thought dampened some of his excitement. "Well, birds, I suppose," then gaining bravado, "or a bear! We'll shoot a black bear, Father and I!"

Nina bit her lip to hold back the laughter. "You're a pretty young warrior to bring down such a big and dangerous beast." She bent closer to him, stroking the silky skin along his jaw. "But I expect you'll bring back something. And I'll tell you what—I'll cook it for you. In a special way, with herbs—thyme and basil . . . Will that be nice?"

He nodded, suddenly quiet, and his blunt fingers toyed with a shiny disk stitched onto her bodice. He stood there for a while. Nina could see that he wanted to nestle closer to her—but he fought it. *Poor motherless mite!* He wanted to stand firm and hold onto his dignity! After all, today he was a man. "I'll bring it to you," he promised, "whatever it is! It'll be for you."

He pulled away with a vigorous wrench that sent the bits of straw flying from his hair. Nina straightened and met Grigol's eyes over the child's head. His well-muscled body was shaking with silent laughter as the boy bumped into a sturdy thigh in blind zeal. Nina had never seen Grigol's face look so relaxed and full of joy. His head was thrown back in a fierce, wild jubilation, and the scar on his bronzed cheek slanted with mirth. A little one-sided smile tugged at Nina's lips. Then she laughed gaily. She waved them away as they went back up the hill, and she went down to find fuel.

It was stacked beyond the wall. To the east, horses, dark and pale, grazed on the tilted green pastures that patched the mountainside. Beyond them, a flock of sheep poured from a rocky funnel like curds from a pitcher. Their hundreds of little brass bells set up a windy tinkling. Beneath her, a harlequin pattern of kitchen gardens and brown fields, plowed or harrowed, stretched right up to the dark border of melded forest trees. But the line of trees bent to a crescent in the west.

The west—where the cliff with the rope rose behind the curtain of dark spruce, and the river ran with silver twilight colors—night or day.

It came to Nina's mind that it would be a pleasant thing to walk in the shelter of those trees once more. She quickly gathered an armful of *kizyak* and kindling and climbed the hill, feeling her back strong and pliant under the load. Irina would go with her, she decided. They'd spend an afternoon in the forest. Who knows—maybe they'd find some mushrooms.

Irina quickly agreed to join her, but Nina soon found she had reasons of her own. It was impossible not to notice her restlessness over the past few days. Nina had passed on Grigol's warning about secret meetings with Noe and, to her relief, Irina had listened, her firm lips tightening with the obvious agitation she was fighting. *How lovely her classic face is in its sleek frame of short hair,* Nina thought. It was a face brought into being by a single type of curve which reappeared in the arch of her brows, the turn of her nose, the line of her jaw, and the swing of that thick dusky hair.

They set out after the midday meal. In the crystalline air the encircling peaks seemed to bend inward, tightening their hold on field, forest, and village. Irina's black eyes flashed as she looked about her. *It's a trap to her,* Nina realized. But to Nina, the mountains were a friendly presence. She felt cradled in the circle of the hills.

"This way," urged Irina. And within yards they stopped at a forest shrine—not a Christian shrine. It was littered with bones and splotched with dark stains. Nina hesitated.

"You've been a cover for me, sister," Irina informed her. "Noe will be meeting me here—our usual place." The lines of her face were strong and harmonious. *No point in arguing,* Nina decided. But there was a hint of apology in Irina's dark eyes.

Nina turned back to the main pathway. How different it looked by day! She remembered that first night in the valley. How she had trembled, following that yellow surcoat of Grigol's. *Sollingen!* What a mystery. He was her friend now. Their unusual position in the village had created a separate little eddy off of the main flow of Khevsur life. They'd had all kinds of talks—at fireside and forge, with Piotr and Noe, and over Loma's little head twisting with curiosity. Like his youthful wanderings, Grigol's mind ranged far and wide. Yet he puzzled her. How could anyone so open be such an enigma? And how could anyone so vulnerable be so . . . so powerful? There was a great unassuaged need in him, and it gave him a grandeur that was unusual and compelling. A *great unassuaged need*, Nina repeated to herself. And it wasn't his need for woman. Although, of course, there was that, too.

She decided to walk to the ford; then she'd go back to the village. The forest seemed suddenly lonely. A few sleepy bird calls sounded in the warm afternoon—yearning calls for something just out of reach.

Nina saw that the ford was much wider, the water more agitated than it had been a few weeks before. The rushing current would catch on the rocks with a spume and a curl, then dimple as it went on its way. Nina tensed and squinted, adjusting her eyes to the bright sun on the water. Yes. There was a dark shape picking its way across. A man. He was wearing a dark suit, such as city dwellers wear, but he was hatless, and the booted feet sloughing across the knee-deep river were clad in sturdy leather. Fear lashed at her for an instant, and she drew back from the water.

"Wait!" he called. She paused in wary silence.

"Tell me," he panted as he splashed onto the bank, "I'm looking for someone. Noe Tcheidze. Noe Tcheidze. Do you understand?" He was meting out the words loudly, one by one. *No doubt he thinks I'm a Khevsur maiden*, she thought. She decided not to correct him. After all, she was better off if he thought the hills were riddled with dozens of her blood-thirsty relatives. She turned, pointing and gesturing towards the village. Her heart was like a stone. What news would this stranger bring?

The dark-clad man was close enough to touch her now. She stepped back to make room for him on the path, then gasped as an ungainly yellow shape nudged her roughly. Why, it was Loma's dog, Rada! As she bent to reward him with a brisk rub above the ear, Loma appeared, followed by his father. Apprehension flickered in the stranger's eyes as they took in Grigol with his rifle and his dagger. But the stranger stood his ground.

"Noe Tcheidze," he repeated.

Grigol swept his arm out toward the village, as though he could sweep the intruder away with the gesture. "There's our village on the eastern slopes. You'll find Noe there. Loma, you can show him the way."

Grigol's brows were contracted with what looked like anger. Their visitor was quick to brush by them, following the boy. Then, having disposed of his latest guest, Grigol turned his attention to Nina. She noticed that there was still a ferocious bend to his mouth.

"What are you doing?" he asked abruptly.

"Walking," she answered feebly. "I was with Irina," she added quickly and was relieved that he didn't pursue it.

"So," she prodded him, "what were you stalking this time of day?"

"Rabbits, squirrel—you'd be surprised. But they were all too clever for us."

"Poor Loma. You'll go home empty-handed."

"Not empty-handed," he said. "I have a captive."

She laughed at him and then wondered whether he were serious. He looked serious. In fact, he looked furious.

The trees began to thin, and the afternoon sun beamed benedictions wherever it could break through the forest canopy.

"The sun's warmth feels so good this time of year," she commented.

"The sun is my enemy," Grigol declared. She raised her eyebrows and looked at him. Why was he so angry?

"The snow is slipping from the sides of the mountains. The gaps will soon be open. Who knows what messengers will come from the outside? Then you'll be gone. And that," he said, "will be a grief to me."

Then he set his arms about her. Nina held her breath in wonder. The wide circular spaces of Khevsuretia had contracted inward to this ring of solace she had found with Grigol. She breathed in peace and breathed out sweet longing. She lifted her hand and traced the contours of that white scar with sure fingers as though she could find out all about him from that thickened ridge of flesh. She lifted her head and looked at him. Grigol's face was open to her; it was wounded with desire and set with restraint. His hand came up gently and pulled her head back onto his breast—he didn't want her to see. So she rested in his embrace; but she had seen and she was content.

Morning came with a lilt of remembered joy, and evening came with the weight of decision. Loma had come to her just past midday with a small leather packet. When he had gone, she opened it and spilled a starry handful of silver into her hand. She held it to the light. It was an exquisitely wrought necklace. Burnished angular bits of silver burst into star shapes and caught at the light, giving it back expressively. *Expressive of what?* she asked herself. What would it mean if she set that shining circle around her throat and went out to face Grigol? She hesitated, wondering.

The question stayed with her all day. In the evening, she took the necklace out again, admiring the masterful skill that had crafted the interlocking tiers of silver. She had seen those metal slivers taking shape over the weeks in Grigol's adroit hands. Had he known even then? Wayward fragments, they had meant nothing then. How they kindled and sparkled as they trickled through her fingers into her palm! Nina held the shining mass for a long time, weighing it in her hand.

XI

The Roots That Clutch

Piotr was struggling his way through "Rassvet" as Noe paced the stone hut, moving his hands in quick, futile gestures—desperately needing a cigarette. Piotr, too, was caught in a kind of blind, animal torment that he found hard to identify. Was it because he had been cut off from everything familiar? Or was it because of the rioting in his blood whenever Nina came by with that confiding friendliness in her beautiful eyes? Or was it the incessant biting of the thousands of lice that invaded his body? Piotr groaned to himself and turned a page. Noe pricked up his ears.

"Finished?"

"Yes, you can have that one." Piotr tore off the page and handed it to his friend, who quickly rolled it into a cigarette. The Khevsurs had plenty of home-grown tobacco, but there was no paper in the village—except "Rassvet" and Piotr's Russian Bible. So Noe oversaw Piotr's indoctrination with double impatience, and Piotr kept close watch on his Bible. God forbid that the impulsive young Georgian should take it into his head to smoke up Holy Writ!

"What do you think?" Noe asked, taking a contented drag on his clumsy cigarette.

"I can't debate with you, Noe. I'm not an educated man. But I can tell you, these words are dry and dead. They lie on my mind like a pile of ashes."

"That's because you're afraid that they're true—and they'd tear up your Molokan traditions by the roots."

"No. That's not my fear. I'm telling you the truth. I can see what your Bolshevik writers are leading up to. After all, even a peasant can see that Christian sectarians and Bolshevik atheists would make strange bedfellows! They see our need for religious freedom as a chink—a convenient little gap that they can shove their heresies into! Then they'll 'reeducate' us poor, ignorant peasant types so that we'll accept their own ideas," Piotr said. "Can you deny it?"

"Of course not," Noe answered calmly. "What's wrong with making a more scientific, correct view of the world available to those who want it?"

"But it's not correct! You think yourselves wise, but you've forgotten God—God who has chosen the foolish things to confound the wise!" Piotr felt suddenly alert. He raked his fingers across his chest in a deep, satisfying scratch. Old Semyon's training was beginning to break through the surface of his confusion.

Noe shrugged. "Words. You yourself admit they are foolish. What it comes down to is this: you think that God is light; I think that knowledge is light—that man in his understanding of himself and his world can change things, build a better life. Then man can create his own history!"

"Light. Yes, that's the thing. But you do admit that there is a darkness. You won't deny that it's pressing around us. From without and from within! You see it in what you call history. I see it there, too. And in what I call sin—*stidna*. But it is Jesus Christ who has broken into history and Christ who shatters the darkness. He shines and the darkness cannot comprehend Him!"

"One says Christ, another Mahammout—"

"Mahammout is dead. Christ is alive . . ." Verses from the Russian Bible came tumbling into his mind. His memory sketched Semyon with his old hands like tree roots pushing into the black and white text. Noe managed to shrug cynically and at the same time cherish the smoldering stub of cigarette. Piotr hesitated. If he had learned anything in the army, it was to be wary of exposing his faith to ridicule. But even if his words deflected off Noe, they were soothing a gnawing ache in his own heart.

"Knowledge you say," Piotr challenged, "listen! 'For it is the God who commanded light to shine out of darkness who has shone in our hearts to give the light of the knowledge of the glory of God in the face of Jesus Christ!' The apostle says that's the only knowledge that can push aside darkness."

"Oh, ho. What an indoctrination! You've got it all memorized."

Noe had come to the end of his cigarette, and he was ready to change the subject.

"Only a bit. Some Molokans know the whole New Testament by heart."

"Well, you'll forgive me if I desist from hearing it all." Noe's attention had wandered; he absently picked up Piotr's Bible and began leafing through it. "Zephaniah, Obadiah—who reads such things? They're not Matthew, Mark, Luke, or John. Maybe you wouldn't miss a page or two of some obscure prophet . . ." His eyes glinted with mischief as Piotr glowered. "Or a genealogy? Who reads genealogies?"

Piotr made a quick grab for his book, but Noe dodged him. His chuckle died though, and Piotr stiffened as they both noticed two men standing in the doorway. One was Grigol; the other, a dark-clad stranger.

The stranger was Zviad Kostava, a festering sort of man with mobile features that stirred and shifted around a disconcertingly fixed stare. His gray eyes were like two steel rivets that held the rest of that quickly changing face together. His broad, flat nose looked as though it had been pulled out of shape by the constant curl of his upper lip and exaggerated lift of his sparse brows. He summed up Noe's abashed pose and Piotr's shocked expression with a quick look. His gaze dropped to the tattered pamphlet on the floor, then cut across to Noe.

"You are Tcheidze?"

"Yes."

"Then I have something for you. The papers for Piotr Gavrilovich Voloshin." His eyes pinned down Piotr while his forehead crinkled and his mouth turned wry. He handed over the papers with a slight ironic bow as Piotr flushed with surprise.

"You should know," Zviad continued, "that your situation has changed as of April 17. The Tsar has signed an Edict of Toleration. One of the things he has promised to tolerate is people like you. You have freedom, supposedly, to practice your beliefs in peace. If you believe in whatever kind of peace the Tsar has to offer."

Piotr lunged at the possibility. "Freedom! It can't be!" he exclaimed. The corner of Zviad's mouth was twitching. *It isn't . . . it's impossible . . . stidna . . .* Piotr groaned aloud as his mind rammed into the obstacle. A dead Cossack lying in his blood. He controlled his face, pretending to study the documents.

"Your Molokan brothers in Baku have been holding a triumphal prayer service," Zviad was saying. "They aren't ashamed to press the bloody hand of the autocrat if it suits them! And the Dukhobors are even more gleeful. They're talking about sending for their emigre brothers in America to come back to Russia. 'A saving manifesto,' they're calling it. They expect it to prevent the revolution." He nailed Noe with his rivet eyes.

"They're wrong," Noe flared. "It's a sop to the liberals. It may take the wind out of the Mensheviks and other Social Democrats, but Lenin and his followers are not so easily defeated. They'll continue to push the autocrats. That's Koba's philosophy. Push them until they respond with such repressive measures that even the most faint-hearted will rise up in rage."

Zviad's features cavorted around his set eyes. "Yes, that's our vision. Our work is not over yet . . ."

Piotr scarcely heard. He was still reeling from the shock of his new position. *So close*, came the taunting thought. *A slip of history, and I could have been free. Free to go home, free to marry. Religious tolerance— but not for me! Stidna—the barrier between me and all that is good.* He swallowed and rose stiffly; Grigol, he saw, was staring at him in concern. The other two were oblivious, talking about Koba. Grigol turned his attention to Noe.

"Your plans are for harm and not for good," he announced sternly. "You hurt the very people you claim to champion. You can't bring about good by forcing others to do evil. It's a twisted way, not worthy of a free Georgian!"

"Our plans are bigger than one little country," Zviad broke in. "Georgia has always been too weak to stand without Russia. Our vision is for a brotherhood of nations—united under a Socialist government. We Bolsheviks will not balk at whatever it takes to bring that vision to life."

"Ah, but your way is to shed the blood of friends as well as enemies. No good can come from such betrayal! You want to buy your revolution with the blood of the innocent. You stand against the Tsar, but you'll put another in his place, and Georgia will still be under the thumb of foreigners. What is the use of a revolution like that?"

Zviad's cheeks puffed and slackened with a sigh. His eyes clicked to Noe, who shrugged.

But Piotr barely heard. The cavelike interior of the hut was suffocating him. He inched his way toward the door. The other two hardly noticed, but Grigol touched his arm as he ducked through the low doorway as though to comfort him. That brief touch seemed to him to be the only real thing in the room. Then the sun was on his face. He leaned against the stone wall.

"Are you a Bolshevik?" He heard Grigol ask in his direct, challenging way.

Noe's voice answered, "I don't know."

Piotr took a path along the woods to the north where the white tips of the highest peaks arrowed upward. He found the place where the valley narrowed to a stone trough for the river. The sloped banks were deeply scored with ragged furrows where the spring torrents had gnawed their way to the river. But he found a flat, sandy shelf near the water. He stripped and gingerly lowered himself into the current, letting the icy rush of water numb his limbs. He stayed there until it seemed that his slowly beating heart was the only part of him left alive. Then he crawled out.

The rough-textured sand gave out a metallic warmth, and Piotr pressed his body hard into the earth. Small rocks and pebbles nudged his skin. He could feel one sharp-edged shard cutting into his breast. *Go ahead, cut*, he thought, still pressing. The steep-sided ravine compressed wind and water sound to a roaring tumult that could be felt in the earth as well as heard on the air.

History. Piotr's mind fumbled with the thought. A wanton twist of events, and here he was—sprawled on a hot rock, stripped of everything. Was it history that had torn him from family and country? Noe would say so. "You are in the hands of history," he had declared. "It'll sweep you along it's path like dust!" Well, he was being swept! Noe would say that the oppressed were victims, slaves of history—Piotr himself among them!—but that the great destiny of the masses was to collectively take history into their own hands and remake society. But, Piotr told himself grimly, the day would come when even Noe would quail at the society created by men like Koba and Zviad Kostava. Yes, it was as Grigol said—they would buy their revolution with the blood of friend and enemy alike! Piotr shifted his torso, finding comfort in the punishing texture of the warm ground.

But they had forgotten the most important thing. History had been invaded! Man's puny defenses of philosophy or law or social order had failed him time and again. The brave new orders were somehow always fueled by the worst in man—and each left its trail of broken victims. Then He came, the God-man Jesus, shunting aside glory to rescue man from history—either personal or collective.

A revolution? That was the real revolution. And He paid for it with

His own blood. A payment the pagan Grigol would understand more readily than the materialist Noe. "No greater love hath any man than that he will lay down his life for his friends . . ." Yes, the nobility in Grigol would snatch at that idea—the idea that had changed history.

For Noe, history was everything—a shaping power. And Semyon? What would he say? It's nothing! Piotr could see the old man flicking the idea away with his knob-fingered hand. All the torments of man—why, they're just manure, mulch from which to grow the eternal! Piotr grinned in spite of himself. No, Semyon would not be shy in shoveling the whole of history onto the dung heap . . . *Ah, but Semyon, Dzedha—those torments still have to be lived through.* Perhaps history was just a setting, harsh or nurturing, against which a man could choose to love or hate.

Piotr rose to his knees and reached for the pile of discarded garments. His documents were folded into his shirt. He looked them over carefully. All in order; he would have the freedom to go to Batumi, purchase a ticket to Marseille, then to America. Freedom for very little else. "My course is set," he acknowledged.

He traced the events that had brought him to this. A law that decreed that he fight for the Tsar or die; Galina's betrayal that made him a deserter, marked for death; a street fight that forced him to kill or die; then the flight to escape capture and death. Death, death again and again! And the worst of it was his enemy's death—that Cossack's young face with the consciousness being ripped from it. *By my hand, by my hand!* Piotr's thought accused.

"Forgive me, restore me," he breathed. "Lord, blot out that part of my own story that haunts me! You alone are my salvation! There are things within me that are shaping a being that You would have to turn from. Tear those things out of me! Teach me to choose love . . ."

He bent, listening. The water gnashed at its forced channel, and the wind lashed at unyielding rock. Peace. It seeped into his mind and took shape in words that soothed and comforted. *Rest . . . rest for your soul. Take it!* The words were an outstretched hand. *My yoke is easy. Take it! My burden, it's light. Learn of Me. I will give you soul's ease.*

Air and water—they were still striving, but peace settled deep into Piotr's soul. *Nothing will tear you out of My hand. Nothing.* Piotr stood, rooted to the hot grainy soil. Listening. The clash of sound around him seemed harnessed now to some kindly greatness. Love. How sternly he had steeled himself to face the disaster of his future. How quickly the steel melted in the warmth of that magnificent kindliness. Something swelled and broke within him. Hot tears seared his eyes, and he shook them away, raising his head to stare into the azure strip of sky channeled above him like a second river. A golden eagle hung there, almost motionless, as though time had stopped. Love. It was brimming up to the crisp edges of the rough-sawn cliffs so that he was immersed in it.

Piotr dropped his gaze and felt himself anchored to the bottom of that raw gash in the mountainside with the wind hurtling down it. A place of beginning. A song of the Molokans came to him, and he sang it out in a strong free tenor as though he were surrounded by a houseful of kindred.

> *Now the blood flames like a fire in my heart,*
> *And my soul is like a star high and pure . . .*

Piotr stooped and picked up his shirt and trousers, greasy with many weeks' wear. They were crawling with lice. He found a flat rock and a smooth, round stone and began pounding. The nits had settled in regiments, especially in the creases of collar and cuff. He ground the fabric between the stones and then rinsed it again and again in the icy water, still singing.

> *There is nothing dearer to me*
> *than if the love of God burns;*
> *my heart is warmed,*
> *and truly unites my thoughts . . .*

It was twilight when Piotr came back to the hut. The iron brazier gave off a sullen light in the center of the room. Zviad struck him with a quick glance that made him feel as though he had been stamped with a rubber seal. Noe's brief glance deflected off Piotr, then back to Zviad. ". . . beyond what we dreamed," Zviad was saying. "All of Georgia from Abkhazia to Kakheti—convulsed by revolt. Our Georgian peasants are made of sterner stuff than the Russians. All during March they were rising against the gendarmes and landlords, murdering them or turning them out. This manifesto now," he continued, suddenly turning to look at Piotr, "it won't stop us. Zordania and his Mensheviks are using it to make peace with the Federalists and other bourgeois liberals—they'll sell their souls for a free Georgia. But their dreams are useless. We can count on the autocracy itself to help us—as it has in the past!"

Piotr was taken aback. "The Tsar? Are you crazy?" he blurted. Even Noe raised his eyebrows.

"That's right," Zviad asserted. "A lesson to you, Piotr Gavrilovich. You and most of your Molokan brothers. You think that you'll never change, but that's because you haven't lost enough blood. That's where the Tsar comes in. The gendarmes and Cossacks have been most cooperative in stirring up the people against themselves. They do it with blood, your blood." Zviad blinked hard and his flexible, almost comical features pulled into a stern mask.

Piotr was having a hard time taking the conversation seriously. His inner exhilaration played havoc with the prescribed Marxist phrases and self-important expressions. Piotr forced himself to listen, but became distracted by the notion that the Zviad's slow, set blink caused each change of expression. Yes—a blink; now his chin was up, and he had the proud, offish look of a misunderstood man. Blink. A questioning look. *Say something, Gavrilovich . . .*

"You think you'll change the Molokans—reeducate them, you say," Piotr said, with a disarming smile, "but they have their own way of looking at things. They think that they'll reeducate you! It will surprise you, but a few of the old Molokans think that the Revolution will be a success, the Tsar will be deposed, and then you Marxists will see the error of your ways and become Christians! Then we'll have Heaven on earth—Marxist and Molokan alike." The impulse to laugh was overriding his caution. Noe was beginning to chuckle, too.

"They really think that?" he chortled. "That's too much! The lion lying down with the lamb!"

But Zviad wasn't laughing.

"Here's a story for you," he said, offended. "It shows exactly what I mean. This Edict of Toleration—a joy to you Molokans—also raised the hopes of the Georgian Orthodox Church. They met just this week to discuss whether they could ask for their own Patriarch—an office they'd had for a thousand years before the Russians came. So they thought they might ask if they could elect one, in keeping with the new religious tolerance. The formula was perfect—for us. The church entered with its incredible naiveté, and the government provided the necessary brutality. Troops and police invaded the meeting, cracking heads, and beating the clergy. Now we have pious believers joining with revolutionary unbelievers to throw off the Tsarist yoke. That's why I say the authorities are an ally."

He turned his face to Piotr. His eyes were suddenly soft and caressing, and this had a frightening effect. "So, you see, the Molokans could be teachable, too. They just haven't lost enough blood." He paused, still looking at Piotr. "They need a martyr." Then his eyes darted upward to Grigol who was suddenly standing over him with folded arms and a fierce expression.

"At any rate," Noe broke in, "we need to discuss how we're going to get out of here. You say we can expect a big strike in Tiflis late in June, Zviad. That will make it hard to get transportation. After that, there may be martial law as there is in the western provinces. So the time to get out is now."

They talked about their needs for the trip—horses, supplies. Grigol was grim and courteous. Piotr noticed that he seemed distracted, and there were purple troughs of weariness under his eyes. When Irina and Nina came in, his eyes flared with something wild and at bay; then he hunched his shoulders and stared at his empty hands.

"A pack mule—yes, I can get that for you."

Piotr looked at Nina. She was wearing the familiar blue skirt and plain white blouse she had worn into the valley. Her hand flew to the simple collar when she saw them, and her face looked stricken.

But Irina leaned forward eagerly. "Our escape!" she whispered excitedly to her companion. "I thought this day would never come!"

"I don't trust this Bolshevik," Grigol asserted. He and Piotr were perched on a rocky promontory above the bleached maze of village dwellings. They had been scouting out the trail that led to the south—over the mountains. Several miles in, they could see that the lower edges of the icy cones had shrunk up over the passes, like the lifted hem of a girl's white petticoat. *A way out,* thought Piotr excitedly.

"He won't be afraid to do you harm if it suits him," Grigol continued.

"What can he do?" Piotr asked. "After all, Zviad's the one who brought my papers—without them I'd be lost. What good is it to him if I meet misfortune?"

"You've pricked his pride, Piotr. And he's a man whose pride rules him as lust rules the stallion. Besides, he himself has said that the

Molokans need a martyr. He imagines that your death at the hands of Russian gendarmes would inspire your kinsfolk to join up with the revolutionaries."

"Martyr! So that's what he meant! I wasn't paying attention."

"That's true enough. You were were wet to the skin and burning with some kind of inner fire yesterday. I could see it in you. But that's no excuse for letting down your guard with men like Noe and Zviad."

"Noe? Noe is harmless. His thoughts may be muddled, but his heart is good."

"If it weren't for men like Noe, men like Zviad and Koba Djugashvili couldn't operate. The only thing good about Noe is that he is vacillating. He can't make up his mind as to whether Bolshevism is worth the price. And it's that animal warmheartedness that makes the price particularly high for Noe."

"What do you mean, 'animal warmheartedness'? It's that open, generous spirit that makes Noe human, likable."

"I don't mean to insult your friend, Piotr," Grigol said, "but he's convivial in the way that animals are—he hates to see suffering because it hurts him, not because his spirit is resolved against it. And that can change very quickly if he puts himself under the mastery of the Bolsheviks. Suffering for them is the fermenting force that brings them power."

"I see what you mean . . ." Piotr drifted into quiet thought. The breeze riffled his hair, and the warmth of the sun radiated from the air and from the rock. Peace. It came to him again in the clear, rarefied air and in the massive power of the mountains.

"What are you thinking?" Grigol intruded sharply.

"Of what you said. I was thinking of how the powers of the world come and go. For thousands of years Tsars and kings and dictators have sent others out to die for them—to do their suffering for them. Not one of them has survived. But the one King who, instead of sending out others to die, chose the opposite—chose to die for them Himself; why, He lives."

"You're talking about Christ, aren't you? The God who dispels darkness. I heard you telling Noe about Him. I've seen Him."

Grigol smiled at Piotr's surprised look. It was a dismal, wintry smile though. Grigol seemed chastened, almost bereft. *He's been like that for days*, Piotr realized.

"In the Armenian church at Vladikavkaz," Grigol explained.

"They have His picture pieced out in bits of colored glass. A marvelous thing. A stern master! There's no thought of joy in His face!"

"That's not Christ. That's an icon. A likeness, and not a good one. If you saw the face of Christ, there would be no mistaking. You would know that you had seen the face of God Himself."

"Have you seen Him then?"

Piotr hesitated. How could he explain that his own inner vision had been transformed by the light-breathing presence of the God-made-man?

"A man has outer vision—eyes that see the world of men and things. But he has an inner vision, too. It's this vision that tells you to mistrust Zviad, and it tells you other things. Well, it's with that inner vision that I have seen Christ; and that vision helps me to keep on seeing Him so that I can follow Him—choosing a different path than others. Choosing love."

Grigol pondered this carefully as the wind skirted the village. He watched as it pilfered bits of straw and old leaves, swept them against the wall, and then fingered the debris carefully, turning over this piece, then that, as though looking for something. But on the higher slope to the east where the temple stood, the wind was fierce, and the wild jangle of hundreds of temple bells broke the air into shards of chaotic sound. Grigol turned his head toward it.

"In Vladikavkaz," he reminisced, "the church bells ring with a deep-throated clamor, and you can see that the sound pulls at people's hearts. Sometimes the men take their caps off. And the women—their faces change. They're praying. Our bells are small—and they call to small gods—gods of woodland, hunting, and fertility. Concerns close to the earth—and to man," he added, glancing up, "and, I can tell you, they can't be trusted. They're capricious as women. But, like women, sometimes they smile."

Piotr shrugged. "And sometimes they frown. The fact is, they don't care. But you, Grigol, you know there is a longing in you for something beyond yourself—beyond what you see with your outer vision. You don't deny it. But what you need to know is that God longs for you with a fiercer longing than you can imagine. And because of that He sent His Son to make for us a way to Him—to rescue us."

"Rescue us? How?"

"By coming to earth as a child, taking up the work of a simple carpenter, stretching out His hand to touch the blind, the lame, the

148

poor—then suffering in our place and dying on a cross to remove our sin far from us so that we can love God and love others."

Piotr paused, breathless with the barrage of thought that shook him. He searched Grigol's face for understanding. His words seemed to him frail, wispy, insufficient to describe the grandeur of God's plan for man. How could he express it? Love. It came to him in the dwelling peace of the mountains. Love. *It was the grinding shock of that soul-deep need that had stiffened Grigol's face*, Piotr thought with a wrench of pity.

"It's love I'm talking about, Grigol. God chose not to abandon us to whatever life will force on us—you know what I mean." Piotr paused, hesitant to touch on the wounds that history or culture or careless choice had left on them both. "God sent for us, in the person of His Son. And those of us who will reach out for that rescuing hand will not perish but have eternal life. It's love I'm talking about. The love that will give everything, unstintingly."

Grigol studied Piotr's face intently, then shook the flicker of longing out of his eyes with a quick movement of his head. The temple bells tinkled with a mad fury.

"If the One God wanted to save the world, He wouldn't have sent a carpenter but a warrior. A god like Tetri Giorgi of the Shining Armor. I can't believe in this dead carpenter and His cross of wood. But I do believe that you need to be rescued, Piotr. Rescued from Zviad's Bolshevik schemes. I think I will go with you when you journey across the mountains."

A charnel stench hung in the air at midmorning. A sticky, unnameable foreboding drew Piotr to the brink of the cliff-hanging path. Below, the Khevsurs were methodically slaughtering dozens of sheep. The blood flowed red on their hands and black on the earth. The doomed sheep huddled in the shadow of the stern cliff walls. Nina came up beside him, watching as the dingy fleeces of the crowded, milling flock churned like gruel boiling in a pot.

"What is it?" she asked through stiff lips.

"Sacrifice," Piotr answered. "They believe it appeases the powers of earth and sky . . ."

She was silent under his studied look. The contours of her face were marked out by violet lines of strain. But she was forcing her eyes to the field below, intent and determined.

By midday the azure sky was hard and pitiless, and the air was putrid. Nina and Piotr were still watching. Just past noon they saw Grigol toiling up the path toward them. He stopped as though stunned when he saw Piotr.

"I'm filthy. I know it," he said, his grin a white gash across his sweat-soaked face. He was shaking for some reason. He drew his sleeve across his damp forehead, leaving a dark smear on his face. He kept looking at Piotr and then back at the teeming, bloody activity in the field below. He was avoiding Nina, trying to obliterate her crisply outlined form from his field of vision. But she was staring at him in dismay.

"You are right," he told Piotr. "These gods are petty traders. Blood for the hope of happiness. But it's my blood. I provide it from my own flock." He paused in the wrench of some inner agony. "But you say there is a God who gives on a great scale—He gives everything; you give everything in return. But the payment, the surety is His—His blood. You say He longs for me. That's the thought I can't get out of my mind. A God who longs for me."

The man was shaking under the duress of his longing. Piotr could see Nina leaning forward with the presage of joy flickering under her transparent skin. *This is it,* Piotr's thought came. He couldn't complete the idea, but an overwhelming sense of purpose steadied him. He put out his hand, felt its firm strength anchor the young mountaineer. "The meeting of two beings who long for one another is the greatest beauty that earth or heaven offers . . . ," he said. Grigol looked up at him with his old straight look. "We'll pray," Piotr said. Grigol dropped to his knees in the dust of the street, bent almost double.

Piotr knelt beside him, but he didn't close his eyes. He watched his friend's face as yearning perplexity changed to release, then to exulta-tion. His mind clutched at the image of that changing face. He let it sink deep into his memory, hoarding it against hard times to come. Grigol's face stamped with the imprint of total love would be the image he would call up when memory tormented him—calling him deserter, killer, forever alien. *It's real—this power of the living Christ, and not just for the Molokans.* Grigol's transformation was unshakable evidence of his own. "Brother," he said as Grigol rose to his feet, "Brother."

They talked long into the night while the orange scatter of live ashes on the brazier winked out one by one. Rain came with the dawn. Grigol lifted his face. "Rain," he said. "You won't be able to leave."

Zviad Kostava thought otherwise. "A day's delay, no more," he con-ceded. "The rain will let up by sundown; we'll leave in the morning."

Grigol shook his head. "The passes will be awash with melt-off. Why are you so anxious? Give me a few days. I'll provide all you need, and you can make your journey in as much comfort as possible. And you'll need an experienced escort. Shota and I will go with you."

"An escort! No such thing!" Zviad remonstrated. "We have our own plans. Don't worry, we'll return your livestock, but save yourselves the trip. We don't need anyone's help."

Grigol bared his teeth in a stubborn smile. "It's not as though you can slither back up that rope to the main road!" he insisted. "You'll be traveling through some rough, wild country, meeting up with mountain tribes and other dangerous folk. We will be coming."

Zviad's flabby cheeks trembled with unspoken objections, but he kept his silence.

"Yes, I think we will come, Shota and I," Grigol repeated with a sidelong look at Piotr.

Noe came in with his sister and Irina.

"They're forcing a wait on us," Zviad complained.

Noe was in good spirits. "What's a few days?" he asked. "I'm as anxious to leave as you are, Comrade, but better to wait than slough over trails mired in floodwater. It's cold in here; hasn't anyone thought to build a fire?" Grigol stood quickly, abashed at having kept guests in discomfort.

Nina stepped forward to help him. Piotr saw that she had on her Khevsur dress again. The red skirt was mottled with rain drops, and her dark hair was spangled with shining droplets. She shook them off, and he noticed the glitter of silver at her throat. An exquisite necklace sparkled in the dim light and threw subtle starbursts onto her face. *Where did that come from?* Piotr wondered. It looked as though it had fallen from the sky.

Grigol, he noticed, was staring at it, too. The bend of his brow and the downward hook of his mouth denied all feeling, but a white zeal burned in the scar on his cheek.

Nina busied herself with kindling. A merry smile caught on one of her upward glances. "We'll build a fire for memory's sake," she murmured to Grigol. "I'll think about that holy tramp you told me about and remember on whose will the universe turns." She paused, tending glowing tendrils of flame. "After all, as we both now know, man is not the axle of the universe."

Grigol looked across her profile to where Piotr, Noe, and Zviad sat. "No," he said. "He is not."

Sleep was elusive that night for Piotr. *There are mysteries here*, he told himself. The hut and its furnishings had become familiar. The noises that came from beyond the partition where the animals were quartered were familiar too. The weak bleat of a lamb, the snuffle of a dreaming dog, the shuffle and stir of straw as a young animal moved closer to its mother. He could put a name to them all! Yet there was something beyond all explaining.

He dipped into a deep trough of slumber. Semyon was there—he saw him so clearly! His head was bent over some work; an awl and an old frayed harness twitched in his bony, searching fingers. His paper-thin eyelids trembled; the pointed clumps of his lashes screened the glitter of his dark eyes. But he wasn't looking at the awl. How well Piotr knew that pose! The old man's thought would be stalking out every need that pricked his concern or pity. By morning the harness would look like it had been mauled by an animal. But the old man was doing his greatest work. Semyon Efimovich Fetisoff was praying. Comforted, Piotr let sleep take him down into deep succoring dreams.

A drumming of hooves awoke him. Horses, more than one, were galloping through the village. Iron-shod hooves slipped and sloshed on the wet stone street. *Quite near*, he thought with a start, *quite near*. Were those voices, a muffled scream, or the neigh of a horse? The patter of rain joined the baffling jumble of sound. Or was it only rain, rattling off the stone walls, rushing down the angled streets, washing away the blood in the field? Piotr sighed and turned over.

At first light a rough hand wrenched him from his dreams. It was Noe. He was half-dressed and flaming with anger.

"She's gone!" he raged, his fingers clutching at Piotr's arm.

"Who?" Piotr blinked in confusion.

"Nina! She's gone. He's taken her—the cursed devil!"

XII

The Day of Indignation

Taken her? Where? Who—Zviad?" Piotr's voice cracked on the raw morning air. His ribs expanded on a yawn, then sprang inward like iron bands constricting his heart as Noe's news slapped him into wakefulness.

"Zviad! Don't be a fool! That barrel-chested brigand Grigol took her. He's defiled my sister—the vermin. I'll kill him."

"Wait." Piotr's hand shot out and gripped Noe's wrist. His thought searched through a haze of bewildered dismay. Signs. He had seen them—why hadn't he taken heed? "Wait. Maybe we don't understand. Maybe he's wanted to marry her—you see? It all makes sense now. Tell me, has Grigol given you anything—a gift of any kind?"

A stunned expression seeped into the anger on Noe's face. He pulled out a beautifully tooled silver dagger.

"This," he said. "And a horse. It's quite a good horse . . ."

"It's a contract. According to Khevsur customs, he believes he's married Nina."

"That's no marriage! Nina's Orthodox—she needs a priest, a church . . . I know my sister. She's very religious."

"I don't know her mind—"

"Her mind? What does it matter? He's ruined her!" Noe shouted and wrenched his head around as another voice came from the doorway.

"I thought you took delight in the ruining of women." It was Irina. Her face was smooth, but the stretched grimace of her mouth punctuated the corners of her lips with two black dots. Other dots—her dilated pupils and widened nostrils—hung beneath the straight, dark line of her brows, so that her stiff face looked like a mask that had been punctured to allow the actor to see, to breathe. *But seeing and breathing would be a stifling agony of work behind that screen*, Piotr thought.

"Danger," she jibed, "sharpens the edge of joy. Remember?"

"Don't throw that up at me," Noe warned. "Nina's circumstances are different."

"Why? Because she's your sister? Of course, her purity must be protected. But me. What am I? A whore?"

"You are what you chose."

"I chose you. Our love. Before I knew it was all hypocrisy!" she flared.

"You call me a hypocrite? I've loved you well enough! We're free of these cultural constraints. But Nina isn't! I don't want to see her life crushed to the ground by this barbarian."

"Who's the barbarian? He's committed himself to her. You're the barbarian!" she flung at him. Then the rage in her face dimmed to ashen composure. "And I," she added softly, "I'm the fool." Unfolding her arms with a swift swoop of a gesture, she was gone.

Noe's eyes sought Piotr's. "She'll get over it." He shrugged. "But Nina won't. And I swear he'll be punished before we leave here. I swear it."

"Don't act in haste, Noe," Piotr begged, swallowing his own fear. "Let me talk to them. There may be more to this than we understand."

"I understand all I need to. He wanted my sister, and so he took her. But he'll pay, believe me, he'll pay."

Looking at his adamant face, Piotr was torn between his fear for Nina and his fear for Grigol. *Poor Nina—what will become of her now? Today of all days, she needs a friend.* Piotr sighed and rose from the straw bedding, stretching and yawning. He gave Noe an oblique look that the latter interpreted as meek acquiescence so that he wasn't prepared for what followed. Moments later a purple-faced Noe was writhing in the confines of twisted rag bonds. Piotr strode off in the cold morning to look for Nina.

How beautifully the mountains loomed in the clairvoyant light distilled from the night's rain! Piotr paused, considering, as the sun's rays sprang from east to west, quickening with power and color. His thoughts skittered wildly. *Nina!* His mind was full of her. Grigol's action had shocked him into realizing all she had come to mean to him.

A month ago, two months ago, she had filled him with an indistinct, barely acknowledged craving. Now he recognized the substance behind that craving. It wasn't only the brigand Grigol who wanted her for his own! Then, too, the wall of his Molokan culture had been breached and was being dismantled brick by brick—leaving him only the foundation—Christ.

He had come to see that he shared this foundation in a more profound way with Grigol than with any other man he had known. Yes, Grigol had forced him to the essentials! The young Khevsur had been willing to fling away huge chunks of his own training to free himself to grasp at that one great thing. Piotr, awed by this grandiose courage, had also begun to pare away deep-rooted tenets and cumbersome traditions that, in his new circumstances, hampered him in his own pilgrimage.

And Nina, the *nynash* Georgian-Armenian—she shared it, too. It would, he now knew, be entirely possible for him to wed her. A stormy exhilaration swept over him, but quickly gave way to bewildered unease. Was it too late? What about this abduction, or kidnapping, or marriage? Grigol had overreached himself this time! He had chosen well, a lovely woman and a Christian. But did she choose him? The thought stung Piotr into a fierce alertness. *If he forced her . . .* Piotr clenched his fists. *If he forced her!*

He scanned the encircling ridges where the pale wash of the morning sky dripped its pastel tones into the drab mountainside. A half-shamed fear began to leach away his determination to find Nina and get the truth out of her. What would he find if he burst into Grigol's hut? A languishing captive or a happy bride?

But it was she who found him. Not many steps from Shota's hut, Nina stumbled toward him, her face distorted with tears. He grabbed her hard by the shoulders.

"Has he hurt you? Answer me!" She was sinking as if she couldn't stand, snatching at Piotr's hands. "Stop it, Nina. Has he hurt you?"

"Grigol? No! I'm married. I am! I'm married—do you believe me?"

Piotr groaned. "Nina—tell me the truth. I'll do anything for you. We can marry—go to America. You don't have to let yourself be trapped. Tell me the truth," he repeated and shook her hard because he was shaking himself.

"What are you saying? I am married to Grigol. I just wasn't prepared for it. I had no idea . . . but it's done. But Noe . . . Shota has been out—he and Grigol are still talking. Noe is planning revenge. I've got to somehow stop him!"

Piotr planted his feet firmly and pulled her to his breast. "Listen, Nina. It doesn't have to be this way. You don't have to sacrifice yourself . . . we can make a new life."

"Sacrifice? I love Grigol. He is the husband of my heart—and my husband according to custom."

"Not your customs. That's part of what inflames Noe. He thinks that you would want a Christian marriage—in church."

"I have a Christian marriage. Grigol is a strong believer, and we are united in Christ—and united according to his people. Piotr, help me—this is tearing me in two! Part of me thinks—well, what do priests and the church have to offer me? I'll tell you what they offered—Mourad Mushegan and the joy of being his half-witted servant wife for the rest of my days.

"But then another part of me is afraid. I think of my mother—what would she say? Of Sirakan. I looked at Grigol's face—sleeping this morning—and he seemed utterly strange, like someone from a different world. Yet I love him so . . . It's frightening to me," she continued, almost whispering, "that I feel no remorse. No desire to go back. I'm all at odds with myself because this marriage is so different from anything I ever imagined. Yet when I listen to my heart, I'm overwhelmed by peace. Everything—the shape of the huts on the mountains, the slant of the furrows in the field—it all seems perfect . . ."

Piotr stood shock-still, letting his own hope drain away quietly. He felt his arms stiffen around her, and he fought a tide of shame. Every sinew in his body cried out to flee—to be alone. What was she saying? And why had he said all that—about marriage? *I've bared my soul.* He winced with embarrassment.

"Noe is not much of a danger right now—to Grigol or to anyone. I have him trussed up like a holiday chicken in there," he informed her, nodding toward Shota's hut. He searched through the blur of distress that was her face and was relieved to find a glint of humor in her red-rimmed eyes.

"Very far-sighted of you," she approved. "But we have two angry men on our hands. When I left, Shota was informing Grigol that his honor had been ground to dust. You know what that means to a mountaineer. Honor is everything, yet Noe has accused him of an unspeakable crime. Noe is not careful at all in the words he chooses. So how do we avoid bloodshed?"

"Let me talk to Grigol." Piotr left her on the pathway, glad to turn away his burning face, glad to seek for a moment the cool, dark shadows that buttressed the sides of the huts.

Piotr was amazed at the activity in Grigol's hut. A couple of old women were folding linen in the corner, chuckling and chatting. Loma was running up and down the steps, and Shota and Grigol were talking as calmly as if discussing crop rotation.

As Piotr approached, Grigol lifted his golden eyes without hesitation. "So you see what has happened," he said. "Are you for me or against me?"

"What have you done?" Piotr asked.

"You know. I've married. Like any other man!" Grigol answered.

"Marriage to you—but what about her?"

"Marriage to us both. I had her consent. Don't talk to me about your Molokan ways. They don't work for us. Besides, it's too late . . ." He nodded toward the old women who, seeing the stranger, bowed pertly and lifted a gray-white bed sheet with mock solemnity. Piotr glimpsed a smear of red before the sheet became as crumpled as the two worn faces bent above it. His heart lurched, and he felt a hot surge of blood exploding within him. He could say nothing for a long moment while Grigol straddled one of the three-legged chairs, swinging his booted leg and watching Piotr.

"So," Piotr ventured, steadying his voice, "is she happy?"

The look of wild jubilation that flamed over Grigol's face passed quickly, but a tender, steady light remained in his eyes, so that he turned them away, toward the window.

"She's well enough now," he stated calmly, "but I'll have her brother's blood on my hands before the day is ended."

"I see. You love her so well, you want to start out your life with her by piling griefs on her head. I thought better of you, Grigol."

"I have no choice. My choice was to honorably marry the woman. Honorable according to *any* measure! Then her brother, whom I treated well—in fact generously—repays my faith with insults. There's no other way but to answer his challenge."

"There is another way."

"No, Piotr," Grigol spoke slowly, sincerely. "It's gone too far. He has insulted my wife, my honor—and done it so that the whole village knows. He cannot back down, and neither can I."

"There is another way."

"Listen. What can I do?" Grigol was still calm, as though explaining things to a child. "A man cannot live in the mountains without defending his honor. With a dagger. I did not choose this, but I stand ready for Noe when he comes to avenge his sister."

Piotr smiled quietly as Grigol's pique grew. "I don't think he'll be coming anytime soon," Piotr explained. "I have him tied up in Shota's hut. He'll be going nowhere this morning . . ."

"You shame him! Him and me!" Grigol spat out the words, and Piotr stepped back a pace, shocked at his fury. "It's not for you to stop him. Let him come! Let it be settled! I've done no wrong, and I'm ready to uphold my honor among my own people."

"Stop a minute, Grigol. The whole path of your life has been changed. You know it. There is another way. Think. Remember how it scorched your soul the last time you took action according to your people's ways. Oh yes, you protected your honor! But remember how it robbed you of your soul's ease. Remember Tetroua."

Grigol's head reared back with a savage force, pushing forth the veins and tendons on his strong, thick neck.

"You would bring that up to me?" he ground out. Piotr blinked in the face of Grigol's mounting rage. But he stood firm.

"I bring it up to you because the pain of it has been lifted from you, as you well know. If you would follow Christ, you'll have to follow Him with your whole heart. You leave your father, your mother, your people and their ways and do His will—no other. And His will in this matter is for you to forgive Noe, appease his anger."

"Appease?" Grigol's tone was low and swollen with concealed rage—or was it awe? "Honor is the life's blood of my tribe. You expect me to pour it out to appease someone else's wrong?"

"Yes," Piotr replied quietly. "Isn't that what was done for you?"

Grigol flung himself over to the window, leaned on the opening, and sucked deep, harsh breaths from the morning-cooled street. When he turned, his face was peaceful and resolved. He was moving the thumbs and fingers of his square, cunning hands as though craving action. But his eyes were clear and steadfast.

"You tell me, Piotr. Tell me what He requires. I will do it."

"There is no blame here, Grigol. Only a problem. For you and Nina, that problem is Noe's anger. Maybe if you married her in a church ceremony—"

"A custom. Isn't that what we're fighting against? You badger and confuse me!"

"But wait. You married an Orthodox woman, in keeping with the ways of your people—so that they understand that you are one before

God. But you haven't married her so that her own people understand that. Doing that could only deepen the bond between you and ease the division in Nina's heart. Besides, it would take the bite out of Noe's anger. But to do that you'll have to turn your face from blood feud and revenge."

"Ah, yes. And be branded a coward throughout the mountains!"

"Maybe. You ask yourself—which best serves the love of Christ and the love of—of your wife?"

Grigol was silent for a moment, brooding. Then a quick lift of his brows pulled all the aching tension out of his face. "You'd better release Noe," he advised. "It would be shameful for him to talk to me as he is."

Shota accompanied them back to his hut. He walked with a suspicious gait, swinging his arms defensively. His morose expression showed disapproval of the way things were going. Grigol, on the other hand, seemed jubilant—as though freed from some restraint. Piotr realized that he was facing a moral unknown as exhilarating as the unknown of lost valleys or hidden cities. Abasement before an enemy or any other compromise of honor were the deepest kind of violation of Khevsur code. Yet Grigol's whole being sprang at this new concept of forgiveness, and his face shone with a combative readiness.

When they reached the hut, they found that Noe was already unbound, standing outside in earnest conversation with Nina. She was explaining something with quick, jerky gestures. When he saw Grigol, Noe's muscles tensed, and he reached for his dagger. He sprang backwards, toward the low wall of the livestock shed. Nina flinched violently and darted toward him. Then she froze. The white-gleaming blaze of metal in her brother's hand drew her gaze like a magnet. Piotr could feel her shudder as he grabbed her shoulder and pulled her away. The girl, Mzia, who suddenly appeared from nowhere, began tugging at her skirt.

"Put it down, Noe," Piotr said. "We're here to talk about a solution."

"A little late for solutions," Noe jeered.

He lurched forward; a flash of silver arched in a clever, threatening jab, but it was Nina who intercepted it. She gasped and a wide slash on her sleeve revealed the white, rounded contour of her arm. Grigol clicked into action, wielding his own weapon with machinelike precision. A scuffling of feet, and the two men were facing each other, circling like wolves. Thighs angled to a bent-kneed crouch, the taut sinews bunching and straining beneath the cloth of their breeches.

They had made no sound, but suddenly there was a crowd hemming in the space outside of Shota's hut. Piotr was amazed. It was as though the spectators had materialized from the gaping cracks in the poorly fitted stone wall. Men, women, children clustered in holiday array. The men shouldered to the front of the throng, their mail coats gleaming redly as the sun lifted above the mountains. The women, too, were in their best—vivid veils, gala embroidery, silver coins dancing on either side of their faces. *Finery fit for a festival*, Piotr thought, then realized with a shock that it was a festival—Grigol's wedding day.

Piotr turned back to the two combatants. Noe held his dagger at a wicked slant, ready to tear into the center of Grigol's bent body. But the whole unswerving angle of the Khevsur's pose aligned with his enemy's hand and arm, not with any vital part. *He'll expose himself*, Piotr chafed. *This is useless.* A feint, a jab—no blood—yet. The crowd murmured. Piotr looked around urgently. A piece of wood—anything to shove between these two madmen! But all he could see was the pressing array of Khevsurs—shining armor, heraldic colors, faces charged with gleeful expectation. Some of the women spread black and red rugs on the ground. An old woman's face cracked in a smile. She made a youthful trilling sound as Noe spun to dodge Grigol's powerful thrust. Then the air was split by a high piercing cry.

There was a shimmer of azure silken cloth. And suddenly young Mzia was there, kneeling between the two men. Her bare head was bent, and her long, tightly woven black braids brushed the dust. Both men stared at the blue veil as though a chasm had opened at their feet.

Shocked, Piotr turned to Grigol.

"It's a sacred law," the Khevsur explained. "If a virgin exposes herself by tearing off her veil and throwing it between enemies, they can no longer fight. But it's a shame to her, to bare herself."

Piotr could see that this was so. Mzia's fresh young face was stained a rosy red, and she was trembling. Nina made a soft noise of concern, quickly retrieved the veil, and draped it over the girl's shining braids. Then she went to Noe, holding together the pieces of her sleeve.

"See what you've done. Let's go in now," Nina begged, wincing at the avid curiosity in the faces surrounding her. "We'll put the daggers on the table and talk." To Piotr's surprise, Noe surrendered his weapon with an abashed look. Grigol, his eyes flashing, strode over to the table and buried his dagger in the soft wood with a loud thud that made Nina jump. Piotr followed them in. They all seemed suddenly limp as the tension of fear and fury drained from them.

"We have a plan," Piotr announced confidently. He paused. A plan? He pummeled his brains, still holding their gaze with an assuring manner. *Lord help me*, he prayed. *What on earth am I going to say?*

"Grigol has graciously agreed to accompany us over the mountains. Of course, Nina will be coming, too. We can go our way through Ananuri—there's a priest there. Perhaps, I hope . . . that is, I suppose he will marry Grigol and Nina." Piotr shot a warning glance at the Khevsur. "And we can all feel that our desires have been taken care of." *Except mine*, he thought, with a quick look at Nina's glowing face. "After all, Noe, Grigol has paid a brideprice, and if they marry in church—what more can you ask? Will that satisfy you so we can all be at peace?"

Piotr hesitated, looking into each of their faces. Grigol's features were fixed in vigorous resolve; Noe was wavering, softening; Nina looked absurdly happy; and little Mzia was still a burning torch of shame. Piotr realized that he had won. They would leave the mountains in peace, Grigol and Nina would marry, and he would go his way—carrying the iron that had entered his soul. His gaze strayed to Mzia's bent head—face red under the blue veil. He would remember that—remember the purchase of shame.

Their plans were to leave the valley early in the next week. Before the day was out, those plans changed. By evening it became clear that Irina and Zviad were nowhere in the village. A farmer informed them that the man in the dark suit had purchased his mule to carry supplies. He supposed that he intended to begin his trek across the mountains that day. Yes, that day. No, there was no woman with him.

They scoured the village and the forest and the rocky outcroppings that loomed over the white-washed hovels. No Irina. After sundown they met at the forge—tired, grim, avoiding Noe's eyes.

"I fear," Grigol said, "that we've been betrayed. If that is so, there may be watchers prowling on the road to Tiflis. We'll have to shun the Military Highway and make use of the hidden paths in the hills. We'll leave at first light."

XIII

The Costly Deliverance

The path sliced into the mountain, heedless of angle or elevation. The quickest way, Grigol said—and east, not south where they would be expected. Piotr paced his long stride to the trot of the handsome bay that was Nina's brideprice. Besides the stolid little pack mule, it was the only mount among them. Their hope lay not in speed, but in secrecy and in cleverly searching out the little-known ways. Zviad and Irina already had almost a full day's lead on them.

They set out at dawn while the red sun's rim stole behind the iron-colored ridges and stretched a bright, fiery line between the mountain-tops and the still-dark sky. They climbed single file, with Grigol in front, Nina and Loma following, Noe leading the horse, and Piotr bringing up the rear. Where the pathway was level enough, they set the boy up on the gelding and quickened their pace.

Grigol's plan was to detour far to the east and then circle back, coming upon Ananuri quietly on the narrow goat paths that twisted down the mountains. The day's journey took them back and further back into an endless unfolding of ridges, ramparts, and serrated chains of rock scored by brief valleys and deep ravines.

At evening they paused on the edge of a precipice, trembling in the icy wind fluting down from the snowfields, drawing its mourner's music from every gap and hollow in tree or rock. Nina and Loma drew back as Piotr approached, their cheeks whipped to brightness. Far beneath them, a long valley funneled into the mountains, widening to the south. Emerald green pastures flanked a river that flowed down to a profusion of flowering cherry trees. The dying sun tinged the blossoms pink, as though a luminous cloud had settled on the valley floor. But gray-white plumes of smoke showed that men were living under that ethereal mass. Piotr could see Grigol tense with caution.

"There's a village," Grigol said quietly. "We'll go to the north." He nodded toward the upward jut of the sloped valley and led them down thorny switchbacks. A skittle of gravel flew at them as a pair of mountain goats bounded up from the path, their horns curled back toward their shaggy shoulders. Then they heard the river, running wide and shallow across a mottled bed of rock. On the other side, made of the same rock, was a shepherd's hut. The hut's humped conformity to the land, the bend of its grass roof, and its rounded pebbled walls made it look like something that had grown naturally beside the river, like a mushroom.

"We'll stop here," Grigol stated, "where our fire won't be seen from the village."

The fire was welcome. The crevasse at the apex of the triangular valley was dark and cold long before the cherry orchard below them lost its rosy glow. After the long day on the mountain, the comforting, enclosing presence of walls, the crackling of pine-scented logs, the waft and caress of fire-warmed air seemed extravagant blessings.

Piotr was bone-tired, but anxiety kept him awake and staring at the embers long after Loma had curled up in a corner. An invisible bird began singing in the bushes behind the hut—extruding pain and glory and the substance of stars in its song. Piotr went to the door, listening to the rise and fall of melody above the wash of the current. An icon-faced moon bent the fulness of its power into the dark ravine, igniting the river and kindling a translucent light within the cloud of cherry blossoms below them.

Nina and Grigol were walking alongside the stream, talking quietly. His eyes followed them until they paused. Grigol put his hand on the side of her neck, and she turned her head toward him. A white blaze of eagerness lit her face, and Piotr retreated from it into the dark, clay-scented cave of the shepherd's hut.

The next day's journey was easier as the ground flattened and widened to accommodate flocks and villages. The fortress of Ananuri straddled two valleys, its ancient battlements overlooking undulating foothills that stretched out into a sizable plain beyond.

The travelers skirted the crenelated walls at midday and entered the town near Assumption Church. Built of golden-yellow stone, the seventeenth-century church gleamed richly under the high-riding sun. Its conical tower thrust into the green of the surrounding hills behind, and its facade was adorned with a relief cross of intertwined vine stems supported by two chained lions. "St. Nino's cross," Noe told them. Cavorting demons squatted above the two arched windows, waiting to snatch at the ripened fruit.

They began climbing the hill behind the church. Everything about the town and its setting attested to the two worlds—the scoring of man's chisel on stone, the scoring of the wind on the mountain; the new growth on the hills and the worn stone on the streets; a round, flat loaf of *lavash* in a child's hand and the deep-cut relief of a disk overlaid with a cross.

The street was lined with what had once been bathhouses, but one had been converted into a teahouse with a cool arbor in back where food and drinks were served. They turned aside under the green archway. Their lively, balding host talked freely, but interspersed searching pauses in his ready flow of words just in case they were inclined to satisfy the curiosity in his hazel eyes. No, there had been no other visitors in the past few days, he reported. A priest? Yes, there was a priest at Assumption Church. His hazel eyes questioned each of them in turn. Then he ducked into the back entrance of his tiny restaurant and reappeared with two bottles of clear red wine.

"A priest," he said smiling, "always means either celebration or sorrow. In either case, you will need something to strengthen you." Grigol bowed his thanks, and they shared tumblers of wine while their host set out a hearty lamb stew, rice pilaf, and wheaten disks of *lavash*. "To fortify you for your religious duties," he commented, unquenched curiosity still brightening his eyes. He shrugged when their only answer was warm thanks.

Then while Piotr and Nina sipped glass after glass of strong black tea, Grigol and Noe went to search for the priest. When they returned an hour later, Grigol's look was black, and Noe's brows were knit in a frown. Nina immediately looked down at the dark liquid in her glass.

"It's no easy matter, marrying among these Christians," Grigol stated. *He must be very tired*, Piotr reflected compassionately. *He's not even bothering to hide his feelings*. The set of his mouth, the slant of his broad shoulders, the turn of his hands on his wrists all told of bitter disappointment.

"It's not impossible," Noe explained, "but there are obstacles. If it does work out, it will take weeks." Piotr was relieved to see that Noe was approaching the matter calmly. *He sees how far Grigol has stepped off the trodden path for him,* Piotr mused.

"Perhaps," Noe continued, "the best plan would be to go first to Tiflis so that Piotr can go his way. That eliminates one danger. Then we can return and see about a wedding."

"What if they will never marry us?" Grigol asked grimly.

No one answered.

They decided to leave immediately, hoping to travel as far as Mtskheta. Grigol was set against staying in the town though. "We'll stay another night on the mountain, away from the eyes and ears of strangers."

"Zviad's no traitor," Noe protested. "Why would he give Piotr papers and then turn on him? But we'll do as you say. Too much secrecy is better than too little."

As they left Ananuri, Piotr was startled to see a black figure detach itself from the shadow of the castle keep and glide toward them. It was a woman in purdah. Abruptly, she snatched the veil away, and the full strength of the afternoon sun struck her face. Yet it took a moment for Piotr to recognize those features. Irina! It had only been two days since he had seen her, but he could not believe the change. Smoky circles shadowed her eyes, and the flesh of her face was reduced as though some hot inner ferment had sucked in the skin beneath her cheekbones.

"I've come to warn you," she said, addressing Grigol. "The gendarmes in Mtskheta have been alerted. Cossacks will be looking for fugitives on the road."

"Zviad!" Piotr muttered. "So you were right, Grigol! A martyr, he said . . ."

Grigol was silent, looking hard at the woman in front of him. She dropped her eyes and slipped past him into the dimness of the narrow passageway. She seemed to waver, avoiding Noe's steady gaze and the slight curl to his lip. "Join us," he invited, with a courtly gesture. She fell in with their pace, keeping her thoughts wrapped up with her purdah-clad body.

They crossed alongside meadows and grazing lands, keeping always to the shadows of the hills. Thick, green grass covered even the rocky places, and the silver of creeks and springs crosshatched the land. At night, they came upon an idyllic camping place nestled between a rippling brook and an enclosing half-circle of bushes. Poplars waved overhead, and the air was warm and kindly. Yet they were troubled, cautious and halting in their speech and loathe to let the fire die so they could sleep. Irina kept to herself. *Punishing Noe, or herself?* Piotr wondered. Her rigid posture and backward glances kept them all on edge.

During the day though they forgot their night-fears and swung into an easy pace, covering several *versts* in the morning. When they came to a major road, Grigol paused, considering.

"We'll have to start veering back toward the west if we want to come out anywhere near Tiflis," he reasoned. "But I'm hesitant to travel so openly by day."

"We're still far from the city—and from Mtskheta. Let's save our worries for then," Noe said. "Our danger, if there is danger, will be coming from the south and east, so we'll be able to see any riders and react."

Grigol eyed him seriously. "It all depends upon where we can expect them to look for us—and that depends on how much they know. What makes you so sure they'll be coming from the south?"

"Think it out. Mtskheta is below us. On foot Zviad is barely arriving there. Besides, all he can know is that we're somewhere between Khevsuretia and Tiflis. I've made this trip a thousand times. The sooner we get into town, the better."

"All the same, I think we'll scout it out," Grigol said. "The women can stay here near the meadow with Loma and the animals. We'll take a quick look and then decide. I'm hesitant to be caught on any road that can be used by horses, many horses." He turned quickly, striding away with his hunter's walk that scarcely disturbed the dust of the road. He stopped abruptly, then turned, and brushed past Piotr and Noe who had begun to follow. He put his hand on Nina's arm. "My wife," he said softly, as though instructing her. "My true wife."

The road tightly wrapped the lapping outline of the hills, but in the distance they could see it climb a rise that would give them a view for many *versts*. When they got there, they found that they shared the way with two shepherds—one an old man in a tall *astrakhan* cap, the other a boy. The brass bells on their sheep tinkled with the rolling, lurching gait as the flock enclosed the three men in a woolly flood.

The flood subsided, and at the same time Piotr became aware of another sound—a thunder of hoofs coming from behind. They spun, looking for cover, but it was too late. Several Cossack horsemen, rifles at the ready, hemmed them in. The horses' breasts formed a wall, so close that Piotr could feel tiny wind-borne drops of sweat and spittle. He had to crane his neck to see the man who shouted, "Halt," in such a commanding bass. He was surprised see a florid, tubby little man who looked more like a bureaucrat than a soldier. Piotr's hand searched out the papers at his breast—would they help him or condemn him? "This doesn't concern you," he told Grigol and Noe sternly. "There's nothing you can do for me."

The rotund commander touched a mustache as sharp as an ice pick and took a long look at each of them. Grigol's face was wooden with self-control, and Piotr felt his own features stiffen. But the light blue eyes drifted past him and settled on Noe.

"I have an order here," rumbled the Cossack, "for the arrest of the terrorist and subversive, Noe Tcheidze."

Nina shaded her eyes against the sun in the east, straining to see the moving blur sweeping across the meadow. Horsemen, many of them. She shrank against the tussle of bushes at the meadow's edge, drawing Loma close beside her. She glanced back at Irina, who was watching, too—intently, so intently. Nina saw her face whiten. Why did Piotr's betrayal bring that dead look to Irina's eyes, and why did the Cossacks come from the north and not, as Irina had said, from Mtskheta?

Irina, her hand on the horse's bridle, took a few steps toward the riders, standing like a black pillar at the meadow's edge. *She has no fear!* Nina thought, watching the tall, lithe line of Irina's body. Then she swallowed her own fear as a group of twenty horsemen surrounded the slender figure. It was a little man who spoke to her, a little man with a voice like a bull and a mustache that poked upward like bent wire. He was questioning her, and Irina was shaking her head vehemently. The skinny mustache pricked upward on a sneering smile; then the Cossack chief signaled to several of his men and cantered onto the road following Grigol, Piotr, and Noe, leaving the rest to wait in the meadow.

"Cowards!" Irina screamed.

"Cowards!" echoed Loma's treble, as he charged forward, his head full of the danger to his father.

"No!" screamed Nina, grasping at the boy's shirt. Irina sprang onto the gelding, and the horse sliced between Nina and Loma. Nina drew her breath in sharply as she caught a glimpse of Irina's blanched face. It was distorted as though a hand had smeared the dark lines of her features with a cruel downward caress. *Such an agony of grief!* And now Nina knew why.

"Cowards!" screeched Loma, wild with fear for his father. Nina lurched toward him, desperately snatching at his clothing. A strip from his shirt came away in her hand as a grinning Cossack grabbed the boy and whipped his horse into a mad gallop. Nina screamed, reaching out her arms and running awkwardly on the uneven ground. With harsh shouts, the remaining horsemen joined with their comrade in a whirling, thundering circle that raised a choking dust.

Nina spun confusedly, her eyes starting as she strove to keep the boy in sight. The first horseman had tossed Loma from the crook of his arm to the pommel of a second Cossack's mount. Loma looked startled, and his deft little hands were clenching and unclenching, trying to hold onto something. Nina screamed again into the dust-filled air. She could feel the grit of it on her teeth. Her eyes widened—where was he? *God help us*, she prayed. He was being dangled by his crooked knee, his head bouncing against a booted foot! *God preserve him!* The boy was crying now, his face red and his eyes screwed up and shining with tears.

"Let him go!" she shouted. "Barbarians!" But only one horseman heard. He pulled his horse back at such a vicious angle that the mare's back legs kicked up on the turn. Then, coming within inches of riding her down, he grabbed at her breast with a lewd laugh. Her diaphragm rose on new terror, but she wrenched herself away—still seaching for Loma in the spinning chaos. A third rider held him now by the waist. The child's arms hung limply, and his head bobbed like a broken doll's.

Her eyes streaming, Nina stumbled forward into the dervish's chaos around her. Something had changed. There were new riders now, plunging into the circle. Nina stood shock-still. They were not Cossacks. These men were Georgians. How cleverly they maneuvered, weaving in and out, wrists and knees urging their small, swift horses. Nina saw one of them pull Loma's limp body away from a burly Cossack while another kept an outlandish damascened rifle at the ready. A wild, tumultuous surge brought the whirling mass of men and horses toward her. The upward swing of a stirrup caught her under the chin, knocking her to the ground.

Dazed, she pressed her cheek into the scrubby grass and dirt. *I have to see*, she reminded herself and painfully turned her body to face the sun. Its relentless brilliance split her vision into dazzling, scattering splashes of color and form. Then the black shadow of a flying hoof crossed her face, and she fainted.

Suspended in a twilight consciousness, it seemed to Nina that the arms holding her were familiar, cosseting arms; that the pounding of hoofs jarring her body tamboured out a message of gladness to come. *Grigol!* she thought with a stab of joy. She remembered the ardent flame in his eyes. *My wife, my true wife.* His hand on her arm had evoked a heady fusion of all shared delights—every glance, every caress—in their brief history together.

Nina shifted her body carefully. Throbbing pain shot through her shoulder and neck, forcing her eyelids open. Her face was pressed into a black shirt—a shirt she did not recognize. A slotted belt filled with silver cartridges chaffed against her jaw. Her body turned to wood, bouncing awkwardly in the grip of a stranger.

"Awake, I see," came a melodious voice from above her. She kept her eyes boring straight ahead, refusing to put a face to that voice.

"The boy is alive. Look there, you see Akaki has him. He snatched him away from the Russians," the voice continued.

Nina turned her head toward the black horse galloping alongside them. Its rider was a small, perfectly proportioned man who sat his horse with exquisite skill. Cradled in his arms was Loma, his pale face tilted in the fastness of sleep. "Alive," Nina murmured and turned a look of thanks to the man above her.

It was a strong, beautiful face. Sculptured locks of gray hair framed deeply tanned features below a black fur cap. Gray eyes, at ease with life, looked back at her from under the glossy sweep of black eyebrows. Two long creases scored the skin on either side of his full mouth. The one was made by laughter and delights of the earth; the other was a dimple that age had extended into a permanent furrow. Nina turned her shoulder into his chest and wondered how dangerous he was.

The land around them had relaxed into pleasant valleys and orchards. Level grazing lands were stenciled with the shadows of high-flying clouds that came swooping down from the north—rimmed with fiery orange-red and trailing extravagant curled tails like legendary birds. Almost sunset. How long had they been traveling? How would Grigol ever find them?

The riders swerved again toward the east, taking a narrow road that

169

cut across a parklike meadow studded with wildflowers and bordered with woodland. At the end of the road was a brick house. Lying low to the ground, it was screened by rosebushes and box hedges. A carved lattice of white wooden balconies graced the second story like lace panels. *So . . . civilized*, she thought, *a manor house fit for a lord . . . A lord! It all fits—the mounted retainers, the chiseled silver ornamentation on the man's equipment, the expensive fur trim on hat and cloak. This man is nobility, an eristav of Georgia!*

Her escort strode over to Akaki and gently took the unconscious child from him. Nina staggered forward, anxious to see that Loma was still breathing. But her head spun, and she tottered on her feet. Her fingers clutched at the horse's mane. Akaki reached out to steady her and helped her into the house; his master followed with Loma.

Nina found herself in a beautiful reception room flooded with light from two arched windows. On an upholstered chair sat a woman. Nina saw at first glance that she was nobility. She wore a creamy silk headdress and a matching dress adorned with two panels embroidered in rose-red and black. The needlework she was toying with froze on her lap as Nina came in. She opened her large black eyes very wide, lifted them toward the ceiling, and then let them drop deliberately on her guest.

Nina guessed that the woman was about forty, although she could have been older. The center of her face, from the narrow forehead to the angular chin, was aquiline. Strongly marked black eyebrows, a curved nose, the long upper lip, and austere little mouth were clear-cut and youthful. But a flabbiness around the border of her face obscured the line of jowl and chin. When she tucked her chin in, as she was doing now, Nina noted, this fleshiness became even more noticeable— like a queen's ruff on an ancient costume. Her pretty hands plucked at her garments and needlework and the sweetmeats on the table in a bird-like fidgeting.

Suddenly, Nina became aware of her own bruised face, the smudges of dust and dirt from head to toe, and her shamefully bare head.

"Loma," she whispered between parched, cracked lips, as though her hostess could understand. "Loma," she repeated, her eyes shearing through the haze into the eyes before her.

"Keke," pronounced the eristav, and the woman's eyes pounced on the dusty little bundle that was Loma. Keke's hands stopped their fussing, her black eyes kindled, and she flung aside her embroidery. Her face was suddenly at one with itself as the strong features pulled the slack-

170

ness from its edges. She called orders to a serving maid, as well as to her husband and Nina. Within moments, Loma was clean and wearing a fresh shirt and resting in a starched linen bed. The maid was smoothing the sheets on a second cot, and Keke was shaking her head and making the sign of the cross over the boy.

Nina kept her eyes fixed on the bruised little face and the quick shallow movements of the small chest. He stirred and blinked. Then with a ferocious frown, he demanded, "Where's Father?"

Something snapped in Nina. She knelt at the bedside, putting her arms around the boy and muffling her face in the crisp sheeting. "Soon," she murmured, "he'll be here soon."

Keke's plump hands pulled her away. "You need rest as well—tomorrow's soon enough for talking . . ." She paused briefly. "Your son?"

"Yes," Nina replied. "My son."

Later, after the clay of the road had been washed from her body and she and Loma had been served broth and bread like children in a nursery, Nina lay awake, listening. In the next cot Loma was breathing rhythmically. Outside she could hear the poplars whispering, and further off, the secretive music of hidden water. It seemed to her that her whole body would be aching with listening until she could hear that voice again. *My wife, my true wife.*

She went quietly to the window and pressed her forehead against the cool glass. The lawn and flowers were dark, but the whole sky churned with clouds the color of tarnished silver, backlit by an invisible moon. *A wicked, boiling brew of a rain about to fall upon us,* Nina thought. The first drops broke and spattered on the glass. Then they came with ungentle insistence.

"Nina," croaked a voice, and a small bruised hand plucked at her shift. "How will he find us? The traces will be washed away . . . are we lost?"

Nina took the tense little body in her arms, holding and rocking him to the rain's tattoo.

"No. We aren't lost. God knows where we are! And He's brought us to kind people who will help us. Your father will find us. I know he will." She stroked his hair, and he turned his blue eyes to her. They were dry and brave and stricken.

"Is my father dead?"

With a moan of pity, Nina picked him up and carried him back to the cot. She put her two hands on either side of his face. "No," she said firmly, "he's not dead. And he will come for us. We just have to wait."

She repeated the words in her own mind as her hands were busy tucking the quilt around the shivering child.

"What if the rain makes it hard for even a very good hunter to find us?"

"Listen. Your father is a very brave and good man, and he loves you very much. God is with him. He will find a way. Now you sleep, little one. We're safe here together." She found a section on his forehead that wasn't black and blue and kissed it gently. Then she made the sign of the cross over him, just as her own mother had always done.

"Nina?"

"I'm here."

"I love you."

"I love you, too, little son," she answered, testing the new word. "I love you very, very much."

The dismal room at the constable's office in Mtskheta became even more dismal as diagonal slashes of rain began to silver the black window. Grigol stopped pacing and groaned. Piotr, who had slumped onto a bench, straightened up and shot a look of concern at his friend.

"What?" he asked.

"Rain. How will I find them? They've given me nothing to go on."

Piotr sighed. "Perhaps Irina may know more. If we can find her."

"Irina," Grigol muttered. They both looked at their feet, trying to forget the look on Noe's face when he realized it was not Piotr who had been betrayed and not Zviad who had done the betraying. By now, Piotr reckoned, Noe would be more than halfway to Tiflis—sent with a mounted guard for trial and sentencing there. Piotr closed his eyes, remembering that bright, exuberant day in Tiflis with Noe. It seemed as though his memory were scanning the length of years, not months, to conjure up a picture of the River Kura and the serene poise of Metekhi fortress overlooking the town. "My future home . . . ," Noe had joked, eyeing the ancient prison. Not an inaccurate prediction as things turned out.

As it was, they were fortunate, he and Grigol, so far. It had taken three Cossacks and some heavy blows to restrain Grigol when he found out that Nina and Loma were gone. But, Piotr reflected, at least he was still alive, and at least he hadn't killed anyone. True, their papers had been confiscated. Maybe they would see that Piotr's passport had been forged, and maybe not. At this point, he felt almost indifferent. But Nina. The Cossacks, avoiding their chief's eyes, had said that she was taken along with the boy by some Georgians. Grigol's demands had been useless. That was all they knew, they insisted, but both Piotr and Grigol had mistrusted their assurances. Taken by unknown horsemen— Piotr's mind balked at what that might mean, and he turned it to other channels.

In the hours of waiting, everything had been decided between them. When, if, their papers were returned, Piotr would go southwest to Gori and pick up the train that would take him across the Surami Mountains to Batumi. From there he would find a ship bound for Odessa. Grigol would go back to the meadow and try to find his wife and son. If there was any sign of them. An ache in Piotr's neck reminded him that he had been staring fixedly at the storm-mottled window. The rain was falling now in undulating sheets with a sound like a mother hushing a child. He flinched, fighting the thought of what might have happened to Nina. And Grigol? How would that fragile, new-born faith survive catastrophe? Piotr glanced at his companion.

Grigol was sitting very still, his hands clasped between his knees and a great strength of quietness settled about his broad shoulders and motionless head. *There's no wavering with him*, Piotr thought in wonder. *It's as though he's bowed under the power of a grand, supple purpose.* Piotr looked steadily across at his friend and Grigol, feeling the pull of his gaze, looked back.

Grigol drew his shoulders back as though he were flexing his whole being. "I will find them," he said. "I have bent my soul in prayer these many hours, and it has come to me that they are alive. Whatever has happened . . ." he paused until his drawn brows forced a firmness into his voice, "whatever has happened, I will find them, and with God's help we'll make a new life together."

Piotr moved his hand in a helpless gesture. "I won't even know," he said through stiff lips. "There's no way I will ever find out . . . Nina, Loma . . ."

"Don't trouble yourself. Be assured that I will find them."

"God grant that you will," Piotr said. He kept his voice level so that there would be no hint of a break in it. "I have you to thank, friend, for my deliverance, but I'm afraid that my escape may have cost you dearly. You know that there is a price I would never willingly pay for my own safety."

"I know it. It wasn't your choosing. Perhaps my foolishness . . . but

God knows." Grigol paused for a moment and then gave Piotr a look he would never forget. "Remember. I have been delivered, too. And at no small cost."

The Black Sea was not black, but slick with limpid, undulating pastels. The sunset colors bled outward from a melon-colored disk sliced in half by the glass-sharp edge of the western horizon. But to Piotr it seemed that the vital, quivering color came from something leaking away within him, turning his legs numb and his wrists weak as he clutched the sticky railing of a ship bound for Odessa. He turned his eyes away from the sun, searching out the east.

A tangle of masts, skinny palms, and eucalyptus trees screened Batumi's waterfront promenade, like marks in a careless tally. Behind this crude screen, the pretty, disheveled town flounced up the hill, charming and contradictory—clinging vines and rebuffing walls, showy foliage and hidden gardens, the stink of dead fish and the perfume of mimosa trees. Colchis, the ancient Greeks had called it—Land of the Sun—and endowed it with strange legends of Argonauts and the Golden Fleece. *Travelers seeking the impossible*, Piotr thought. *Like me*.

The deck beneath him began a churning vibration that thrummed with the pulses of his own body. Suddenly, voices came from below. A kind of panic seized him and a tumult of memories broke free.

Pohod! It had started for him. The Molokans' heroic flight to refuge. For fifty years, Molokans in Transcaucasian villages had marched in procession to prefigure the coming day—the day of *Pohod*. Now that the day was here, it seemed less real to him than the mock pilgrimage enacted on a village street.

Pohod! The prophets had said that a time of great menace would shake the whole earth. The flight to refuge would come on the crest of this mighty turbulence. Suddenly, Piotr was seeing not a sparse forest of masts and trees, but a procession—a clambering assortment of people, his people, striding with measured tread from one end of the village to the other. The old men were in front, long beards torn to flying shreds in the wind. Behind them farmers, craftsmen, holy women, housewives, children all pressed eagerly toward that obscure future. Old Semyon was there, holding his Bible aloft. The quick valor of the gesture was a lunge toward heaven. Those behind him crowded around him as though they were bearing him up. And, because they were Molokans, they sang as they went.

"*Pohod.* That's the real *Pohod*—not this lonely, furtive departure." But the idea caught on another memory. Himself. Stripped and bereft—and alone—in a rough-hewn rift in the rock awash with love and new purpose. And Grigol. Piotr's mind grabbed hold of that moment when the dead weight of bewilderment had fallen from his friend. And he remembered the courage with which the Khevsur steeled himself to confront whatever had been left to him of his future. "I will find them. We'll make a life—with God's help . . ." Grigol's face lit by that familiar smile that showed both his top and bottom teeth flashed in front of him.

Back in Mtskheta the Cossack commander, his mustache limp as dangling mouse tails, had returned their papers as that long, anxious night was ending. Grigol opened the door, and the odors of stale smoke, ink, and mildewed paper gusted away with the fresh scent of morning coming up from the rain-washed stone street. And, in spite of everything, he managed to smile, just once. Then he was gone, alone.

Pohod. Piotr's mind returned to the puzzle, and a lifetime of connotation slipped away. *Every man's journey,* he mused, *is made alone, as Christ walked the way to Golgotha alone.*

Piotr turned his eyes back to the town. To the north and south, promontories reached into Batumi harbor like encircling arms. The light lingered on the contours of gentle knolls and softened the outlines of the houses of the Muslim Ajars. Behind that, as he knew from his journey across the Surami Mountains, rose rougher climbing hills and tea plantations and then the higher mountains—all connected by a uniting skin of land to Tiflis, to his native village, then Khevsuretia and across the Caucasus Mountains to Tambov province and the Volga regions where his ancestors were buried. And bound to that land and inseparable from it were its people. He could see them. They crowded his mind, blocking out the strangers' town: Semyon calling on God with a gesture that defied age or death. Galina pushing her son toward God with all the pain of a woman giving birth. Gavril counting out his life's earnings into his son's hand. Andrei and his beautiful Natasha, and that odd little Fenya ambushing him from beneath her kerchief with those blue, blue eyes. Noe with his trickster's mind and generous heart. Sirakan groaning at risk, yet sharing it where the sharing would help. Lovely Nina shunning the fraud and finding the true. And Grigol. He would remember Grigol.

The light faded, and the ship began struggling through the water. The two arms of the harbor relinquished them. But it seemed to Piotr that the grinding of the engine had anchored the ship and that it was the land that was slipping away, forsaking him and receding into the mystery of a future he would never share.

Piotr watched until he was surrounded by blackness pricked below by flicks of light reflected from the ship's lanterns and above by the fierce jottings of thousands of stars. *Another tally*, Piotr thought, as the sticks of mast, spar, and tree disappeared. *This pilgrimage of mine has cost each one of them. Cost them painfully.* He struggled in a confusing welter of emotion. *Choose*, he instructed himself, counting and sorting through the chaos within. *Either bear the guilt, or humble yourself to accept the gift.* He wanted to grieve with them, his kindred and friends, and somehow it seemed that letting go of his guilt, his responsibility for everything that had happened, would belittle all that they had done. Yet the sacrifice of love could not achieve its end if he clutched at his old life instead of reaching for the new.

"I have been delivered, too," he murmured softly to the widening chasm of dark water below him. "And at no small cost." He lifted his face in sudden kinship with the stars.

XIV

The Voice of the Bridegroom

The more Nina knew of the eristav's wife, the more she admired her. Keke would come each morning to check on Nina and the boy—and her strong face would take on a bewildered look. Nina was neither daughter nor servant nor social equal, and Keke wavered in a moment's loss as to how to treat her. But the sight of a bandage, a bruise, or the dark circles under Nina's sleepless eyes would send her into cluckings of pity.

Except for a broken left arm, Loma was surprisingly sound of limb. The ugly bruises that covered much of his body would be black for many days, but the freely bleeding cuts on his head were already healing— thanks to Keke's kindly touch. With care, Loma's young bones would knit, and then they'd be able to go. But where?

"He's doing so much better," she told Keke thankfully. "He slept all last night—see how rosy and healthy he's looking."

"But you didn't," Keke observed. "Every day I look at you, your face is pared down a little further. If your husband has done no wrong, no wrong will befall him. You squeeze your heart with worry—all that winsomeness will be wrung out of you."

"I know he's innocent of wrong," Nina replied. "But my mind goes round in circles wondering how to let him know where we are. It would be hard for me to find my way back to the village with Loma, especially as he is now. And how could I find him if he's been taken to Mtskheta or Tiflis? Yet we could stay here forever, and he'd never find us."

"You could stay, and welcome," Keke offered. "But think—the first thing he'll do when he's free is to go back to where he left you and look for signs. I don't know what signs there will be, but the next thing he'll do is see if the shepherds can tell him anything. And I've taken care that they will tell him plenty. I sent Akaki out the day after you arrived to spread word that you and the boy are here. Your Grigol will be here any day."

"Any day!" Nina's heart lunged at the word. Grigol with his adroit hands and firm mouth and broad protective shoulders. *My husband, my beloved*, she thought. Hope increased the intensity of her listening—for the sound of a door opening, or of sudden footsteps on the porch, or a far-off manly voice.

"Come, you and the boy. We'll have tea, and I'll tell you some stories that will make you forget your troubles," Keke suggested. Nina and Loma followed her to a beautifully set, linen-draped table beside a window overlooking a lovely formal garden. But Keke's stories of honor and wild feats of arms were far from comforting.

"The bodies of the dead at Ananuri were piled as high as the ancient walls," she intoned with satisfaction, "and the severed head of Prince Bardsig decorated the castle keep, the very keep you saw last week. You see what these abductions can lead to, Nina." She tucked her chin into a welter of wrinkles and aimed a black glance at Loma. His mouth gaped, and his eyes begged for more. Keke smiled at him, then at Nina, sure of her power.

"It all happened because of a pair of pink pantaloons," she continued. "Prince Bardsig, the Eristav of Aragvi, was feasting with his kinsmen and friends when he happened to glance out the window and catch sight of a great lady riding along the valley with her chaplain, her two falconers, and other retainers. Well, one of the prince's friends saw that the lady was the wife of Prince Chanche, the Eristav of Ksani—and Bardsig's bitter enemy.

"As she drew nearer, the prince could see that the lady was young and beautiful. He and his companions had dined well and were in a rollicking mood—so they needed no other invitation. They mounted their horses and calling to their men-at-arms, they charged into the little party, chased away the chaplain, the falconers, and the serving men and carried off the princess. An hour later, her pink pantaloons were flying like a standard above the keep.

"Naturally, when the princess returned home, her husband, Prince

Chanche, was furious. He swore a great oath to exterminate the whole cursed brood of the Eristav of the Aragvi—every one of them.

"But this was no easy matter, for Aragvi was a powerful prince. So Chanche, though a Christian, allied himself with the Mohammedan Lesghians and seized the fort of Khamchistsikhe. Then he marched on Ananuri where the sight of his wife's pink pantaloons floating above the keep infuriated him even more. He swore another great oath—to replace this symbol of shame with the head of the Eristav of Aragvi.

"A long siege—and a bloody one. But in the end the garrison at Ananuri was massacred; the pantaloons were taken down and replaced with poor Bardsig's head. But the pink pantaloons have been preserved through the generations in the family of the Eristav of Ksani—a token of valor and revenge!"

"Vengeance is mine, I will repay, saith the Lord . . ." A husky, oddly breathless voice came from behind Nina, and she turned quickly. "So you see what comes when man takes God's work into his own hands."

Keke was up, stretching her hands out to a thin young man with the face of a consumptive and the cassock of a Georgian Orthodox priest. The hem of the cassock was splotched with mud and layered with the dust of many roads.

"Father Panteley! He's our conscience here, Nina. I spout off with this or that—God knows what—and he'll nudge it into alignment with God's will. At least as he sees it!"

"I'm your chaplain, Lady, so that's my job," Panteley said with a mock bow that pushed the end of his brown beard into his narrow chest. "And from the stories you tell, it's a dangerous one!"

A jerk of his head sent a piercing smile toward Nina. Then he turned his attention to Loma. "Who is this little fallen warrior? He looks as though he's been dragged through the village by wild horses!"

"That's about what happened to him," Keke explained. "Christ have mercy on him! It's taken me these many days to get him on his feet again—and as you can see, he's bandaged and splinted like a war hero. In fact, he should be off to bed this minute."

Keke ordered more tea and told Father Panteley the whole story. Nina's searching glances took in a man still quite young whose whole outer shell seemed restless, almost agitated—snatching at time. When animated, the angles of his thin body jerked awkwardly, and sudden, startling intakes of breath through his teeth punctuated his speech. Yet when he was quiet, his repose was so deep nothing could touch it. Now his focus was firmly fixed on Keke, but there was a glimmer of preoccupation about his manner—as though the inner life behind his clear brown eyes demanded as much attention as the outer—as though he kept an exquisite mental balance between the two.

Father Panteley's eyes were housed between deep, bruised-looking dents on each temple and very high cheekbones, like clear pools sheltered by a rocky outcropping. His whole face was like that—bony promontories and gray hollows. Yet there was a gentleness and wisdom in the beautiful eyes, and humor twitched at the corners of his lips. As the priest looked back at Nina, his whole being congealed in a quick understanding. A wisp of comfort threaded Nina's thoughts. She let herself drift back into Keke's description—and was stunned by what she heard.

"So that's how it is with her, dear Father; she's neither fish nor fowl." Keke shook her head sympathetically. "As you can see, we'll need to plan the wedding. You can officiate. But first we'll need to find the groom," she said with ponderous gravity.

Father Panteley pulled a long face and replied with leaden tones, "Of course, find the groom . . ." But a droll light shone in his eyes, and Keke caught herself and began to laugh, pushing the tea things about with brisk fingers.

A welling bubble of emotion broke in Nina so that she laughed, too. "Find the groom," she said, wiping her eyes. "Find the . . ."

But there was an edge of hysteria to her merriment, and when Loma nudged her and insisted on hearing the joke, she had nothing to tell him.

Keke and Father Panteley continued their conversation, sipping strong, black tea from Sochi as their talk ranged far and wide over the valley, the five villages, into the doors of peasant huts, into the lives of needy people. Names of peasants and workmen, sick or disabled or widowed, crossed the table—they knew them all. Father Panteley's weakening health had not kept him from attending to his flock and, as for Keke, Nina had already seen that the prick of pity would send her into rough, tender action. *This is what they live for,* Nina thought. *Their ears are full of the cry of human hearts, and everything else is a faint buzzing that they have to put up with. And it's made them the closest of associates— friends.*

Later, the handsome eristav, Dzhumber, came in with Akaki, and the conversation turned to riots and unrest. Throughout Georgia, princes and priests, landlords and constables were being slaughtered in bloody uprisings.

180

"Prince Nakashidze has been murdered," Dzhumber reported. "And things have come to such a pass that not a single gravedigger could be found to dig his grave."

"The Social Democrats had placed him under a boycott, you see," Akaki broke in.

"Listen to this," Dzhumber continued. "Listen to this—not a coachman could be found to take the prince's grieving relatives to the funeral! Three priests were summoned, but only one showed up, and he was too frightened of the revolutionaries to officiate. The whole countryside is seething with treachery—but it will turn on them in the end—as it did in '58.

"In my father's time there were uprisings. The landowners and princes and Tsarist generals taught them a lesson they'd never forget. The rebellious villages were laid waste and burned; orchards and vineyards were cut down to the very root. Utter beggary was their punishment."

"It seems they've forgotten the lesson," Father Panteley murmured gently, "in only one generation."

"Yes, you are right," Dzhumber quickly agreed. "Thank God, my own father was too wise to leave his own people—and his own lands—with that kind of scar. Besides, we've given our people many freedoms and tried to buffer them from Russia's corrupt officialdom as best we can. That's why it's been quieter here," he reasoned as his eyes shifted uneasily from the priest to Akaki. But Akaki's mind was still full of the red glare of Georgia's trial by fire.

"The nobleman Urushadze—murdered," he said, almost absently. "And in Azerbaijan, the governor of Baku—also a Georgian prince—has been assassinated by Armenians. There have been mass slaughters of Armenians there. It's coming . . . it's coming."

"Not here, not here," the eristav denied. He reached out and put a soothing hand over his wife's where it clattered among the dishes. "No point in frightening Keke and our beautiful guest."

Keke's quick upward glance was baffled and a little bored, and Nina realized she hadn't been listening. But Nina had, and she was frightened. Any government official in any circumstance would be slow with the questions and quick with the reprisals. A chill foreboding darted through her as she thought of what might have happened to Grigol and Noe and Piotr. Then, too, Akaki's words had conjured up old fears. Did Dzhumber and Akaki realize that they were sipping tea with the daughter of an Armenian storekeeper?

Keke, who did know, seemed unaffected. *She responds with such unwavering simplicity,* Nina realized. *She never sees people as part of groups or movements, but only as individuals—body and soul knit together for some purpose which she will instinctively help, not hinder.*

Later, Father Panteley motioned Nina aside. "I know her," he said, indicating his patroness with a nod. "She'll have your life all planned out for you—a baptism on Wednesday, communion on Thursday, and holy matrimony on Saturday!

"She should have had a dozen children to pour out her love on. As it is, she has none—but the people benefit. Her husband would be shocked to learn that the villagers restrain themselves because of her charities, not because of the political maneuverings he's so proud of.

"But enough of that. Come out with me to the porch and we'll talk. As far as your marriage is concerned, I will answer to God, not to Keke, and I need to know what's in your heart. And in the heart of this man you would marry."

Nina followed him to a pleasant spot on the shaded verandah. She watched the first roses in Keke's garden dip and sway with the weight of their bloom, and she told him her story—and Grigol's. When her voice faltered, she would turn her eyes back to him and his glance—so bright and alive in the midst of those dead tissues—would infuse her with the strength to go on. She told it all and then stopped abruptly, looking at her hands twisting in her lap.

Father Panteley was silent. Finally he spoke. "This is like something that would have happened many hundreds of years ago when the gospel of Christ was so new—invading the borders of dark cultures, rescuing men of fierce courage like your Grigol. And these men become the pillars on which Christ builds His church." Nina could see that he was deeply touched by their story. He stood up in sudden agitation and paced the length of the porch. The hollow echo of his steps and his gasping, consumptive breathing filled her ears.

"It isn't easy for a man to tear himself away from everything he's been taught," he said. "That he would turn his hand from revenge and absorb reproach is a great thing—a great thing. But you—what would you be willing to do? Would you give up Grigol if God required it of you?" A taut pause lay between them and stretched until it pulled all the warmth and color from Nina's face. Numb and stricken, she turned her eyes to him, hiding nothing.

"No, no, forgive me." Father Panteley waved the question away. "He doesn't ask that of you—why should I? It's just that I'm amazed at this mountaineer of yours, this pagan. He was so quick to understand why he needed to thrust aside his whole culture for Christ—and for you, his wife."

"His wife?" Nina questioned.

"His wife. Soon. The Word of God tells a man to give himself for his wife as Christ gave Himself for the Church. Grigol has shown this kind of love more clearly than many a couple whom I've led to the altar. You examine your conscience and prepare your heart, Nina. And we'll pray that your Grigol returns safely. Not all would agree with me, but for my part, I'm willing to marry you. God forbid that we should cheat Keke of her wedding! You can see her heart is set on it!"

Nina smiled warmly. Alongside the garden, the trees murmured and quivered, shaking a bright metallic shimmer from their leaves into her eyes. Behind them, she could see the stony, austere flanks of distant mountains, and beyond that more mountains tinted a chalky lavender that dissolved into the misted air of early evening. The further peaks had an insubstantial, mythical look to them, like something longed for yet unreal. But Nina knew that they were real. *My home*, she thought, staring into the overlapping triangles that sawed across the sky. *We'll go north, Grigol and I and the boy, and we'll start a new life.*

The priest, quiet and preoccupied, walked across the porch and went into the house. Nina wandered around the corner to the western face of the house and watched the pale road that cut through the meadow. She kept her eyes on the road until the sun slipped behind the saw-toothed ridges and the dark shapes of the trees melted into the dark shape of the mountains. And as she watched, she listened.

That night Nina coaxed Loma into a peaceful sleep. She folded her clothes carefully, freed her hair and brushed it out over her white shift with deft fingers. But her heart somersaulted with a wild restlessness. The room was dark except for the red lamp in front of the icon, the yellow flame of the candle on the table, and its flickering reflection in the window. Her eyes darted from one point of light to the other and back again as a deep, yearning intensity began to build inside her—an intensity that could only find its release in the strong, stalwart spirit she had found in a lost village, in trackless mountains, in a cleft of rock at the back of the wind. "Grigol!" she whispered.

Examine your heart, she reminded herself, remembering the priest's words. Marriage. According to Father Panteley, it was far more than worn tradition or cynical economics or the craving of the body. It was an image, in fact, the only earthly image of an unearthly love—the love of Christ for those He had chosen. A holy and passionate image—for wasn't Christ's passion the price of love's release? An image framed in words took shape in her—where had she heard it? From Piotr? "A man will be as a hiding place from the wind, and a cover from the tempest. As rivers of water in a dry place, As the shadow of a great rock in a weary land."

The prophecy, she knew, was about Jesus. But for the first time she understood what the word *husband* meant. Peace enveloped her like an embrace and she drifted into slumber.

A sharp cry from Loma tore her out of her first deep sleep in days. The predawn air was cold and clear and brittle as dark glass. The boy was tossing on his cot, and she hurriedly put soothing hands on him, caressing his cheek and pulling at his hand to wean him away from nightmare. His blue eyes started open.

"I was upside down!" he told her in a trembling voice. "The ground and the sky had changed places just like that—and I was upside down!"

"You were upside down on the horses, but God protected you. We found you and you're right side up again. Just as you should be. Remember? Akaki galloped right alongside you and snatched you away from those wicked men. And now we're safe."

"Safe," he repeated. "Is Father safe, too?"

"I think he is. I think we will see him very soon. Will that make you happy?"

Loma smiled crookedly through the bruises and swellings on his face. Nina stroked his hair and told him stories. Her young lion cub had lost his taste for bloodthirsty tales of warriors and the old, capricious gods, so she told him about a little lost lamb tumbling about in the topsy-turvy world of a dark chasm and of the Good Shepherd who came to rescue him, who would always come—no matter what.

"Did the lamb have a bell on him?"

"Yes. All the sheep in the flock had brass bells tied around their necks."

"That's how He found him then. He could hear the bell tinkling."

"Maybe. But even without the bell, He would have found him. Because of His love."

"And that's why Father will find us, right?" Loma asked, his voice beginning to blur with sleep.

"Right. That's exactly why."

Nina knelt by the cot until Loma's breathing became deep and regular. The skin above his eyebrows was still knotted with concern, and she longed to smooth it out with her fingers, but she didn't dare wake him. The silence of the house and all the lands around it settled on her in layers. *Dawn is still a long way off*, she thought, thinking of dawn as something that traveled in space rather than time. But beneath her skin, her limbs rebelled with a yearning to move, to act, to listen.

She pulled on her battered russet boots, slipped her wool skirt over her shift, and went outside. The long meadow grasses were wet and gray, and the trees were languid under the damp weight of the night air. Dawn was slow in coming, snagged on the other side of the barren, jagged mountains of Dagestan. But the morning star burned with piercing power, and the moon put a wedge of shadow at the base of every rock in the road.

Nina stepped out on the road cautiously, feeling that the hushed sound of her tread was an intrusion. She paused, letting the night air seep into her pores. A pleasant, herbal scent lingered all around her. She walked past the meadowlands, just reaching a wooded copse as the sun broke free from the mountains. An old woodcutter's hut squatted in the dark of the trees. Its roof had caved in long ago, and the clutter of sawn branches, old thatch, and piled-up brushwood made it hard to distinguish from the tangled thicket behind it. Standing beside it, prosaically munching on straw and watching her with docile, unsurprised eyes was a dark brown mule. And next to the mule, propped up on the mottled slope of brushwood, was Grigol—sleeping the sleep of utter exhaustion.

Nina caught her breath and knelt beside him. His face was thinner, hollowed out with the ordeal of their separation. The russet edges of his hair fanned out on the litter of branch and brush beneath him. She put out a hand and smoothed the hard gnarl out of his forehead and his tawny eyes flared open.

He pulled her toward him with a bruising crush of arms, and his mouth sought hers with a sweet insistence. He said nothing, but the heave of his breathing, the heat of his body, and the strength of his yearning were a vow and a declaration. Then he drew back gently and began touching her face, her hair, her arms, as though to assure himself that she was real.

"My wife," he murmured.

Nina merely looked at him, her heart too full to answer.

"The boy?" he asked.

"Well. Bruised, a broken arm, but mending," she whispered.

"And you? You haven't been hurt?" His eyes raked her face and his fingers gently stroked the ugly bruise on her jaw line.

"No, no."

He sank back on the brambly pile, setting up a rustle as bits of bark and twig settled. He drew his brows together in a pained concentration and looked away.

"I've been thinking—something Piotr said—weeks ago when I was first getting to know you. He was, well, shocked . . ." He flicked a glance at her with the word, "at our ways, our way of choosing a bride. 'You're just ravishing her,' he said. His ideas seemed so strange to me. I didn't understand it! And my own feelings were so strong. I had no doubts. But now."

"Now?" she prompted.

"Now I do. I wonder if I've done wrong. And I wonder about you. About your . . . feelings. What I wonder is this—did you have a choice?" He turned roughly, watching the first stroke of light bring out the brutal shadows on the northern mountains. Nina studied his averted face. *I've seldom seen him afraid*, she realized, *but he's afraid now. Afraid to ask me if I love him!*

"No," she replied firmly, "I did not have a choice. Listen!" She grasped his hand as his face stiffened. "Ever since I was a little girl, it seemed to me that I lived in a broken world. I was torn—half-Georgian, half-Armenian. And my growing up was torn, too. My parents, they kept to the customs, but there was an emptiness—the old pattern was there, but the meaning of the pattern was gone. I was caught in the crisscross of this barren design, an oddly shaped little piece that didn't fit—and it crushed me.

"I longed for something, someone strong enough to break through and make something new of it. So I took my risks—and God sent you to me. Look at me, Grigol! You are my beloved. I had no choice but to love you. It was in me from the day I was born!" He reached for her silently, cradling her in his arms, so that her voice was muffled as she continued.

"God sent you to me, Grigol," her hushed words mingled with the rustle of cracking twigs and sliding debris as she nestled closer to him, "to teach me what love is!"

"My wife . . ." he said so that she scarcely heard, and his kisses now were soft and warm and alluring.

Later he told her about Noe's arrest, Piotr's departure, and his own long search. Nina watched day's color strengthen on the vineyards and orchards to the south and listened. *My brother!* she grieved when Grigol described their clash with the Cossacks, *what will become of Noe? And Irina. How that mighty passion has turned on them! The flaw in it has consumed the good. And Piotr. A steadfast friend—we will never see him again.* Grigol's lowered voice meted out the losses, one by one, and she took them in, silent, with dry intent eyes. But all the while her soul drank in a strange contentment as she listened to the rise and fall of Grigol's voice.

In turn, she told him about Loma's rescue, Keke's kindness, and Father Panteley. "He will marry us. He is willing," she reported. Grigol drew her closer and they made their plans.

"We are this far south," Grigol considered quietly, "so there's no reason why we shouldn't take another day's journey so that you can see your mother and older brother. Then we'll travel across the mountains to Vladikavkaz and see if we can find a place in one of the villages of the northern Caucasus. There are many there that may have use for a smith."

Nina followed his narrowed gaze. The great peaks of the north had detached themselves from the muted sky. The snow-jeweled diadem of Sarkineh and Zedazeni sparkled in the sun and sky-clearing Kazbek gleamed like eternity itself. Every trick of light and color played across their rocky ramparts and wooded slopes to describe majesty, defense, and habitation. A trill of pure joy sang through her, and she pressed closer into the cover of Grigol's arms and shoulders.

"Why are you waiting here?" she thought to ask suddenly. "Why didn't you come to the house?"

"It was too early. I didn't want to creep up on the eristav while it was still night," he whispered.

"Why are we whispering?" She laughed softly. "There's no one around."

"Because. This moment. It's sacred," he replied seriously and pressed the smile from her lips with another kiss.

"And becoming more profane by the moment," she teased. "Come—there's someone waiting for you. Loma will be overjoyed."

They walked back to the house and, entering by a side door, slipped into the nursery. Hand in hand, they sat quietly on Nina's cot and waited for Loma to awaken.

Father Panteley's predictions proved accurate. Grigol spent much of the next two days in deep conversation with the priest while Keke was beside herself preparing for a Saturday wedding. Nina and Loma were too full of bliss to concentrate on anything—which was fine for the boy, but Nina found herself under the lash of Keke's tongue more than once.

"See this? It's perfect for you," Keke exulted holding up a silk gown in a vivid rose shade. "Look at the color! What's wrong with you? Don't look at the window; look at me." Nina forced her attention to the dress and schooled her face to smile and show interest while her eyes strayed to the garden where Grigol and the priest walked. Her ears strained for the rise and fall of their voices.

But on Saturday morning as she dressed for her wedding day, she was more than thankful for Keke's faithful attention to detail. The older woman helped her as she stepped into deep rose silk so heavy it would almost stand by itself. The dress was made in the Georgian style with a gently flared skirt, tight sleeves, and fitted waist. The sleeveless overgarment with its divided, three-quarter-length skirt was a fragile pink. It was edged with a tracery of silver embroidery that meshed into filigreed borders and then dispersed into glinting, flying filaments as intricate and insubstantial as spider's web. The bodice, made over to hug Nina's slender waist, was laced up with a silver cord, and Grigol's necklace encircled her throat. They wove her dark hair into two thick braids that fell to her waist and then covered her head with a shimmer of pink veiling that floated around her like a cloud of blossom.

Nina felt as light and insubstantial as her clothing as they made their way to the eristav's circular chapel. It was ancient—much older than the rest of the house and dark inside. Frail wisps of light sifted down from small, narrow windows onto a throng of village folk. The ring of candles that lined the curved stone wall aided the light so that she could make out Grigol's stern expression as he caught sight of her, framed in the doorway. She stepped from the morning light into the enclosure, and the tread of her steps set up a gasp and a whispering all around her. But Grigol's eyes didn't move. A hush—then Father

Panteley's husky voice, with its peculiar stops and gaspings, chanted the ancient rite. Grigol took it up, his voice quiet and sure; then her own voice, clear and without doubt.

She dropped her eyes, and the glitter of embroidery was like moonlight on water. She raised them, and candlelight flared yellow from Grigol's eyes. He answered again, according to his instruction, and her ears were full of the sound of promise.

XV

A Gathering of
Shadows

The fields were gold stubble under the sun, shaped and shaven to the cut of the scythe. The hot, dry air, scented with buckwheat and rye, was so still that chaff settled on every railing and ridge, like dust in a closed room. Even the birds, wheeling and stooping to meet their shadows on the bristled ground, looked dusty.

Fenya pulled her sleeve across her sweat-soaked face and squinted across the only green in sight—her neat rows of cotton plants. In a far corner of the fenced field, Vassily chopped away with his hoe. Fenya opened the gate and shooed in a flock of gray and white geese. Valued helpers in the business of cotton growing, they would nip away at the tough steppe grasses that invaded the field, but ignore the cotton. Oblivious of the heat, they cackled and hissed and began weeding ardently while Fenya started breaking up the sun-baked ground with her hoe.

She and Vassily were the only ones working the fields. The hot days were a brief respite between the grain harvest and the grape harvest; most of the villagers occupied themselves with quieter tasks. In the little lopsided hut, the other Kostrikins were putting the last touches on preparations for Natasha's wedding tomorrow. Up at the big house by the mill, Mikhail Voloshin was entertaining the Bogdanoffs and other guests from Delizan.

Fenya cultivated a few rows, then screwed up her eyes against the glare, and surveyed her work. The plants were a lush green, tall and beautiful against the dry clay—too tall and too beautiful. All their strength had gone to leaf and stalk, and the bolls were few and small. It would be a meager harvest for all their hard work. Fenya let her eyes rest a moment on the fresh green shades that had cheated them of plenty; then she searched out the bent back of her father in the field. He straightened to meet her gaze.

"Go open the sluice," he called to her. "We'll irrigate these rows here."

She let herself out by the crude gate and went to the mud-caked channel to the east, grateful for the feel of cooler earth under her feet. The brown water gushed with a blue-white curve over the wooden slat, and she bent to rinse her work-hardened hands. But as she shook the sparkling drops from her fingers, her heart froze.

A dog was barking—a dog harrying the helpless, earth-bound geese! She flew to the open gate and sighted a mongrel happily bounding after the terrified geese, his long pink tongue hanging down almost low enough to lick the ground. The geese scattered, frantically beating their clipped wings as their webbed feet awkwardly flapped across the turned-up soil. Fenya knew that they would run until they dropped of exhaustion. She could hear Vassily shouting and her own voice yelling as she ran headlong toward the invader. The dog took joyful leaps after a young gander. Its long neck stretched forward, the bird spread its wings in a pitiful attempt to fly. The goose collapsed as Fenya came up, and the dog, confused at such a quick end to his chase, sniffed at his prey and panted at her with an expression that said, "Now what?" She shoved him away with her knee, and Vassily caught him by the scruff of the neck and hefted him over the fence.

Fenya knelt beside the goose. Its neck lay slack across the ground, but the beautiful, splayed-out wings twitched feebly. The beady eyes, still bright, flicked toward her, then died, and quickly glazed over in the heat that radiated up from the ground. She turned the bird over, touching the soft downy feathers at its breast. Then, gathering it into her arms, she sat on the rough, crumbled crust of the earth and wept.

Vassily stood beside her, shrugging and muttering. "No worry," he said, awkwardly patting her bent head. "We'll pluck it and use the down." He didn't say it, but no Molokan could eat a fowl that had fallen in the field. The goose would be wasted.

"Shush, girl. It doesn't matter." But Fenya was shaken by harsh, shuddering sobs. "Stop that! Enough!" he admonished. Frightened and confused by her unchildlike grief, he went over to the fence and put his hands on it, as though holding himself up while he stared up the road toward the village. "Enough," he groaned, looking up at the harsh blue sky. He went back to her and gently took the dead bird from her lap. "There's no need—" he began, then flinched back when she raised her face.

He went to the gate, holding the goose under one arm, and with a brief backward look at the crumpled form of his daughter, he trudged up the road to the village. Suddenly still, Fenya watched his slow gait, the dead gander's neck bobbing in his grip. He didn't turn down the hill to their hut, but kept going, up toward the mill, up toward the house with the blue tile roof where Voloshins were preparing for a son's wedding.

Fenya propped herself up on her hoe and watched him for a long moment. *Now he's upset, too,* she chided herself. *Stop it!* But she didn't stop. She could feel the tears crawling down her dirty face as the irrigation water began to crawl along the furrows, turning the pale soil to dark brown. The slow-moving water winked with white sparkles before it disappeared into the thirsty earth.

She could hear their voices through the thin partition—Vassily and Anna's—raised in the heat of discord or muted in a bitter swallowing of grief. The rough wood between the best room and kitchen was not thick enough to hide a grim striving—whether against each other or something from the outside, Fenya couldn't tell. What was it that had stolen the joy of Natasha's marriage from them? Like a fox among grapes, troubles were snapping at their happiness! And snatching away their sleep—just when they needed it most.

She shifted her body wearily, thankful for the coolness of the kitchen floor, careful not to awaken Luba sleeping beside her. A blue block of light—a chunk of night sky shaped by the window—struck Natasha's beautiful profile and Tanya's broad back. Vanya's white-skinned leg, clean for once, hung over the side of the stove. Coming from behind him, she could hear the even little whistle in Misha's breathing. Fenya's gaze settled on the two girls—one would be a bride tomorrow. The other had been spoken for, but was without a dowry. Was that the trouble? Pretty, robust Tanya was almost a year younger than Fenya, but everyone forgot that. *I've worked too hard this season,* Fenya told herself. Labor had toughened and thinned her body. The suggestion of womanly growth that had showed in the spring had been siphoned off in the hot, back-breaking days of summer.

Anna was weeping now despite Vassily's comforting murmurs. Her grief was sharp, clear-cut. There was an awful sureness about it, Fenya acknowledged to herself. Some very specific woe had befallen them. Then she heard it. "You've sold our daughter . . ." The aggrieved sob swelled and broke. "Sold her . . . sold her . . ."

They marched in a joyous procession up the hill, a score of young men in long, embroidered *kosovorotkas* sashed with silken tassels, each carrying a loaf of bread under his arm. Their high boots gleamed with polish so that sword strokes of unsheathed sunlight flashed with each stride. Rounded shadows trundled after them, changing shape with the groomsmen's movements and with the contours of the road. The girls followed—Fenya, Tanya, and Nadya Voloshin in bright skirts and full-sleeved blouses, then Natasha in her wedding dress and veil.

The morning sun, just before midday, curled the edges of flower petals and brought out a glow on the young faces. But at Voloshins the brick-walled house had stored up a damp breath of coolness to exhale on them. Fenya joined the group inside and glanced back at Natasha standing at the threshold, framed in white light with blurred edges. *How lovely and ethereal she looks*, Fenya observed. Joy played under her delicate features like the secret flow of water under ice just before it breaks in the spring.

Inside, Andrei fell to his knees, bending low under the prayers of the elders. Mikhail placed his right hand on the glossy sweep of straight black hair. Marfa's hand hovered over her husband's and, higher still, trembled their old bunya's hand, Marfa's mother, Agafya Bogdanoff. Semyon's ancient voice was swollen with the strong intent of his prayer, and the old woman's frail, veined hand fluttered in the current of his thought. Andrei bent his head further, and his black hair fell over his face, but Natasha held herself straight and queenly.

The congregation moved back with a great surge and made their way to the church for the final ceremony and feast. Fenya paused briefly in the best room after they had all filed out. On the wall by the door was a rectangle covered up with a white cloth. It was, she knew, a mirror in a wooden Tartar frame, draped so as not to offend the stricter Molokans. "An implement of the devil," some of the brethren would say, "an image where God commands no graven image." In olden times, she had heard, superstitious peasants had used mirrors for divination, believing that a girl's future could be seen in the long corridor of repeated images that opened when two mirrors faced each other. A frightening thought! But Marfa Andreivna Voloshin, worldly and rich as she was, only used the glass to smooth her hair and tie her kerchief just so. Timidly, Fenya lifted a corner and took a quick look.

A pale oval sprang out of a surface both dim and shiny. Fenya pushed her kerchief back to reveal the very white rounded forehead. Even in the dusky light, her eyes blazed with intense blue tints—and with curiosity. Below the eyes, her face was much darker, hollowed out by hard work and toughened by the sun. Her nose, slightly scooped at the bridge, was tipped with a suggestion of a square, which was repeated in the shape of her full lower lip and the jut of her firm chin. Fenya drew back with a sharp intake of breath. *I've been cut in two*, she thought, *white on top and brown beneath*. She adjusted her kerchief as she ran to catch up with the others, pulling it forward to shade her eyes and conceal her thoughts.

Fenya hurled herself into the moving mass of brightly clad Molokans. Zealous sunlight lavished a sheen on silks and satins and awoke the dazzle in the many-colored embroideries on hem, bodice, and collar. But the dust-laden trees and the empty huts, plank and thatch, were still and chalky-pale, faded as old, blurred memories. A hint of remoteness crept into Fenya's blood. *Ah, it's all so dry, too dry for me to stick to*, she mused.

Then they were in the church, and Semyon's sure voice was pouring over the young couple. When he finished, Andrei recited, "Let now all servants of the Lord, in the courtyard of the house of our Lord, raise your hands in holiness and bless the Lord; the Lord bless you from Zion, who created heaven and earth . . ." He bowed again to Andrei's father and mother to ask their blessing.

Mikhail snapped his head back and pronounced, "Be blessed, our child, by the high God, and the Lord bless you from Zion, and may you see the holy Jerusalem in the days of your life and see your sons' sons, peace in Israel, and may peace be on your head for ever. Amen."

Fenya caught a glimpse of Aksinia Bogdanoff's sweet, red-lipped smile. *Will she remember me?* Fenya wondered. And there, in a space framed by one woman's shoulder and another's kerchief, was a section of Galina Antonovna Voloshin's face. Her eyes were misted, her jaw set. Fenya wondered if she was seeing Piotr's features beneath the smooth fall of Andrei's hair. *She will never see her son's wedding,* Fenya realized. She turned her eyes back to Andrei's face, savoring the cousinly resemblance. *Will Piotr remember?* she wondered. *Does his mind hold a place of lodging for me?*

There was a shuffle; people moved to make way for Andrei and Natasha to face each other beneath the plain square of white cloth. The crowd bristled with a jostling, a hushing, an old woman's voice, "Ah."

Natasha's gray eyes beneath the white edging of her veil shone with light and promise as her voice joined with her groom's in the oath-taking; Andrei pushed his hair back and recited the words through stiff lips, staring into her face as if the words were written there.

"We, the here-named servants of the living God, swear before Almighty God and before His holy Gospels and before His holy Church that according to the order of the law of God we wish to live in legal marriage, with the blessing and agreement of our parents, and by our own will, so that without breaking the Lord's commandments between us will be observed fidelity and modesty . . ."

Andrei put his hand forward, but did not touch the girl facing him. "I will not have any other wife except the one to whom I now swear," he said loudly and dropped his hand.

Their voices joined once more. "In conclusion of our promise, we swear fidelity and truth forever."

From every corner, the voices of the Molokans attested, "Listen, men . . ." three times. Then Vassily stepped forward. He took Natasha's hand, led her the few steps toward her groom, and put her hand in Andrei's.

"I give you my daughter to wife; take her according to God's law to your father."

The crowd milled joyously into the courtyard while tables were set up for the wedding feast. Vassily and Anna stood beside the young couple, receiving the well-wishers. But Fenya noticed Vassily's glance flitting toward her with an abashed nervousness.

Guests churned in a circular frenzy that spun Fenya to the outskirts of the group. Behind her, the branches of the trees along the stream arched and dipped under their summer's weight of leaves. The leaves themselves were as dry and lusterless as mummified hands, curled inward as though to hoard the dense clotting of gloom that hid the trees' boles. But the darkness was shot through with occasional flashing points of light from the water.

Aksinia found her there. She was shaking her head even before she came within earshot; then her plump fingers came up and pinched the tanned skin on Fenya's cheek.

"You've worked yourself into a dried-up stick, dearie," she scolded sympathetically. "There's no need for it."

Fenya rubbed her face self-consciously, but she was glad to be remembered and at ease in Aksinia's overflowing kindness.

"Jam and pancakes and lots of butter—that's what you need," the young wife decided. "Praise be, we have a good two weeks before we leave Delizan. We'll fatten you up then! It's not good to start a sea voyage without a little extra meat on your bones."

Fenya looked at her in astonishment. "Delizan!" she almost choked on the word. "How would I be in Delizan?"

Aksinia's ruddy cheeks grew even ruddier as her hand flew to her mouth. "What a fool I am, jabbering on! I've spoken out of turn . . . I suppose your father wanted to wait until after the wedding to tell you."

Realization began to wash over Fenya in waves. *Pohod*, her heart whispered—but she was afraid to say it.

"Tell me what?" She forced the words out.

"*Pohod*! That's what. God has remembered you. And me, too, I should say. You're to come with us to America! It's all worked out to the good."

"*Pohod*," Fenya murmured. Astonishment, fear, and a heady excitement began tugging at her. "How could it be?"

"I don't know what turned his mind, but your father came to us yesterday. It was a strange meeting! He was all atremble with arranging things with us—cradling a dead goose all the while as though it were a dear little babe! But it seems his mind is made up that it's the best for you. Then, too, it seems he's hard up right now—one daughter married and another soon betrothed."

Fenya opened her mouth to say something, but Aksinia was bursting with her news.

"Don't worry," she interrupted with a smile, "it will all be taken care of. We'll pay your passage; you'll help me with the twins. Then when it comes time for you to marry, you can repay us from your *kladka*. I've heard that the Molokan lads in America will pay well for a bride—there just aren't enough girls to go around."

Pohod! *God has remembered me . . .* Fenya reeled under a sudden awkward joy. Voloshins had spared no expense for the wedding feast, but the steaming bowls of *lapsha* and heaped platters of *kasha* with meat and raisins were wasted on Fenya. She was aware only of a strange, shining future, the sudden jab of Vassily's stare, and the sting of Anna's stiff smile and desolate eyes.

"We lived together and chewed bread together, and God prospered us, dear ones." Granny Bogdanoff's shrill, wavering voice hearkened back to her own marriage more than fifty years ago. "May He do so for you! May peace be on your heads!" She waved a blessing to the newly-weds with one brown, speckled hand and anchored herself to the cart with the other. Since it was the cart that the young couple would be leaving in, Fenya gently pried her hand loose and reattached it to Aksinia's firm elbow.

It was early evening, and the guests were dispersing, except for those invited for the last part of the ceremony—bedding the bride and groom at his parents' house. Mikhail and Marfa had gone on ahead to prepare for their guests. Andrei and Natasha were settled into the flower-decked cart surrounded by bridesmaids and groomsmen on foot and by close relatives of the young couple.

Fenya joined the cluster of other bridesmaids behind the cart and went over the wedding traditions in her mind. When they reached the groom's house, the girls would comb out Natasha's single braid and replait it into two, as a sign that she was part of a couple now. The others would be feting the groom; then Marfa, as the groom's mother, would take the couple out to the barn and lock them in with suitable instructions. Fenya looked at her sister curiously, overwhelmed by the importance of the night.

Trofim, who as *druzhko* (best man) was driving, whipped up the team, and the handsome Dukhobor horses eased into a steady trot. He drove them into the square to make a smart turn, rounding his shoulders and flourishing his whip playfully. Then Fenya saw his broad back stiffen. He reined in cautiously and turned halfway to say something to Andrei. Andrei jerked his head around, and Fenya followed his stare.

A knot of Georgian youths blocked the road in front of them. Four, perhaps five—they were laughing and cursing—sodden with drink. The sight of three powerful horses, each garnished with a summer posy, sent them into gales of uproarious mirth. One ripped a wilting dahlia from the harness, and pretending to sniff it ecstatically, kissed it and scattered the torn petals.

"A kiss from the bride," he demanded, and the others chimed in.

"A kiss, a kiss . . . " "Right. Why should the rich man have it all?" "The poor make love as well as the rich—better!" Joking, laughing, they began stripping the floral decorations from horse and cart.

"Have a care, brothers," Trofim admonished. "Leave us in peace— and Christ be with you." But his words were swallowed in a wild scatter of shredded blossom and merriment.

Then the young men grew suddenly quiet, their eyes stern and resentful. Fenya began to be afraid. "Look at the beauty his rich father has bought for him!" one said bitterly.

Andrei wedged his body in front of Natasha, holding out his arms. They started pelting him with the flowers, then with refuse from the street. The bridesmaids began edging backwards into the darkness of the square. Trofim lumbered down from the cart. Fenya expected that the size of him would daunt them, but the leader had worked himself into a self-righteous resentment.

"Kulak!" His scream tore away any pretense of calmness from them. "You wallow in your riches while we scratch to make a living. Go on— take it all—take it for your bride! You've bled us dry, you carrion!" Fenya's scalp prickled with shock as she watched hate contort the handsome young face. He really believes it, she thought. He thinks that Mikhail Voloshin's house and livestock and mill and high-stepping horses have somehow robbed him. And his soul is filled with all the fermenting anger of a wronged man.

"Kulak! Kulak!" The man's companions took up the cry. Andrei jumped down from the cart, and Fenya climbed in to shield her sister as the two brothers faced off the drunken men. Other groomsmen moved forward, creating a wall between the cart and the Georgians. Fenya saw a youth with thick, black brows and flashing white teeth clench his raised fist. She could not turn her eyes away from the pain on his face. The power of his hatred was as forceful and as personal as a blow to the face. They hate me, she thought with astonishment, and they hate Natasha who has lived her whole life in poverty.

One of the Georgians tore the spectacles off Andrei's face. "You've a beautiful wife," he said bowing jovially. "We wouldn't want you to see too much of her." He let the glasses fall from his hand and then ground them beneath his heel. Trofim's enormous form blocked Fenya's view; there was a thump and a curse, and the agitator sprawled on the roadside. Without a word and with methodical ease, the huge Molokan dispatched a second nuisance. The others backed away, and he and Andrei clambered back into the cart.

Andrei's weak eyes looked odd and stunned without his glasses, but they widened and hardened as he took in Natasha's strained face and trembling hands. Oblivious of anyone else, he pulled her toward him, shielding her eyes with his hand. His heavy black forelock hid his face as he leaned toward her.

Without discussion, the Molokans grouped themselves around the cart, each holding to railing or harness with one hand. "*Kulak!*" An angry shout broke the air. They ignored it and started up the hill to Voloshins'. "*Kulak!*" The word lashed after them like the crack of a whip. The Molokans kept walking. Then a hesitant voice started a song. The other Molokans took it up, one by one, and the Psalm grew in strength and beauty as they marched up to the groom's house.

Fenya took her last look at the village. The Kostrikin hut sank into its hollow; the busy stream glinted a last farewell in the early morning light; the three firs in the square loomed, then slanted away. The haphazard woodpile and the acacias at the village edge, the familiar fields and vineyards—they all disappeared in turn as the Bogdanoff's cart lumbered toward the Old Post Road that would take them to Delizan.

Fenya held each detail in her heart. Her fingers reached out to prod the plump cloth-wrapped bundle that contained her things—more things than she had ever thought to own. The touch of them stung her with joy and pain.

Last night, Anna had served *blintzi* and jam and clotted cream—Fenya's favorite. It was only a few days after the wedding, but still Natasha had run over to join them, bringing a gift of a new padded jacket. Anna, determined not to frighten her daughter with tears, had a gift, too.

"I couldn't sell it," she explained, handing a cloth-wrapped package to Fenya. "Not after I'd seen it on you."

The package contained the beautiful merino dress with its glowing sunflower embroidery. By that time, a confusing lump of emotion had lodged in Fenya's throat. She nodded mutely as she stroked the soft fabric. Vassily was standing behind her, and she became aware that he was nudging a smooth block of wood at her. She took it. It was a carved box. Not very large, maybe the size of a lady's jewel box, but the lid was carved with a border of intricate geometric shapes—an exact duplicate of the carved decoration on the posts and shutters and lintels of the

Kostrikin hut. "There, you see, you'll take a bit of your home with you—out there to America . . ." He bit off the words with a tuft of mustache and began chewing.

A *bit of home*, Fenya mused. The village was still in sight beyond the fields. Then a fold in the land swallowed it. *Old things have passed away*, she thought. They were far beyond the fields she was used to working, and now only the Surami Mountains on the horizon were familiar. She looked at them with yearning intensity. "Old things have passed away . . ." From throat to midriff, she felt as pummeled and porous and receptive as cultivated earth.

The cart creaked and groaned as they approached the turn-off to the smoother Post Road. Fenya's eyes skirted the rows of vines lining the road to the south and fastened again on the retreating blue line of mountains. Would there be vines in California—and mountains?

"You sons of Satan, you don't have to find every rut in the road!" Ivan grumbled at the horses. Fenya glanced back. Aksinia's complaisant face and full body half-reclined at a relaxed slope against a pile of cloth bundles. *She doesn't torment herself with wonderings*, Fenya thought. *She just takes what is*. The jarring movement hardly affected her well-padded body, but Granny Bogdanoff jumped as though she'd been stung with every bump. She would nod with a satisfied air, smiling at Fenya as if to say, "That's right! We're being knocked about—just as we should be!" Her bony body seemed to be flying every which way and, Fenya supposed, her face would be that way too, except that she tied her kerchief on so tightly that the deep scored lines along her nose, across her forehead, and beneath her mouth were pushed even deeper. *Her face*, Fenya thought, *looks like it's been taken apart and put back together—and it's only that old kerchief that keeps it from falling apart*. But her tiny smile was very sweet and her eyes, milky with cataracts, were as bright as a cloud with the sun behind it.

Little Valentina perched on her mother's stomach. She grabbed a handful of Aksinia's skirt and began gumming at it with a worried pucker to her face. She occasionally took it out of her mouth and studied it with a disappointed expression. Nikolinka, the little boy, was teething, too. He pulled himself up, holding to the cart railing with both hands and looked out with his mouth wide open and astonishment moving in flickers over his shining bluish-brown eyes. A sudden jolt slammed his jaw shut, and he lunged toward Aksinia, bellowing his outrage. Fenya quickly took the little girl, while Aksinia cradled and stroked her son, and Ivan moved his cap and turned to give them all a disgruntled one-eyed look.

"You see how it will be," she said to Fenya. "One thing after another with these two! Can you think of what it will be like on a ship? Get me through all this, dearie, and I'll buy you *likirovnii tooflii*—patent leather shoes—when we get to Los Angeles."

"Los Angeles?" Fenya repeated aloud. Aksinia, as usual, had filled her with astonishment. *Likirovnii tooflii!* Who else would ever think of such a thing?

"Why, yes. Los Angeles. That's where we'll live when we get to California."

"California!" old Granny Bogdanoff broke in. "My soul and body will be like that," she held up two tightly crossed fingers, "until we get to California. My heart is set on *Pohod!*" Tremors of quick little noddings shook her tightly wrapped head, and she smiled her sweet smile, as innocent and gummy and moist as the babies'.

"Do you know what this Los Angeles is like?" Fenya asked.

"No. No, dearie. God knows, and He'll provide the way. I just follow."

Fenya smiled back at the old bunya. An immense sense of relaxation flowed over her, and she felt that something very new, something she did not understand, was taking place in her soul. *I'm like a weary swimmer, all beat up with striving—and suddenly, I've been caught up by a strong and gentle current,* she mused. She let the thought buoy her up and began looking around at the unfamiliar landscape as eagerly as the curious Nikolinka.

Valentina began fussing and arching in her arms. She had had enough of the taste of calico and was ready for something more substantial. Aksinia began unbuttoning her blouse, and they switched babies.

"You see?" Aksinia insisted, but her face smoothed over with tenderness as the babe took the breast.

Fenya bounced Nikolinka on her knee, and the cart turned onto the Old Post Road. She took a last look at the mountains and then turned her full attention to the energetic, adventurous little boy.

"*Likirovnii tooflii,*" she marveled. "What next?"

XVI

The Place of Refuge

It was mid-August when the Southern Pacific Railway deposited Piotr in Los Angeles, simmering in its circle of mountains. He blinked in the bright sun as he stepped down from the train, feeling weak and shaky. After leaving ship in San Francisco, he had survived on candy. His lack of English made it difficult to get food, but there were always plenty of candy vendors at the depots.

The next step, he instructed himself, *is to find the Molokans. How?* He struggled with the queasy agitation churning in his stomach. Of course, they wouldn't be expecting him—or if they did, it would have been months ago. Well, then, they were in for a surprise!

Piotr forced himself to sort out the confusion around him. Whistles blew, metal doors clanged, and commands rapped out in the strange, clipped language of America. Uniformed porters, men in brown business suits, and women in shirt waists, flaring skirts, and picture hats swirled around him. A horsey-faced woman floated in front of him, waving a handkerchief at someone getting off the train. Her billowing dress had huge sleeves, narrow at the wrists but so wide and puffy through the shoulders that her waving arms were like the beating wings of a bird about to fly off. She pushed past him.

Then there he was—a robust old Molokan in a high-necked tunic, knee boots, wide peasant trousers, and a lavish fanfare of beard—summoned to life by the clear, southern sunlight. Relief coursed through Piotr's body. Six months! He marveled. It had been six months since he had seen one of his own people.

The old man's face creased in a welcoming smile with a wince behind it as Piotr clambered down the steps. His fluffy mustache moved indistinctly; whatever he said was lost in the confusion of arrivals and departures. But he took Piotr firmly by the arm, shouldered one of his bundles, and they walked up First Street toward the Molokan settlement. Piotr stumbled alongside, taking in the assortment of one- and two-story buildings and storefronts—all plastered with a mad profusion of enigmatic signs. Letters, words, and slogans on walls, on placards, on windows, even stuck on sticks here and there. Shops, cafes, pool halls—each space carried its proclamation, but there was no meaning in it. Here and there behind a dark, dusty pane, he glimpsed an averted face. *There they are*, he thought, *human beings living their hidden lives* . . .

"I'm Ilya Valoff," said his companion. "You'll get used to it. It'll be easier when you're with your own folk." His childlike curl of a smile pushed the bronzed cheeks up to narrow the keen, kindly blue eyes.

"So," he continued, "you've come by way of the horn! Most folk are coming through Bremen these days—it's shorter going across the Atlantic." The day dimmed around Piotr. No, he wouldn't tell his new acquaintance that the long overland train trip through Russia and Poland to Germany was much too dangerous for a deserter—and a murderer.

"Way of the horn . . . ," Piotr repeated. "Yes, I've been zigzagging all over this half of the world."

"Well, you're here now. Here with your own people. You've made your flight to refuge!"

Ilya led him up First Street, touching his arm every now and then as though to reassure him. "East—there. The mountains." Piotr squinted at a faded, humped blur on the horizon. "There, now go up that way and you'll get to the downtown, the business district on Spring Street.

"See—look at that." Ilya pointed. Piotr glimpsed a jumble of oil wells apparently sprouting up right in the middle of a neighborhood. "A man named Doheny found oil out there, and the Americans have been digging up their front yards, even their living rooms, looking for the stuff. Splat in the middle of town!" Piotr took another astonished look at the cocky belt of derricks.

"They're a strange, unaccountable folk—these Americans," Ilya confided. "On the first of the year, thousands of them come out here to Pasadena and, what do you think? They have chariot races! Right on the street."

"Chariot races?" Piotr's head was starting to ache, and he was beginning to think that there was another reason for Ilya's chatter. *He's keep-*

ing something from me, some bad news, Piotr thought. A growing dread took hold of him as he followed the old man's vigorous steps.

"Chariot races—with horses. On a whim! Just like the gentry, they are. An unaccountable folk! But we haven't forgotten the old ways. We're getting settled—you'll see."

Ilya's free hand never stilled as he tried to describe the first waves of the Molokan migration breaking over the streets of Los Angeles. The fervent flow of *Pohod* had sluiced into a small section of the eighth ward just west of the Los Angeles River near the railway tracks. The Russians huddled between east First Street and Aliso Street and Alameda, wedged between the Mexicans of Olivera Street and the Japanese of Little Tokyo.

"At home, we're at war with them. Here, they're our neighbors! God is trying to tell us something, eh?" commented Ilya. "But we're making a place for ourselves—you'll see! Most of us rent these three-room frame houses. They have running water; some even have electricity. But it's hard all the same, hard for the women, hard for everyone."

They turned aside toward a clapboard house painted in two shades of soft gold, and they mounted a step that jutted out of a tangle of scruffy Bermuda grass. Then a dim and distorted, but recognizable bit of old Russia shut out the hot August afternoon. The front room of the house was fitted out with a brass bed, very foreign-looking with its knobs and loops of shiny metal, but it was smothered in the down bedding and embroidered slipcovers so dear to the heart of a Russian housewife. Odors of cabbage and corned beef and good Russian bread came from the kitchen. Through the narrow doorway, Piotr glimpsed a samovar set up on a redwood picnic table. Ilya's fresh-skinned wife appeared, dimples and wrinkles competing within the circle of her kerchief.

They treated him to a good meal and then handed him the letter from Gavril. They must have sensed the bad news in it. The old woman busied herself around the stove, and Ilya went out to the best room to leave him alone.

So Semyon was dead! Of course, he would die; after all, the old man was well past ninety. Piotr bent his head again to pick out the steady pace of Gavril's words. Cholera. An epidemic. There were other troubles, too. Gavril hinted at them vaguely. Political troubles.

   ... Best stay where you are. You will find good work

with Maxim Merlukov. Stay. We are praying. All is well with the rest of us.

Piotr could almost hear Gavril's calm voice, but he could find no assurance in the words. He folded the letter carefully with forboding. *What else?* he thought. *What else will I lose?* Ilya appeared again—diffident, not looking at him.

"Maxim Fersich Merlukov will be here in the morning to take you out to his farm. He has quite a set-up out there in Montebello. Is he family?"

Piotr nodded. "My mother's cousin, though I've never met him. They come from Delizan gubernia; our village is nearer Tiflis. But my mother has told me about him."

"Ah, they're the lucky ones! The rest of us are cut off from the land. We can't even afford to buy houses, much less farmland. But your cousin must have been rich."

"Where is his farm?"

"Not far, not far. A few *versts* across the river. Good land—if you can find enough water for it. They grow walnuts and lima beans."

"Walnuts and lima beans. That'll be new for me." Piotr drew an attempt at a smile, and the old man looked relieved.

"Yes. That's right. A whole new world for you! Walnuts and lima beans!" His eyes twinkled shrewdly, as though he were giving sage advice.

The next morning, Piotr left for Montebello in a wooden farm wagon. He sat next to a blond-bearded, taciturn man he had never seen before.

"Come see us again," Ilya urged from the porch steps. "Come on a Saturday, and we'll all go out to Santa Monica—to the beach. We'll take the trolley—the Big Red Car. That's the way we do it here!"

Piotr bowed his thanks.

"Don't let him work you too hard," the old man joked, and Piotr twisted his head to give him a departing grin. But Maxim Merlukov did not smile.

"The earth is calling me . . . ," the old people used to groan when they felt the number of their days dwindling. Old Semyon had never said that—his call came from elsewhere. But he was dead all the same.

Piotr shoved his weight into the handles of a McCormick harrow, watching the steel spikes rake through the pale clay, tearing up alfalfa by the roots. Its fragrance rose strong and sweet, but not strong enough to disguise the old, powerful scent of turned-up earth. *The earth will have its due*, Piotr thought.

He wrenched to a stop, pulling up the team suddenly. Semyon dead! "Dzedha," he murmured. And by the time he had heard anything of it, the old man had been weeks in his grave.

"Pete, Pete." A high, nasal voice began pecking at him. Piotr ignored it, keeping his eyes on the harrow and the speckled haunches of the horse in front of him. A collection of five flies jumped up and resettled on the sweating rump. He wanted to think about Semyon, wanted to take in what it meant that the old man was no longer walking the earth.

"Pete, wait up, *amigo. Despacio, por favor* . . . Hey, the boss wants us to move the pipe in the grove."

Piotr stopped in his tracks and shifted the thrust of his broad shoulders from the harrow into a shrug. He turned to confront a copper-colored face shaded by a straw cowboy hat. The young Mexican smiled ingenuously. *Eduardo Rodriquez is always smiling*, Piotr thought, annoyed. He pulled a rough sleeve across his face and looked beyond his companion toward the foothills of the San Gabriel Mountains.

Beyond the torn-up alfalfa field, ruler-straight rows of lima beans sketched green lines toward a dusty walnut grove in the east; and behind that he could see the blue, hazy outline of the mountains, far away and alien in color and stature. Low, blunt-looking, hammered down by time—these California mountains had none of the chiseled immensity of the Caucasus. The highest of them, the one the Americans called "Old Baldy," was only about 10,000 feet, little more than half the height of lofty Elburz. There was no trace of snow.

A booted figure in a peasant smock and peaked cap appeared and began hacking at the earth with a hoe as though inflicting pain on it. Maxim Merlukov—the boss. *And Maxim with his familiar clothing and blond beard*, Piotr thought, *is more alien than anything else in this strange landscape!*

"*Alcánzame, amigo.* You'll have to open the valve while I set the line." Eduardo kept at it with both hands and his mouth. "He's looking; we'll have to be quick about it." Piotr narrowed his eyes and searched his memory for the few scraps of English that he and Eddie used to communicate.

"Water?" he asked, knowing full well what Eduardo meant. Even when the words were strange, the young Mexican's gestures left little room for doubt.

"*Si!* Yes! Water!" Eddie beamed and nodded encouragingly and then darted a concerned glance back at Maxim.

Piotr sighed. By now he was at the end of a row, so he turned the horse and tethered it to a stake without unharnessing the equipment. If he had learned anything in the past weeks, it was that Maxim hated delays. Intent on the inexorable swing of his hoe, he didn't even glance at them as they passed by.

The shade of the walnut trees fell on them with a soothing coolness. Stray patches of alfalfa lay like little carpets between the trees. Piotr and Eduardo Rodriquez set the irrigation lines with the quiet camaraderie that had grown between them.

"Dinner, huh?" Eddie pointed to the low, green bungalow at the edge of a pale, wheel-rutted dirt road. "It's time."

"Sure," said Piotr.

"You sound just like an American," Eddie approved, flashing his perfect, white teeth under a pencil-thin mustache. Piotr hid his irritation behind a halfhearted grin. He knew why Eddie was so helpful, why he was constantly beaming approval, why he took on the hardest tasks whenever he could. Eduardo Rodriquez felt sorry for him.

Maxim Fersich Merlukov was Galina Antonovna's second cousin. He had a broad, flat build and big, sinewy hands. His straight, straw-colored hair was cut in a fringe across his forehead, like a Ukrainian, and a broomlike mustache and beard concealed the lower part of his face. Very little expression stirred in the remaining rectangle of skin. Maxim had the shuttered eyes and stinting gestures of the instinctively secretive person.

His wife, Lukeria, Galina had said, was accounted one of the great beauties among the Delizan Molokans. *But that,* Piotr thought, *must have been long ago.* Before Maxim and America had taken those regular, balanced features and pressed them into sculptured bitterness. When Piotr had looked for the first time at the renowned Lukeria, he saw the discontent and disillusionment on her face before he noticed the straight, perfect nose and large, black-lashed eyes.

She ignored him for the most part now, but those first few days she had had a thing or two to say. "California? Life is a struggle anywhere. But here." She paused, her bold gray eyes under the arched brows boring into him, but not seeing him. "Look around you. Not a soul. No village. Nothing but fields. Little bean plants gasping for life in the middle of a desert! And those pathetic walnut trees! Oh, he'll make money off of it, he'll make money," she muttered.

Piotr noticed that she never referred to Maxim by name. It was easy to see that "he" was the source of all her misery. It was Maxim who had pried her away from her life of queening it in a sizable Transcaucasian village and caged her in a peeling bungalow on a bean field in Montebello. She never openly confronted him, but she showed her resentment in a thousand small ways. The house was stifling in them.

Piotr and Eddie washed up outside while Lukeria mechanically set out roasted meat, cabbage, and black bread for their midday meal. The bread was literally black. Lukeria had insisted that Maxim build her a traditional Russian-style outdoor oven at the side of the house. To her fury, he used rough adobe. It would never bake properly, she insisted, and made sure that she was right. The bread always came out charcoal black on the bottom.

"*Sozhshoni opyats!* Burnt again!" she would mutter in grim satisfaction as she lurched away from the opening with a lump of scorched dough at the end of her shovel. This ritual would always make Piotr's stomach tighten. But he ate the bread. The work was unending, and he was always hungry. He was hungry now as he and Eduardo approached the house, slowing their steps as the wolf slows his gait when he leaves the shelter of the forest.

They washed in the barrel by the porch. Piotr went inside to fill his plate from the bread and cheese and meat left out on the table. Lukeria was watching with that familiar expression that made him feel awkward and clumsy about taking food. He went out again to sit on the stoop with Eduardo, leaving Maxim and Lukeria to their domestic happiness. It was her habit to leave Eduardo's lunch on a tin plate out on the porch. She didn't want him touching her things.

A lethargic fly droned past, and Piotr's eyes followed it into the dim kitchen where he glimpsed Lukeria's bent head, her cheeks slack with dull, unexpressed resentment. Maxim was chewing with characteristic inexorable indifference, the skin on his temples moving in and out like the throat of a frog. Lukeria arched her brows and looked at him with stupefied wonder. *How can you be such an animal,* said the curl of her lip. Fortunately, he never looked up.

208

Piotr shrugged and looked at his companion. Eduardo treated both of them with exaggerated respect. *I wonder what he really thinks?* Piotr asked himself. The young Mexican balanced his tin plate between his knees—it had a bend in it that made it especially suited for this—and wolfed his supper with a carefree air, smiling at Piotr all the while. Then he rolled the soft part of the bread into pellets and ate these more slowly. He tossed the last of them toward the chickens in the yard. One sleek young hen came over to give it a cursory glance, then strutted off, unimpressed. For some reason, this delighted Eduardo, and he chuckled. Suddenly, he sighed, looked around as though at a loss, and then sprang up energetically.

"Come on, Pete, let's go get some tortillas!"

Piotr grinned. Tortillas he understood.

They skirted the bean fields and crossed the road to the shack where the Rodriquez family lived. The shack was jumping with excitement. Children were everywhere, tooting on tin horns or flaunting bright paper party fans in red, magenta, turquoise, and yellow. Esperanza Rodriquez smiled over her brood benevolently—no cause for worry! Today was Saturday, and on Saturdays there was plenty! The benevolence intensified as she spied the two young men.

"*Ven, ven! Acompáñanos!*" she welcomed, folding her hands over the white apron hitched high over her protruding stomach.

Twelve-year-old Lupe ran over to meet them, her tightly braided pigtails pulling a slant into her black eyes. The ribbons on her swinging plaits were as pink and fresh as the color that touched her cheeks and lips.

"Try this," she said, offering a brown bottle. Piotr took a cautious sip and then snorted as the bubbling liquid frothed up his nose. She laughed delightedly.

"Root beer!" she explained.

Esperanza handed around warm tortillas, and the children rolled them up and bit into them greedily, suddenly quiet. Things were sparse on Fridays, but on Saturday Carlos Rodriquez came home at noon with his week's pay and passed out pennies to the children. They wasted no time in squandering them on candy and cheap toys. Later in the evening, Eddie would come home to contribute his share and then go to town to meet his friends.

It wasn't often that he showed up at midday, so the children had something extra to celebrate—and celebrate they did, with a noise and energy that astounded Piotr. "*Cállate! Cállate!*" yelled Esperanza. But they blew louder on their tin tooters and grinned at her. And she grinned back, shaking her head.

"*Pobrecitos,*" she said good-naturedly. "*Qué les pasarán?*"

Even the sudden lull that came when Maxim appeared didn't last for long. One young ragged boy, the loudest tooter of them all, looked up curiously. Esperanza wiped her hands on her apron as though she were going to do something—she didn't know what—and Eddie stood gracefully. "We're finished," he told Piotr casually. He slapped his hands on his trousers, and the warmth of his smile refused to break on the ice in Maxim's glare. Piotr jumped up awkwardly, remembering the still-hitched team.

"You can finish the alfalfa field before dark," Maxim told Piotr coldly. "The horses have been standing in harness—you may as well make use of them before the day is over." His eyes flinched at the jumble of bodies and toys and junk in the Rodriquez yard. He turned to Eddie. "You go and muck out the barn. Quick." Eddie beamed as though he had just been waiting to hear that. He gave a jaunty tweak to the brim of his straw hat and set off across the fields. "*Chacal!*" Eduardo pronounced courteously, and Maxim gave him a quick sharp glance.

Five-year-old Carlos, his huge brown eyes taking in every nuance, suddenly sprang forward, right up to Maxim Fersich and blew an earsplitting blast on his tin horn. His impish grin faded when he saw that the Russian was not at all impressed but stood still as a statue. Piotr stifled a laugh and tried to look serious as he and Maxim strode away.

"Tooters and licorice and trash today, and by Friday they'll be begging for corn meal." Maxim was sincerely appalled. "It's shameful. They're just dragging themselves into the dirt . . ." *It's not our way.* He didn't say it, but Piotr heard it all the same.

Lukeria was pulling bunches of green Thompson grapes off of the vine that draped over the front porch as Piotr and Maxim walked up. Her movements were quick and agitated, and she kept looking at them to see when they would be within earshot. "Look," she said, pointing. Coming up the road were two Molokans. Piotr strained his eyes toward them. One was a beardless young man with curly blond hair; the other was a big-boned, middle-aged man with the sun gleaming on his bald head. Their attire and posture and the way they strode along the dusty road flanked by flat fields seemed so familiar, so Russian, that Piotr was filled with an odd excitement. *They could be any peasants in Russia, walking across the steppe to their native village,* he thought.

Eduardo stood a little to the side with a questioning look on his face. Maxim grimaced and pointed silently and firmly at the barn while his wife pursed her lips and gave each young man in turn a knowing glance. Eddie shrugged and disappeared into the barn, gently murmuring what Piotr strongly suspected were Spanish maledictions.

"Go finish harrowing," Maxim told Piotr. "You can come in when you're finished." Piotr drew his head back in surprise. In any other family, guests were cause to throw down all work and keep company with the visitors—unless it was the middle of harvest. The two men were closer now, and Piotr could see that the younger had a rather soft, good-natured face. He looked as though he'd be good to talk to. Piotr hesitated, but too much depended upon his work with Maxim. He felt suddenly ashamed of his eagerness. He lowered his eyes and went off to finish tearing out the alfalfa.

When he came back at dusk, the silence in the kitchen told him that the visitors were gone. There was no sign of the evening meal, so he went out to the barn to find Eduardo.

Eddie didn't smile. Instead, his face mirrored the glum look Piotr gave him. He shrugged expressively, then said something in English which Piotr didn't understand. But his tone was sympathetic, and his eyes flashed with derision as he nodded toward the house.

Suddenly, his face took on a serious look. He pulled the red bandana from around his neck and tied it around his head, like a peasant woman's, while Piotr watched in bewilderment. Eddie minced up to the pitchfork, took up a forkful of hay from a pile of bales, and lurched away. "*Sozhshoni opyats!*" he muttered in a strained falsetto, wriggling his eyebrows. The likeness was unmistakable, and Piotr felt the whole incomprehensible harshness of the day exploding away from him on gales of laughter. Eddie threw the straw into the air and waved the bandana in front of his face. He fell backwards onto the hay while Piotr laughed so hard his sides ached, and he had to sit down.

After a while, they quieted down, occasionally looking at each other with satisfied chuckles. When Eddie wriggled his eyebrows again and said, "*Sozhshoni opyats!*" they were off again in choking gasps of laughter.

After that Eddie would break the stern drudgery of many a day simply by moving his eyebrows and muttering, "*Sozhshoni opyats!*"

Whatever news the two Molokans had brought must have been good. Lukeria was more animated than Piotr had ever seen her, and even Maxim seemed more human. *I won't ask,* he told himself, still smarting under their earlier rudeness. He put on a cool, nonchalant air, which neither of them noticed and which quickly evaporated when Lukeria told him the news. The Molokans of Los Angeles would be holding their first meeting of all the pilgrims on September 3—a *sobraniya,* she said, such as had never been seen since the first days of exile!

During their first months in California, the Molokans had been gathering in homes, usually grouping together based on their old villages. But they had no central gathering place. A Methodist minister, Rev. Dana Bartlett, had tried to aid the colorfully dressed folk who thronged the eighth ward in settling into their new life. He had offered use of his church auditorium, but the Molokan elders had strenuously objected. The hall was furnished with seats in rows from front to back.

"A foreign, ungodly arrangement," Maxim contributed. "*Stidna!*"

"The Americans have no fear that some members will be shown preference over others, though the apostle forbids it," Lukeria added, pursing her lips.

Piotr looked at her strangely, remembering her treatment of Eduardo—and himself, for that matter. Lukeria seemed a poor thing to him just then, pulling the tattered shreds of her lost life around her.

Rev. Bartlett, unperturbed and even admiring, turned his unquenchable helpfulness to the task of finding a more flexible facility. "Better to be a good Molokan than a poor Methodist," he said and managed to arrange use of the Stimson-Lafayette school building for the new Angelinos.

Piotr welcomed the news with his whole soul. Hope sprang up in him and scrubbed away the dead crust of loneliness formed in long days of isolated labor. He decided to walk to Los Angeles the evening before the *sobraniya* and stay with Ilya Valoff. Then he could feast his eyes on the souls gathered to the place of refuge.

On Saturday Piotr walked the nine *versts* from Merlukov's to Ilya Valoff's. It was a warm, sultry evening, and the streets were full of people. A crowd of Mexican youths strolled by, turning to laugh at his peasant breeches and *kosovorotka.* The ice-cream man, dressed in a white suit and carrying a tall bucket on his head, threw Piotr a searching glance out of black Indian eyes. A blue-suited policeman swerved his bicycle across the trolley tracks and stopped to buy an ice. A Chinese vegetable seller, pulling his almost empty hand-drawn cart, hurried by head down so that his shiny black hair was all Piotr could see of him.

Piotr crossed over to Vignes Street, observing the changes in the eighth ward where the Russians had fashioned a new life for themselves. Jews, Japanese, and Mexicans had watched with open or covert astonishment as booted, bearded men and kerchiefed women in bright peasant garb set about transforming the new community. Housewives had grimly surveyed small, dried-up front yards choked with dandelions. They hung up embroidered curtains to shut out the too-bright light and the city noise. "The place of refuge!" proclaimed dogged old men with undulled vision as they sat on porch stoops and looked into the distance at mountains devoid of snow or as they walked along a river destitute of water. God would be with them! "His ways are not our ways. Their ways are not our ways!" *"Pust khuzhe, da nasha!"* "Let it be worse, but let it be ours!"

Young men shouldered burdens in the lumber and railway yards. "It's not Russia!" they'd say, shaking their heads and looking at each other with bewildered eyes. Matrons built their old-style, outdoor ovens and fought the truant officers to keep their daughters at home to help with the young ones, the endless tubs of laundry, and the arduous task of scraping meals together for exhausted men. And the young girls—well, there just weren't enough of them.

The few who could afford to buy houses built traditional *banyas* in their backyards. The Molokans could steam away the grime of the city and swat at their work-hardened bodies with eucalyptus switches. Piotr smiled as he noticed the stucco walls of California bungalows sprouting clumsy, clay-covered ovens, as much like the old country as the limitations of adobe brick and the Los Angeles fire marshall would allow.

The welcoming sound of his native tongue chattered out at him as he strolled up the sidewalk toward Ilya's house. The Valoff kitchen was crowded with women in aprons and kerchiefs preparing special foods for the *sobraniya*. Names of families and villages wafted around with the cooking odors. Tikhonov, Kobzeff, Samarin. . .Vorontsovka, Golovinovka, Chinari . . . Listening, Piotr found it hard to piece together a single sensible sentence. The whole purpose of the women's talk was to seek out connections, some thread attached to both the old life and the new. And when the familiar found its match, Piotr noted, joy, reassurance, even relief would murmur through the busy women like the breath of a hot wind.

"Denisov? No, not from Malaya Tiukma—no, no, Ardahan. They're from Ardahan."

"Ardahan! We knew a family from Ardahan . . ."

"Volkoff? Who knows? There are so many Volkoffs. Nikolai Ivanovich? Never heard of him . . ."

The crisp old voice grew peevish, but a younger one cut in. "Nikolai! My father's sister-in-law's nephew! It has to be!" A pretty young matron turned beet-red so that a smudge of flour stood out on her cheek like face powder. "A miracle. I can't believe it!" she said, almost fainting with excitement. "Of course, I've never met him—but I've heard of him all my life. Here, take this . . ." She fervently pressed an oven-fresh *piroshka* into Piotr's hand, as though she needed to reward someone for the good news.

He took it with a grin, laughingly making a lavish display of eating it in front of the pleased women. Ilya's wife, Yelena, came in from the outdoor oven, smiling over an arm load of beautiful golden loaves. "Piotr Gavrilovich!" she welcomed him. "Go out to Ilya—he's been hoping you'd come early."

He found Ilya on the porch polishing the family samovar.

"Quite a party—listen to them!" he exclaimed, his smile curling into his fluffy whiskers. "Chattering away like birds, they are."

"It will be a big day for them, for all of us," Piotr commented.

"Big? Ah, not so big as it will be. More are coming every week. Our back room looks like—what do the Americans call it? A flophouse! Not an inch of space to put your foot down, what with all the sleeping pallets. A flophouse!" Ilya repeated, pleased with the word.

Piotr laughed. "That's what I hear. You meet every train and bring all the stray Russians home—as you did for me, God be praised."

Ilya shook his head. "What else can I do? I can tell you, my own first days in this city were bleak. A place of refuge, I thought—no work, no land to live from, no village—how can we survive here? And my Yelena, she just looked at me like a stunned animal . . . Ah yes, we suffered in those days."

Piotr didn't reply, but watched a pale scatter of light shifting in the lacy foliage of the pepper tree in the front yard.

"We're still suffering." A voice broke into Piotr's musings. A young Molokan with a stocky build and the neck and shoulders of an ox came out to join them. Sighing, he sat heavily on the stoop, looking first at Ilya, then more closely at Piotr.

"Look," he began, searching the balmy evening air with brooding eyes, "in Russia this time of year, the air would be like crystal with the hoarfrost beginning to form—ah! Remember what the first days of hoarfrost were like? I'll never forget it—the sun coming bright in the morning, scattering diamonds over everything—because of the frost . . ."

They were all silent.

"Winter was our respite then," the young man continued. "We bent our backs from dawn 'til dusk at harvest. But as soon as the snows came, we were nomads—carters carrying goods from town to village with a team and a sledge. It was a free life for us! Here there's nothing but work—and what work! They drive us like animals . . ."

Ilya's eyes lit up with reminiscence. "We were like Gypsies, we were! We didn't carry goods, but for us winter was the time for visiting friends and relatives. In bad weather, we'd repair plows, harness, household stuff. And the women, they'd spin all winter—until it was a good day for piling into the sledge. Then off we'd go!"

"I remember it," Piotr said quietly. "It was like that for us . . ."

The newcomer, Gerassim, looked down at his knees and his face darkened. His expression grew more and more morose as Ilya continued talking about the old ways in his cheery, gentle manner.

"There is no respite here," Gerassim interrupted, his voice hoarse with stored-up grief. "They drive us, they drive us . . . See this?" He began stripping off his shirt, looking from Piotr to Ilya. The flesh on both of his powerful shoulders was deeply gouged; the crisscrossing of old white scars, puffy red flesh, and fresh scabs was so pronounced that his body looked deformed. Piotr winced and looked away.

"You see how they use us. But there's no other work. It's the lumber yards or starve. The boss there—how he gloated when he saw me! 'There's a strong one,' he says to himself. 'He'll carry more than quota.' And I do! I do carry it because I want to survive. And at the end of the day when he nods to me, I smile even though I hate that nod, hate his shiny, slicked-down hair, and the greasy sideburns that look like something unclean is oozing from his ear. He doesn't give a tinker's cuss what becomes of me or my body as long as he meets his quota. But I smile at him, and I feel ashamed . . ."

Ilya was shaking his head. "No, no, brother, don't let hatred eat at your soul. Suffer a day, live an age. Calm down! Yelena will make you some more of those pads for your shoulder. We'll wad you up so's you won't feel a thing."

Gerassim hitched his raw, ugly shoulder and pulled his shirt around him as though suddenly embarrassed.

"There's no solace here. A man can't even find a wife to comfort him. There are so few girls, and where would I take a bride? My father's house? Why it's halfway across the world! If I could, I'd go back to Russia."

"Don't sin," Ilya said sternly. "God stirred up the tumult that sent us here—here to refuge. The Lord of Heaven doesn't play so with human hearts. It's not His way. You just wait. That's your job. Wait and endure."

Gerassim bent his head back and let his dark angry eyes slide away under their thick lids. "Refuge," he muttered bitterly. "There's as much refuge here as there is water in the Los Angeles River."

The vacant lot behind the Stimson-Layfayette building was studded with a gleaming line of samovars in brass and copper and base metal. Piotr's heart was leaping within him, and he found it hard to concentrate as he hungrily eyed the men and women and children beginning to fill the yard outside the hall. Angelinos in their Sunday best slowed their gaits and stared curiously at these new townsfolk. *No wonder they're looking*, Piotr thought.

The Americans were tastefully turned out in tailored summer suits; their wives and daughters wore crisply starched dresses or skirts and waists in white and navy or soft pastels. Their eyes under their fashionably tilted hats widened with astonishment as they took in the exotic assortment of Russian peasants. The Molokan men were resplendent in long *kosovorotkas* worn over their trousers and girded like smocks. Some wore bloomerlike peasant breeches tucked into high boots. Beards, long and short, gray, white, blond, dark and auburn, clung to their shirts and tangled as the men grasped each other by the shoulders and kissed emphatically. The women's peasant skirts belled out from their waists in vivid shades of red and blue and green, trimmed with yellow or blue braid. Their full-sleeved blouses were green or purple or buttercup yellow. Black and red embroidery or white lace decorated the crisp kerchiefs that bound their long plaits of hair.

Piotr searched the crowd, looking for a familiar face—someone from home, from his village, or a family resemblance. Maxim and his handsome wife appeared; Lukeria's green and yellow printed skirt was stiff with starch, and she held her head with its exquisite lace kerchief proudly. Piotr looked away and went into the hall.

As the service began, the outer noise and confusion subsided. But Piotr's inner confusion and agitation increased. He scanned the group of "speakers" in front of him; Ilya and Gerassim were the only ones he recognized. His eyes darted to the back rows. No one. Piotr's gaze scaled the walls. Then he closed his eyes. *We're all looking,* he thought, *craving something familiar. But what are we? A bunch of strangers with crisscrossing glances hemmed in by four walls in a foreign land.*

A numbing sense of isolation clamped down on him as the elder came to the front and addressed the group. The man's sparse beard was still threaded with traces of brown. Piotr's throat tightened; it seemed all wrong! What was it? Semyon! In his twenty-one years, Piotr had never attended a Molokan service without the familiar sight of his great-grandfather striding to the front and confronting his people with an open Bible in his sinewy hands. *That was it,* he acknowledged. *Semyon's life is severed from the earth, and this other is standing in his place.* Surprised at his own detachment, Piotr watched the usurper begin the readings. *I am like a stranger,* he mused. *Maybe Semyon was my link to this people . . . and Semyon is gone. But there are other links,* he reminded himself quickly—*my family, my people.*

The Molokans started singing. Disparate, halting, then gaining strength, the melody took on the strong, hammer-stroke rhythm of an old Russian work song. Each stroke had its own power of thought and harmony. Grief. Redemption. Consolation. Word and note struck at the foreignness and the fear and the bewilderment. And the music welded them together. They were one, Piotr marveled—a malleable lump of Russia lodged in the strangers' land. With the clear objectivity of an outsider, he watched Ilya's affability transform to joy, Gerassim's bitterness melt into a cleaner sorrow, Lukeria's discontent change to yearning. *One,* he mused, still feeling himself separate.

Later, while the tables were being set up for the meal, he joined a group of Molokans clustered around a youngish man dressed in a dark suit and holding up an American newspaper.

"News from home," he said, excitedly shuffling through the pages. "I've been keeping track for weeks. Amazing how much there is on Russia in the *Los Angeles Times!* Listen. Count Witte is here! In Portsmouth, New Hampshire. He's meeting with the American Tsar, Teddy Roosevelt, to talk about a treaty with the Japanese."

Piotr pressed forward. So the war he had tried to escape had ended—and ended here, of all places!

"And here—back in August." Paper crackled in the translator's eager fingers. "Listen to this. 'If the Bouligan scheme is adopted, Russia will enter upon a period of catastrophe compared to which those previous experiences and ordinary revolutions of the 19th century will be child's play . . . ' That's Count Ignatieff. Catastrophe, he's saying. Just like the Prophet warned. Klubniken knew what he was talking about. And here, wait . . ." The assured, ebullient voice stumbled a bit and went on more slowly. "A horrible massacre in the Tiflis town hall—Cossacks killing peaceful demonstrators. They expect it will set off more uprisings." The Molokan cleared his throat. "And this—epidemics of cholera and smallpox reported in the Caucasus . . ." He peered over the edge of the paper as he folded it. His audience fell silent. Piotr walked off. *Semyon*, he thought. *And who else?*

He passed a tangle of overgrown oleanders sprinkled with pink and white blossoms. This meeting had not been what he had expected. *You cannot graft on what's been cut off*, he thought. Molokan traditions and customs had the power to touch his heart, but could not strike at that higher allegiance forged in a mountain chasm in Khevsuretia. *It's You I follow, You only*, he prayed. *But what's it for? The drudgery, the aching loneliness, the exile. Why?*

When the call came for mealtime, he went back to the hall with reluctant steps. He sat with Gerassim and a fair-haired young man whose father was a Molokan butcher. Gerassim made it evident that he considered both of his companions more fortunate than himself since they worked at what he called "easy jobs." The other young man, Matvei Ilyich, was preoccupied with the few single girls sitting with their families on the other side of the elders' table.

Piotr forced himself to smile and listen, but he was all stirred up inside. Memories—from Russia—from the past several months—were twisting around inside of him. Semyon—moonlight awakened every silvered tuft of that sumptuous beard, and his dark steadfast eyes bored into Piotr. What was in his mind as he watched his great-grandson rattling away on Sirakan's cart? The image faded. *I never thought it would be forever*, Piotr grimaced, then tried to smile away the affronted look on Gerassim's face. What had he said? *Whatever it was, I didn't respond the right way . . . And girls, yes, Matvei—the girls are pretty, but where is there a woman like Nina Abajarian?*

Suddenly, an elder stood at the front table and said something that fused Piotr's anxiety and isolation into new purpose. The Molokans of Los Angeles, in spite of their hardship and poverty, had been led by God's Holy Spirit to collect money to bring one hundred people from Russia to

218

refuge! Piotr had no idea who these fortunate pilgrims would be, but he was seeing Galina with Dausha pulling on the fringe of her shawl and Nadya, her skirt billowing in the sea wind, and Gavril, tentative and watchful, hovering over his loved ones. Resolve hardened in Piotr. *I'll do it!* he vowed. *I'll pour myself out to earn enough to bring them here.*

In spite of his sense of distance, Piotr began coming to the Molokan meeting every Sunday. New families arrived every week, and every week the Molokans gathered in front of the school auditorium and the names of newcomers rose like incense. Tolmacheffs from Vorontsovka, Bogdanoffs from Delizan—yes, six of them, a man and wife and two children with their grandmother. The sixth, oh yes, a lovely young girl. Blonde as the palest wheat. Piotr went in and stood in the singers' section. Tolmacheff, Bogdanoff—there was no one for him. But someday, he vowed, he would be one of those eager, joyful ones reuniting with family at the door.

After the service, Maxim came up and grasped his sleeve. "Listen," he muttered, looking around furtively, "it's hot. Almost October, but it's hot. The seedlings will burn in the rows unless you get out there and set the lines. You'll have to go." His eyes traveled over to where Lukeria was standing, looking at them from under her bold, black eyebrows. "Go. You'll have time before it turns into a scorcher." He turned away before Piotr had a chance to respond.

Piotr shrugged. So much for a good Russian meal! As he turned away from the excited crowd, he caught a brief sight of the newcomers. The young matron, plump and glossy, almost overwhelmed her thin husband in an effusive, brilliant display of skirts. Next to them was a frail old woman, standing with her feet spread wide apart, obviously for balance, although as it was, she tottered precariously with the jostling all around her. But that didn't keep a childishly joyous smile from sending ripples of wrinkles colliding with the edge of her tightly tied kerchief. A young girl—yes, the long, long braid was the color of pale wheat—turned to steady her, but she wasn't too steady herself. She swayed slightly on black, shiny, pointed shoes that peeked out from under a printed cotton skirt. A sudden movement of the crowd prevented any glimpse of her face.

Feeling cheated and somehow vulnerable, Piotr turned away and began walking back toward Montebello. The now-familiar blue line of the San Gabriel Mountains looked bludgeoned by the heat. Slick, wet mirages haunted the strip of paved road all the way down Sixth Street.

"A dry and thirsty land, where there is no water . . ." The words ghosted up with the mirages and the heat haze wafting up from the street.

He was steaming with sweat and ravenously hungry by the time he reached the farm, but he irrigated the rows and then helped himself to some grapes, stale bread, and warm milk. The weather astounded and appalled him. *But*, he reminded himself, *this climate will help me buy my own share of happiness*. In frostless California the lima beans could be planted and harvested every few months. The more harvests, the closer he could come to his goal of bringing the Voloshins to America.

The Merlukovs were late in coming from church; Piotr reckoned that they must have gone visiting with the Molokans in the city. When he heard the wagon draw up, he retreated to his room and pretended to be asleep. A hot wind began blowing in from the Mojave Desert, pelting the little bungalow with leaves and debris. The night filled up with odd knockings and moanings and the far-off baying of a dog.

Piotr jolted out of sleep suddenly, grabbing at the fleeing remnants of a dream. It was Semyon; Semyon had been there. In his dream, the old man was lying on top of the stove, shuddering under the duress of sharp, repeated pain. Every filament in the snowy tangle of his beard burned white-hot. A barefoot girl came up and gently tucked a quilt up to his chin. This seemed to quiet him, and he closed his eyes briefly; then they flew open, and Semyon looked around with that familiar fierce glance. The beautiful dark eyes continued to kindle and gleam as he fixed them on something beyond the girl standing by his side, something afar off. Then the delicate eyelids curtained the flame, and the old man subsided under the quilt. The girl turned toward the door, and Piotr saw that she had a bundled-up baby cradled in one arm. As she put her hand out, he heard himself calling, "No, no, don't open it . . . Don't let it happen . . ." But she opened the door, and the room was immediately filled with a roaring tumult. The wind snatched away her white kerchief and sent bits of thatch and debris flying through the room. But old Semyon lay still as a statue on the stove. Not a hair of the magnificent beard stirred.

During the next week, his plans for the Voloshins were seldom out of his mind as he plowed up Maxim's fields with new purpose. A growing unease gnawed at him as he remembered his family, but at other times his soul spiraled upwards, alien in a way that was not hurtful but free and whole.

This sense of freedom and wholeness was shattered that Sunday. As he idly scanned the kerchiefed heads in the women's section, his eyes came to rest on one bent, earnest face. The girl raised her head, and her profoundly blue eyes looked and looked, gathering in every loss and every triumph and every day of labor and sorrow that had marked the time between them. Fenya Vassileyvna Kostrikin! He was stunned. He pulled his gaze away abruptly. A shade of unbidden, unexpected responsibility fell athwart his plans, but at the same time he longed to look into those eyes and tell her, without stinting, the truth about everything that had happened to him.

XVII

The Mountains
of Bether

Fenya could see that all the boyhood had been leached out of Piotr's face. The strength of the broad, beautiful bones was laid bare to catch at the light and to fortify against the onslaught of expression when he caught sight of her. What mystifying things had happened to him? He was both strange to her and, at the same time, a more intense version of what he had been. The play of dark and light in his eyes reminded her more than ever of old Semyon.

When he came up to her, Fenya didn't wait for him to ask, but began telling him everything she knew about his family and his native village. She talked as she had never talked before, piecing together a vision of the Voloshin home, Semyon's last days, Andrei and Natasha's wedding. She had never been much of a talker, but something in his face pricked at her heart so that she cast about for details to wad her description and tuck around him like a quilt. *Cover it, cover it,* she thought in pity, seeing the look on his face. His eyes never left hers, but she knew he wasn't seeing her but his loved ones—and she didn't care. She wanted him to see them and to find comfort.

"Semyon Efimovich—you know how he is." The words flowed from her. "He said the prayers for Andrei with his bent old hands stretched out over your cousin's head and all the light in the house quivering over his beard."

Fenya's own thoughts about her sister's wedding, held close to herself in silence all these months, came pouring out. They began walking, past bushes bristling with long spear-tipped leaves and studded with roselike flowers.

"You remember how he prayed," she said, watching Piotr. "Well, he prayed for Andrei and Natasha, and it was as if bands of steel were being hammered out to hold them fast together. It was as though nothing could break those bonds . . ."

She told him about the incident with the young Georgians after the wedding feast and saw him wince and look away. "Never on a single day have I seen such love and such hate," she told him. She picked at a rose-hued flower and began twisting it in her hands.

"Hate—that's it," he replied. "There's a great store of hatred building up in Russia, and I fear for our families—I fear for them. Here, don't touch that; it's poison." He gently took the flower out of her hand and threw it on the ground.

When the meal was over, Fenya noticed Ivan in lively conversation with a pleasant-looking young man in fine leather boots. She saw no sign of Piotr. Aksinia took her by the arm and led her toward the two men. "A new acquaintance," she said, smiling. The young Molokan bowed his curly head toward Fenya. "Matvei Ilyich Kalpakoff," Aksinia pronounced. The youth's attractive, blunt features crinkled in a grin, and Fenya gave him her searching gaze before her eyes wandered to where she could see Piotr crowding into an assembly of intent men.

A Molokan in a dark European-style jacket was reading from a sheaf of newspapers. She strained to catch his words, but his back was toward her; her eyes flitted to Piotr's tense face, and she edged a little closer to the group—and to Matvei whose greenish eyes twinkled with pleasure. She could hear now—just barely.

"Baku is burning . . ." She saw Piotr's lips moving to echo the words. "The city is deemed unsafe . . . fighting between Tartars and Armenians at Bibiebat and fires in Sabunto and Nomani oil works . . . disturbances . . . the Viceroy of the Caucasus has dispatched troops from Tiflis, but they are not enough . . ."

Baku burning. Something flickered over Piotr's face as though the charcoal shadows of those oil-fed flames were blotting out the brightness of the California school yard. The crinkle of folding newspaper became the crackle of red destruction in Piotr's eyes. Fenya looked away.

"I'm just telling your uncle here about the produce market in Los Angeles . . . ," a good-natured voice sounded at her elbow. Matvei. What was he saying? "So many farms—not at all far from the city. Anyone with a wagon and a team can cart fruit and vegetables to Los

Angeles and sell them. Like the Chinese—only on a bigger scale . . ."
Fenya absently nodded encouragement. Fruit, vegetables—it all
sounded so commonplace, so practical. *Matvei's helpful, down-to-earth
voice is soothing, pleasant,* Fenya thought. Her eyes drifted off to Piotr's
face again. His expression made her turn and lean anxiously toward the
dark-suited speaker.

"'In other parts of the Caucasus, bands of peasants have organized
against the nobles and are invading their domains and seizing all the
farms . . . '" The self-appointed herald paused significantly.
"Catastrophe—such as Russia has never seen. The blood is flowing.
Praise be that we're here and not there . . ." Fenya was still looking at
Piotr, her mind refusing that last comment. *No,* she told herself. *He's
there, not here. Leave it, Piotr,* she chided him inwardly. *Leave it.*

"Yes, that's what I'm told. A grocery store for Molokans," Matvei
was saying. "Meat slaughtered according to Molokan ways, good black
bread. They'll need some produce. It's a good opportunity for the right
person."

Fenya saw that Ivan was listening with acute interest. He kept
reaching out to touch Aksinia's arm or skirt in absorbed excitement.
"Listen to this!" said his whole manner while Aksinia's sparkling glance
wandered merrily over the gathering. Ivan tried to pin her down with
a quick, sharp look every now and then, but she was overflowing with
joy and couldn't restrain her restless eyes. She did, Fenya noticed, manage to focus a little when she heard her husband invite the talkative
Matvei for tea. Fenya gave a last look at Piotr, still standing with the
knot of men in the yard. For the first time, she felt herself a servant. She
had no home, no right to catch Piotr Gavrilovich by the arm and bring
him in to tea.

They collected Bunya and the babies and strolled back to Vignes
Street. Matvei dropped back to walk beside Fenya, pointing out the
unique trees lining some of the streets. Jacaranda—a smoky profusion
of lilac blooms roiling around a silver-gray trunk; crape myrtle—dusty
pink flowers held on a slender stemlike bole, like a lady's bouquet in a
holder. And palm trees, some tall with a feathery sweep of branches like
an exotic bird's plumage; others stumpy with stiff, fanlike leaves.

Aksinia set out the samovar and some rich dark tea from Sochi
along with buttery tea cakes dusted with powdered sugar. "We're all at
odds," she apologized. "Everything's all which-a-ways, like a Gypsy
camp . . ."

224

"All which-a-ways," repeated Bunya, nodding in delight. "No stove to lie on, but we have a table to sit at and food to share, God be praised."

Matvei and Ivan continued their conversation. "Soon the local farmers will be growing much more," Matvei was saying. "All the area to the north—the San Fernando Valley, they call it—well, it's a grain-growing area now, dependent on seasonal rainfall. But now they've started this Owens River project. Clever people, these Americans! They're rerouting an entire river to bring water to the city and irrigation to the farmlands. The San Fernando Valley will be a garden of fruits and vegetables—all kinds—you know what the growing season is like here."

They were silent for a few minutes. Fenya knew they were thinking—as Molokans were apt to do—of the land, rich and yielding and just out of reach.

Aksinia sighed. "Few Russians could afford to buy farmland here. At home, we had over sixty *desiatiny*; here we can't buy even a dried-up sliver of lawn to put a house on."

"If I'd have stayed in Russia, I'd never have seen that!" Bunya said, pointing a trembling finger at the overhead light bulb.

Ivan ignored her. "The problem," he said, looking at Matvei, "is English. Almost all of the farmers are American. How will I be able to talk about prices and such—a man could be at a disadvantage. The world is full of dishonest folk."

"Oh, you'd have to learn English," Matvei said. "You will anyway. My father's in the same situation—he has to buy cattle to butcher for the Molokans. But I'm the one who takes care of that. I'm learning English at night. The classes are at Los Angeles High School. Just sign up and start learning!"

Ivan's brows flew up, then drew down suspiciously. "English, eh? Who're in this classroom?"

"Russians, mainly. They have a special night session for us."

Ivan was already shaking his head. "It's not for me," he intoned, gulping tea. "I'll have to find another way."

"Listen," Matvei threw a quick glance at Fenya and leaned forward excitedly, "why not send Fenya? That's what my father did; he didn't want to go, so he sent me. She'll learn and help you out!"

Ivan choked. "A girl? Why she barely knows Russian! She can't even read. English is a crack-jaw language—no woman could learn it. No, no—a woman's place is in the home. There's work and enough here with Aksinia and the little ones."

Aksinia shook her head. "It's not so bad, dearie. The babes are getting older. I can spare her for a class or two." Fenya noticed that Aksinia was quieter than usual, busy scrutinizing Matvei. She obviously liked what she saw.

Matvei shrugged. "It's survival here, Ivan. Sometimes you need to change if you want to get by in a new place."

"Change? God knows, I've changed enough," Ivan grumbled. "I'm not about to have women giving themselves airs with book learning and all."

Aksinia sighed gustily. "Ah, well. There's plenty of work at the lumber yards. No need to spend our good money on a wagon. We may need it for food. I've heard the yards don't pay so well."

Ivan gave her a bleak look. "My mother didn't give birth to me so's I could bend my back under a load of wood. You don't understand anything! Buying a wagon and team would take every ruble we have. What would become of us if things didn't work out? We need to take things carefully. Step by step—that's the way."

"Maybe it's time to step a little faster, dearie. We need to get settled," Aksinia insisted. "You've been wandering around the neighborhood for two weeks now, and still we don't know what we're doing. I've been afraid to unpack anything—or get anything to start a home with. We're sleeping on the floor; the babies are sleeping in orange crates. All we've got to show for our new life are two pairs of patent leather shoes."

"*Likirovnii tooflii!*" exclaimed Bunya in wonder.

"New American shoes already?" joked Matvei. "You haven't wasted so much time."

"We got them at the Broadway on Spring Street," Aksinia reported. "Ninety-eight cents. But I'll never do that again." The bright color deepened in her round face. "Why, I was like a carnival curiosity," she told Matvei. "Ivan and I would have given up and come home except that I promised Fenya the shoes. She's such a good girl. God knows, I'd never have gotten here without you, dearie." She smiled at Fenya. "But you're lucky you missed all the gawking and giggling I put up with that day! And that caved-in stick of a clerk pinching at my bare feet with some kind of metal vise! It was beyond anything!" Again, a red tide of indignation swept from her throat to her hairline. Aksinia shook her head. "From now on, I'll stick with my own kind."

"That's what I'm saying!" blustered Ivan. "God brought us to this land—but not to this folk. We're a separate people. Why should I put myself in the hands of their teachers? We have our own. English classes?

Not for me! I'll learn what little I need to barter with. But," he added, threading his long, nervous fingers into his sparse, sandy-colored beard, "I will buy us a wagon and team."

In spite of Ivan's decision, the sense of tentativeness continued in the Bogdanoff house. Aksinia padded her awareness with an exaggerated complaisance. Ivan drummed his fingers on the table and furrowed his brow and muttered numbers to himself—rubles and dollars and cents.

To Fenya, it seemed that Ivan's numbing apprehension, Aksinia's lethargy, her own uncertainty, and the complexity of the life outside were slim, strong strands that kept them incapable of action. *It's like those first days in Bremen*, Fenya remembered. *How quickly our excitement turned to fear when the ship's doctors put us in those wire cages to see if we were fit enough to emigrate!* They were days of anguish for Aksinia. Usually, it was the very young or the very old who were rejected and forced to return home—either with or without their families. They had seen some tragic partings through that web of wire! It was a miracle that Agafya had passed—a miracle that Fenya thanked God for daily. Life without the old woman's trembling serenity would be bleak indeed!

As it was, Agafya was the only one unaffected by her son's anxiety. The old bunya took a childlike delight in the electric lights and in the porcelain kitchen sink with its on-tap water. She was also entranced with the tiny water closet in the hall with its modern toilet. The irrepressible Nikolinka avidly shared this interest, but Valentina would scream in terror every time a great whooshing flush shook the little house. Fenya learned to anticipate bathroom use so that she could hold her hands over the little girl's ears.

Several times a day, Agafya would totter out to the front yard and stand under the jacaranda tree by the curb. Fenya saw that she was out there now, changing to a greenish color under the droop of lacy foliage. Agafya put her hand on the trunk and looked up and down the street with a keenness that owed no thanks to her fading vision.

"The place of refuge!" she would murmur. When she said this, her usually vague expression became so concentrated that it seemed to Fenya that some vital essence was coming up from the tree roots into the clinging little hand with its mushroom-like skin. Then she came back into the house.

"We'll abide," she announced with surprising loudness. Ivan lost track of his counting, and his face went slack with bafflement.

"Abide," Fenya repeated to herself, and she recalled Vassily's gift to Natasha—not so much the exquisitely carved wedding chest, but the words that went with it: "Abide in Me, and I in you." The thought was as clear and radiant as the honeyed sunlight streaming through the window. "As the branch cannot bear fruit of itself, unless it abides in the vine, neither can you, unless you abide in Me . . ."

And joy. Fenya remembered the part about joy. ". . . that My joy may remain in you, and that your joy may be full . . ."

She knows, she thought, watching the old woman go into the kitchen. *It's not that she knows what she believes so much as she knows Whom she believes . . .*

Fenya followed as Agafya approached her son. "We'll abide," she assured him. "You buy the wagon. God's hand will not fail to provide for us. You buy the wagon."

The next day Ivan went downtown with Matvei and returned with a team of sturdy gray horses and a used Weber wagon—a wonderful thing painted green with red, black, and yellow striping and the Weber decal in red and yellow. Inside the wagon was a metal bedstead, enameled white—a wrought-iron assurance that housekeeping had finally begun for them! Aksinia, startled out of her apathy, ran out to exclaim over the new purchases; then she bustled inside to move the boxes from the front room to make way for the bed.

After that, they couldn't move quickly enough—washing, ironing, hanging curtains. Soon the bed was covered with a snowy down quilt decorated with a red tracery of stitching that caught up crosshatched acorns, birch leaves, and exotic birds with broad tails like beavers in a regular procession around its edges. Fenya hung red and white linen panels from the best room windows. And Aksinia gave her long strips of cotton embroidered with pastel flowers to hang at the bedroom window. Fenya stacked orange crates under the window, covered them with a white cloth, and set out the wooden box Vassily had given her.

"A bit of home," she murmured, her eyes cherishing the intricate designs on birchwood in the bold morning light of California. Later, Ivan announced that Matvei had prevailed upon him to let Fenya begin night-time English classes at the high school.

"Don't hearken to any foolishness," he warned her. "Just learn what you have to."

For Fenya, the day when Ivan came home with the wagon and the day she started school became the beginning of their "real" life in their new home.

A strife of mockingbirds woke Fenya. Long, shrill whistles, raucous calls, and melodious warblings poured through the partially open bedroom window. *Today we begin our new life!* she thought. She looked around the crowded room. The babes in their crib were still quiet, and Bunya was snoring softly on her mat in the corner.

Carefully, Fenya spread out the sprigged blue and yellow cotton dress she had worn to Natasha's wedding on her sleeping mat. She placed the precious patent leather shoes nearby. Tonight she would dress in her best and go out to school; her whole soul cramped up with exhilaration and fear when she thought of it. School! For an illiterate peasant girl. She pulled on her old patchwork skirt and slipped out into the front yard.

A day for rejoicing! A fine misty rain from the ocean had washed away the smoky haze that clung to Los Angeles. A fresh breeze ruffled the few remaining clouds. Puddles on the street and sidewalks repeated both the blue and the ruffling. The trees dropped blots of shadow on the ground, so shining and crisp around the edges it seemed that she could pick them up in her fingers and hang them on a line to dry! Fenya shaded her eyes and looked to the east where the overlapping ridges of the mountains emerged in shades of faded blue and sage green and peach, like torn strips of calico.

Drawn by the birdsong cascading from the apricot tree, Fenya strolled around back to look at the new brick oven. The bricks were in place and the mortar set. *I suppose Ivan will cover it with clay today, since the weather is so good*, she thought. A cocky mockingbird flitted his gray and white tail feathers in the arched opening until a scraping noise frightened him off. Fenya turned to see Bunya shuffling up behind her. Her sweet smile curled around the pink tip of her tongue. She didn't have enough teeth to keep her tongue from slipping out. But the old woman was quivering with joy. It was as though she had forgotten that there were trees and birds and sky and all these things were a shining revelation to her. Her cloudy eyes shone with the bright awareness of a child.

She breathed in the sharp clear air and pointed her brown speckled hand toward the dappled swell of the San Gabriels. *Can she see it?* Fenya wondered.

"Refuge!" she stated with prophetic sureness. "Mountains of spices." She skipped a little as she said this, as though she were jumping along with the Molokans at service. Fenya looked into her face, seamed and mottled as the mountains themselves, and gilded like them with a golden light that spilled out of the morning sky.

"Mountains of spices," Fenya repeated, smiling into Agafya's face. But other words sang in her mind, and she recalled a little boy's voice in a far-off land:

> Until the day breaks,
> And the shadows flee away,
> Turn, my beloved,
> And be like a gazelle
> Or a young stag
> Upon the mountains of Bether.

She thought of Piotr's face as she had seen it on Sunday, and she began to pray earnestly for him. But the brightness of the morning and the beauty of the old woman's spirit fused and sharpened into a bright shaft of hope. *All will be well with us.* Fenya caught at the assurance. She flexed her fingers in an ardent craving for action. She wanted to hang curtains and set out pots and create a home!

An earnest babbling poured out the bedroom window. Bunya tilted her head and lifted a finger. "Ah, they're talking," she said.

She was right; Nikolinka and Valentina were deep in their early morning conversation. The two would bandy sound back and forth while a most judicious play of expression crossed their faces. It was almost impossible to believe that their words had no meaning. Fenya and Agafya shared a mirthful glance before they went in to get the children.

"No need to tell it all," Fenya jokingly chided the talkative Nikolinka. "Save some for later!" She and Bunya took the two into the kitchen and settled them down for their morning oatmeal. Aksinia bustled over from the stove to coddle her little ones, and even Ivan smiled at the rosy bobbing faces.

"You're a talkative one," Bunya scolded. "Be quiet long enough to take a bite." She waved a wooden spoon at the sputtering little boy.

"Dzrukorf gaaaa bom," he announced seriously and threw a questioning look at Valentina.

"Mmmurf," she replied unequivocally and let her eyes slide away with a cool, poised expression.

"You see?" Agafya insisted. "They're talking right enough. It's the American tongue, no doubt."

Aksinia and Fenya burst into laughter, but Ivan shot an affronted look at his mother.

"American? I won't have them gabbing the stranger's speech in this house."

Agafya lifted her chin stubbornly. "It's not Russian they're talking," she insisted with a sage nod. "The words come with the land. It's only natural for babies to speak the tongue of the land that grows them."

"Don't talk such foolishness," Ivan grumbled. "They'll talk Russian right enough . . ."

Fenya and Aksinia beamed wet, despairing looks at each other as they shook with silent mirth.

"God help us." Aksinia's sigh broke on a giggle. "What a family! You can start teaching your son and daughter Russian," she told Ivan. "Fenya and I have work to do."

"I'll do that," Ivan retorted. He turned his attention to his young pupils. "Table," he boomed, pounding on the pinewood surface. Nikolinka grinned in understanding and pounded, too. He aimed a long string of syllables at his sister, who raised her eyebrows in comprehension and began beating the table with her rosy little fist.

Fenya and Aksinia burst into new gales of laughter and set to work in the best room. By midday they had emptied all the boxes, and the house was clean and orderly.

"It's beginning to look like a home." Aksinia beamed. They bundled up the little ones while Bunya napped and strolled down toward Amelia Street. They passed under the shade of a huge sycamore tree, then stopped enchanted by the shrill music of childish laughter coming from a school yard. The yard was filled with Molokan children exuberantly exploring every possible use for the play equipment. Boys climbed on iron bars like squirrels, and the girls sailed high in bright arcs on the three swings. Entranced as they flew higher and higher, the girls let their full skirts bell out shamelessly, their sturdy little thighs flashing white in the sun.

Fenya noticed two American girls in matching blue dresses looking on with wide, astonished eyes. The eldest was around eight or so, she guessed, and the younger not much more than a toddler. Fenya could see that the older girl was distressed about something. Taking her sister by the hand, she approached the Molokan children and said something in a firm voice. The Molokans fell silent, staring at the interlopers. The girl made some request, very earnestly and loudly, but the Russian children, obviously confused, began backing away. She shook her head vehemently; then with an exasperated expression, she pushed her little sister forward, pulled up her skirt, and pointed to the lace-trimmed bloomers beneath it.

So that was it! Fenya choked with laughter and grabbed Aksinia's arm. She, too, was shaking with merriment.

"Well, who'd have thought it," she giggled. "The Americans wear little trousers to cover their nakedness in such cases. My, she's worked herself into a snit about it!"

"She's really offended." Fenya laughed.

It was true. The American girl's distinct brows were knit with concentration, but she finally shrugged and walked away, leading her sister by the hand. Their eyes glued to the retreating challengers, the Molokan children tentatively put a hand or a foot on a bar or swing chain. In a minute, though, they had forgotten all about it and threw all their energy into rollicking play. A tiny girl with a red-blonde braid caught sight of the watching women; her small hands flew to her head, and she quickly pulled her pink kerchief over her bare head and retied it demurely. *God forbid*, Fenya chuckled, *that her head should be shamelessly bared in the sight of one and all!*

"There's no telling about the strangers' ways," Aksinia sighed.

Fenya shook her head. "No telling," she agreed, but for her a little cloud had darkened the day. The incident put a doubt in her mind. She wondered what kinds of mistakes she would make when she went to the American school and whether she, too, would be the brunt of jokes or an unwitting offender.

Los Angeles High School was the most imposing building Fenya had ever entered. She waved to Ivan as he left her on the steps of the four-story brick building, and then she ducked inside the arched doorway. The sheen of newly waxed floors and the scent of furniture oil were inviting, but Fenya retreated to the steps, looking out toward the city. She was early, and there was no sign of other students. Matvei had promised to meet her and explain her situation to the teacher, Miss Annie Green, but he would not be coming until his father's shop closed for the day.

The high school was set on a low hill. Fenya could see the sheer burnished orange and flaming magenta of a vivid California sunset dwindling behind the squared jut and trough of four- and five-story buildings. The buildings merged and blackened as the blaze of color guttered and sank into the cut-out spaces where the streets and alleyways were. A brooding darkness gathered for a moment. Then a gauzy, mysterious light began to emanate from between the buildings as the electric lights on Spring Street and First and Broadway winked on.

Fenya watched a trolley lit with a row of yellow lights crawling up the hill. *Going home*, she thought. And the distant lights at the service of strangers stirred up an aching remoteness in her—as though she were set apart for some quest or journey, denied the friendly succor of her kind. *It's true; I am separated. This is* Pohod—*my pilgrimage*.

She sat on the cold cement step and pulled her padded jacket around her. She started when a sheepskin cap plopped beside her, followed by a pair of once-black leather boots so scraped and cracked with rust-colored scuff marks they looked like tree bark. Piotr Gavrilovich's lean body folded next to her. She smiled.

"Those are Gavril's boots, aren't they?" she asked.

"They are," Piotr said comfortably, "and for a long time they were the most valuable thing I owned. My mother had stitched every ruble I had into the lining. It's funny you would recognize them."

He scrutinized her upturned face. "It's nice to have my old boots recognized. Usually I'm so anonymous."

"Well," she hedged, "I just barely recognized them . . . I think they've gone through some hard times."

"Hard times . . . yes," he repeated hollowly.

"Look," he said, nodding toward the moving trolley. "People are coming home from work."

The jeweled arc of lights below them, the silent hulk of the brick building behind them, the distant hum of home-bound traffic wrapped them in a quiet intimacy. Fenya savored it in silence, watching with Piotr, seeing as he saw.

The lights in a classroom behind them sprang on, and their shadows zigzagged down the steps. Fenya turned toward him, seeing the muscles tighten as he pushed away the moment of peace. The hollows in his face were very noticeable now. She studied the deep scoring of lines that bracketed his firm mouth.

"What happened to you?" she asked softly.

"I'll tell you. Sometime. Not yet," he answered. He put his hand out to stroke her upper arm, as though sealing a promise. Then he turned, and she followed him into the bright, cheery classroom.

Matvei was there, as he had promised, talking to a kind-faced woman in a white shirtwaist and brown skirt. Miss Annie Green welcomed Fenya with a warm smile and signaled for the class to be seated. She introduced Fenya to the handful of students and then took up a glossy, blue ball held in a brass bracket. The ball was covered with blots of color—pink, yellow, green, and peach—that whirled into a stippled blur as the teacher spun it. She stopped it with a deft movement of her hand, and pointing to a yellow blotch, she said, "California." Fenya strained every bit of her attention on the shiny ball. What was she saying? The teacher rotated the blue sphere a half turn and indicated a large pink splotch and said just as seriously, "Russia!" Was she saying that Russia was in the ball? She must be joking! The keyed-up alertness building in Fenya all day broke into a shaky titter.

Miss Green raised her eyebrows. No one else was laughing; several students turned to look at her in amazement. A hot flush surged through Fenya, and she could feel her pulse throbbing just where her kerchief was tied. She loosened it and took a deep breath. *Better be on guard*, she told herself. *I'll need all the wit I can muster to figure out what's happening here!*

She saw no sign of Piotr when the class ended. Matvei was waiting to walk her home. "How could you know?" he comforted her. "Why you've never even seen a map!" Just as they were passing under the sycamore tree, Fenya looked back to see Piotr silhouetted in the lighted doorway, his sheepskin cap outlined unmistakably under the arched entrance.

After this, Fenya's life settled into a routine, which for her was rich and full and exotic despite its predictability. In the mornings she would accompany Ivan as he drove to the farming areas outside of town and helped him bargain for produce. In the afternoons she pitched in to help Aksinia with housework and meal preparation. On Sundays they joined with the other Russians for service and for the traditional midday meal, visited with other Molokan families, and returned to the auditorium for evening service. Once a week Fenya walked early to the high school to meet Piotr on the steps, and together they'd watch the sun go down and the lights spring up in the town. After class Matvei would walk her home and come in to drink tea with Aksinia and Ivan.

Each day she knew exactly what she would do, but still questions cudgeled her mind as the glowing autumn days shortened into the mild California winter. Ivan, she knew, was withdrawing into a dejection so heavy that the weight of it began to press even on Aksinia's effervescent spirit. The strangeness of the land, his helplessness in even the smallest matters, and the week-to-week scraping to make ends meet dragged on him.

He fears for his family, Fenya realized, *and there's nothing more he can do for them.* In Russia the Bogdanoffs had been wealthy by peasant standards, but here they were forced to struggle in what often seemed an unequal fight. The small economies and "making do" that were part and parcel of life for Fenya Kostrikin were an awkward, unnatural burden for someone like Aksinia.

Even Granny Bogdanoff grew somewhat subdued; Ivan had taken the light bulbs out of all the sockets except the one in the kitchen. The old woman would sit at the table sharing a bowl of oatmeal with the babies. Her one great comfort was that the twins were beginning to speak Russian. Encouraged by this, she would croon Psalms and old Cossack songs to them by the hour, and the little ones would croon back, imitating her slurring, lisping old voice.

Matvei was the one spark of brightness during this time. He came by frequently, sometimes bringing a gift of meat from his father's shop. The young Molokan was full of practical suggestions for Ivan's route. "Don't let fear get the best of you," he encouraged. "It's like this for everyone the first year . . . we've all survived, one way or another." His greenish gaze slipped over to Fenya as he said this, and an agitated mixture of dread and excitement forced her eyes downward. When she lifted them, Aksinia's pleading glance raked up the pity and fear and wonder in her. *What can I do?* Fenya asked herself.

She had plenty to think about. It seemed that Matvei was always there with his quick bright smile and common sense and genuine concern for their plight. But the ways of the old country were shifting and changing and had not yet adapted to the new. The customs of couples' games and village walks and matchmakers were lost, and heaven only knew what would take their place! What did it mean when a young man walked you home from school? Or made a point of assisting your foster family in any way he could? Or was it only kindness such as he would show to anyone?

Fenya knew that Ivan and Aksinia would be overjoyed at such a match. The Kalpakoffs' butcher shop offered a steady, secure income. After all, they were the only butchers who slaughtered livestock according to Molokan tradition, so everyone who could afford meat bought from Matvei's father. Plus, Fenya acknowledged, there was no denying that the young man was both attractive and likable. If he offered for her, she had no good reason to decline, and she knew that the payment of *kladka* for her brideprice would be more than relief for the struggling Bogdanoffs. How could she deny them? They had been so kind . . . and yet how could she marry Matvei when her heart was knit to Piotr Gavrilovich? And what reason could she give if they insisted, as they had the right to do since they stood in the place of parents to her?

And Piotr. The thought of him always tilled up that old gnawing need in her. He had visited the Bogdanoffs too, but he had been taciturn and preoccupied.

She showed him Vassily's carved box, and Piotr was quick to recognize her father's handiwork. He traced the intricate designs with a slow finger. "It's your *izba!* I remember it—the carving on the door posts . . ." He seemed excited and pleased for a moment, but when he left, Fenya thought he was sad, and she wondered what kind of home Lukeria Merlukov made for him.

Later she sat for a long time, pressing her fingers into Vassily's skillful woodcuts, finding impressions of her family and home in every jut and dent. She opened it and took out a silk scarf with a rich burgundy background. A final gift from her parents, it was the betrothal scarf she would one day give to her future husband. She studied the shining lines of bronze-gold and silver-blue which curved into a riotous symmetry of paisley. *Who would wear it?* she wondered.

As the first day had come, so came the last. Late in February Ivan decided that Fenya had had enough English. They were just coming in from Pasadena with a wagonload of lemons and oranges and had stopped at the hardware store to buy a colander for Aksinia. Ivan's eyes narrowed to slits as he watched Fenya shyly approach the young man at the counter. She had no idea what the English word for colander was,

236

so she waved at a collection of pots hanging on the wall, and the scrubbed-looking clerk with his flat, shiny hair was quick to take one down for her.

She shook her head and said, "No, with holes, like this." And she poked imaginary holes in the bottom of the aluminum pot with her finger.

The attentive clerk tugged at his suspenders in bafflement.

"A sieve?" he asked.

She shrugged expressively; then with a brilliant smile of inspiration she explained, "Water go, noodles stay!"

His freckled face broke into a grin, and he confidently brought her a graniteware colander.

"Just right!" She thanked him and offered twenty cents for the twenty-five cent item. He took it with a bemused smile.

Fenya flashed a triumphant look at Ivan, but her cleverness turned on her soon enough. Ivan was so impressed by this performance that he concluded that Fenya knew all the English she needed to handle any likely circumstance for the Bogdanoffs.

And so, she told herself, squeezing her feet into the pointed patent leather shoes, *today will be the last class for me and the last meeting with Piotr Gavrilovich.*

Fenya could see Piotr's shadowy form on the steps as she drove up with Ivan. Something in the pose of his body told her that he had been waiting for a long time. She sat down beside him and looked at him expectantly. Piotr sat with his legs drawn up and his wrists resting on his knees, his long hands dangling. It was the way his hands dangled that made her think that he had bad news. He glanced at her briefly and then returned his gaze to the city. Lights, both fixed and moving, seemed to be suspended in a wavy liquid that slowed and distorted everything.

"He's paid me," Piotr began. She knew he meant Maxim. The Molokan farmer had begged off paying Piotr until he knew what his year's earnings and taxes would be.

"Less." There was a rasp on the word. "Much less than I expected."

Fenya's eyes followed the incomprehensible movements of bits of light in the strangely illuminated city.

"I don't understand it!" he continued. "I've worked so hard. You don't know how I've worked. As though my life depended on it. And it does! Everything I've earned in six months will only pay for one person's passage. My family. How can I help them?"

Fenya looked at him, offering everything she knew of love and comfort and hope. She knew that he saw. His hands came up, and his head came down to meet them.

"I fear for them, Fenya. It's been months, months since I heard anything. My father's last letter came in November. August. It was dated in August. Do you know what's been happening in Russia since then? The worst part is, I can do nothing. Nothing! Here I am; safe in refuge. Refuge, they call it!"

"No. You can do nothing." Fenya could feel a swelling throb of sureness in her voice. "Nothing except abide."

"Abide?" He jerked his head back with the aggrieved combativeness that comes when pain has no logical answer.

"Abide," Fenya repeated. She was very sure of what she had learned. She pulled at his hand. It was wet.

"Listen. In Russia I worked myself raw—until I was scarcely human—hoping that I . . . that *Pohod* would work out for me. You know how it was for us. But all my striving was nothing; it was God's kindness that brought me here. To refuge." He shoved her hand away, refusing the word.

"And even yet," she continued, "I didn't understand. It's Christ we abide in. He is our refuge—not California or any other place—though I had to come here to see it. I had to be separate—alone—to see Him that way . . ."

This seemed to quiet him, and when she slipped her hand back into his, he left it there. When he turned to her, there was an expression of wonder on his face.

"Alone, you say. That's how it is! I've felt it, too. Not with the Molokans—that's not how it happened with me."

She shook her head. "No. Not that way . . ." And she saw an agitated excitement flare from under his eyelids.

"I need to tell you . . . Sometime I'll tell you," he began. Then words were drawn out of him—stronger than the bones of the earth— and older, far older:

"A man will be as a hiding place from the wind
And a cover from the tempest,
As rivers of water in a dry place,
As the shadow of a great rock in a weary land."

She looked into his face, understanding everything. Then the spangled glory of Los Angeles was blotted out by a greater glory as Piotr pulled her into his arms. She clung to him, burying her face in the rough, sour-smelling peasant coat. He bent his head and kissed her.

"*Dushok*, darling." It was a soft breath's burst of a word—did she hear rightly? A tremor shook her, and she dug trembling fingers into his arm.

"What did you say?" She had to know, and her tone left no doubt of it.

Piotr shook his head. "I can't say it! Don't ask me to!" But the drumming of his heart under her cheek and the movement of his throat as he swallowed told another tale. A sudden beam of light from a classroom window struck them. But it was awhile before they had any strength for moving. Finally, Piotr pulled away and stood looking down at her with both sternness and longing. Fenya recognized both the purpose and the yearning. *Come back, my beloved*, she cried inwardly.

Another square of light blinked on, sketching their two shadows across the steps surely and distinctly, as though they had never been one. They went in to class.

XVIII

The East Wind

W hy do you put up with it!" The anger in Eddie's voice
mounted in dry ridges of sound. "He treats you like he treats
us Mexicans. Except we have no choice. Just about everybody's going to treat us that way. But you . . ."

Piotr didn't bother to look back at him. He leaned into the plow,
digging through the hard clay of the new thirty-acre parcel Maxim had
bought. What choice did he have? He didn't say it, but his whole face
became rigid, and the set of his shoulders was like a cross beam fixed to
his spine. He kept his attention on the earth. The land had never been
worked, and it was the color of ash and the hardness of rock, fringed
with twiggy puffs of tumbleweeds trembling on the edges, waiting to
trespass.

"He's paid you no more than he pays me—it's a cheat!" continued
the indignant Eduardo.

"I have my room, meals . . . ," Piotr muttered back at him.

"Sure! I know what kind of a home that she-demon makes for you.
You don't need it. Look . . ." Eduardo jammed his sandaled foot hard
onto the moldboard, and Piotr pulled up short and looked at him stubbornly. But Eddie grabbed at his arm before he could pull away and
roughly jerked the sleeve up.

"Look," he insisted, prodding Piotr's bare arm just above the tan
line, "you're white as snow! You speak English as good as me! You can
be an American! Do you know what I'm saying?"

Piotr pulled his sleeve down and grinned affectionately. "Yep, my
English is just like yours. But then you're the only one I talk to around
here. Miss Green is amazed at my progress, but she can't figure out my

accent. 'You have the brain of a Russian and the tongue of a Mexican,' she says."

"Well, it's my brain that's helping you with all this," Eddie grumbled. "And my brain is telling me you'd be better off out of here. Why do it?"

"For my family. What else?"

"But you can go elsewhere for work. I've seen him. He flaps a few dollars at you—his eyes sliding right off his face because he can't look at you—and he shrugs. Sorry, he says, that's all he can spare. Then he's down at the land agent's buying thirty acres. It stinks."

"What do I do? Work at the lumber yards? I'd have to find a place to live, buy food. Things cost here. My money would be like grain through a sieve." Piotr narrowed his eyes and morosely surveyed the fallow field.

"My work is here, on the land," he added grimly. He urged the team forward and let the strength of his body fall into line with the angle of the plow handles and the slant of the moldboard.

"You peasants," Eddie groaned, but with an edge to his joking. "Tied to the earth . . . Go ahead. Work! Make old Maxim rich!"

Piotr kept his eyes on the monotonous uptilling of the earth. Hardened clods churned out on either side, revealing darker clay under the bleached crust. The movement hypnotized him, numbing his thoughts and forcing a dull, alien endurance on him. He wrenched his eyes away. The air was uneasy, and the tumbleweeds wobbled in the vacant fields. Maxim was beyond them, goading the earth with some implement. Piotr fixed his eyes on the now-familiar band of mountains. It seemed to him that something lurked on the edge of his world, some force seeking to annihilate him, but the more he felt it, the more an independent power of life grew within his soul.

Abide, he reminded himself, thinking of Fenya and her sweet courage and steadfastness. "'Lord, You have been our dwelling place in all generations. Before the mountains were brought forth, or ever You formed the earth and the world . . . '"

But Eddie's advice had forced a wedge into his thinking. Piotr was filled with an agitation akin to panic whenever he thought of the Voloshins in Russia. But another idea had crept in as his sense of alienation grew—the thought of himself as an ordinary American wearing denim trousers and taking some easy job in the city. But whenever his torn confusion drew him into prayer, a third image took shape in him. A pale-haired girl with keen eyes and a soft expression, melting against him, returning his kisses as no maiden kisses a man unless she will marry him. This last thought threw him into an anguish of yearning that he fought with all his strength. To marry at all would be difficult. To marry and rescue his family from the chaos of Russia would be impossible.

On Sunday there was a new face in the church—a dark-haired man with a swift glance and a receding chin, paler than the rest of his face. Probably in his midthirties, he was much too old to be beardless. The Molokans began sprouting whiskers as soon as they married as a matter of principle. Piotr prodded his memory. There was something familiar about those darting eyes . . .

Drawn by his stare, the newcomer caught sight of Piotr, and his face lit up with recognition. In the same instant Piotr knew who he was— Aleksei Davidovich! From his own village! The magnificent wedge-shaped beard that had been Aleksei's most outstanding feature was gone—who would have guessed that weak chin lay under those lush, black whiskers! As soon as the service was over, they both shouldered their way through the crowd and met, planting firm kisses on each other's faces.

"So you managed to slip through the Tsar's fingers," Aleksei began. "I remember that day we talked by the stream. 'He'll be gone,' I told myself. 'That's another one marked for *Pohod*!' When I heard of your supposed death, I said, 'Oh, yes, he's dead—and the afterlife is in California!'"

Piotr laughed excitedly. "I remember it! Maybe you knew—but I didn't. But you—you didn't sound at all sure about emigrating."

"Well, I wasn't. But things happened to make me sure." He lowered his voice with a familiar wry twist to his lips. "The things happening in Russia—it will turn your blood cold. We had to leave—things were that bad for us."

Piotr stood rock-still, letting the moving crowd of churchgoers flow around him. "Tell me," he urged.

Aleksei's restless eyes stilled and hardened. "The Caucasus has become a killing field," he said. "Uprisings, murders, strife—especially between Tartars and Armenians. But it's affected some of our folk, too."

"My family?" Piotr questioned.

"I don't know. They were fine when I left, although your Uncle Mikhail has made the Voloshins far from popular. When I saw the way things were going, I took my wife and sons and fled. We spent months trying to get onto a ship. There have been epidemics, and they're quarantining anyone from southern Russia. It took every kopeck I had, but we got out just in time. I told your uncle he'd better leave, too, but you know how he is. Too much to lose—that's his problem."

"So they're still there . . . I wonder how it is for them."

"Not good, brother. Baku is a smoldering ruin; Tiflis like a city under siege. You heard about the massacre in the town hall? Cossacks charged into a peaceful meeting and began killing people—men, women. Did you know?"

Piotr found that he was breathing fast as Aleksei's report stirred up memories. Oh, he knew, he knew! He remembered the brutal revolt in Baku, the striving for justice that turned into a class war in Tiflis, the elemental power of hatred in the Georgian—Koba, the casual toying with murder in the Kirghiz eyes of a young Cossack. He had seen it well enough, and he had been marked by it! He had killed in the grip of its power. The ugly, inhumane images evoked a terror for his loved ones and a terror for himself. *That ugliness is within you,* an inward accuser railed, *and it's cut you off from your people and from the help of God for those you love* . . . But the challenge came immediately, and a vision of Grigol's transformed face blotted out the thought. Piotr sighed and returned his attention to Aleksei.

". . . and massacres of Armenians. Did you hear? Every Armenian in the village of Khankend was killed, murdered . . . Sirakan from our village, you remember Sirakan, well, he fled. With his parents—"

"His sister," Piotr forced out. "He had a sister. What happened to her?"

Aleksei shrugged. "They had set her up for a marriage to a rich Armenian, but the girl would have none of it, and she ran away. The young people are wayward these days. Last I heard, she had married some mountaineer."

Married, Piotr thought, *to Grigol.* A sense of rightness and comfort took hold of him.

"But it's good," Aleksei was saying, "to see a face from my village."

"I barely recognized yours," Piotr remarked.

Alexei's hand came up to cover his shame-faced grin.

"Oh, yes. My pride and joy. Sheared away by an American barber—no Russian would do it. You don't know how naked a man feels, but it's the price of survival. The creamery offered me a good job. I told them I could make French butter, and they could see I knew my stuff. 'We'll pay you well,' they said, 'but off with the beard!' 'Nothing doing,' I told them. Then I went home and talked to my missus. 'Well,' she exploded, 'what are we going to eat—geraniums? You go back there and tell them you'll take it.' I could see she was about to take after me with a razor herself, so I ducked out pretty quick."

The Molokan touched his face with delicate fingers.

"Yes, my old mug's been mutilated. It's like an amputated limb; I'm always tugging at it, and it's not there." He lowered his voice confidentially. "The wife, she's happy with the money. On weekdays she's proud of what I can make—but on Sundays she's ashamed of me."

Ilya Valoff came up, throwing out his hands to grasp both their shoulders. His face was elated. He was always elated when family or old friends found each other.

"Praise be! A reunion!" he rejoiced, pulling them into his generous bear hug. "We'll have to keep this one in the fold," he said winking at Aleksei. "It's the shorn sheep that feels the cold."

His perceptive blue eyes narrowed as he looked at Piotr. "I can see that Maxim is working you too hard. You come with us on Saturday. Yelena and I are putting together a picnic for the young folk. We'll take the trolley out to Altadena and have a feast in the meadows—just like the old days. You come . . . don't you forget, we're counting on you." He moved off to another group, wagging a chiding finger at Piotr.

Aleksei was laughing. "I see the elders haven't forgotten their duty," he said. "They want to make sure you have a chance to meet plenty of good Molokan girls so you won't be drawn off by some pretty American miss."

Piotr raised his eyebrows in amazement. "Why, I hadn't thought of it. So that's what he's about."

"He's a wise old man," Aleksei said.

The bright red trolley was packed with a high-spirited assortment of Russian peasants that next Saturday. The girls were dressed in their best—for them this was the outing of the year—and the young men had trouble reining in their glances. Piotr was having trouble, too. Fenya had appeared in a lovely brown sarafan bordered with golden bursts of sunflowers. He could hardly keep his eyes off her. She turned the blue intensity of her gaze on him for a moment and then ducked her head in that self-effacing way of hers. She moved toward the back of the car and sat gazing out the rear window.

Piotr stationed himself a few seats up from her, standing and watching the dense jumble of buildings space out until he could see the open acreage of small homesteads. As they moved toward the foothills, the broad sweep of land began to undulate, beautiful and inviting—and quickly gone as the trolley ate up the tracks.

The Americans on board were also in a holiday mood. The women were decked out in pretty, brimmed hats and snowy shirtwaists. The men wore dark suits with silk vests festooned with gold watch chains. Their hands clasped smooth-crowned bowler hats. The women, young and old, kept a lively eye on the scenery and on the Russian passengers. Their tongues were lively, too, and Piotr found he could understand many of their comments.

"Why, they're just like something out of a storybook. Look at those colors!" exclaimed an older lady with an oblong face.

"Red, purple, yellow—ugh, what a combination," commented her companion.

"Oh, I like it. They're so full of life—you know we're sort of drab with our white blouses and dark skirts. And look, every one of them is pretty. Look at the rosy cheeks on that one . . . And see that young man looking at us? Yes, the one with the brown lock of hair falling over his face. Quite handsome."

Piotr turned red when he realized she was talking about him. He put a hand up to hold onto the strap and looked studiously out the window. He sensed a movement at his elbow and looked down into Fenya's eyes. Her beautiful, quirky face was a study in determination and wonder as she bent to glimpse vineyards and flowering trees and the roots of the mountains.

"Why, it's like home!" she exclaimed.

"It is," he answered, smiling down at her.

The vineyards ended abruptly, and the land spread out into wide meadows flaming with the springtime bloom of thousands of red, orange, and yellow poppies.

"Stop!" hollered the American lady. She reached across Piotr and tugged wildly at the bell. The trolley lurched to a rolling stop, and Piotr reached out to keep Fenya from being pitched into the lap of a dapper American businessman. The long-faced lady beamed as she informed the conductor that they'd all be stopping for a few minutes to pick flowers. He shrugged good-naturedly.

"Sure," he agreed, "but when I clang the bell, we'll be off—so you'd better come running."

The Americans filed out while the Russians exchanged worried looks.

"They've just stopped to pick flowers," Piotr explained, pointing to the merrymakers scooping up great handfuls of poppies. "We'll join them."

The Russians tumbled out, and soon they were all harvesting bunches of brilliant blooms. The wildflowers trembled with the slightest movement of air so that their translucent, papery petals overlapped into startling bursts of new color. Fenya stood as though transfixed, then crouched suddenly. *She looks like she belongs here,* Piotr thought, *with all that color moving over her face like firelight.*

He came to stand beside her as she tilted her glowing face up toward the mountains, so close at hand. The snow glistened on Mount Wilson and on the lower peaks of the San Gabriels.

"Snow," she said, shaking her head and looking at Piotr. "So far away."

Her face was taut with longing and homesickness and a kind of burning gladness.

"The mountains are named for an angel," she commented. "Did you know?"

He nodded. "It makes me think of Kazbek—The Mountain of Christ—in the Caucasus. The snows there are eternal. The Ossetians say that God lives on the summit, and anyone who comes near will be stopped by unseen forces or a terrible storm. They say that Abram's tent is there on the top and a cradle supported by unseen hands with a sleeping child in it. It's only one of their legends, of course, but the mountain—well, the light springs up from it into heaven. It does have a way of catching at your heart."

Bells clamored over the field, the conductor waved his hat, and they all piled in for the rest of their journey. The Molokans picnicked at the end of the line near the foot of the mountains. Yelena Valoff had provided a sumptuous array of treats. Piping hot samovars anchored each end of the long picnic cloth heaped with colorful bouquets and fringed with yellow mustard flowers. After their meal, most of the young folk began singing, but Piotr and Fenya wandered up to where the roots of the mountain plunged into the meadow. The day was crystal clear. They could look past the tidy vineyards and graceful orchards of Pasadena, all the way to the Pacific Ocean glimmering like a piece of silver foil, hammered thin and moving with subtle tremblings. They found a crusty little arroyo cutting into the sandstone hill.

"Let's go up a little," Piotr suggested. "Maybe we can see the Island of Santa Catalina."

They followed the gully up the side of a chaparrel-covered hill scarred with flesh-colored fissures. A brown thread of water turned into a steady trickle and then a musical gush as they climbed higher.

"Look," Fenya joked. "Water. In a dry and thirsty land . . . That's the first moving water I've seen since we've been here!"

"Amazing!" Piotr bantered. "Actually, even the Los Angeles and San Gabriel Rivers show a little moisture this time of year—but they'll dry up soon enough . . . I've heard that there are fuller rivers far to the north—called Kings and Merced. And vast tracts of farmland where ordinary folk can buy farms. The land there is watered by snow melt from huge ridges that hold back the great desert to the east."

"Sounds like a place where Molokans could be happy . . . ," Fenya commented.

They found a flat nub of granite projecting over the stream and sat down, looking out toward the west. Far away the oblong, ghostly shape that was Catalina Island rose from the ocean. They did not look behind them, but the looming strength of the mountains gave a raptness to their vision of the sea. The texture of sandstone, the herbal tang of mountain greenery, the gurgle of water fretting at rock sent shock waves of memory through Piotr.

"It's comfortable, sitting like this," Fenya offered.

He gave her a serious look. "You are sitting with a stranger," he said.

Her widened eyes told him that she was prepared to hear whatever he had to say. And Piotr began describing his departure from the village, his day in Tiflis with Noe, and the demonstration near Sioni Cathedral.

"A Cossack—he found me crouching in a doorway. He was a stranger, and he was my brother. His eyes were slits spurting blood-lust, but they challenged me, too. 'Don't think you're any different than me,' they said! He was right—he plunged four inches of steel into my shoulder, tore it out to rip the flesh, and then smiled at the work of his hands!"

Fenya whitened and seemed to grow smaller on the rock ledge, but he didn't spare her.

"So I showed him. I hit him, and he toppled like a tree, and I pounced on him to make sure he was dead and could no longer smile the way he was smiling."

"You had no choice," she defended him. "He was going to kill you."

Piotr snorted. "I wasn't cringing with regret when I killed him. There wasn't a drop of pity in me. I was full of rage—rage like that is death to the soul."

"A man's heart is a dark forest," Fenya murmured. "But God does not let us out of His hand."

"No. I found that out." He told her about Grigol, about his own encounter with the God of love, about everything that had happened to him in Khevsuretia. He searched her face for understanding and found it, as he had known he would.

"Up until then, my life with God was a tidy little set of beliefs and customs—as just about everyone has. But the God I met in that mountain chasm could not be contained in anything made up by man's mind. We think our traditions are the answer—they aren't the answer. At best, they're a useful vessel for holding parts of the answer so that we can work it into our lives. It's God Himself shown to us in the face of Christ Who is the answer. Sometimes when I think of everything that's happened, I wonder whether I can even call myself a Molokan—or whether I want to."

He looked at her, and the comprehension in her face made him glad. Her kerchief had fallen back. The pale, glistening strands of hair shone lighter than her warm, golden skin tones. To Piotr, she seemed so compact, so complete, sitting quietly on her granite stool, mysterious in a way to pique and familiar in a way to cherish.

"It's true you can only find God alone," she agreed. "Sometimes I've thought that is what *Pohod* is—a lone person seeking after God—not a huge migration of thousands. At least that's what it has been for me. Your people can give you ideas about God, but they can't give you God Himself."

"That's true! That's what we've been given. The giver is Christ, and the gift is a love bond with God Himself." *Love bond.* The idea ascended like smoke, loomed in the looming of the mountains. *Much as it had before,* Piotr thought, *in a chasm on the other side of the world.* But this time, the sense of peace was even fuller and deeper. *It's because she's here,* he realized, *the one my heart longs for. She grasps it all. She has the faith and understanding to blunt the edge of life's pain and the practiced hope and keen charity to sharpen all delight.*

"But as for your people—they have their place," she added thoughtfully. "Otherwise, whom would you serve?"

Piotr put his hand out, lightly touching the shining floss of hair. His fingers traveled down to lift her chin. Her hair smelled of sunshine and mint. He held her close and kissed her, and she responded with artless honesty—as she had before. Then she pulled away and tugged her kerchief forward to shield the concern that crossed her features.

"I have to tell you something, Piotr," she said. Her eyes sought refuge in the tufts of sage along the Sierra Madre, but she held onto his hand tightly. "Matvei has offered for me."

"What did you tell him?" The blood rushed to Piotr's heart and set up a swollen throbbing that reawakened the pain in his old wound.

"The only thing I could. Ivan and Aksinia have gladly accepted his offer—they are so much in need of the *kladka*. What could I say? I owe everything to them. But I told Aksinia why I was hesitating. And I told her that I'd like Matvei to write to my father . . . It will give me time." She hesitated, then went on matter-of-factly.

"I know that it would be hard for you to marry while your family is still in Russia. You couldn't . . . forsake your family."

"I can't. I can't forsake them. But I can't forsake you—"

"What will happen then? The Bogdanoffs can insist that I marry. They're kind, but you don't know how things are for them. To them, this is the answer to hardship . . ."

"I don't know. I only know this. There's a space carved out in me—and you're the one who can fill it."

They sat quietly holding each other until the clang of bells called them back to the meadow and the red trolley. Clumps of faded poppies lay here and there on the green field like dying embers. They stood side by side on the way home, holding onto one strap and swaying with the lurch of the car, as though their two bodies were ruled by one impulse.

Piotr was out plowing Maxim's new eastern parcel when he saw Ilya and another elder crossing the road. As soon as he saw them pass by the house and walk toward him across the field, he knew why they had come. Piotr stopped in his tracks, pulled up the team, and sat down beside the plowshare to wait for them. A leaden weight of dread pressed him to the earth. The dry, hot Santa Ana winds were scouring the land, and brown tumbleweeds quivered intensely as they strained against their delicate root-moorings.

Ilya's face confirmed his fears. His reddened, bleary eyes flinched as they took in Piotr's rigid form. The other man, Efim Tolmacheff, wore an expression of compassion that was thoughtful—but also exalted—as though whatever had evoked the pity had also evoked a strong, heady interest.

Ilya said nothing, but sat beside him on the ground. He leaned over to kiss Piotr on both sides of his face. Efim sat too, heedless of his fine wool trousers, and reached into his jacket to retrieve a stained and creased envelope.

"The Lord has chosen to sift us like wheat! The news is from your uncle—written to the church here, but he added a note asking us to find you, to tell you . . . It will not be easy reading for you, brother . . ." His warning died away, and Piotr took the envelope, staring at the postmark. Persia! How could it be?

Piotr read while the wind tried to wrestle the paper out of his fingers, and the two men sat still on either side of him. He knew they were praying.

> Truly the Lord God has spoken to you . . . And truly it was by His hand that you were led away from this place . . .

Piotr's heart lurched. Mikhail was asserting that he was wrong about *Pohod* in the strongest possible terms. What had happened?

> Uprisings, threat of death to me, my family . . . We prepared to leave, but too late. At night torch-bearing rebels accosted us. They fired the barn and led my children, Trofim, Andrei, and my dear daughter-in-law Natasha into the glare of the yard. The beasts left no work of their father, Satan, undone. They tore at the girl's hair and clothing and defiled her while her husband and brother-in-law were forced to watch. It was the last thing they saw. The devils took sharpened stakes and put out their eyes and drove them into the forest at the mercy of wolves and bears.

Piotr bent his head down to his knees, and his one hand scrabbled in the crumbled clay.

> The flames brought us help, too late. Marfa and I fled across the lower Caucasus into Persia. Others, both

Molokan Russians and Armenians, have also fled the village. Word has come to me that my brother Gavril, along with his wife and daughters, left the village, hoping to find succor here in Persia. But in the weeks and months since then, I have not been able to find them. I can only thank God that their son, Piotr, has escaped to refuge. This must be their greatest comfort. He is one of the remnant—chosen for God's work in a new land. And a remnant, too, for his family. He is the only Voloshin son to survive. . . .

If in the long days of hardship among an alien people, your souls complain against God, remember what you have escaped. . . .

Piotr dropped his head into his hands and began shaking violently. His dear ones—swallowed up—lost. And his cousins. Andrei's agony, Natasha's shame and horror, Trofim's suffering—how could he bear it? Ilya was holding him, shaking with him. Efim's hand was strong on his knee. They stayed, anchoring him, until his powerful young body absorbed what his mind refused.

Finally, he looked up. The wind was stronger now, and the tumbleweeds had broken loose and were crowded against the stick and string boundary Maxim had made. They heaved and jostled like a pack of animals. Then the string broke, and they came bounding helter-skelter across the field so that the horses shied, and Ilya put out a hand to soothe them.

"Piotr," Ilya said gently, "let's go in. We'll ask Lukeria to make us some tea. Come in with us."

Piotr shook his head vehemently. "No. Let me stay. I need to stay."

The two men remained beside him quietly until the sun left the sky and an aching chill began to rise up from the ground.

"Come in," Ilya persuaded once more, but Piotr had set his face like a rock. The Molokans stood in silent respect for his grief for a few moments; then they left. Piotr could just barely make out their shadowy forms entering the Merlukov's house and then leave soon after.

It was completely dark when Maxim strode up.

"Come in, Piotr," he urged, his voice softened and unfamiliar. "Lukeria has some supper set out. Come in."

Piotr refused, and after a few minutes Maxim shrugged and led the horses and plowshare away, leaving Piotr alone in the windy field. He stayed until the moon rose. He stood to watch as it detached itself from the blanched mountain ridges. In whiteness and in the delicately etched traceries of craters or fissures, they looked to be of the same substance—as though the mountains had birthed the moon in some mysterious life-giving. Awe entered Piotr and he whispered:

> "A man will be as a hiding place from the wind
> And a cover from the tempest,
> As rivers of water in a dry place,
> As the shadow of a great rock in a weary land."

He turned to look back at the bungalow. They had left a light on for him, but he couldn't bear to go into that house again. Instead, he went into the barn and spent the night with the two plow horses and the four cows. Wind noise and the doleful scratching of tree branches against the wall kept the animals restless and wakeful. But Piotr pulled some burlap sacks around himself and slept like a dead man until dawn.

At first cockcrow, he stole into the house, cleaned himself up for church, and slipped out to walk to Los Angeles. It was still windy out, and the fields and yards were littered with debris. He bought some sunflower seeds from an Armenian vendor and ate them alongside the auditorium, watching the empty husks skittle around like beetles. He waited until the hall was almost filled before he went in, keeping to the back. He stiffened under the pitying looks a few of the men cast his way. But most, he figured, didn't know.

The singing stung his eyes. He glanced at Ilya. The old man was weepy and trembling. Piotr closed his eyes tightly. When he opened them, he saw that Efim was standing in front with Mikhail's letter spread out in front of him. At the same time, he caught sight of Fenya's eager face in the women's section. *She doesn't know!* The thought shot through him with fresh pain. *Natasha is her sister; and she doesn't know!* He glanced again toward the front. *I can't believe it, he's going to read it, and she doesn't know.*

"Truly, the Lord God has spoken to you . . . and by His hand you have been led from this place . . ." Efim's commanding voice rang out. Fenya's face tilted up with that receptive openness. *I can't bear it,* Piotr groaned. *I've got to stop him.* He reached out to make a way, jostling his neighbors—too late.

". . . defiled . . . last thing they saw . . ." He saw the words register on Fenya's face. Then she disappeared. A circle of women's kerchiefs, bending inward, lined the hole she had fallen into. They drew back suddenly, and Fenya was running blindly toward the door.

"Her sister . . ." "God help us!" Voices followed her. Piotr forced his way through them. Aksinia was suddenly beside him, tears streaming down her face.

"Find her, find her." She grabbed his sleeve, and he tore loose out into the wind-blasted morning.

Piotr caught up with her in a vacant field not far from the school auditorium. He passed under a pear tree, white with its lovely, sour-smelling bloom, and saw her near a eucalyptus row lining a wooden fence. She was standing very still, but everything around her was moving, waving wildly. She looked toward him as though she had been expecting him. Then her face changed, and he crushed her in his arms, stroking her silky hair and wet face.

He pulled her down by the twisted, splintered trunk of a eucalyptus. The grass flattened under the wind, and the treetops groaned with strange, oceanic murmurings. Sickle-shaped leaves in muted pastel colors scythed through the air around them. Piotr kept holding her and rocking.

He knew that tomorrow he would go to Ivan Bogdanoff and offer his earnings as *kladka* for Fenya Vassileyvna. Then he would take up work in the lumber yard to earn enough to make a home for them. Married, he would grow a beard and set his love on this vigorous, bewildered, struggling folk that God had called to refuge. He narrowed his eyes, looking toward downtown Los Angeles and held onto his broken, trembling beloved more firmly. The life of the city and the life of the earth and the pulling of tree roots for nurture and the shifting of air between the mountains and the sea—all these things bound them and drew them into a place of impossible peace.

The wind tore the pear blossoms from the trees and swept them up against the redwood fence like drifts of snow.

Glossary

astrakhan—Loosely curled fur made from the pelts of very young lambs originally bred near Astrakhan.

banya—Wooden outbuilding used for steam bathing.

blintzi—Thin pancakes wrapped around clotted cheese or jam and cooked in hot milk.

boyar—Aristocrat in old Russia (prior to Peter the Great).

caravanserai—In central Asia, an inn with a large central courtyard where caravans stopped for the night.

desiatiny—2.7 acres.

druzhko—Best man in Molokan wedding; driver

eristav—A Georgian nobleman.

gornitsa—"Best Room" in a two-room izba.

gubernia—A province in prerevolutionary Russia.

izba—Traditional Russian peasant house; usually constructed of wood, it consisted of one main room with a clay stove in the corner opposite the front door.

kasha—Porridge of cracked buckwheat, wheat, or barley, sometimes served with meat.

kladka—Money paid by the groom for his betrothed prior to the wedding, usually kept for her by her mother.

kosovorotka—A side-opening peasant shirt with an upright collar. It was usually worn long over trousers and tied with a rope or sash.

kulak—Well-to-do peasant farmer who employed workers.

lapka, krugi and **gorelki**—Village games played with a stick and pieces of wood, in which a young man chooses a bride.

lapsha—Noodles, usually served in soup.

lapti—Plaited bast shoes.

lavash—Georgian or Armenian flatbread.

nagaika—Cossack whip or knout.

Narodnik—Member of a nineteenth-century movement which regarded the peasantry as the source of the future revolution and of healthy Russian values in general.

papachka—Tall Georgian cap made of lamb's wool.

piroshka—Bread pastry stuffed with meat or cabbage.

pridanoe—A bride's marriage portion consisting largely of clothes, bedding, and drapery.

sarafan—Traditional Russian peasant dress with a high neck and embroidered strip down the front, worn for special occasions.

sobraniya—A special gathering; for the Molokans usually a religious gathering.

uezd—Next governing unit below gubernia in prerevolutionary Russia.

verst—.66 mile (approximately one kilometer).

zemstvo—Prerevolutionary government council responsible for educational, medical, and farm advisory needs.